Bone
of Contention

FORGE BOOKS BY ROBERTA GELLIS

A Mortal Bane
A Personal Devil
Bone of Contention

Bone
of Contention

Roberta Gellis

A Tom Doherty Associates Book   New York

BONE OF CONTENTION

Copyright © 2002 by Roberta Gellis

Book design by Jane Adele Regina

A Forge Book
Published by Tom Doherty Associates, LLC
175 Fifth Avenue
New York, NY 10010

www.tor.com

Forge® is a registered trademark of Tom Doherty Associates, LLC.

Library of Congress Cataloging-in-Publication Data

Gellis, Roberta.
    Bone of contention / Roberta Gellis.
        p. cm.
    "A Tom Doherty Associates book."
    ISBN 0-765-30019-2 (hc)
    ISBN 0-765-30554-2 (pbk)
    1. Great Britain—History—Stephen, 1135–1154—Fiction. 2. Oxford
(England)—Fiction. 3. Woman detectives—Fiction. 4. Ex-prostitutes—Fiction.
I. Title.

PS3557.E42 B66 2002
813'.54—dc21   2002069253

First Edition: September 2002
First Paperback Edition: December 2003

Printed in the United States of America

0 9 8 7 6 5 4 3 2 1

To my brother Roger with love

in particular for the warmth and hospitality with which
he has so often welcomed us into his home

Bone
of Contention

PROLOGUE

Spring 1134,
Near Culham

Carl Butcherson quietly followed after the maidservant he had been futtering toward the small, grassy clearing where her mistress was waiting for her. The maid was a tasty piece, but he had an appetite for sweeter, softer flesh. If he could catch the maid's mistress in the indiscretion the maid had confessed to him, the mistress might well spread her legs for him to keep her secret. If she coupled with one, why not with two?

He heard his doxy cry out in surprise or pain and wriggled quickly to where he could see. He expected to get a fillip of pleasure from seeing the girl beaten because he had made her late, but what he did see made his breath catch in his throat. Him! He had seized the maid and was holding her with her back to him. And he saw what was at the maid's feet.

Carl would have torn himself free of the bushes to run away, but he was paralyzed with fear and so he saw the man's hand rise and plunge down, saw a long knife, dripping red, emerge from the maidservant's throat, saw the blood fountain down her breast, saw the man push the girl so she fell forward . . . next to the other body, the body so battered about the head that he would not have known her, except for her fine gown. Carl choked back a cry of terror and began to squirm backward, out of the ring of brush. As he freed himself, the killer turned his head.

Carl leapt to his feet and ran, and ran, and ran until he could run no more. Then he found a place to hide and he lay still, first shivering with fear but when he realized no one was following or searching for him and his terror eased, thinking. He lay hidden all night, and did not return home. The next day he ran again, right out of Culham. He had a friend in Sutton who could teach him how to defend himself.

Four years later; spring 1139, Oxford

A shadow shifted in the niche in the attic that funneled sound from the comfortable solar below. The man crouching there had discovered by accident that a strange quirk of the construction or some crack that formed in the settling of the building produced the effect. Two feet away one could not hear a thing, but just here everything his master said in his private solar could be heard, clear as a church bell.

The shadow in the niche had almost forgotten that he had once been Carl Butcherson—until the voice of the man who had unintentionally given him his new life reminded him, reminded him of everything. He breathed in deeply but silently. How fortunate that the man should come to his attention here, not far from the manor where a local but powerful baron likely still mourned a murdered daughter and sought her killer.

No greater impulse moved Carl to betray the murderer now than he had felt when he saw the maid stabbed and her mistress lying dead. He only felt that he finally had a desire important enough to extort a favor from the killer. Also, he thought, smiling grimly, he was no longer a terrified, simple butcher's son; he was a practiced man-at-arms, who had no need to fear the killer's strength.

He crouched still as death, hardly breathing, while civilities were exchanged between his master and the murderer. Those civilities told him where the man now lodged and to whom he was sworn. He could find him when he needed him. Now he had a tool that would deliver to him the rich orphan his master and the king's clerk had been talking about a few days ago.

Carl was growing uncomfortable and would have left then, but the men were too close to the opening that carried the sound. Perforce, he heard his master say, "We know that treason is intended, but it is too dangerous to wait until there is proof of that. We must find a cause to strip them of their power before they act."

The murderer then made a suggestion and his master laughed. "It is certainly worth a try," his master said. "If it happens early enough it will be an irritation, even if it does not succeed—and we will have time enough to try again."

"Oh, it will succeed, my lord," the killer said, "if you will suggest to the king's steward that the lodging provided for his retainers be inadequate and uncomfortable . . . and very near some foreign lord who has more space than he needs." There was a sly suggestiveness in the voice.

"I do not . . ." his master began uncertainly and then burst out laughing. Carl heard the scritch of a chair's legs against the floor and then his master's voice fading as he moved away. "But I do! I do know the perfect 'victim' to be abused."

Carl Butcherson listened idly, learning the name of the lord whose men were to be used. However, as soon as he realized that the plans would not involve his master's troops and so were irrelevant to him, he lost interest. It was more important to escape from his profitable oubliette before someone heard him. He had all the information he needed.

CHAPTER 1

The thin, dark man in correct, if unusually sumptuous, priestly garments, nodded briskly at the whoremistress of the Old Priory Guesthouse when she opened the gate for him. Magdalene la Bâtarde, who had taken in his expression in one swift, practiced glance, opened her mouth to tell him he had mistaken his direction. Neither dissipation nor guilt marked his fine-featured face. In Magdalene's extensive experience, a priest who entered her premises was bound to show one or the other. What stopped her tongue was his indifference to her appearance, which implied he had seen her before, and the confident way he led his horse past her. In addition she had a vague feeling that she knew him.

Then, as he walked the horse toward the stable, momentarily a silhouette against the low rays of the evening sun, she remembered. This was one of William of Ypres's clerks and the reason for his guilt-free, easy manner was surely that he had not come to sample her wares but on business. Business. Magdalene frowned, but she did not follow the priest to the stable. If the business concerned her, she would soon know; if it did not, it would be wise not to display any curiosity about William's affairs.

Magdalene left her visitor to care for his own horse—a custom of her house that ensured the privacy of her clients—and returned to the common chamber, leaving the front door invitingly open. She glanced around swiftly to be sure that no client had left any telltale item, but the large table on the right-hand side of the room was clean and empty as were the two short benches that flanked the head and foot and the two longer ones that provided seating on the sides.

The shelves that were built onto the walls to either side of the open door to the corridor that led through the house carried only their usual array of dishes, cups, and flagons. To the left, the four stools arranged comfortably around the hearth were also empty, the workbaskets beside them tidily closed. The only work visible was the piece on Magdalene's own embroidery frame; her lips twitched. The altar cloth she was embroidering with a variety of religious symbols should be soothing to her guest.

She was considering whether to seat herself before her embroidery frame, which would draw attention to the altar cloth, or at the table when a footstep behind her relieved her of needing to make the decision.

"Mistress Magdalene," the priest said, as she turned to face him, "we have met before, but it was briefly and you might not remember."

"I never remember the name or face of any man who has been in my house," Magdalene said, her expression blank. "Neither do my women. It is a rule of my business."

The priest laughed. "We will need to abrogate that rule for a few weeks, at least with regard to me—but since I am not a client perhaps the rule would not be broken anyway. My name is Father Etienne de Dreux and I come as a messenger from Lord William of Ypres."

Magdalene nodded and gestured toward the table. She and the priest seated themselves at right angles. "Lord William is a most charitable man," she said. "He has tried from time to time to alter my condition for the better."

Father Etienne's dark eyes widened a bit. "I do not believe I have ever heard quite as ambiguous a remark. I know that every word is true, but I doubt anyone less familiar with your situation would learn any truth from them. Still, I am glad to hear you acknowledge the debt. Lord William needs your service. He wishes you to come to Oxford as soon as possible."

Needs your service. The words cast Magdalene back in time. Now her name was Magdalene la Bâtarde and she was a whoremistress. But once she had been Arabel de St. Foix, a lady . . . not a great lady but the mistress of her own manor house and outlying farms. Her husband, long dead of a sharp (as in a well-honed knife) disagreement between them, had been while he was alive a sworn liegeman to a vassal of old King Henry. That king had brooked no disobedience from his men, and when he demanded their service, swift retribution fell on those who failed to answer his summons promptly.

Although King Henry was dead and buried, and it was much easier to flout King Stephen's will, Magdalene had been well schooled in the response of a vassal to his overlord. It was her duty to obey William. Of course, Magdalene thought, William of Ypres would likely have had a fit laughing if he guessed how Magdalene regarded their relationship . . . but he might not; William had a surprisingly penetrating mind. And even if he had laughed to think of the whoremistress, who occasionally served him sexually, as vassal to his overlord, he would be quick enough to take advantage of her fancy.

Magdalene's eyes were fixed on the well-dressed cleric who sat across the table from her, but she was seeing William of Ypres instead of his minion. William looked, and frequently acted, like a coarse brute. His face was blunt and broad with small blue eyes that blinked frequently. It had none of the distinction of Father Etienne's fine, thin features, nor did William have the priest's neat black moustache, which grew into a well-trimmed beard that surrounded his mouth and covered his chin, leaving his cheeks bare.

That elegant beard would look ludicrous on William. He was clean-shaven—more or less, since he did not shave often enough so that his cheeks and chin were usually covered with an untidy stubble. Actually the unshaven stubble suited him as did the tousled disorder of his mud-brown hair. It was liberally streaked with gray now. . . . Magdalene blinked and drew a little broken breath as her heart contracted. He was aging, her William.

"I do acknowledge my debt to Lord William," she said hastily, "and if he needs me in Oxford, I will come."

"That is excellent," Father Etienne said with considerable relief.

The relief was a clear warning to Magdalene. It told her there was nothing casual about William's message; she guessed Father Etienne had been told to get her to Oxford in any way that was necessary. Magdalene knew that William's coarse brute manner was a deliberate screen behind which he concealed himself—not that he was not coarse and brutal, but he was much more. He was brave and steadfast, too, and, more significant, his wit was far sharper than the sword he wielded as leader of the king's mercenaries—and he kept that sword honed to a fine edge because he used it often. If William said he needed her, she must come; on the other hand William would use anyone without regard to any convenience but his own, even those of whom he was fond. So, if there was no dire, immediate emergency a delay would be useful.

"But what does 'as soon as possible' mean?" Magdalene asked the priest. "Must I start for Oxford this afternoon? I have a business—"

"Yes, yes. Lord William is aware and wishes no harm to come to your business. He said—" the priest looked a little surprised but repeated carefully "—that your business had served his purposes from time to time. He is also aware that your women are not fit to operate on their own. He said something about the blind, the mute, and the simple." Father Etienne cocked his head inquiringly.

Touched because William had thought of her need, Magdalene smiled. "He meant that to ease my clients I have chosen women who, they believe, could not identify them. Letice is mute. Ella has no ability to remember. And Sabina is blind. However, Sabina is now married and no longer works for me."

Father Etienne's eyes had widened again at the list of the whores' infirmities, but he did not seem to notice Magdalene's remark that her clients *believed* the whores could not identify them. He merely nodded, displaying a mild satisfaction as he said, "Ah, now I understand my role better. Lord William desires me to oversee your household to make sure the clients pay what they should and do not mistreat your women in your absence."

For a moment Magdalene felt as if her heart had stopped and she had to struggle to keep her face bland and expressionless. Considered her need? If William had sent a priest to greet her clients, he had, for some reason she could not even guess at, determined to destroy her. Or had he merely lost patience with her insistence on protecting her clients' privacy? Did he intend Father Etienne to record the names and businesses of those who used her house? Magdalene swallowed the bile of fear that had risen in her throat.

"Lord William told you to live here and deal with my clients?" She curved her lips into the travesty of a smile. "But surely that would not do your reputation any good, Father Etienne. News of your employment—and no doubt speculation as to how you were being paid—would soon enough come to the bishop of Winchester, who owns this house, and—"

"No, no. I did not plan to live here. As you know Lord William has a lodging on the grounds of the White Tower. I will live there."

"Then how can you oversee my household? Clients come at all hours, although most have fixed appointments." She waved at the empty room. "All my women are now at work, but as you saw I came to answer the bell. Do you intend to answer the bell and invite men in? to ask which whore they have come to see? or, if they have no preference, suggest which of the women would be most satisfactory and then make light conversation while the client waits. . . ." Her fear lessened when she saw the consternation that spread over his face, and she dared ask, "Just what *did* William tell you to do?"

"To assure you he would see you suffered no loss from answering his summons. I assumed he expected me to attend to your interests—" he laughed suddenly "—but I am afraid I did not think too much about what that would entail . . . for a whorehouse. My mind was on some other business I need to accomplish for Lord William."

Magdalene laughed too, almost giddy with relief. "I wondered whether he wanted to destroy you or me," she said, then shook her head. "If I can delay leaving for one more day, I will be able to arrange for a substitute to take my place. Then you would need come only once each evening to check on the receipts—I will leave a list of what they should be—and to listen to any complaints the women might have."

"For me to come every evening . . ." Now aware of the perils of being so intimately connected with the whorehouse, the priest was uneasy.

Magdalene smiled at him. "No one need know. This house backs upon the grounds of St. Mary Overy priory and some scores of years ago this was the priory guesthouse. There is still a gate between the church grounds and my back garden, which the prior kindly leaves open so sinners in this house can confess and be absolved. You can come at Compline, entering at the abbey gate. From there you can walk around the church and come here through our back gate. When your business is finished, you can leave through the abbey gate."

"Thus I will not be seen to enter a whorehouse every night and your clients will remain unaware of my visits." Father Etienne nodded. "Lord William often speaks of how clever you are and how useful. He is not mistaken, I see."

"He is always generous in his judgments," Magdalene said noncommittally. Since a number of her more anxious clients used that path the idea was not as clever as the priest thought, but Magdalene never spoke of her clients voluntarily. "But I must ask you for one more indulgence," she continued. "Lord William pays me a monthly fee for entertaining any of his men that he gives permission to come here. I will have to ask you to beg them not to use that privilege while I am away."

"That I can do, and most willingly." He frowned. "In any case, I think Lord William is recalling most of the men to Oxford. Sir Niall Arvagh and his troop have already returned to Oxford. I think Lord William plans to have the men camp well outside of the city—the weather is warm enough for them to live in tents." He shrugged. "The city is, indeed, so crowded that not only the houses are filled but the churches and church-yards."

He went on to expand on the problems raised by the new eagerness to attend on the king. Magdalene listened only enough to be sure he was repeating what she already knew. She had heard about the crowding in the city from those of William's men who had been sent away from Oxford and had stopped in at the Old Priory Guesthouse.

Half the tradesmen in the city had been displaced or had men quartered on them. Magdalene wondered where *she* would stay and felt a new prick of anxiety. Would William want her to live with him? His primary use for her was a safe house to conduct political business. Any man from any party can come to a whorehouse without raising suspicion. However William did occasionally wish to lie with her. She had always agreed, although he was a terrible lover, driving to his own quick sat-isfaction, usually without foreplay or consideration for his part-ner.

On the other hand, William was most moderate in his sexual demands. He was far more interested in politics and the man-agement of his many estates than in the pleasures of the flesh, but if he were *very* anxious it was possible he might feel the need for continued physical comfort. Magdalene swallowed uneasily. She was very fond of William, in fact she loved him, but . . . not that way.

The thought brought to mind the man she *did* love . . . that way, and Magdalene swallowed again. Bell. Sir Bellamy of Itchen, as clever as William and just as proud, although he did not come near William in wealth and power and made his living as one of the bishop of Winchester's knights. Bell would have a *fit* when he heard she had agreed to go to William in Oxford, and if he heard she was living with William . . . Magdalene managed to restrain a shudder.

She had warned Bell when she finally allowed him into her bed that from time to time there would be, must be, other men, that their coupling could only be for a temporary pleasure, not a symbol of any permanent bonding. She had insisted from their first meeting that she was by profession a whore and would not change.

Magdalene did not sigh because she was aware that Father Etienne was looking at her while he talked, but she felt like sighing. Bell gave lip service to acceptance of her profession. Perhaps his head even acknowledged the truth of her warnings, but she feared his heart did not. Well, he would either learn to control his jealousy or they would come to a parting of the ways.

A funny hollow feeling in Magdalene's midsection made her shift on her seat. That was wrong, she told herself. To become attached, to desire too much to please, that way lay disaster. She could never again be one man's woman. Three men were dead from trying to keep her. And, because she had been a whore for many years, even if she agreed to abandon her trade and her business, even if she were as faithful to her man as a nun is to Christ, no man would ever trust her. To any man, no matter what he said, she would always be a whore.

It was a very good thing, indeed, that William had summoned her. She was growing too . . . too wifelike. She must distance herself from Bell and retain her independence. Still, to live with William . . . Magdalene began to think over the friends and acquaintances she still had in Oxford from the years when she had managed a whorehouse there.

"The king's power is now nearly absolute," Father Etienne was saying, "although the bishop of Salisbury and his 'nephews' still do much of the day-to-day governing. They have done it for so long—years under the late King Henry and since King Stephen came to the throne—that they are obeyed without question by all the sheriffs and most of the local barons. This is making the king uneasy."

Something in the priest's voice snapped Magdalene out of her own thoughts. She peered at Father Etienne's face, but she could not make out his expression. The room had become too dim. She glanced toward the open windows. It was still light outside and would be for some candlemarks yet because of the long evenings of summer, but the small windows did not let in enough light at this time of day.

"Let me bring some candles," she said, rising and suiting the action to the words. "And surely you would like something to drink and a bite to eat?" She went to the banked fire in the hearth and lit a long sliver of wood.

"I would be grateful for a cup of wine," Father Etienne agreed, and smiled self-deprecatingly. "I have been running on, have I not? But Lord William is uneasy . . ."

"Oh, no," Magdalene assured him. "I am very eager to hear anything you are allowed to tell me. My usefulness increases the more I know, as I am then unlikely to say the wrong thing to the wrong person."

Father Etienne laughed. "I cannot imagine you saying the wrong thing to *any* person, but I will be glad to tell you what I know, which, unfortunately, is more guess than fact. Before I go on, though, I must not forget to ask when it would be best for me to meet your women. They should know me, I think."

"If you can stay until Vespers, they will all gather for the evening meal. Ella has a partner for the night, but he will come later, after dark. My women should be leading their present clients out at any moment."

As if her statement had sparked the reaction, a door opened in the corridor and Ella's little girl voice said, "You do not need to go so soon. See, the sun is not yet set. If you like . . ."

A man's low rumble followed and Ella gave a lusty sigh.

"Oh, very well. I know I must not importune you to stay when you say you must go. But we did have a good time. . . . Well, I did! I hope I didn't displease—" Her voice cut off sharply—perhaps the man kissed her—and was followed by a giggle. "I'm glad."

The sound of a smacking kiss came and then another giggle, but fading, as if Ella was moving away. In another moment another door opened and closed and returning footsteps heralded the entrance of a girl who made the priest's eyes widen once more. She was short and beautifully rounded, high white breasts peeping above the low décolletage of a pale blue robe, which obviously covered a naked body. Her hair hung in pure golden ringlets and waves to her hips; her eyes were large and as clear blue as a cloudless summer sky . . . and just as empty.

When she saw Father Etienne, she stopped short and her

rosy lips made an O of consternation. She began to back away, saying, "I am so sorry, Magdalene. I didn't know you had a client with you."

"No, no, love," Magdalene said, getting up and going to the girl, whom the priest would have taken for a blushing innocent as color rose in her cheeks if he had not heard her with the man who had left by the back door. "Come in, Ella, do. This is Father Etienne."

The look of smiling welcome disappeared from the girl's face and she stiffened slightly. Then she dropped a curtsey and said, "Father," in a frightened voice.

Magdalene slipped an arm around her waist and drew her into the room. "There's no need to fear Father Etienne," she assured Ella. "He is William's clerk and has come on business."

"Oh." The smile returned to Ella's lips and her eyes sparkled. She was startlingly lovely. "Lord William's man," she said, happily. "He will not lecture me and threaten me with being eternally damned." Then the smile dimmed. "But you said he was here on business. Does that mean he cannot come and play with me?"

Father Etienne's lips twitched. "I'm afraid I cannot do that, pretty Ella. My calling forbids."

"Oh, but—" Ella began, but before Magdalene could speak or even gesture, there was the sound of another door opening.

"Do not be so silly," a rich contralto voice said. "You know it is my pleasure to pleasure you, and it *was* a pleasure. You've taught me something new, which is a miracle. Would you be angry if I . . . ah . . . used it again?"

"Course not." A male giggle. "That's why I taught you, because I like it."

"But that means you intend to come again." The rich voice was full of hope and expectation.

A male laugh, not girlishly high but not a man's full-chested tone. "M'father said to come and paid. Said it was worth being a little thin on other things. He's no fool, m'father. He was right, but I'll lay odds he won't short me, that he'll come up with the silver. I'll be back as soon as I can touch him for the price."

The back door opened and closed. Father Etienne looked expectantly toward the opening to the corridor. A moment later he was rewarded by the entrance of a woman of ordinary height—but that was the only thing ordinary about her. Her eyes were as bright and clear as the emerald glass in a church window. Auburn hair, brown but with enough red to give a hot glow, tumbled over back and shoulders to her hips in deep waves. Her skin was very pale, almost the milky white of a true redhead but with a gleaming lustre, and her smile was an invitation to confide.

"This is Diot," Magdalene said, patting Ella on her bottom, and telling her to run and tell Dulcie there would be an extra person for the evening meal. "Diot is neither silly, mute, nor blind . . ."

As she said the words, Magdalene faltered and a great weight she had not even realized was crushing her dropped off. There would be no need for her to seek among the retired whores or whoremistresses she knew for a substitute. Diot had not been with her long enough for complete trust, but she would be far more trustworthy than anyone not connected to the Old Priory Guesthouse. She was happy here and would not want to do any damage to the business, and overseen by Father Etienne, she would not be able to steal. Not that Magdalene suspected Diot of thieving under ordinary circum-stances, but the temptation to keep unexpected revenues for herself would be strong, particularly as she would be doing double duty. She would have to manage her own clients and others . . . Magdalene pushed the thoughts away. There would be time enough tomorrow to explain to Diot, who did not lack for sense.

". . . and she has the patience of a saint with self-important younglings," Magdalene went on with only the barest hesita-tion.

Diot laughed. "Ah well, it's easy enough to pretend the old, old ploys are new and that they enthrall me. It tells me what the younglings like and what will not shock them, poor in-nocents. And at least I do not need to exhaust myself to bring their standing men to attention."

"I cannot imagine any man—myself included, although I am forbidden to satisfy the impulse—being slow to rise to your invitation," Father Etienne said, grinning.

Diot's brows lifted questioningly and Magdalene said, "This is Father Etienne, who has come as William's messenger. I will have to leave for Oxford the day after tomorrow—" She turned and said to the priest, "That will do, will it not?"

The priest's brows drew together. "Ah, how long will it take you to reach Oxford? A baggage train—"

Magdalene shook her head. "I need no baggage train. I will ride and take a mule to carry what I need. If any of William's men are going back, I could ride with them, or I could hire a man or two from the Watch to accompany me. In any case, if I leave on Saturday, I will be in Oxford either late on Sunday or early on Monday."

"You should not ride in late on Sunday. You will be sleeping in the street if you do, I am afraid."

"Oxford!" Diot exclaimed. "But are there no whores in Oxford that Lord William must—"

"None like Mistress Magdalene," Father Etienne said.

Magdalene twitched her fingers, and Diot bit her lip, indicating she knew she had spoken amiss. Magdalene saw her glance uneasily at Father Etienne, but his eyes had moved toward the corridor, where Letice had scraped a slipper against the wall to draw attention. He shrugged his shoulders, taking in a totally different kind of near perfection. Letice's skin was dark, her eyes nearly black, and her hair a smooth, shining curtain that hung to her knees and had something of the sheen of a crow's feathers.

She came forward, smiling, extending a hand, and although she made no sound, it was clear that Father Etienne felt her welcome. Magdalene smiled with satisfaction as she performed her introduction again. Letice could not speak but now she could read and write. She had made enormous strides in the two months since Magdalene had begun to teach her, her desperation to find an outlet to express herself changing the drudgery of lessons into a precious gift.

As she watched Letice silently charm the priest, Magdalene dismissed her worries about how the Old Priory Guesthouse would function during her absence. Letice had worked in the place for a long time, and she had come as a volunteer. Despite her name, she was neither English nor Christian; she had communicated to Magdalene that in her culture whoring was an acceptable profession—not as honorable as being a wife, but not reviled. Letice had every reason to ensure the continued success of the Old Priory Guesthouse.

Lettice knew how the whorehouse worked; she knew most of the clients; she knew the prices. Father Etienne could do the accounts, but he would not know if there were subtle disruptions in the services provided or minor dissatisfactions among the clients that would make them resent the high prices Magdalene charged. Letice would know, and now she had a way to transmit even involved information. And since Diot could not read and write, she would never know that Letice was compiling a day-by-day account of what was happening.

CHAPTER 2

About midmorning on Friday, Magdalene checked once more that her undertunic was tied in a chaste bow around the base of her throat, that her linen gown was unsoiled and not laced too tightly. The color was a soft blue-gray, suitable for a warm day and modest enough for a merchant's wife's everyday wear. She drew a light veil the same color as the gown over her hair and the lower part of her face, felt for the letter concealed in the pocket tied around her waist, and set out for the bishop of Winchester's house.

She had been there several times before, and when she was admitted, she did no more than glance around the large, stone-vaulted room. It looked even larger today because it was far emptier than on her previous visits. There were no writing stands near the windows set between several of the arches and only four men lounged on the benches at right angles to the stone hearth about midway in the room. The fire was banked to dull embers in this mild weather but never allowed to die because the stone walls retained a chill.

She was by now accustomed to the surprise that showed on

the face of the servant who had admitted her. The bishop of
Winchester, abstemious in his habits, received few women, and
Magdalene told the servant quickly that she had come to leave
a message to be sent on to Winchester. He waved her toward
the back of the room, where a partition provided a private area
for the bishop to talk business. In front of the partition was a
handsome table. Magdalene approached the priest, who sat on
a stool behind it.

He looked more shocked than the servant, but said, "The
bishop is not here, mistress."

"I know," Magdalene said. "I am one of the bishop of Winchester's tenants. Sir Bellamy of Itchen collects the rent . . ."

Behind her veil she smiled bitterly as the young priest stiffened and moved back on his stool. Sir Bellamy was one of the
bishop's knights, a strong secular arm to enforce the will of
the prelate when Churchly admonition failed. He was no simple bailiff and collected rents only where there might be danger, which was nearly always from the whorehouses owned by
the Church. The young priest, Phillipe something-or-other,
had realized she was a whoremistress and recoiled.

"I must leave Southwark," Magdalene continued, "and I wish
to inform Sir Bellamy that there will be no one who can pay
the rent for several weeks. I will, of course, pay the full sum
as soon as I return. I have been a tenant of the Old Priory
Guesthouse for over five years and have never been late or
short with my rent."

While she was speaking she had thrust her hand through
the slit in her skirt and pulled her pocket through it. As she
opened it to extract the letter, she noticed that the rigidity of
the priest's body relaxed somewhat when she named the Old
Priory Guesthouse, and she wondered whether Bell had spoken

of her or whether young Father Phillipe remembered the involvement of her women in solving the murder of the papal messenger back in April.

"If you will be kind enough to send this letter on to Sir Bellamy in Winchester, I think he will be willing to let my account ride for the time of my absence and not frighten my women with demands for money they do not have."

"But Sir Bellamy is here," Father Phillipe said, sounding surprised. "He is in the bishop's chamber."

"Ah," Magdalene said, her face expressionless despite her shock. So Bell was in Southwark, and he hadn't let her know. "Then I can give him my letter myself."

"Wait!" Father Phillipe exclaimed as she started to turn. "You cannot go into the bishop's chamber."

"Of course not," Magdalene agreed. "I was only putting my pocket back under my skirt. Shall I wait here, or will you tell Sir Bellamy to come to the Old Priory Guesthouse?"

Despite the pain she felt over Bell's abandonment, she had to make a conscious effort to keep from smiling at the agony of indecision in the young priest's face. He could not decide whether it was worse to have her standing by his desk, contaminating the atmosphere with her sinfulness, or to send Bell to the den of iniquity that was a whorehouse.

"Wait there," Father Phillipe said, "I will tell him you are here and he can decide whether he wishes to speak to you or not."

He rose from behind the table and went through the door in the partition into the bishop's chamber. Magdalene blinked once or twice to clear a slight mist from her eyes. There had not been the smallest sign that Bell was tiring of her the last time they were together. In fact, it had been a Sunday, and they had had such a lively night they had both slept late. And then he had lingered so long over breaking his fast and laughing with and teasing her women, that he had told her he would have to ride far into the night to arrive in Winchester at the time he had promised the bishop he would be there.

Could he have been set upon by outlaws? Could he have had some other accident on the way to Winchester that made him think he had been punished for sinning in her company? She drew a deep breath. Well, if that were so, at least she would not need to quarrel with him over obeying William's command. Perhaps she should just leave the letter . . . No, she couldn't do that! It was full of affection and apology. She must—

"Magdalene!"

She had turned toward the outer door but swung back to face Bell when she heard his voice. He was dressed with his usual elegance in footed dark blue chausses cross-gartered in pale green. His tunic, short enough to expose his powerful thighs and give him freedom of movement if fighting became necessary, was also light green, faced and collared with an elaborate multicolor pattern bordered in dark blue. Magdalene's lips tightened. That embroidery was her work.

There were new touches to his clothing, however. His broad swordbelt was now decorated with gold wire, although the well-worn grip was still plain wrapped leather as was the hilt of his long fighting poniard, also sheathed on the belt. The eating knife was another story. That was new; it had a chased silver hilt with a semiprecious stone pommel—a typical gift from a woman.

"Sir Bellamy." She bowed her head very slightly.

Her voice had been cold, but he came toward her without

reluctance, holding out his hand. "How did you know I had come?"

"Father Phillipe just told me."

"Then what are you doing here?" Now he hesitated, frowning.

"I find I must leave Southwark for several weeks, so I—"

"Leave Southwark? To go where? Why?"

Magdalene widened her eyes as if she were surprised by his questions. The fool. A rent collector would not care where she went or why. She deliberately looked over his shoulder at Father Phillipe, who had also come out of the bishop's chamber, and then around at the servants and the men-at-arms near the hearth, who were looking toward them.

She ignored the questions and continued her own sentence as if he had not interrupted. "So I wanted to let you know that there would be no one at the Old Priory Guesthouse to pay the rent. I hope you will allow me to pay it all at once when I return. You know I have never failed to pay—"

He made an impatient gesture of acceptance. "Yes, of course. I will let the bishop know. But where—"

Magdalene shook her head at him, annoyed. Bell was not usually so slow to understand. It was, after all, for his sake, not hers that she acted as if their relationship was only that of tenant and rent collector. She was a known whore and her reputation could not be damaged by association with any man. He was the bishop's knight; he would not be much criticized for using a whore, but befriending one was another matter entirely.

Then Magdalene saw that his fair curls were tousled, far more unruly than the ordered waves in which he usually combed his hair, and the skin beneath his blue eyes was dark

and bruised looking with lack of sleep. A gleam of hope that
it was business rather than indifference that had kept him away
lightened the gloom of acceptance of separation, but she suppressed it firmly.

"You are tired, Sir Bellamy," she said. "I will not keep you
any longer." And she started to walk away.

"God damn it, Magdalene!" he roared. "I'm too busy—"

Something heavy hit the ground. Magdalene hoped Bell
hadn't run into poor Father Phillipe as he attempted to follow
her; she repressed a giggle but she didn't turn around. Perhaps
that wasn't wise. A lowly whoremistress should obey the
bishop's knight, but he hadn't issued any order, merely expressed his exasperation. Then she heard the door to the
bishop's private room slam and her amusement died. Bell hadn't
been following her.

She was much tempted to go back to the Old Priory Guesthouse and have a good cry, but the self-pity did not last very
long. By the time she had walked from the house to the gate,
stepped out into the road and turned left, her impulse to weep
had changed to one for slightly bitter laughter. Whores did
not cry over men . . . and anyway she had a great many more
important things to do before she could start for Oxford the
next day.

She needed some items for the trip. It had been so long
since she left the London area that her travel baskets had been
adapted for other purposes. She would have to get at least one
new one so her gowns would not be too badly wrinkled. For
the rest, her undergarments and toilet articles and such, she
thought a good strong piece of canvas and two leather straps
should serve. Then she must be sure that no necessary item
would be used up in the Old Priory Guest-house while she

was gone. First and foremost sheets—keeping the linen clean in a whorehouse was very hard on sheets; they tended to thin from being washed so often and then tear when the action abed became vigorous.

Musing on other supplies that might be needed before she returned, Magdalene walked briskly along the wall of St. Mary Overy priory, past the gate, which was only a hundred feet or so from the gate to the bishop's house, and on toward the river. At the end of the road was a small dock belonging to the priory. Magdalene glanced at it, but there was no boat tied up there and it would take longer to try to signal one than to walk to London Bridge. Besides, the bridge was lined with merchant's stalls. She might see something she wanted.

In fact the fine spring weather had caused the merchants and peddlers to spill off the bridge itself into a broad apron around it. Magdalene tightened her veil around her face against the tugging and brushing it would receive in the press of people ahead. A curious glance or two, because it was not customary for women to veil their faces—especially on the Southwark side of the river where prostitution was a major business—made her reflect unhappily on the flawless beauty that would gain far less welcome attention if she walked bare-faced. She had been told she was beautiful enough to stop a man's breath. Perhaps, but unveiled she was more likely to experience grabbing hands than breathlessness.

The wry thoughts slipped away as pie-sellers thrust trays at her, ribbon vendors offered multicolored streamers for her inspection—Magdalene did stop to look; she and all of her women embroidered and ribbons were always needed, but these were too coarse—and shouted praise of these wares and those drew her attention from one side to another. Despite a resolution not to be seduced, she was a handful of sweetmeats the poorer by the time she got onto the bridge itself.

Here were the established merchants, those who owned stalls along each side of the bridge, although one still had to push past and around itinerant sellers of small items and food as well as by purchasers and passersby who just wanted to cross the bridge. She could only thank God that the bridge was not roofed; even open to the air and the sky the noise was deafening. Journeymen and apprentices bawled their masters' wares, peddlers bawled their own, purchasers shouted offers at merchants who shouted back higher prices, and those who wanted to cross pushed and excused themselves and cursed as the mood took them.

In fact, Magdalene found her travel basket on the bridge. It was actually a pair of long, narrow baskets, just about the length of a horse's body so they could be mounted on pads or a frame without getting in the horse's way. The baskets were long enough to hold a gown and one fitted into the other. There were open handles woven into both baskets about a third of the way from each end. One could pass a rope or a strap through those to secure the baskets together and attach the bindings to straps on the animal's harness. Magdalene paid for the baskets and left them with the merchant to be picked up on her way back.

She was good about resisting temptation as she worked her way to the other end of the bridge, then turned left to walk north toward the East Chepe on Gracechurch Street. Fish Street would have been nearer to her next stop, at Master Mainard's saddlery, but she preferred not to be splashed with fish guts and filthy water.

When she reached the Chepe, Magdalene turned right and

walked nearly to the end of the street. Henry, who sold the products of Mainard's labor, smiled broadly at her and stepped aside so she could come around behind the counter, which held reins, saddlebags, stirrup leathers, and even two saddles, and enter the door of the shop. Cody, the journey-man, saw her when she crossed the open door of the workroom and called out to Master Mainard, who laid down his tools at once to greet her with considerable pleasure.

Hearing Magdalene's voice, Sabina came down from her rooms above the shop. She was more beautiful than ever, glowing with health and happiness. Magdalene told her that she would be away from the city for a few weeks so there was no need to visit the Old Priory Guesthouse. She saw the flash of pleasure on the saddle-maker's face; he never protested against Sabina's visiting her old place of business and her "sister" whores, but it made him uneasy. He could never forget the horrible birthmark that disfigured his face, and despite the fact that he knew Sabina, being blind, could not see it, he still feared she would come across a more attractive man and leave him.

Then Magdalene mentioned the leather straps needed for the travel basket and asked if Mainard had any on hand. He did not, but the journeyman said it was no matter at all. If Magdalene would give him half a candlemark, straps would be ready for her. She asked the price; Mainard and his journeyman both looked offended. The journeyman stammered that he could not charge someone who only the month before had saved him from hanging. Mainard nodded agreement and said she had done as much for him, saving him from a lifetime of suspicion that he had murdered his monstrous wife. There would be no price.

Magdalene said she wouldn't take the straps without paying; that probably William of Ypres would return anything she spent anyway, so there was no reason for Mainard not to take a decent profit. They spent a pleasant half candlemark haggling and worked out a satisfactory arrangement in which Magdalene would pay costs and labor, and the straps would be ready when she returned from her visit to the mercer.

The sun was declining from noon by the time she got back to the saddlery burdened with sheets, pillow slips, stockings, and half a dozen of the thinnest and softest shifts she had ever seen. She had bought three for herself and one for each of her women. Sabina touched them, murmured something about the softness of the garment . . . and Mainard got the name of the mercer from Magdalene, showed the shift to Cody, and sent him out to buy three more for his beloved wife.

Sabina protested that she had shifts enough and Mainard should not spend so much on her, but Mainard said they were not for her but for him, for the pleasure he would have in seeing her wear them. That silenced Sabina, and then he diverted her by pressing Magdalene to stay and take dinner with them. Sometimes Magdalene found the overgreat sweetness of Mainard's and Sabina's relationship faintly sickening, but today for some reason it lightened her spirit, and she agreed at once to stay. She did not have to live with them, Magdalene told herself, so their doting fondness and Mainard's tendency to treat Sabina like a witless child—which she was not by any means; she was only blind and was well able to take care of herself—was pleasantly amusing.

By the time the meal was brought from the cookshop and consumed, it was nearly time for the first set of clients to arrive at the Old Priory Guesthouse. Magdalene said a hasty farewell and began to gather up her bundles, wondering how she would manage the travel baskets atop the others. However the problem did not arise. Cody and the oldest apprentice removed the packages from her hands as soon as she came down the stairs and said they would accompany her home.

A sense of cold weight, which she had managed to hold off, began to descend on her as they approached the Old Priory Guesthouse, but she could not indulge it. Cody and the apprentice brought in the fruits of her shopping and Ella burst into tears at the sight of the travel basket. It took a little while to convince her that her simple world was not coming to an end, that nothing would change at the Old Priory Guesthouse, that Diot would solve her problems and not scold her, and that Magdalene would be back in a few weeks.

Distribution of the new shifts went a long way to distracting Ella's mind, and before her fears could rise again, her first client appeared. Magdalene breathed a long sigh of relief. When Ella was with a man, her attention was totally focussed. Then Letice's client, who was new and had been recommended by Master Buchuinte, wanted to ask a host of questions. Since he was a wealthy grocer whose wife had died some months past and was just the kind of client who might be very profitable for a long time, Magdalene had Letice bring out good wine and sweetcakes and did her best to satisfy his doubts and soothe his anxieties.

The delay and Letice's understanding that a first-time client must not be rushed and must be completely satisfied made her late for her next client. Since he planned to spend the whole night, he did not feel as if he were being cheated of precious time and was not impatient. Magdalene kept him busy with light chatter, and when that ran thin began a mild complaint about the inconvenience of family obligations, which were dragging her away from her business to Oxford.

"Oxford!" he exclaimed, shaking his head. "This is a terrible time to go to Oxford. Had you not heard that the whole realm has responded to King Stephen's summons to this Court sitting? I hope your family has some place for you to sleep."

"They had better," Magdalene said, smiling—but she did not think that William would have troubled himself to think about where she would stay, unless he intended her to stay with him. She repressed a shudder and leaned forward to refill the client's wine cup. "They bade me come. I did not offer, I assure you. But why is this Court so crowded? I do not remember that there was so great a press of people, even at the Court at Westminster at Christmas."

"Those who came to Westminster could lodge in London," he said. "Oxford is much smaller. The thing is that after the king's victories in the west and the Battle of the Standard, which routed the Scots in the north, most men believe that King Stephen is too strong to oppose. Thus, everyone wishes to display his loyalty by appearing at Court."

Magdalene sighed. "That is reasonable, I suppose, even if it is inconvenient for me."

The goldsmith grinned. "It may be reasonable, but that does not make it the whole truth. This is one of the times I am very glad to have been born a goldsmith instead of a lord. The earl of Gloucester's defiance to the king has made Stephen suspicious, and the great lords are trying to show they are not looking Gloucester's way. To fail to appear at Court might mean one was gathering men and supplies to burst into rebellion as soon as Gloucester crosses the narrow sea."

"Surely not? Why should they? Stephen has been a mild and merciful king, has he not?"

"Perhaps too mild and merciful. I have heard it said that rebels would likely escape punishment, and as for reasons . . . there are always reasons—" He looked up at the sound of soft footsteps to see Letice smiling at him from the doorway to the corridor. He smiled too, but turned back to Magdalene to say, "And for those who *are* rebels, what better place to meet and make plans than a king's Council where you and your confederates have been summoned? Who could say your meeting was for an ill purpose?" He shrugged as he rose to join Letice. "I hope these are only fanciful fears. No merchant likes war, and a war of rebellion least of all. Your family is not political, is it Magdalene?"

"No, not at all. They are small folk of no importance."

"So much the better," he said soberly. "This is a good time to be overlooked."

When Letice's door closed behind them, Magdalene put away the flagon of wine and carried the cups into the kitchen to be washed. The bell at the gate rang as she was coming back along the corridor, and she frowned slightly, trying to think who could be arriving at this time. Another new client? Anyone who knew the ways of her house would be aware that no woman would be free until Vespers and that if he wanted to be entertained without an appointment he should come closer to that time.

I will send him away, she thought, as she went out to answer the bell. *I will explain that this is a bad time because I am leaving tomorrow*. But she walked slowly, still undecided. Turning away a new client on his first visit was not good business. On the other hand, she really did not want to spend the next few hours

entertaining an impatient man. She wanted to pack before Ella
was free to notice and begin to wail again.

The bell rang again, a short irritable peal, just as she reached
for the gate. That made up her mind for her. She didn't need
any more clients who were short tempered and demanding.
She snapped the gate open harder than she had meant, beginning to say "I am sorry—" before the angry face on the other
side made an impression.

"Sorry about what?" Bell snapped.

"Oh, I thought you were a new client and I was about to
try to explain that this was a bad time because I am going
away."

"What difference could that make to a new client . . . Unless
you are taking clients again?" His color rose with temper as
did his voice.

"It would be none of your affair if I did!" Magdalene snarled,
pulling the gate all the way open, and yanking him forward.
Since he had not been braced to resist and Magdalene was no
weakling, he stumbled through. She slammed the gate behind
him and pulled in the bell cord, so that no one else could ring.
"It so happens that I want to do my packing before Ella is rid
of her client because she begins to cry every time she's reminded that I'm going away."

"To cry? Why?" Bell asked, momentarily distracted.

"Who knows?" Magdalene replied impatiently, walking past
him toward the door. "You know she's like a child. I suppose
she is afraid that I won't come back or she will be mistreated
in my absence. Actually, she won't even notice that I'm missing
once I'm gone if everything runs smoothly, but if she sees me
packing she'll weep and wail all the time I'm away."

"Surely not when she's abed," Bell said, grinning.

Magdalene closed the door of the house behind them and
waved him toward the stools by the hearth. "No, not then,"
she replied, also smiling. "To futter is her ultimate comfort, so
her clients won't be deprived, but if she doesn't realize I'm out
of the city, she won't bore them to death by rehashing her
fears with them. And, truthfully, I would just as soon most of
them didn't know I was from home."

"Home," Bell repeated softly. "Do you really think of a
whorehouse as home?"

Magdalene stared at him for a moment, then sighed long
and loud. "Yes, I do," she said in a mildly exasperated voice,
looking around at the orderly, handsome room. "It *is* my home.
I am comfortable here, happy."

"Yet you are going away, and for some time if you are packing enough to make Ella notice."

"Several weeks, I fear."

"And you will not tell me where you are going?" He looked
at the hands clasped between his knees.

"Of course, I will tell you. Why in the world should you
think I would not? I came to the bishop's house to leave a
letter for you explaining everything."

"But you did not leave it."

"No." Magdalene stiffened, remembering her pain when she
realized he was in Southwark and had made no attempt to see
her. "You did not bother to let me know you were back in
Southwark, so why should you care if I go away?"

He blinked at her. "Let you know? When did I have time
to let you know? I arrived after midnight. Would you have
thanked me for waking the entire street and disturbing your
clients by coming here? And I have been going through Winchester's correspondence since dawn—" He stopped abruptly

and lifted a hand to rub over his eyes and then down his face.

Magdalene smiled slightly. "I've forgotten already what you said."

Bell burst out laughing. "Thank God I do not have to hold my breath until I believe you. I would surely turn blue."

She lifted her brows, acknowledging that he knew she rarely forgot anything but also knew that it was extremely unlikely she would repeat it deliberately or let it slip by mistake. But all she said was, "You arrived last night?"

"Yes, from Oxford—"

"Oxford!" Magdalene echoed. "But that's where I'm going."

"You are going to Oxford? What for?" And then, his lips pursed as if he had tasted something bitter. "I fear any man rich enough to afford your fees will be too busy with the concerns of the realm to have time for your soliciting."

Magdalene laughed again. "I have no need to solicit for custom. As you know we frequently have more business than bodies to satisfy it. I have been thinking of starting a search for another blind girl. There are those who still ask for Sabina. Apparently her hands had a special delicacy of touch—"

"Magdalene . . ." Although his voice was no louder, it gave the impression of a roar. "Why are you going to Oxford?"

She did not sigh although she felt like doing so. She had begun to hope that Bell would go on to Winchester with whatever information the bishop needed and that she would escape having to tell him that she had responded to William of Ypres's summons.

"Because William sent a clerk to tell me he has need of me. He is my . . . patron. I owe him my comfort and most of my freedom from fear of persecution. If he needs me—"

"Needs you?" That time his voice did rise, and Magdalene

held up a hand for quiet. When he spoke again it was little above a whisper, but he might as well have been shouting. "How can he need you? Are there no whores in Oxford?"

"Diot said the same thing." Magdalene giggled, then said more soberly, "I lie with William if he asks me, yes, but I doubt his desire for my body is why he has summoned me all the way to Oxford. However, you are right insofar as he wants me because I am well known among those who serve the king as William's favorite whore. What he wants is my presence in a place where any man of any party can seek a woman's com-pany. With that excuse, he may speak to whom he likes with-out suspicion." She frowned. "One of my clients says that there is much uncertainty among the king's men over the defiance of Robert of Gloucester."

"Uncertainty is a mild word," Bell said, his lips thin and grim. "And Waleran de Meulan is whispering in this ear that the bishop of Salisbury and his son and nephews have stuffed and garnished their keeps for war in readiness to join with Glouces-ter as soon as he arrives in England."

"Good God, you do not mean it!" Magdalene whispered. "The bishop of Salisbury was King Henry's other self for thirty years and was loyal and steadfast. Whenever King Henry went abroad, Salisbury ruled in his stead and Henry, who was no wooly lamb, was satisfied. Salisbury accepted Stephen and swore to serve him, saving his duty to the Church—"

Bell's lips twisted. "Saving his duty to the Church . . . that can cover many things. Remember—or maybe you do not, such things are not important to women—that King Henry forced his barons to swear to support his daughter Matilda as queen."

"Oh, I remember." There was bitterness in Magdalene's

voice. "My h—" she choked back the word "husband," swallowed, and substituted "—father was so enraged he beat me,
because I was a woman and he said it was unfit that men should
swear to obey a woman and have her for queen." Then she
shook herself as if shaking off the memory and frowned. "Did
the bishops also swear?"

She hoped the question would divert Bell from her slip. She
had told him the standard tale of how she became a whore,
that she was a love child that her father had recognized and
raised in his household, but when he died she had been cast
out by his wife, who hated her for her beauty. She had no
desire for anyone, even Bell, to know she had been married.
To know so much, might open enquiries into what had happened to her husband. If he had died a natural death, some
arrangement would have been made for his widow.

Although she did not really believe Bell had not noticed, he
only answered her question, saying, "I do not remember if the
bishops swore to Matilda. I am not sure I was in England then.
I served some years as a mercenary on merchant ships before
my father found me a place with the bishop. My mother feared
me dead each time I set sail and gave him no peace until he
found me safer work."

"Then I must thank your mother," Magdalene said, smiling,
"because I am glad you did not drown."

"Probably because I was born to be hanged," Bell said lightly
and then shook his head. "Or because I was born to die on a
battlefield. If Salisbury *does* turn rebel, it will be a disaster."

"It will, indeed." Magdalene pulled back the hand she had
extended to move her embroidery frame closer and clasped
both hands. "Merciful Mother, the whole government is in
Salisbury's hands. He is the justiciar. Roger le Poer, his son, is

chancellor now, but he just does as Salisbury tells him. And his nephew Nigel is the treasurer."

"Which may be why Waleran de Meulan is whispering that they must be stopped before they shift to Gloucester's camp."

"Stopped? Stopped how? Surely the king would not attack a bishop!"

"Openly? God knows, but I am afraid that Waleran is urging Stephen to strip Salisbury of his secular offices and castles. That is the king's right, but when I sent word of those rumors to Winchester—" He stopped speaking abruptly, and then said, "I must ride back to Oxford tomorrow."

"That's wonderful!" Magdalene exclaimed. "I must go to-morrow also. We can ride together, which will save me from needing to hire men or ask Father Etienne to send some of William's men with me."

"Who is Father Etienne?"

So Magdalene told him of the arrangements to preserve her business from damage, managing to conceal her temptation to grin at Bell's sour expression. She knew he thought that if her business was not so profitable, she might give it up and become his woman, but that was impossible. To a man, once a whore always a whore. No matter what she did he would never trust her. And lack of trust led to beatings and threats of worse, to a body bleeding out its life . . .

She wrenched her mind back to the present to hear Bell say, "I do not think Oxford is a safe place for you to be."

"Why not?" Magdalene shrugged. "No one will bother a whore conducting her usual business. What does a whore care who rules? She does not care who pays her. All she wants is peace in which to ply her trade."

"I don't mean that there would be any threat to you as a

particular person. I just feel that this Court will not pass without violence."

"Violence? But surely the king's peace is enforced during his time of holding Court. All men have safe conduct to come and go . . ."

Her voice faded. She remembered some weeks past that a group of William's captains had stopped at the Old Priory Guesthouse on their way to Rochester. They had complained that their men had been sent out of Oxford because there was no room for them. At that time she had remarked that such an order was foolish. Who better than William's foreign mercenaries to keep the peace? They certainly did not care about English parties. And one of William's captains had said that perhaps someone did not want the peace kept.

Bell had been watching her face. Now he shrugged. "I hope the rule of safe conduct may hold. King Henry was strong enough that he could suffer a man to defy him in Court and let him go free because he could punish him later. Stephen has beaten back his enemies, but I doubt he believes himself able to confront the really powerful among his own men. That is why I fear some move will be made against Salisbury . . . but I do not know what. Salisbury has given no real cause for Stephen to act against him."

Magdalene sighed. "Well, it does not matter. I still say that unless the whole city of Oxford goes up in flames, I will be safe enough. And I have already given my word that I will be there by Monday morning at the latest. So, will you let me ride with you, or shall I make other arrangements?"

Bell looked sour and then laughed. "I should know better than to try to change your mind after it is fixed. Of course you will be welcome to ride with me." He stood up. "And you had better finish that packing. If I stay the night, which I hope you will allow, I have no more desire than you to hear Ella wailing or asking over and over why you must go and what will become of her."

CHAPTER 3

Aside from several showers, one severe enough to force them to seek shelter, Bell and Magdalene had no trouble on the road to Oxford. He was not surprised, since he had four well-armed men and he himself wore mail and helm. Moreover they did not look to be worth attacking, since the mule that carried the baggage was not heavily laden and the woman who rode with them wore simple clothing without a ring or a chain for ornament. A poor knight and his wife, thieves would think, with no money or jewels worth fighting five armed men.

Ordinarily the most dangerous part of their journey would have been the passage through a heavily wooded area and then crossing the ford just outside of the town, but there was a whole concourse of people, several with larger meinies of armed men, on the road that morning. As they slowed behind a heavily laden baggage cart until the road widened and they could pass, a mounted man waiting by the side of the road hailed them. He waved his meinie to ride behind and brought his horse to Bell's other side. Magdalene was surprised to see him, but her face showed only mild curiosity, as for a stranger. He glanced at her and then away.

"Is the bishop here?" the young man asked Bell eagerly.

"No, Lord Ormerod," Bell replied. "I am sorry to say he holds by his decision to remain in Winchester. However, the dean is here. He is at Wytham Abbey and will welcome you."

The young man frowned. "The dean will not do. It is that old trouble about the farm my father bought just before he died. You know I have a quittance and the bishop witnessed it, but the man now says that was only the first payment. I hoped the bishop would ask the king to settle the matter. Winchester *is* the king's own brother. And I think the king feels an especial desire to please the bishop just now."

"And so he should," Bell snapped, then set his jaw. After a deep breath, he went on, "There is such a great attendance at this Court that I am not certain the king will have time to look into all the claims raised, but he usually does try to settle clear cases. It might be worthwhile for you to approach him. However, with the press of business, I cannot think of a way to bring yourself to his attention."

"Sir Bellamy!" The young man's voice was raised in mingled shock and reproach. "I never thought—"

What he would never have thought was cut off by someone coming in from a side lane, who called out, "Bellamy of Itchen? Is that you?"

Bell turned, stared, and then lifted a hand in salute. "It is, indeed, Sir Ferrau."

A shade of annoyance flicked over Lord Ormerod's face, but he let his horse drop back as Sir Ferrau took his place beside Bell and replied, "You remember me? It has been more than ten years."

Ferrau smiled as he spoke, and Magdalene looked at him over the draped veil that hid most of her face. His smile was genial, his teeth good. He was dark-eyed and dark-haired, the hair fashionably cut in a bang across the brow and a smooth edge at the bottom of his ears. His tunic, split fore and aft for riding, was of good mulberry-colored cloth and he wore a short scarlet cape that Bell eyed with a touch of envy. He was broad shouldered and had as easy a seat in the saddle as Bell's.

"Of course I remember you," Bell replied. "How could I forget the drubbing you gave me when I said I wished to be a knight—I could hardly walk for a week. But it was kindly meant, I am sure."

"It was, indeed," Sir Ferrau replied, laughing again. "One of your teachers—Brother Simon, I think it was—asked me to show you that the profession of arms would bring you no joy. I could have told him he was wrong. I could see it in your eyes when you took hold of the sword I lent you. Well, and so—" he took in Bell's rich surcoat and the well-polished coat of mail that could be seen on his arms and through the surcoat's open sides; the inner edge of Bell's shield, which showed around his body although the device on it was hidden; the fine destrier he rode "—I see that you have acheived your ambition and been knighted."

"Oh yes. I left Abingdon when I was fifteen." Bell grinned. "But I took your lesson to heart and used all the money my mother sent me for sweetmeats and other toys to buy lessons from the men-at-arms that Lord Sutton owed to the abbey. They had not all the knightly skills but taught me enough to let me sell my sword to a merchant ship captain as a mercenary." He grimaced. "I learned more over the next few years, and by the time I returned home my father had resigned himself to the fact that I would not be a priest. So I spent another year as squire and was then knighted."

"And you have come to Court to forward your fortune?"

"I am not so high in the world yet as to need the king's favor," Bell said, smiling. "I am presently at the service of the dean of Winchester. But I could ask you the same question. Have you come to argue some case for Lord Sutton of Culham? I hope he is well. I heard about the great tragedy in his household some time ago, that his daughter was beaten to death and her maid was murdered also."

Sir Ferrau paled. "I am so sorry! I had not heard! I knew the girl as a child. I am appalled! When I left Lord Sutton's service all was well with him and his. He is a good man, but content with his small place. I was not. I am now in the service of Count Alain of Brittany, earl of Richmond." He shook his head. "I must ask leave of my lord to visit Lord Sutton and give him my condolences. He was very fond of the child. Did they catch the killer?"

"Not that I had ever heard."

"How terrible for Lord Sutton." Sir Ferrau sighed then shrugged. "Was there some reason . . ."

"I don't know." Bell had lost interest in the old story, distracted by an idea that might help Lord Ormerod.

He turned around to gesture Ormerod closer. Seeing the gesture, Magdalene fell back to make room and Sir Ferrau cast an interested glance at her.

"Is she your wife?" Ferrau asked.

Startled, Bell replied, "Alas, no," and grinned. "I am not rich enough to support a wife. The lady is a tenant of the see of Winchester and requested my protection on her way to Oxford. I was glad to agree. She is good company."

"Her husband would not escort her?" Sir Ferrau's eyebrows rose almost to the bangs that crossed his forehead.

"I know nothing about the lady beside her tenancy." Bell's voice became noticeably colder.

Magdalene grinned behind her veil. She was momentarily tempted to intrude herself into the conversation, just to tease Bell and see his fair skin turn as red as Sir Ferrau's cape, but she quelled the impulse. Sir Ferrau might take her boldness as an invitation. Then she would be in trouble because she would have to refuse him. . . . She hesitated over that thought. Why would she have to refuse him? He was an appealing man. No, it was too dangerous to take any man she did not already know until she understood in what William was involved. Even as the thought formed, she knew she was lying to herself, but she did not wish to seek for her true reason, and she fixed her mind on the men's conversation.

Sir Ferrau had clicked his tongue in response to Bell's repressive remark. "Sorry. Idle curiosity. My besetting sin. I hope you and the lady have lodgings in the town. Count Alain is well bestowed, so I am also well lodged, but the town is packed like a barrel of herrings."

"I am staying at Wytham Abbey with the dean," Bell said. "Monseigneur"—he patted his horse—"needs the exercise, and I don't mind the ride."

"It is no great way," Ferrau agreed, but his voice was absent and he glanced back speculatively at Magdalene.

She was again tempted to mischief, but modestly lowered her head. Then she was sorry about her deliberate act of propriety because Bell smiled. He did not smile at her—he was not a fool and doubtless guessed what her reaction to such a gesture of satisfaction would be. He was looking straight ahead, but there was something about the back of his neck and the tilt of his shoulders that betrayed his pleasure in her action. Likely he thought she did it for him. She sighed. Likely he was right.

Meanwhile as Ormerod drew closer, Bell said eagerly, "I have just had a thought about how you could bring yourself to the king's notice. Go to the castle and ask for Bruno of . . . of . . . yes, of Jernave. Tell him the problem. He is a Knight of the Body and may well know whether the king will be able to listen to your plea."

"A very sensible man, Sir Bruno," Sir Ferrau put in. "He arranged Count Alain's lodging. How do you know him?"

"I usually attend Court when my bishop does," Bell said. "I like Sir Bruno, who is a real favorite with the king but never puts on airs." And, as if those last words reminded him, he added, "Forgive me, Lord Ormerod, I have been remiss. Let me introduce to you Sir Ferrau. Sir Ferrau is in service with Count Alain of Brittany who is also earl of Richmond."

The young lord nodded pleasantly and then an expression of deeper interest crossed his face. "Richmond is none so far from that contested farm. Is Count Alain in Richmond often? Could I present the case to him?"

"He is most often with the king," Ferrau said warily. "And not wont to interest himself in local problems. Perhaps you had better consult his bailiff." He bowed slightly in the saddle and then said, "If you will excuse me, Sir Bellamy, Lord Ormerod, I see two of my master's men over there."

Bell was surprised at the abrupt decision to leave, but said only, "If you do find time to visit Lord Sutton, remember me to him. We met once or twice when he visited Abingdon Abbey, and he even once came to watch me practice with one of his men, and praised my . . . ah . . . energy."

"Gladly." Sir Ferrau smiled back over his shoulder. "I hope to get to Culham before the Council is over."

Bell was smiling when he turned back to Ormerod and was surprised again to find the young lord staring hard at him.

"You know Lord Sutton of Culham?" he asked.

"Well, not to say 'know.' Culham is not far from Abingdon Abbey where I was schooled, and Lord Sutton has several farms deeded to the abbey in his care. He pays his rent with a small troop of men-at-arms, who guard the abbey. I took my first lessons in sword and knife play from those men." Bell raised his brows. "How do *you* know Lord Sutton?"

"I was betrothed to his daughter—the girl who . . . who was killed."

"I am so sorry!" Bell exclaimed.

Lord Ormerod shrugged. "Don't waste any sympathy on me. I only met the girl once and, to speak the truth, we did not take well to each other. I was younger then, of course, but I did not think the dower lands offered with her were worth a lifetime in her company. Also she hinted pretty broadly that there was another she preferred—" he wrinkled his nose. "And what could have offended Sir Ferrau in what I said to him?"

For a moment Bell was silent remembering his surprise at Ferrau's abrupt departure, and then he shrugged. "It was not that he took offense. I think he has not influence enough with Count Alain to suggest that he hear a stranger's case, and he did not wish to admit it."

"Ah—" Ormerod began, but stopped speaking as Magdalene, who had seen the road ahead widen enough to pass the cart blocking them, kicked her mare into a trot.

Lord Ormerod quickly followed her. Bell brought Monseigneur around more cautiously. The destrier was not beyond taking offense at a cart and biting the driver or the mules that drew it. When Bell caught up with his companions, they had passed the party to whom the cart belonged and were riding side by side, conversing easily.

"Did you bring Magdalene to Oxford, Bell?" Ormerod asked, grinning.

"You introduced yourselves?"

Ormerod laughed. "No need for that. I've known Magdalene a long time. M'father brought me to the Old Priory Guesthouse . . . what? five years ago? Said he didn't want me to get a taste for serf girls and maidservants and wanted me to know what futtering *should* be like. I lay with the mute girl that time." He laughed again, snickered. "Didn't make a sound, but she taught me. Unless I'm too drunk to see or smell, I leave the common women alone. M'father was no fool. Well, you know that, Bell."

"I do know it. And I know you have a pretty wife, too."

"Yes, she is." Ormerod grinned. "And a good woman also, but sometimes . . . that Ella!" He sighed then grinned again at Magdalene. "Haven't been to the House in a long time, but—" suddenly his eyes were full of tears "—m' father died."

"Oh, I am so sorry!" Magdalene exclaimed, and neither man doubted that she truly felt grief. "He was not a frequent client, but he was so kind and good humored that all the women were eager to go with him. Sabina will weep. I will not tell Ella, if you do not mind, my lord. She would be so upset. It is so hard to explain to her."

"No, don't tell her. If she remembered next time I came, she'd ask me . . ." He swallowed hard, then found a smile. "I've been so busy. I haven't had time for much except the estate. When I can . . . I'll come for a night in his name."

"I will see that it is special for you," Magdalene promised.

"So you are still whoremistress there?"

"Of course." Magdalene laughed. "It is my livelihood."

"Ah . . ." He looked sidelong at Bell. "I thought perhaps since you had come with Bell that you and he . . ."

"No, no. I only begged escort from him. I am here on business. I do not think you know that Sabina has left us. One of her clients found he could not live without her. He married her. I found another woman, but business grows better and better and I could use at least one more. An old friend here thinks she may have found what I want."

"You picked a terrible time to come," Ormerod protested.

Magdalene sighed. "I know, but the whoremistress of the Soft Nest might not be able to hold the girl long without using her—especially when so many highborns are in the town. You know my women love their work and that my house is special. I do not want the girl frightened or broken. Oh, look, is that not the gate? Thank God we have arrived."

"At the gate, perhaps," Bell said drily, "but not yet in Oxford. Look at the crowd." He shook his head. "I think we can accommodate you at Wytham Abbey, Ormerod, if you have no other place."

"I am not so behindhand. I am staying with an old friend—" Ormerod chuckled "—well, he is some years younger than I. I was senior squire when he was still a page, and he looked to me for help. He has a manor at Osney." He sighed. "Usually it is quickest for me ride across Oxford. Osney is no more than a third of a league or so on the road west and then a little way south." He snorted. "Today I would have done better to ride around. I knew it was crowded, but this . . ."

However, it did not take them as long as they feared to get through the gate. It turned out that most of the delay was caused by a cart with a broken wheel, and that was dragged away only a few moments after they arrived. Once the way was clear, the people poured through quickly, the gate guards making no attempt to stop and question anyone.

Having taken a good look at the stalls of merchants and the slowly moving mass of people, Ormerod said he would go out the South Gate and around the farm lanes. He raised a hand in farewell and turned left to follow the wall. Magdalene waited until he was away and then said to Bell that they could take the same path.

"We will come out by St. Friedesweide's church. We can then turn north on the road that goes to the Carfax. The Soft Nest is on Blue Boar Lane, and you can leave me there. If Florete does not have room for me, she will ask around for another place that I could stay. I will leave a message with her for you if I must go elsewhere."

"I could wait—"

"No. I want to find out what Florete knows, and she would be less than frank in your presence. You can just ride north along the same road, which will take you to the North Gate, and there you will find the road to Wytham Abbey."

"You know Oxford all too well," Bell said flatly.

"Of course I know Oxford well." Her voice was angry, hard. "My first 'keeper' died here in contest with another man who wanted me. When the second man was killed in a drunken brawl in which I was again the prize, I decided there had been enough blood shed because of me and that I would never be any one man's woman again. So I worked in the Soft Nest for Mistress Lysette. William found me there and set me up in a house of my own."

"So much for not being one man's woman," Bell said.

"I was *not* his woman. Never. He knew I would take other men and he approved of that. In fact, he brought other men to me. I worked like any other whore, except that I could choose which man I would serve and which I would not—"

"Except for the ones Lord William brought."

Magdalene's lips thinned. "Yes, except for those. But then I found Ella, and that problem was solved."

While they spoke they had followed the wall for a little way, then Magdalene turned right into a lane that was not quite a street but was wider than an alley. At its far end it debouched into a large vegetable garden with a low house at the edge of the field. A cart track separated the garden from a graveyard, across which they could see St. Friedesweide's church. They rode past the graveyard and the church and Magdalene turned right again on the broad street by the church. They passed several merchant's houses, stalls out in front and well patronized, although the crush was much less than on the street leading to the East Gate. Then the mouth of an alley opened. Magdalene pointed at it.

"That is Blue Boar Lane," she said. "Do you want to come in and meet Florete so she will know you? If not, I can just give her your name . . . or any name you want to use if you prefer not to be known by name to a whoremistress."

"As if I were not already so known?"

"But that is business. You are the bishop of Winchester's knight. He is my landlord. You come to . . . ah . . . collect rent, to answer complaints, to . . ."

Bell burst out laughing, his good humor restored. "Do not work so hard to make me innocent. It is some years since I was pure." Then he frowned. "Is it true that this Florete is keeping a girl for you?"

"Unfortunately no. I have put out word that I would like to find a blind girl who was new to the craft, but I have heard nothing. That was only an excuse for my coming here at this time. I cannot admit William sent for me until I am sure he wants that known. I believe he does . . . but guessing is dangerous when mixing in his affairs."

"But you *are* looking for another girl."

"Yes . . ." She sighed. "But even if I never lie with a man again, will I be less a whore?"

She reached out and patted his hand just before she turned her mare into the alley mouth. Bell stared at her back bleakly for a moment, then followed. They passed an alehouse, its front yard full of idling men, some crouched over rolling knucklebones, others cleaning weapons or checking boiled leather armor. A few of the men looked up at the passersby, but most paid no attention.

Just beyond the alehouse Magdalene passed through an open gate into a yard in which several horses were tied to rails between sturdy posts. Beyond the rails, which prevented the mounts from coming too close to the building, was a wide-open door. Bell dismounted and tied Monseigneur at the far end of the yard, well away from the other animals. Then he returned and lifted Magdalene down from her mare.

"Will Monseigneur be safe there?" Magdalene asked, knowing the destrier was worth as much as a good house.

Bell sighed. "I just hope he doesn't kill anyone for coming too close. Yes, *he'll* be safe."

Magdalene shrugged. Any man should be able to recognize a destrier caparisoned for war; if he approached the animal he was a fool or had ill intent and would deserve what he got. She walked quickly through the open door and then stood still for a moment in the poorly lit corridor suppressing an old tremor of fear and a frisson of revulsion.

The Soft Nest was better than the lowest form of stew. There were no couples humping in the dim corridor, nor to the left in the corners of the whoremistress's large reception chamber. That was open in a wide arch to the corridor, but the way was blocked by a long, sturdy table. Behind the table the whoremistress presided, keeping an eye on the men and women who used her premises. At each end of the table was a stool. On one a large man sat, clearly a bullyboy.

Along the wall to the right of the table were two long benches, one to either side of the window that lit the room; another two were set to the right of the hearth. To the left of the hearth, against the far wall, was a large, curtained bed. Farther down along that wall was an open doorway.

Only a few women sat on the benches, talking or dozing, waiting in case a man came in to chose one. He would then pay the whoremistress and take the girl through the door beyond the foot of the bed into a large dormitory. The price was two farthings, higher than that in a common stew, but it paid for a pallet that was not too infested with crawling things— the straw that filled it was discarded once a month and the covering washed—and a modest space around the pallet. In the worst houses the pallets were never washed and would be set edge to edge. It was not unknown for two copulating couples to roll over onto each other.

This early in the day most of the women were still sleeping

on the pallets they used in their work. Magdalene guessed that a larger number than usual were doubly occupied with men who were willing to pay extra to stay the night in greater comfort than their tight-packed lodgings provided. When the town was not so crowded, only a few women stayed in the whorehouse. Most sought out safer, quieter rooms elsewhere, but because of the king's Court, all of them had been driven out to make room for better paying lodgers.

The seat behind the table was empty, but the whoremistress could not be far because the bullyboy had not risen or called out. Before she stepped up to the table, Magdalene looked down the corridor. Her eyes felt dry and hot and she had a bitter taste in the back of her mouth. The torches had been allowed to gutter out because the open door provided enough light, but the corridor was never really dark.

Pairs of torches were provided so that anyone traversing the narrow corridor would be forced nearly to touch the curtain-hung doorways that lined it. In those doorways a woman could stand, barely clothed and within easy arm's length, to smile, move suggestively, even touch in order to entice a man into her room rather than another.

As she thought it, two women came to lift a curtain. Seeing Bell, they posed and smiled. Magdalene swallowed more bile. She herself had stood in one of those doorways when she served in the Soft Nest. Any man had been free to push her in or walk past her into the small, windowless chamber behind the curtain. When it fell, she had been on her own. If a client thought she asked too much, she would be beaten, and the whoremistress would not interfere. The condition of the tiny chamber and how she protected herself and collected and kept her payment had been up to her. For that privilege, she had paid a penny a night in rent.

From behind the two closed curtains nearest them came characteristic sounds of sexual engagement—mostly grunts and groans, but Magdalene did hear one masculine laugh and a feminine giggle. At least those were sounds that told of a well-regulated place. There were no thin shrieks of abused children, no screams of agony, no snarls of sadistic rage.

Magdalene swallowed once more, and walked up to the table. "Is Mistress Florete here?" she asked, speaking English rather than French.

The man, who had been looking at Bell, expecting him to ask for a chamber or some other accommodation, turned his head to Magdalene. "Out back. She—oh, here she is now."

A medium-sized, sturdily built woman was coming down the corridor. Magdalene saw with relief that her shift, which was tied a decent inch above her cleavage and well above the edge of her low-cut gown, was clean and white. The gown itself, a pleasant shade of light green, was also unstained and clean, its folds those of the chest rather than of the bed. Her hair was clean, too, a glossy brown, worn in two thick plaits, one falling over each shoulder.

As she approached, Magdalene was sorry to see that Florete's brown eyes had lost their sparkle and were without expression and that her lips had become thin and tightly drawn to give nothing away. But in the next moment, her whole face changed. The eyes brightened and opened wide, the lips softened and tilted upward.

"Magdalene!" she cried, running forward. "Magdalene! What in the good earth are you doing here?"

"Not setting up a rival establishment," Magdalene said, laughing.

"Nor looking for work," Florete said, examining Magdalene's riding dress, which was a soft gray-blue, simple until one noticed the quality of the cloth and took in the elaborate embroidery around neck, sleeves, and hem.

"No." Before Magdalene could control it, a shudder passed over her. She suppressed another and smiled. "I have a long tale to tell and a huge favor to ask, but I don't want to keep Sir Bellamy from his duty any longer than I must. I just wanted to make him known to you so that, if I cannot stay here, I could leave a message for him so he would know where to find me."

Florete blinked, looked from one to the other, then smiled at Bell. "I am not likely to forget him."

Bell smiled back. "My name is Bellamy of Itchen, and I serve the bishop of Winchester. If any message besides those from Magdalene should be left for me, you will be well rewarded if they come into my hand and into no other."

An expression of anxiety crossed Florete's face. "For a friend of Magdalene's, I promise to do my best to make it so, but you must understand . . . we are whores here. If we are questioned straitly, we answer before worse befalls us."

"Good enough," Bell said, pleased with her honesty. "If you do not offer information, I will be satisfied." To Magdalene, he said, "You know where I will be. A message left with the dean will reach me. I doubt I will be able to come back to Oxford today. Will I see you tomorrow?"

"Yes, unless William sends me away from the city. In any case, I will leave word for you if I am not here."

He bowed slightly and left. Florete stared at his back, then bent sideways so she could watch him cross the yard. When he seized the reins of the destrier and mounted, she turned back to Magdalene.

"I thought you swore you would never be any one man's woman again."

"And I have kept that oath. That Bell would like me to break it is neither here nor there. He is welcome in my bed only on the understanding that others will be welcomed there also."

"Does he understand the honor bestowed upon him?" Florete asked, her eyes full of laughing mischief for a moment.

Magdalene laughed aloud. "Almost. He has even stopped flinching when I mention William."

The mischief in Florete's eyes was replaced by wariness. "The same William?"

"Yes, the same."

For a moment Florete was silent, then she went to the door and across the yard into the street. She looked both ways. When she came back, she told the man at the table to call her only if necessary, beckoned to Magdalene and went to her bed. Having crept inside the curtains and gestured for Magdalene to join her, she said softly, "I cannot go out now. Business will begin to increase soon. This is the best I can do for privacy."

"It is enough for now," Magdalene assured her, speaking no louder than she had. "I have no great secrets to keep or to tell. I am indeed here at William's behest, but I know no more than that. All his clerk told me was that he needed a safe house." She sighed. "Naturally he asks that of me right in the middle of the greatest concourse of men to take place in years. Do you know of a small house that I could empty temporarily? My old house? I can pay."

"What about here?" Florete asked.

"The cocking chambers are not large enough," Magdalene said at once. "There are likely to be several men, and the curtain at the door does not give enough privacy."

Florete repeated "Cocking chambers?" and looked surprised. "How could you think I would suggest a cocking chamber for *that* William's purposes?" Then she shook her head and laughed shortly. "I forgot you were gone by the time I added the back chamber."

Magdalene raised her brows and Florete shrugged and went on, "Well, you know we never used the garden. This is better than a stew but not like your house, where noblemen are cozened with talk, tidbits, and wine if a woman is not ready." A note of bitterness had come into Florete's voice.

Magdalene uttered a single bark of laughter. "And you are likely to make a powerful enemy if the entertainment is not sufficient or his lordship doesn't like to be reminded that his sword is not the only one that dips into that sheath. Do not envy me too much."

The tightness in Florete's expression relaxed and she shrugged. "To each her own joys. But anyway that's what I did with the garden. I built a room where a man could be really private—if he were willing to pay." She shrugged again. "I learned from you that a whorehouse is a good place for meetings that should not be taking place. I get some of those. I get some wild parties. I also get men who desire to dress as women, who desire to be together rather than with a woman, who want several women who will permit unnatural acts, preferably all at once." She sighed. "All kinds."

Magdalene's face lit with hope. "Oh, let me see. If the room is suitable and I can be assured that no one else will have it for the week I am here . . ."

They got out of the bed and Florete led the way to the back of the corridor. The heavy door was suitable to protect the back way into a house. However, instead of opening on a lane or a yard, the door opened into a long, narrow, but surprisingly pleasant room. To the left was a large bed with curtains looped back. Past them, Magdalene could see a small hearth in the corner and an open window, large enough to let in light and air but well barred against intrusion. The room had other windows, all barred, two in the back wall and another in the wall to the right. A second bed stood against the right-hand wall.

In addition to the beds, there was a chest under the window in the left wall, a single, high-backed chair with arms, and perhaps half a dozen stools arranged around the room. A tall candlestick with a thick, very white candle stood beside each bed, and brackets for torchettes were fixed to each wall. One could have, Magdalene could see, as much or as little light as one chose.

"How much?" Magdalene asked eagerly.

"A shilling a week," Florete replied, then bit her lip as Magdalene merely looked surprised without answering. "I wish I could offer it for nothing or ask less, but—"

"Less?" Magdalene exclaimed. "But you are asking far too little already. You must make double that by renting the room by the day or night in ordinary times, and you could make double or triple *that* while the city is so crowded."

Florete grimaced. "Yes, if I wanted a troop of men-at-arms in here. Can you imagine the havoc they would wreak with my women and my business? My boys are good boys, but they could not manage a troop of armed men. That is why the room is empty." She seemed to hear what she had said and closed her eyes and sighed. "Sorry," she muttered. "You can have it for nothing, Magdalene. I am growing so hard that even what I owe you grows dim in my mind."

"And so it should," Magdalene said, putting an arm around the woman. "You owe me nothing for a simple act of Christian charity. And even if there were a debt, it is not the kind that can be paid for in coin."

"I *know* it." Florete put her cheek against Magdalene's hand, which lay on her shoulder. "It was my *life* you gave back to me when you picked me out of the gutter—"

"Perhaps," Magdalene interrupted sharply, "but that has nothing to do with a fair rent for your room." She gave Florete a brief hug and released her with a laugh. "Likely I will not be paying for it anyway. I am reasonably sure William will make good." She looked around the room again. "Three shillings for a day and night is fair. . . . Yes, I will give you a pound for the whole week. That would be more than your regular fee, but for this time it is not unreasonable."

Florete blinked back tears. "You have not changed. You could have taken my offer and told your William that the price was a pound for the week. He would never have known—" She stopped, catching her breath a little at the horror on Magdalene's face.

"Never! I would *never* tell William a lie, not a small one about money or a large one in which my life hung in the balance." She shivered.

Florete stared at her then shook her head. "Your life must get very complicated if there are two men to whom you are pledged."

"Why?" Magdalene laughed. "I never said I wouldn't tell *Bell* a lie. I tell him what it is best for him to know." She sobered. "And I do not tell William more than *he* needs to know either. I simply never tell him a lie."

CHAPTER 4

With the most urgent problem of lodging settled, Magdalene asked Florete for a messenger. She produced a reasonably clean, nice-looking boy of about twelve, left on her hands by one of the whores who had died. Diccon was a clever boy, she said, tousling his hair affectionately, and accustomed to carrying messages.

That seemed to be true enough, for he nodded at once when Magdalene told him Father Etienne's description of the house in which most of William's captains were lodged. "In the small lane that goes off the road around the castle," he said. "The armorer's shop or the mercer's?"

"Oh that silly man," Magdalene sighed. "He didn't say, only that it was the largest house in the street."

The boy grinned and nodded again. "That'll be the armorer. Who gets this?"

"Lord William of Ypres, but I doubt he will be there. I believe he himself is lodged in the castle. Ask for Sir Niall Arvagh or Sir Giles de Milland. If not them . . ."

"Any knight in Lord William's service?"

Diccon's eyes were knowing. Service in the whorehouse had made him quick to recognize the difference between gentry, merchant, and peasant. He would not mistake a common man-at-arms for a belted knight. Magdalene nodded to his question, only cautioning him to make sure that Lord William's men were still lodged in the armorer's house or that Father Etienne had not made a mistake when he indentified the place. Not that delivering the note to the wrong person would be a disaster. It said only, "I am lodged in the Soft Nest on Blue Boar Lane. Magdalene."

She then told Diccon to wait for an answer but to leave at once if he were told there was no answer. And when he turned to go, she touched his shoulder and gave him a farthing. His slightly widened eyes and broad grin showed both surprise and pleasure with such largesse. Few of the women in the house would pay him; to their minds they had better uses for their money than paying for service from a boy who already got his food and lodging free, but a grateful and willing messenger might be valuable to Magdalene.

Her most pressing duty done, Magdalene began to settle into the Soft Nest. She arranged for the care of her horse and mule with one of Florete's men, who told her the animals could be kept in a shed in the small overgrown space that was left of the garden behind the house. There was some grazing there, and he'd bring them water. He also offered to bring in her traveling basket and canvas carryall.

Magdalene noticed his eyes on her, fixed on her face at first and then traveling downward to take in her dress. He looked away, then back, and his mouth set in a dissatisfied line, showing he had marked her as beyond his touch. Still, hope springs eternal and he said he was very ready to do any service she

requested. Magdalene thanked him, but to make perfectly clear
that she would not, like many whores, trade sexual favors for
work done, she gave him a penny, telling him to buy fodder
for the animals, and to keep any amount that remained after
the transaction.

He hesitated for just a moment, glancing sidelong at her
unveiled face, then sighed, took the coin, and went out. A
moment later she went to the common room to speak to Florete, who was presiding at the entrance. Magdalene wanted a
table for her room so that William and whoever he was meeting could sit and talk. There was nothing like having one's legs
under a table to discourage men from leaping up and launching
blows at each other.

That was easily arranged, but Magdalene was heartily annoyed when two men in the act of paying over their fees both
immediately chose her and began to quarrel over who should
have her first.

"Neither!" she snapped. "I do not work here. I am long retired and I have come to collect a woman for my house in
London."

"Retired?" one of the men said, laughed, and reached for
her. "Not with a face and body like that."

Magdalene pulled away as Florete said, "No!" The man
bringing in Magdalene's baggage set it down and reached for
his club, which was leaning against the table. Florete's other
man stood up. Magdalene slipped by them and retreated to
the back chamber, once more cursing her own beauty.

Fortunately no harm came of the incident, but it demon-
strated clearly that she would be deprived of one of the pleasures to which she had looked forward. It would be impossible
for her to sit with Florete and gossip about old friends and old

clients. She occupied herself with cleaning the bed and the
chest while Florete's man brought a small trestle table down
from the attic. When he had set the tabletop over the trestles
and moved the stools around it, he went out, casting a single
longing glance back at her.

Magdalene cursed and then sighed as she took clean sheets
from the bottom of her basket and made the bed by the left-
hand wall, hung her gowns from pegs, and moved her undergarments to the chest. She felt a trifle guilty at using the man,
but not nearly guilty enough to give him what he wanted. And
she had issued fair warning by paying him, she reminded herself.

Before she had finished unpacking, Diccon returned to report that he had given Magdalene's note to Sir Giles de Milland. Sir Niall Arvagh, her first choice to carry her message to
Lord William, was not at the armorer's house and was not
expected at any particular time. Diccon giggled; Sir Niall was
out courting a local girl.

Interested, for she liked Sir Niall, who had a quick wit as
well as a skilled sword, Magdalene probed for information.
Several men had come in together, Diccon said, and when he
had asked for Sir Niall and explained he had a message from
Mistress Magdalene to be carried to Lord William, Sir Giles
had explained why Sir Niall was away and that no time was
set for his return.

Diccon had then handed over his message, but he had heard
one of the other men make some pointed remarks about Sir
Niall's good luck.

"And that was all you heard?" Magdalene urged.

Diccon looked at the floor and admitted the men had paid
no more attention to him and talked among themselves after

he had handed over the message. Then he fell silent. Magdalene chuckled. More likely, she thought, Diccon had deliberately hidden himself in a corner to listen, but she was even
more interested and produced another farthing. Diccon
grinned.

"She's Loveday of Otmoor," he said. "That's what they called
her, and said she was a heiress in the king's ward."

"Lord bless me," Magdalene murmured. "What is Niall doing
courting an heiress in the king's ward? Stephen will want her
for one of his highborn paupers."

"Nah," Diccon stuck in. "She've not got enough for that nor's
born high enough."

Magdalene's brows shot upward. "Now how do you know
that, you little limb of Satan? Out with it! You've had two
farthings of me, and the next thing you'll get is a whipping."

"I was going to tell you," he said indignantly. "The man said
a king's clerk told Lord William about this Loveday. Another
said—I didn't get his name either—that the clerk was looking
for Lord William's favor and thought the girl would do for one
of Lord William's men since she wasn't grand enough for the
king's cronies. That man sounded a little sour, and Sir Giles
snapped at him. He said the reason Lord William sent Sir Niall
was because he remembered Sir Niall came from Murcot,
which was not far from Otmoor."

Now that it was brought to her mind, Magdalene also recalled that Murcot was possibly half a league north of Otmoor,
but she was reminded again of William's acuteness. It was as
if he kept the placement of every vill in the kingdom in his
mind. Magdalene frowned. She could not call to mind any
manor called Otmoor.

"That's all I heard, honest," Diccon said.

Magdalene wrinkled her nose at him. "I doubt it," she replied, but then smiled and asked, "Where do the women get dinner?"

"Cookshop just up the street near the Carfax, but they eat late. Busy time here at dinner hour. Men like a bit extra in their time off."

"And the cost of a meal?" Magdalene grinned at the boy, who had hesitated. "I'll be going out myself tomorrow. If you lie to me, I'll skin you."

"Two farthings for the ordinary," he said sullenly.

"Good enough. That sounds right." She handed him a penny. "Get two dinners and you can have one."

The boy's eyes brightened. "Ale or wine?" he asked. "I gave you the price with the drink."

"Ale."

Magdalene shook her head as Diccon ran off. Likely the meal was only one farthing and the drink a second, but he hoped to get away with giving her the higher price by pretending he thought she would want a drink. It showed his cleverness, however, and Magdalene felt that two farthings was a cheap price to pay for the information she hoped to extract and with no one the wiser about her curiosity.

She obtained her money's worth, for she invited Diccon to join her while she ate. He was enormously pleased and relieved, which made Magdalene suspect that half or more of his meal might disappear down other gullets if he were caught with it. She began by remarking that Florete had told her how crowded Oxford was and asking if Diccon happened to know who was already in the town.

The knowledge that he was safe and could eat and drink in peace oiled his tongue. He not only knew who was in the town, but by virtue of being used to carry messages, he knew where most of the great lords were lodged. He also knew who among them were friends and who were at odds because of the behavior of the men-at-arms of different meinies to each other. And there were others, he said, who were supposed to be friends—the men would greet each other civilly—but the way they looked at each other told a different story.

He mentioned the earl of Chester, and asked if it were true that Chester ruled like a king on his great palatine estates bordering Wales and cared little for King Stephen. He mentioned the lodgings of meinies of the earls of Surrey and Warwick, Pembroke and Leicester. Magdalene bit her lip; she remembered that the king had told William to send his men home because there was no room for them, but all those earls were relatives by blood or marriage of Waleran de Meulan.

Diccon named others, but they were mostly the king's own creations and had little weight or influence beyond the king's will. Absorbed in her anxiety for her friend and protector, she ignored the boy's light voice until he said, "They're all asking about the bishops of Salisbury, Lincoln, and Ely. Seems there's a house kept empty for them on Castle Street but they haven't come. Men are betting that they'll seal themselves into their castles and wait for Robert of Gloucester to come."

"Who is betting that?" Magdalene asked sharply.

"Oh, Lord Waleran's men mostly. Surrey's men bet against them. They said the bishops have to come 'cause Gloucester ain't ready yet and they need to look innocent 'til they join him."

"But Surrey's men are just as sure the bishops are in league with Gloucester as Lord Waleran's men?" She frowned. "Are you making this up, Diccon? Where would you hear such talk?"

"In the common room," Diccon said indignantly. "They act like me and the girls are deaf. If they have to wait because there are too many for the private rooms or their favorite girls are busy, Florete sells wine and they drink and talk. They could take the common girls, but they don't." A look of cunning crossed his face. "Sometimes I wonder if they come to talk to each other more than they come for the women."

It was certainly not impossible, Magdalene thought. William was clever, but he could not be the only one who realized a whorehouse was a place where men would come in contact and yet not be seen actually visiting each other's lodgings, or gathering in groups in the street. A whorehouse was a good place to spread rumors, too. And Magdalene did not like either of the rumors. If the king took away the bishops' offices either for defiance or for some other cause, who would manage the country? Who beside Salisbury and his son and nephews understood the exchequer? The sheriffs were all Salisbury's appointees. Who else would they obey?

Finally Diccon had no more to tell and Magdalene let him go. She repeated the significant pieces of information to herself to commit them to memory so she could tell William, although she doubted anything would be new to him except that the Soft Nest was being used as a place of meeting. And then she wondered if he knew even that, and had summoned her for that reason.

Even as she arranged what she must say in her mind, she felt uneasy and restless, as if she should be doing something more than sitting in a chair. She looked at her hands, resting idly on the table, conscious that something was missing—and then she burst out laughing and let out an exasperated sigh. In the chaos of getting ready to leave, and with Bell in her bed and taking up all her attention her last night in Southwark, she had forgotten to pack her embroidery.

The windows showed it was still light, and Magdalene was about to go out and buy herself the wherewithal to work when Florete came to the door. Business would be slow for a little while, she told Magdalene; if she were allowed to leave the door open so she could watch the men come and go in the corridor, she would like to stay and talk over old times. Magdalene was only too happy to accommodate her, and the two women exchanged gossip and renewed a friendship dimmed by time and distance.

Moreover, Florete confirmed everything that Diccon had told Magdalene. "What will happen?" she asked anxiously. "I have good arrangements with the sheriff's men in Oxford and with the bishop's people too. Is everything going to be changed? Will I have to pay double bribes?"

"I don't know," Magdalene confessed. "I only know that William is worried, which is why he sent for me. My bishop is safe—he is the king's brother and the papal legate, too." She sighed. "All I can say is that if too much trouble overtakes you, come to me in Southwark. There is room for a house like this one—not so pricey as mine, but decent and well managed."

"Thank you, love," Florete said, getting up. "I hope it never comes to that, but I will remember."

The afternoon shadows were long now and clients who wanted to be finished before Vespers were coming in. After dusk there would be another busy time, as those men who planned to stay the night arrived. Florete returned to her post at the entrance, and Magdalene went about placing torchettes in the holders on the wall. She took one of the night candles from the stick near the bed on the right-hand wall and set it on the table, reminding herself to ask Florete for a branch of candle holders when there were fewer men around. She would need the light if she bought embroidery materials the next morning. For now she sighed with boredom and wished that William had gotten her message and would be able to come.

That wish was granted. The bells of St. Friedesweide were just ringing for Vespers when William of Ypres came striding into the Soft Nest, never stopping at Florete's table, and bellowing, "Heyla Chickie, where are you?"

Florete signalled urgently to her men to sit still as six men in helmets and boiled leather armor followed their master through the door, but she sighed with relief when Magdalene flung open the door to the back room and ran forward into William's bearlike embrace.

"Perfect!" he exclaimed, peering cautiously into her chamber, then pushing her back into the room and slamming the door behind him with his heel.

"I'm so glad you approve," she replied, voice laced with irony, "since I haven't the faintest idea where else to go."

He gave her a rib-bending, affectionate hug that squeezed the breath out of her, then put her away from him to smile down at her. "I was worried about where you would find a place," he said in a more moderate tone. "I even thought of emptying out that house you used to rent, but the way things are, I couldn't have done it quietly. There would have been howls of protest. It would have become known that I took the house, and I'm not sure everyone would have believed that I would go to so much effort only for a favorite whore."

"Then God must favor you, because it was sheer luck that Florete was afraid to rent this room to anyone. She thought she would end up with a troop of men-at-arms in there who would make merry with her whores and pay nothing."

He laughed. "Likely she was right." But then his smile disappeared, and she noticed the gray in his hair, the new lines on his face, the gray tone under the weather-beaten brown of his skin, and how he blinked his eyes, as if to clear them.

"You look tired, love," she said. "Come, sit down." And she led the way to the chair. "Shall I send the boy out to get some wine and food? I have had no chance yet to buy in stores."

He sank into the chair, put his elbows on the table, and rested his head in his hands. "Don't bother. I have *another* meeting for the evening meal." He sighed. "My spirit is tired, Magdalene, not my body. God knows, I've done little enough but stand around in the Court making stupid noises."

"Is there something I need to know to mind my tongue, William?" she asked anxiously.

He shook his head helplessly. "I don't even know if there is something *I* need to know," he growled.

"Will this help?" she asked, and repeated what Diccon had told her about the wagering between Waleran's men and Surrey's.

"In the common room of a whorehouse," William said softly, lifting his head. "I knew what they were saying, of course. Waleran has been whispering his warnings in the king's ear since we all arrived and the king was kind enough—" his lips twisted "—to pass those warnings to me, since doubtless I would be the one who would have to winkle the bishops out of their castles. But I am a little surprised that the suspicions were common knowledge in the town and among the common men-at-arms. So his men are deliberately spreading the doubts to all. But why?"

Magdalene ignored a question she knew was not for her,

but she shivered. "William, what will happen to the realm if Salisbury and his son and nephews are turned out of office?"

There was a silence and then William said softly, "Why do you think I cannot sleep at night? I don't know, Chick, I don't know." He took a deep breath and squared his shoulders. "Except that there will be war and I will do what is necessary to save the king's groats."

"Stephen is a fool!"

"Yes. Sometimes."

Magdalene sighed. "Will this place be safe for you, William, if Waleran's men and those of his blood kin come here?"

He laughed and put out an arm to pull her close, ignoring the fact that the arm of the chair was cutting painfully into her thighs. "Sweet Chick. I think sometimes you really do care about me."

She dropped a kiss on the top of his head and blinked back tears. His hair was not only graying but thinning too. "Well, I do," she said, making her voice light, "even though you don't know your own strength and you will break my legs and cripple me if you don't let me go." He released her, but swatted her sharply on the buttocks, and she sighed. "Answer me, William. Will you be safe coming here? I will find another place if it will be better for you."

"No!" He grinned up at her. "And of course I will be safe, you silly woman. Waleran wouldn't harm a hair on my head, especially when there is fighting coming along. Do you think he wants to risk his precious hide on the field? As long as I am alive and well, the king will send me."

"A fool, but he knows whom he can trust."

"In war . . ." Now William sighed, but then he smiled and gestured for Magdalene to sit down on one of the stools.

"Maybe you spoke aright when you said God favored us. That this place is a known haunt of Waleran's men is perfect. You remember Raoul de Samur?" Magdalene wrinkled her nose and William laughed once more and went on, "Yes, yes, he is no prize, but he has been of use to me. A place where it is known his fellows all come will make him feel safe. He will be willing to bring news to you of Waleran's meetings and doings more often and even speak to me in your chamber directly—in which case I am sure I will be able to squeeze from him even more than he thinks he knows."

"I suppose so." Magdalene grimaced. "But he is not likely to look on *me* with favor. I threw wash water in his face, Sabina crowned him with her staff, and Dulcie finished him off with her frying pan."

William roared with laughter. "Is that how you subdued him? Poor man. I am glad we are on such good terms." Then he shrugged. "He will not dare touch you or even misspeak you. He knows how I value you."

I will have to warn Bell, Magdalene thought. *Raoul will not know that William's protection covers Bell—if it does.* William had never shown the slightest sign of sexual jealousy over her, but he seemed to realize that Bell was more than just another body in her bed. Would he doubt her loyalty when he learned that Bell was also in Oxford, or would that arouse his sense of possession?

Unaware of her thoughts, William continued, "And that was interesting news you gave me about the betting. Can you arrange to hear more of what the men who come here say?"

"I think so. It was the boy who carries messages and fetches food and wine for the women and the clients who told me. He's clever, and I gave him reason to like me . . ." William raised his brows and she laughed. "No, you evil-minded man. The boy is barely twelve years old. I gave him two farthings and a meal. He will be glad to listen for me and bring me what he hears."

"I do not believe I was much above twelve when I had my first woman," William mused, grinning. "Ah, well. I imagine I was a likelier lad than any half-starved whore's brat. At least while you are here he will be better fed. You do tend to take in the lame and the lost."

"And find good use for them," Magdalene said sharply, then suddenly cocked her head. "Which reminds me, William, could I ask your men to keep their eyes open for a pretty blind girl? I am looking to replace Sabina."

"I thought you had, with that green-eyed slut."

Magdalene laughed. "Why is Diot more of a slut than I?"

William stared at her, blinking his eyes to clear his vision. After a moment he said, "You did what you must . . . as I at times do what I must. Diot does what she likes."

Magdalene stared back at him. "You are very perceptive, William," she whispered.

"Which is why I am still alive."

He looked away, staring into nothing for a long moment, then pushed back the chair and began to rise. Magdalene rose also, her hand going to the tie of her shift, which showed above the neck of her gown.

"It is not only 'must' with you, William," she said.

He looked down at her and drew her to him, gently for once. "I wish I could," he said, resting his cheek against her hair, "but I am pledged to share the evening meal with Lord Hervey at Alain of Brittany's lodging. Curse the man, he looks down his nose at all of us as if we were bugs to be trod underfoot. And Stephen usually has little patience with such airs. I cannot think why I am sent to dance attendance on him."

That comment was not meant for her either. Magdalene only said, "Let me change into a bedgown, William. There is no reason to let Florete or anyone else wonder what we have been doing."

He nodded and released her and went on irritably as she swiftly removed her clothing and replaced it with a tucked and embroidered linen bedgown, "This Hervey is not even a decent Norman. He is all French from his overcurled hair to his long-toed shoes."

The continuation of subject implied that William did want an answer from her. "Then he must be connected to King Louis's court and Stephen wants something from the French king."

"I know that!" William snorted.

"A wife for Eustace?" Magdalene ventured.

William groaned. "Another reason for the king to show himself strong and in total control of his realm." He shook his head. "The boy may ripen into something—" he sighed "—but I see no sign of it." He went to the door and opened it. "You are always a pleasure, Magdalene," he said as she followed him out. "I will be back as soon as I can find the time."

Hearing his voice, his six armed men came out of the common room, where they had been teasing the whores. They stepped out the door and William paused by Florete's table. Magdalene tightened the tie on his shirt as if she had not done it up properly. He flicked a finger against her nose.

"Be good, Chick."

He turned away just as a big man, with a badly bruised face, a black eye, a swollen nose, and split lips, pushed past Florete's table and almost collided with Magdalene. What more could be seen of him was stringy, somewhat matted black hair, a dark eye—the blackened one was swollen shut—and unshaven stubble on his cheeks and chin.

"A penny for the likes of them?" he lisped over his shoulder as if his teeth were loose. "Common whores they are, no better than I could buy for a farthing."

Florete stiffened a bit, and Magdalene gave back a step and then tried to sidle around the complainer to follow William to the front door, but the man sensed the movement and seized her arm.

"Well, where've you been hiding this one?" In addition to the indistinctness caused by the loose teeth, the big man's voice was thick with drink, and spittle spotted his broken mouth. "Here's one to make up for the whey-faced sack of wet mud I'll be wedding tomorrow."

"Let me go," Magdalene said coldly. "I do not work in this house."

"In a bedgown in this house, you work here," the man snarled. "My money's as good as his—" he gestured with his head toward William, who was just stepping out the door.

"You are hurting me!" Magdalene exclaimed, her voice rising. "Let me go!"

"Sir!" Florete half rose from her seat. "Let her go! She speaks the truth. She does not work here. She is a visitor on business."

While she was speaking, another man came around her table. He said, "Aimery, this is a decent house. If the woman is not willing . . ." His voice trailed away, denoting some discomfort about Magdalene, at whom he was staring.

She had been struggling to draw her eating knife, but hesitated with her hand clasped around the hilt, twisting her head toward the new speaker. His voice sounded familiar. She would prefer to have her attacker's friends take him away than to stab a man in Florete's house.

"Sir Ferrau," she cried, recognizing the second man. "Tell this creature to unhand me."

His eyes fixed on hers, and recognition dawned on his face. Doubt dawned also. Magdalene could see Sir Ferrau trying to decide how to react to the plea of a woman to whom he had been introduced by a respectable knight but whom he discovered in a whorehouse. While he hesitated, a large hand fell on the shoulder of the man called Aimery.

"Let her go. Now!"

The bellow could have wakened the dead. Several of the curtains in the corridor twitched half open. Sir Ferrau gaped and his eyes widened.

"Aimery," he cried, rushing over and trying to loosen the drunkard's grip on Magdalene. "For God's sake, let the woman go. That is William of Ypres."

"And Waleran de Meulan is my master," Amiery growled, drunk and sullen. "I don't need to fear Ypres."

At that moment Magdalene's eating knife came free of its sheath and struck down at the hand gripping her. It was not a large knife, but it was pointed and very sharp for cleaning and paring fruit, and it went right through the man's hand. Furious, Magdalene twisted it as she drew it back. Aimery's half-uttered shriek was cut off as, almost simultaneously with Magdalene's blow, William's hands wrapped around his throat and squeezed.

"Don't, William," Magdalene gasped, seizing his arm. "He isn't worth a quarrel with Lord Waleran."

William looked into her troubled face, and his hands slowly relaxed their grip.

Two heartbeats later Sir Ferrau pleaded, "I beg you my lord, don't kill him. He is drunk."

As soon as William had ordered Aimery to let go of Magdalene, Florete's bully boys had started to rise from their stools and reach for their cudgels, but they had not been able to decide how to accost their prey without interfering with William of Ypres or Magdalene. Now when William released the semiconscious man, they leapt forward, seized him, and dragged him out the door. Sir Ferrau did not follow, but only stepped back out of Lord William's sight.

"You all right, Chick?" William asked roughly.

"Oh, yes," Magdalene said, looking up at him from cleaning her knife, "I'll have a bruise . . ." She grinned. "But your affection sometimes gives me worse. Go ahead, William. You'll be late."

His lips twisted. "That would never do." But he did go out, his step quickening as his men formed around him.

Sir Ferrau came forward as William disappeared. "What a beautiful woman you are," he said. "You were veiled when I met you on the road with Sir Bellamy, and I had no idea . . ."

"What in the world are you doing here with that . . . animal?" Magdalene asked.

Ferrau laughed deprecatingly. "I wasn't *with* him. I met him in the street outside of St. Friedesweide and he asked me where I was going. Like a fool, I told him. I didn't realize how drunk he was when he said he would come along with me. But if we are asking questions, I would like to know how you came to be traveling with Sir Bellamy?"

Magdalene smiled sweetly at him. "Exactly for the reason he

told you. I keep the Old Priory Guesthouse in Southwark and the bishop of Winchester is my landlord. Sir Bellamy collects the rents—some of the stews make trouble, although not my establishment—and the bishop believes in stopping trouble before it starts; Sir Bellamy is good at that. In any case when I told him I needed to travel to Oxford, he said he was himself going there and offered to escort me."

"You know him well?"

She shrugged. "He has been collecting my rent for some years, and I pay in silver . . . every penny. Sometimes we exchange a few light words. The prices of the Old Priory Guesthouse are too high for a simple knight."

"You mean they are too high for me also?"

"I have no price for any man but William of Ypres," she said flatly.

Every word she had spoken was the literal truth, too. Bell didn't pay her at all.

CHAPTER 5

20 June, Cornmarket, Oxford

Magdalene retreated to her room again, vowing not to come out into the public areas of the house other than fully dressed. She hoped she had not made any trouble for Florete, but was relieved of that worry when the whoremistress later came in for a cozy snack, which Diccon fetched, and to apologize for the fracas.

"It is I who should apologize," Magdalene said. "I hope that drunken fool will make no outcry against your house."

"Oh, no." Florete sipped her wine and nibbled placidly at a sweetcake. "The boys will have taken him up to the Carfax and dumped him behind some wagon or crate. Likely he won't even remember what happened and will think he came drunk out of one of the alehouses and just fell down. If he does remember, he will hold his tongue. The Soft Nest is well liked. He'll not want to say he was thrown out."

They talked a little longer and then Florete was called forward to settle a contest between two men over a girl. They were both drunk, too, but good humored about it, and Florete was skilled at soothing them and finding another woman "like," she said, "as two peas in a pod," to the one over whom they were quarreling, and then setting them to match straws for the girls. As soon as Magdalene was sure the altercation would not erupt into a riot, she wrapped up the remaining sweetcakes, covered what was left in the flagon of wine, locked her door, and went to bed.

She woke early to a blessedly quiet house and a mild day. It had showered earlier, she saw, by looking out the window and seeing the leaves and grass all wet. The sky was partly clouded, but the sun was out now and Magdalene was determined to stock her room with such tidbits as William would nibble if he did not want a full meal, some decent wine, and— to give her something to do in her idle hours—two needles, some embroidery thread, and some ribbons.

The remains of last night's cakes and wine made a satisfactory breakfast. Then, dressed in her sober traveling gown, Magdalene veiled her face and went out. There were puddles in Blue Boar Lane over which she had to lift her skirt, but they were mostly water with only a hint of other, less savory, substances. Both the alehouse on the corner and the Soft Nest generally served decent merchants and had arrangements for collectors to remove solid waste.

Although she was a trifle apprehensive about the reaction of the men-at-arms quartered in the alehouse because there was no way of concealing that she came out of the Soft Nest, Magdalene passed its yard without worse than a couple of called invitations. The men-at-arms now lodged there had been warned that they would be evicted if they offended too often and they believed it, since every day more than one captain of other troops came to beg for accommodations.

Once she was away from the Soft Nest, Magdalene strode

more confidently into the South Way and walked north. Early as it was, the street was unpleasantly crowded with far too many armed men. Magdalene kept her head down as much as she could while making sure she did not bump into anyone. However, once across the Carfax and into the Cornmarket, the worst press of men-at-arms diminished. At least the large groups marching from the east and west remained on Castle Street. Some armed men mingled with the other shoppers in the market, but they were unthreatening, looking at the goods in the stalls alone or in twos and threes.

Despite its name, a great deal more than grain was sold in the Cornmarket. Almost every variety of shop thrust a stall into the street, and only a few yards from the corner Magdalene found a rough basket that would do to carry her purchases and was not too expensive to leave behind when she returned to London. Not much farther along, a grocer's shop provided dried fruit and leaf-wrapped flat cakes of candied violets and rosebuds.

Magdalene shook her head over spending far more than when Dulcie made the delicacies, but she had no cook, no kitchen, no garden, and two men with mouths to fill. Still, the expense made her set down a very tempting plaited-grass sack of fresh strawberries she had been examining. They were so perishable, and she had no idea when William would be able to come again. Unfortunately it was too early in the season for any other fresh fruit.

Suppressing temptation, she crossed the road. Cakes came from a baker she remembered, whose shop was still in the same place. The baker exclaimed in surprise when she leaned forward to look at a long loaf of dark bread and her veil drooped and exposed her face. He greeted her with warmth, and wanted to know where she now lived and why she was in Oxford, but there was a compensation. For an old friend, the baker sliced the dark loaf in quarters, the quarters in half, and smeared one side of each quarter liberally with butter.

When he had tucked that carefully into the side of the basket so it would not fall apart, Magdalene stepped out and looked up the street toward the shop of the mercer who had supplied almost all her embroidery materials—and sold her work, too—for most of the years she had been in Oxford. She took about two steps in that direction, then turned sharply about and went back across the road to the grocer. William's was not the only mouth that could eat strawberries; she had a right to pleasure too. And though she sighed over her folly, with her mouth watering she purchased the berries.

With a mingled sense of guilt and righteous self-indulgence, Magdalene pulled her veil down to pop a strawberry into her mouth, pausing a moment to savor the sweet/sharp taste. Sighing with satisfaction, she set out again for the shop of Master Redding, the mercer.

Two more strawberries, the reddest and softest, were saved from possible decay. Magdalene slowly chewed the second while she examined the broadest ribbons on the mercer's counter. Having sucked any possible strawberry stain from her fingers, she pointed out two ribbons, one a dusty blue and the other a bright green. Then she turned her attention to the thin hanks of thread hanging from three wooden trees fastened to the counter; she asked the prices, chaffered over them, and, satisfied, began to lift off those she wanted. There was no need to restrain her buying of embroidery yarn; sooner or later she would use every bit.

While the apprentice took her money and folded the thread

inside the wide ribbon, which he rolled up tightly and secured with a string, Magdalene returned her attention to the grass bag of strawberries. She was examining the contents carefully, seeking the ripest, when a hand seized her arm. Crying out softly, she gripped her shopping basket even more tightly and tried to pull her veil back across her face while she raised her head to scream for Master Redding to come to her defense. The shout died unborn.

"Sir Niall!" she exclaimed. "You idiot! You frightened me half to death."

"Why should my taking your arm frighten you?" he asked, and then shook his head impatiently and added, "Never mind that. Come inside." He urged her around the edge of the counter toward the shop door. "I think you are the answer to all my prayers."

"I think you are drunk!" she riposted tartly.

Nonetheless, Magdalene let him draw her into the shop. He didn't look drunk, for one thing, and for another, she was reasonably sure Master Redding would not allow her to be assaulted on his premises.

"That is Loveday of Otmoor," Niall said, drawing Magdalene toward the far end of the counter in the shop where a young woman with a worried expression was conversing with Master Redding, the mercer.

Magdalene stopped dead in her tracks and looked up at Niall. "You fool!" she whispered, turning away. "You do not introduce whores to—" *Loveday of Otmoor?* she thought. *Where have I heard that name?* And then it came back to her, Diccon saying that Sir Niall was courting an heiress named Loveday of Otmoor. Her eyes widened. "You do not introduce whores to young ladies you are courting with hopes to marry!" she muttered fiercely, pulling free of Niall's hold.

"Where did you hear that?" he asked, looking stunned.

Magdalene had retreated to the other end of the shop and Niall had followed her. "Go away!" she urged. "I don't think she's noticed me. Pretend you don't know me!"

"No, listen to me. Loveday will be safer with you than being alone on her manor, and I can't stay . . ." He drew a deep breath. "You don't know what's happened."

At that moment it became too late to escape notice. Loveday left the mercer and came across to where Niall and Magdalene stood. For the moment, although she glanced at her, she did not acknowledge Magdalene. She looked up appealingly at Niall.

"Edmee is gone to London. Master Redding was afraid to keep her here with the streets full of armed men, not to mention that he expects his house to be forced to quarter some of them either today or tomorrow. He said I could have stayed here, except for that, but I wouldn't want to stay unless Edmee were in the house with me."

Then the mercer joined them. "Ah," he said, "so you've found a chaperone for Loveday, I see. Why don't you all go up to my solar where you can talk this out in comfort. I'm sure you'll find some satisfactory arrangement."

He at least did not seem to have recognized her. Magdalene started to shake her head, but Loveday was already thanking Master Redding and Niall had taken her arm again and was steering her toward the steep stair that rose along the wall not far from them. Magdalene despaired of trying to be diplomatic and sparing Niall Loveday's anger, and when the girl came up the stair and walked across the room to join them on the benches near the hearth, she dropped her veil.

"Mistress Loveday, I don't know what is in Niall's mind, but I am no fit chaperone for any decent young woman. My name is Magdalene la Bâtarde, and I am a whoremistress. Now I am sure Niall does not seek to sell you to me, not that I have ever bought a young woman who was not already in the trade—"

"At least you will not try to marry me and seize my property," Loveday said bitterly.

"You believe Niall is trying to seize your property?" Magdalene's voice was high with surprise. "Then why are you with him? I think he would be a good husband, but I suppose he *would* wish to manage the manor—"

"No, I would not," Niall said. "Loveday does that far better than I could. Likely I would stay with Lord William for a few years more and then, if we could find suitable grazing, I think I'd like to raise horses. My father would sell us some decent mares, and let us use his stud."

"That's a very good idea, Niall," Loveday said enthusiastically. "About the horses I mean. I'm not sure I'd like you to risk yourself in Lord William's service, though."

Magdalene put her free hand to her forehead. "Are you both mad? What am I doing here? Did you bring me up here to give you a good character, Niall? That you know me at all is already a mark against you, in proving you unchaste." She looked at Loveday. "What kind of character can a whoremistress give? I can tell you he doesn't try to beat my women and that he is kind even to the childish girl who often makes others impatient. He is cheerful when he has to wait . . ."

Niall's fair Irish complexion was now bright red, and Loveday was laughing. "Actually, that is a very good recommendation," she said. "Considering his profession, I never thought Niall would be a celibate saint." Then the laughter faded from her face and she shuddered. "I have reason to know that there are worse men than Niall Arvagh."

"You aren't here to give me a good character," Niall said. "Loveday needs a safe house in which to hide."

"Safe house?" Magdalene echoed. "A whorehouse?" And then seeing Niall and Loveday exchange glances and nod, she asked "What is so dreadful that hiding in a whorehouse would be considered safe in comparison?"

"The day before yesterday," Loveday began, slightly pale now, "a man came to the gate of Noke Manor and asked for me. We have been keeping the gates closed because of the influx of men-at-arms in the area, but one man . . . I suppose we should have kept him out, but he was wearing a lord's house badge. He wasn't one of the ragged hangers-on—"

"He was wearing Waleran de Meulan's house badge," Niall interrupted indignantly. "Of course, Loveday didn't know that when the steward let him in." His face reddened again, but this time with anger. "That clerk that came to William with the news about Loveday and went out with a gold piece for thanks . . . the treasonous bastard, he must have gone to Waleran first."

Loveday put a hand on his arm, and he subsided. "When I came down to the common room from the solar, this . . . creature . . . seized my hand and said we were to be married by order of Lord Waleran de Meulan. He was looking around the common room, at the plates on the wardrobe and the tankards. He never even looked at me beyond one glance. At first I was too frightened to speak, but I managed to pull my hand away and get behind a bench. Once I was free of him, I remembered why I was not married already. I told him that I was the king's ward and that only the king himself could order me to take a husband."

Niall began to mutter something, but Loveday held up her hand and he fell silent.

"For one moment the man looked taken aback, but then he laughed and said it *was* the king's order, that the king's clerk had come to Lord Waleran and bidden him find a husband for me."

"That treacherous clerk!" Niall burst out.

Magdalene frowned. "I know the clerk said that Loveday was not sufficiently highborn nor rich enough to make a marriage prize for one of Stephen's own poor noblemen—"

"Thanks be to God!" Loveday exclaimed. "One of those would strip Noke and Otmoor bare in a year to pay for his fine clothing and his gambling."

"I agree," Magdalene said, still frowning, "but I am very surprised indeed that Waleran should send a common man-at-arms. I should have thought he would have chosen, as did William, one of his captains, who would be a knight and of decent if not noble family."

"Apparently I was not worth so much consideration." Loveday's voice was stiff and ice-cold. "But it became an advantage. Because I saw that he did not truly have any knowledge of what being a king's ward meant, I gathered my wits and told him I would take no man's word on a matter so important to me as my marriage. I said I must see the order in writing with the king's seal before I would agree. He was angry, but my steward was there and he left, saying I was a fool to resist and start off on the wrong foot with him, that he would come back with the order." She shuddered. "I would rather die, I thought, than have him. He stank!"

"I do not always smell fresh as a flower," Niall said tentatively, touching her cheek.

Magdalene thought he probably did smell somewhat of flowers that day. He was clearly scrubbed clean and newly shaven, his hair washed . . . but not combed? And then she noticed that his sleeve was cut and so was his tunic, as if someone had attacked him with a knife, and the knuckles on the hand he had raised to touch Loveday were skinned and swollen.

"No," Loveday said to him, smiling, "nor did my father smell like flowers nor my brothers. Like them you smell of horses and honest sweat." Her eyes came back to Magdalene and her voice sharpened. "That animal smelled of stale beer and wine and piss and vomit." She shuddered again. "I was not certain what I would do if he did come back with the order. First I thought I would not let him in, but what good would that do? I thought the king would send many men to force me. So then I decided to let him in and look at the order. If it really was from the king . . . I would have the steward and the menservants from the house kill him!"

Magdalene fought back a grin and said, "Better that than a life—a short one, I suspect—as his wife. But I hope you bethought you of how to hide what you had done."

Loveday sighed. "It did not come to that, but almost. He came with a document, but it was not an order from the king and it bore nothing beside the signatures of two witnesses. There was no seal. It was a betrothal agreement yielding all that was mine to him without any safeguard for me. It already bore my signature—" she snorted contempt "—an X with the words 'Loveday of Otmoor, her mark,' beside it. The fool did not even know I could read and write."

"Can you?" Magdalene asked, surprised. It was an unlikely skill for a woman.

"Yes, father taught me after mother died. He traveled a lot and he wanted to know in detail about what was happening and in particular how the priest was behaving. There had been trouble years before with a dishonest priest. Not this priest. He is new here but a very good man. I don't know what that other priest did, but father never forgot and he did not want me to be dependent on the priest to write my letters. I find it very useful."

"I too," Magdalene said, smiling. "So you knew the document was a forgery and even had some proof."

"And so I told him," Loveday snapped, "and I bade him leave, but he laughed at me and said what he had was quite enough and that I should be delighted with Lord Waleran's choice since he had sent a strong man who could defend my property. He came close while he spoke and grabbed for me and said we should settle the matter at once by consummating our union, but I hit him in the nose so he let me go and I threw a bench at him and shouted for my menservants. He *was* strong. He knocked my steward down and it took three men to wrestle him down and cast him out of the gate."

Niall snorted. "Strong? Maybe, but not skilled. It took me a quarter of a candlemark to beat him unconscious, and only because you yelled at me not to kill him, Loveday."

Magdalene's eyes widened. "You mean all this was going on right in front of Niall?" she asked, thoroughly confused.

"No," Loveday said, frowning at Niall, "you are making me tell this story all wrong. Niall came the day after Aimery St.—"

"Aimery?" Magdalene repeated.

Could it be the same man who had tried to seize her in the Soft Nest the preceding night, she wondered? It must be. The name Aimery was not uncommon, but an Aimery who had obviously been badly beaten? The coincidence was too great.

"He said his name was Aimery St. Cyr, but he did not know a single word of French. Anyway as my men were dragging him to the gate, he shouted that he would make my servants sorry they had ever been born and before he was done with me I would be glad to take him into any hole I had in my body, that his master would give him a full troop to take my manor and burn it to the ground . . ."

"Stupid lout," Magdalene hissed.

"He is," Niall said, "but how did you know?"

"He tried to take me in the Soft Nest last night," she said, lips thinned with distaste. "You are right, Loveday, he stank! I heard his name then and saw he had been badly beaten, so I suppose it was the same man." Then she shook her head. "That doesn't matter, and I suppose he didn't burn the manor down. What did you do?"

"To tell the truth, I was frightened to death, but I had never before heard the names of the witnesses, so I thought they might be nobodies, and I decided I would try to plead my case with the king."

"Better had you sent to your neighbors for help," Niall said. "The king is overwhelmed with business."

"So you did not receive any answer from the king?" Magdalene asked.

"I had no chance even to send my appeal. By then it was growing dark, and Niall showed up at the gate the next morning. I almost didn't let him in until he called me by name and then when I saw him, of course I remembered him. His sister had just his look, that red hair and white skin. She was a sweet girl. I was so sorry when she died . . . and my brother too, of course."

For a moment Loveday's face looked old and drawn, its clean lines sagging as she recalled past grief. She was not beautiful, Magdalene thought, but certainly did not deserve St. Cyr's description of her as a "whey-faced sack of mud." Her hair was an indeterminate shade of brown as were her eyes, but those eyes were bright with intelligence, her skin was lovely as was the soft curve of her mouth. And her body was not sacklike at all; her full breasts lifted her gown becomingly and her waist and hips were all that a woman's should be.

"Well, of course I asked why her gates were locked and why I was being threatened with pitchforks," Niall said, "and she told me the whole story. I was . . . annoyed."

Loveday giggled. "He was steaming mad. His face was so red, I thought his head would burst into flame." Then she looked up at him with adoring eyes. "But he didn't yell at me or hit me."

"Why should I hit *you*?" Niall said in a choked voice. "I wasn't angry at *you*."

"Yes, well." Magdalene sighed. "With some men, their wife's innocence is less important than having something to hit."

Niall snorted. "Just as well then that St. Cyr chose that very time to show up. The steward called a warning that four armed men were approaching and I came running out—"

"Unarmed?" Magdalene asked.

"Oh no. There have been such grumblings and rumblings that I had my mail shirt on under my surcoat, and my helmet and shield are always on my horse. I was angry enough to ride out and take all four of them, but I have not been Lord William's captain for some years without learning when to swallow my bile. I warned the men on the manor to get long staves or pitchforks and keep St. Cyr's companions from taking me from behind. Then I bade the steward to open the gate. As I said before, I could have cut him down in two strokes, but Loveday shouted at me not to kill him so I beat him off his horse with the flat of my sword."

"And the other men?"

"Two fled as soon as they saw me knock aside St. Cyr's sword and realized the pitchfork men would not run. Two younglings had got out their slingshots and were pelting the third man with stones until he withdrew beyond the gate. Then I dismounted to cut St. Cyr's purse to get the fake betrothal, and he drew a knife on me, so I used my fist on his head, threw him belly down on his horse, and drove it out."

"Why in the world did you tell Niall not to kill the man?" Magdalene asked Loveday. "Now the chances are that for revenge he *will* come back with many more men and really try to burn down the manor and kill the servants."

"I was afraid Niall would get into trouble," she said. "If that man was truly at Noke by Lord Waleran's order—and how else would he have known about me—and Niall killed him, Lord Waleran would certainly hear of it from the men who fled. Who knows what vengeance Lord Waleran would take for the despite done him in killing his man?"

"Yes," Niall put in in an exasperated voice, "and that is why I daren't take Loveday to my father to keep her safe. Lord Waleran could squash my poor father like a bug. Nor, of course, dare I take her to Lord William. He *must* not be embroiled in any fracas with Lord Waleran right now and, besides, what would he do with Loveday?" He hesitated, and then added uncertainly, "Could he ask the queen to house her?"

"She *is* the king's ward," Magdalene pointed out, but she sounded doubtful. Even if the king were willing for his wife to take Loveday into her Household, that could not possibly be arranged in an hour or two.

Before Magdalene could voice her doubts, Loveday said, "No. From what Niall has told me, Lord Waleran is so much a favorite with the king that if he went to Stephen complaining of Niall's interference, I might be handed over to be delivered to St. Cyr."

"So you have to take her and keep her safe until this matter of the forged betrothal agreement is exposed."

Magdalene stood staring at Niall, eyes and mouth open in shock. Finally she swallowed and said, "You are serious? No, you are mad! I am a whoremistress. You *cannot* entrust a maiden to my care."

"You are also the most honest woman I know, Mistress Magdalene," Niall said. "If you say Loveday will be safe in your care, she will be."

"Niall, do not be a fool. I am staying in a whorehouse. Last night I, myself, was nearly assaulted by a drunken client. I *cannot* swear to keep her safe."

"But you did get away from the drunk," Loveday said slowly, clearly thinking as she spoke. "And you did not expect it to happen, so usually you are safe from such affront. That means when you were attacked you must have been out in a public room for some reason—"

"I was seeing a client out," Magdalene said pointedly, wanting to make her situation clear.

"Yes, well, of course—" Loveday offered a small smile "—I

would not need to be out in a public part of the place for that reason. And I doubt the men who come there would invade your private quarters, even if they were drunk." She thought another moment and then added with perfect calm, "Indeed, Mistress Magdalene, I will add my plea to Niall's that you allow me to lodge with you."

Magdalene drew a deep, exasperated breath. "But Loveday, even if you were physically safe, your good name would be sullied if anyone discovered that you had been staying in a whorehouse. And the Soft Nest is frequented by just the kind of people you know—merchants and substantial yeomen."

"I still think it better than if I were caught by St. Cyr."

"But people will talk. And in the future if your husband hears of it, he may begin to harbor doubts about your virtue, which could lead to some painful misunderstandings."

"How?" Niall asked. "I will be her husband and since the whole thing was of my doing, how could I doubt?"

"And who will know of my staying with you? No one besides Master Redding knows I am in Oxford. If I veil myself so that no one sees my face . . . Mistress Magdalene, I doubt I would survive longer than it took to marry me and kill me if St. Cyr lays his hands on me—"

"And I *must* tell Lord William about that treacherous clerk." Niall drew a sudden breath. "Good Lord, Magdalene, what if the clerk's *purpose* was to embroil Lord William with Lord Waleran? I must go warn him. I must go *now*."

Magdalene's eyes widened. Maybe *that* was the reason Waleran had chosen a totally unacceptable man, so that Loveday would refuse and whomever William sent—any one of his captains would have been more to Loveday's taste—would defend her and involve William.

"Very well," she said. "Go and tell William what has happened, and for God's sake, tell him you have left an innocent maiden in the Soft Nest, and he must find other arrangements for her as soon as possible."

"Bless you, Magdalene," Niall exclaimed, bussed her loudly on the cheek, and ran down the stairs.

"I am not so innocent as all that," Loveday protested with a grin. "What with spending half my time deciding which horse should cover which mare and what bull would best freshen this or that cow, not to mention watching to make sure we get our money's worth from the stud if he does not belong to my own farm, I am scarcely ignorant of the coming together of male and female."

"Oh yes, I was once a country girl myself," Magdalene agreed thoughtlessly, laughing, then looked down and bit her lip, annoyed at what she had exposed. She covered by adding quickly, "But somehow it is different when it is men and women rather than horses and mares. I hope you will not be shocked."

Loveday raised her brows. "I have servants, too, who are not always perfect." Then she laughed. "I will not be shocked, but I hope you have an explanation for my sudden appearance."

Magdalene laughed too. "It so happens I have. The true reason I have for being here is private, so I have been telling everyone who asked what I was doing in Oxford that I came to pick up a girl for my house in Southwark—" she sighed "—as if London had no girls. However, it is a convenient excuse. You can be that girl. I will call you . . . Maeve. But I am afraid I will have to tell the whoremistress of the Soft Nest the true tale or she might succumb to bribery and agree to use you."

Loveday readily agreed. Magdalene picked up her shopping

basket and gestured Loveday toward the stair. Fortunately, de-spite Magdalene's qualms, Loveday's establishment in the Soft Nest went without any difficulty. Master Redding, who had heard the tale of the attempt to force Loveday into marriage when Loveday sought refuge with his wife, quickly offered to contribute a veil and a light cloak to change Loveday's ap-pearance. His cooperation surprised Magdalene until she re-alized that his purpose was to be rid of Loveday before Waleran de Meulan could learn she had appealed to him for help.

He even sent an apprentice to lead Loveday's gelding, still loaded with her travel basket, through the back alley and ride it to Blue Boar Lane. There Magdalene called Diccon to take the horse out back and leave him with her own mare and mule, and the apprentice was sent back to Master Redding's shop. Then Magdalene simply led Loveday to the back chamber, mouthing "Come when you have time," to Florete as they passed.

She felt Loveday stiffen after they entered the Soft Nest and she saw the women in bedgowns and thin shifts in the common room and by the curtains that lined the corridor. However, the girl relaxed when they entered the back room and cheer-fully asked if she could help put away the items from Mag-dalene's shopping basket. Magdalene waved toward a shelf near the left-hand bed, meant, probably, for a man to put his purse or other valuables on. Loveday carried the basket over and removed the long, buttered loaf, now wrapped in a napkin. She exclaimed with surprise when she saw already on the shelf a thin roll of parchment bound around a tightly stoppered ink flask and several quills.

"Could I—" she began, and was distracted when she found

the strawberries. "Where shall I put these?" she asked.

Magdalene looked at what she held and laughed. "In your mouth . . . and mine." And she gestured Loveday to bring them to the table where they promptly sat down to finish them.

Niall came in before all the berries were gone but only stayed long enough to snatch a few for himself and say that William begged Magdalene to keep Loveday for the night, or at least until he had a chance to ferret out what was going on. Niall also told Loveday not to worry about Noke, that he was returning to the manor with ten men to be sure it and her servants would be safe.

Magdalene saw him out, and stopped by Florete's table to ask if she could rent clean sheets for the second bed. Then, unable to resist the bemusement in the whoremistress's eyes, she told a brief version of who Loveday was and her need to avoid an unwelcome suitor. And to engage Florete's sympathy, she pointed out that the man who claimed Loveday was the one Florete's men had disposed of the previous day.

"Pretty little thing," Florete muttered. "And she doesn't need to walk on our road. She's got lands. Yes, I'll keep her secret and I'll do my best to keep her safe."

Satisfied, Magdalene returned to her room. Together she and Loveday made up the second bed. Then Loveday asked Magdalene if she could use the pen, ink, and parchment on the shelf.

"I will gladly replace them or pay for them," she said. "I wish to write to the king and protest the forged betrothal." Then she drew a determined breath and added, "I will tell him not only that I can sign my own name and do not need to mark an X, but that I could never have agreed to such a proposal because I am already betrothed to Niall Arvagh of Murcot."

CHAPTER 6

But—" Magdalene began to protest.

The door slammed open and William of Ypres stood in it, looking from one woman to the other. He then examined Loveday more closely, walking up to her and then around her, very much as if she were a mare, then teetering back and forth, heels to toes.

"All right," he said, "so it isn't your face that's in question, it's the lands. What are you worth, girl? Do you know?"

"To the penny, Lord William," Loveday snapped back, her voice a feminine echo of his flat, practical tone, a flush of irritation brightening her eyes.

Magdalene bit her lip and went to close the door.

"Well?" William asked.

Lips thinned with anger, Loveday told him.

He shook his head. "Nice," he said. "Just what Niall needs, but not worth Waleran's interest. Not worth mine either, except . . . who is this St. Cyr?"

"I have no idea. I had never seen him nor heard of him before he appeared at my manor."

William snorted. "You saw him then, girl. He was threatening to marry you. You refused. Why?"

"He stank!"

Magdalene stifled a giggle as William rolled his eyes heavenward. "She doesn't understand what you want, William," she said. "Loveday, what Lord William needs to know is why Waleran de Meulan should take enough interest in St. Cyr to drop a wealthy orphan in his hand. Was the man French? Was he a man of birth who had fallen into low estate? What did you observe that might help us understand why Lord Waleran chose him?"

"He wasn't French," Loveday replied immediately, interest replacing irritation in her face now that she understood where Lord William's questions were leading. "I told my steward in French to get several menservants to drive the creature away, and he didn't understand me. As to fallen into low estate? I cannot be so sure of that, but I think not." She shook her head. "There was something about him that shouted 'lowborn.' There are things one does not unlearn, no matter how drunk and dirty fate makes one. His English was coarse; he never learned that on any manor. The way he used his hands to gesture—"

William nodded abruptly, cutting off her description. "All right, then the man was nothing and no one and there is no open reason for Waleran to offer him a prize. I need to take Niall's warning then, that the clerk and the whole accursed business might be designed to show me as eager to frustrate Waleran no matter how harmless his action. I cannot show myself in this."

"But if Niall appealed to you as his master?" Magdalene asked. "Could you carry a protest from Loveday to the king?"

"What has she to protest? Niall said something about a betrothal agreement—"

"A forgery!" Loveday exclaimed. "I can read and write. I
would not sign my name with an X. Beyond that, how could
I agree to a new betrothal when I am already betrothed?"

"What?" William scowled. "To whom?"

"To Niall," Loveday said.

It was the second time Magdalene had heard the claim and
she believed it no more this time than the first. Still, she had
taken a strong liking to Loveday of Otmoor. Few maidens,
herself included, would have stood up to William of Ypres as
Loveday had. So Magdalene tried to keep her face bland and
blank as if this were old news of an established fact.

Meanwhile, William blinked at Loveday, then shook his
head in a dazed way. "No. Niall would have told me. Woman,
what are you about?"

Loveday met his eyes steadily. "It is a very long story, going
back to before my father's death. Since I know Niall was in a
hurry, likely he thought the tale of our betrothal could wait.
It has waited more than four years, a few days longer would
not matter."

"But when I first told him to court you—"

"Did he say he didn't know me?"

"No. No, he didn't. He said 'Loveday,' and then smiled."
William laughed. "I thought he was smiling at the name, but
that clever devil was having a little joke at my expense."

"Not a joke, my lord," Loveday said, smiling now. "He was
going to impress you with his charm and ability. He was going
to ride back and say everything was settled and then you and
his companions would admire his address with women—"

"Phah!" William exclaimed. "So when did this betrothal take place?"

"I am not very sure exactly when, but it must have been nearly four years ago. Six years ago my brother and Niall's sister were married. Less than nine months later, they were both killed in a stupid accident. At first we were all too shocked and grieved to do anything but mourn, but about a year later when my father had recovered, he decided that he was still in favor of uniting the families, so he spoke to Sir Brian about renewing the bond by joining Niall to me. It took some time for my father and Sir Brian to come to terms. Sir Brian had the better birth, but my father could afford a good dowry. I gave my approval, but to tell the truth I do not know whether Niall was even in the shire at that time."

"Well, if you have the document—"

"Alas, there is no document. It was a word-of-honor agreement. The priest was supposed to write it all down, but within a week or two of the final agreement, possibly while a messenger was seeking Niall, the plague struck. My father and my two remaining brothers died." Her voice wavered and tears filled her eyes. "The priest died too."

"Then it is not so easy. I have only your word . . ."

"Sir Brian Arvagh will remember, as soon as Niall can get to Murcot and mention it to him."

"I am sure he will," William said with great solemnity, although the laugh lines around his eyes were crinkled.

"Then I will write to the king—in my own hand—to protest this false betrothal. I will explain the whole case. My steward and the other old servants will also bear witness. Can I send this letter to you, my lord? To what place? At what time? Will you bring it to the king?"

He stared at her hard, then nodded. "Write. I will send a messenger to pick up the document tomorrow morning." Then he turned to Magdalene, who had been standing silent near the door. "Magdalene, come with me. I want a word or two with you."

They went out together, and William pulled the first woman standing by a curtained alcove into the corridor. "Out," he said. "Magdalene will pay you later." Then he pushed Magdalene in and a moment later followed her, his hand on his knife hilt.

"What is it?" Magdalene asked anxiously. "Did I do so wrong in taking Loveday into my care?"

For once William's voice was low enough that only someone with an ear pressed to the curtain could hear him. "I don't know yet about that," he said, "but you know something about that betrothal that I don't. I saw it in your face when she first claimed to be troth bound to Niall."

Magdalene smiled, but she couldn't help being a little annoyed. Her bland expression had not fooled William. Again his bluff face had made her forget his keen mind . . . and he knew her at least as well as she knew him, possibly better. Doubtless he had watched her more carefully over the years, still unsure of how much he could trust a whore.

"Oh, that," Magdalene said. "She's no more betrothed to Niall than I am, but I didn't say anything because it doesn't matter a bit. She's quite determined to have him, and I suspect there are few things that Loveday of Otmoor wants that she cannot get. The servants will all swear just as she says—they would swear that the sky was green and the moon blue if she asked."

William nodded. "And Sir Brian will swear the same—unless he's mad. From what Niall has told me, the Arvaghs are poor as mice. I doubt Sir Brian will cavil over the girl's birth or whether or not she and Niall were betrothed four years ago when she brings rich lands with her."

"And William, she's a nice girl. Do you remember the man you choked last night?"

"Filthy sot."

"That was the man Waleran sent to Loveday."

William stared at her, blinking and blinking. "How do you know that?"

"Sir Ferrau—the man who rushed out and begged you not to kill the one you were throttling—when he first tried to make that drunk let go of me, called him Aimery. Niall said he beat this St. Cyr unconscious. And Loveday says St. Cyr's given name was Aimery. How many Aimerys all bruised and broken are likely to be in Oxford at this moment?"

"I see. Well, first I'll set Giles to discovering whether Waleran has any relationship to the girl or wants her lands. They are in a good place, I must say. I would like very much to have a loyal man of mine perched just a bit out of the way but near enough to Oxford to come down in force if needed. It was why I sent Niall out to speak to the girl so soon. Or could Waleran just have taken a hate to her? No, that's impossible. Who was her father?"

"Joseph of Otmoor. He was a breeder and shearer of sheep. Otmoor has perfect grazing for sheep, according to Loveday. But he's been dead for at least four years."

William shook his head in puzzlement. "This whole business grows more ridiculous by the moment. I almost cannot believe it happened at all, but Niall is not given to imagining battles, nor were the knife slashes he bore figments of his mind. Still, before I act on Loveday's letter, I must know whether Waleran is bent on some revenge against her. If not—" his mouth grew grim and hard "—that filth St. Cyr was deliberately chosen to force me to interfere."

He shrugged and put out a hand to pull the curtain aside. Magdalene slid in front of him to come out into the hallway first. She looked both ways into an empty corridor. "Be careful, William," she said over her shoulder, and pulled the curtain farther aside for him to pass.

"You always say that to me." He laughed. "It makes me feel pleasantly like a young fool," he said, and bent to give her a firm kiss on the lips.

"Will you come back tonight?"

A shadow darkened the front doorway as she asked. William turned away from her, his hand on his sword hilt, unable to see who it was against the light. But his laugh had alerted his guard, and they came out of the common room. William turned back to Magdalene.

"No. I will linger in the Court tonight, dropping St. Cyr's name here and there. I hope this is all some kind of mistake . . ."

He turned away on the uncertain word and strode toward the door. Whoever had come in had wisely stepped into the common room to be out of the way. Magdalene stood looking after William, her brows creased in a worried frown. The whole business was unbelievable. Great lords like Waleran de Meulan and William of Ypres did not contest over a girl with a few farms and a few flocks of sheep.

"I see you have enough company without me," a tight voice snarled almost in her ear.

Magdalene jumped. "Oh, Bell, I'm so glad to see you," she said, paying no attention to his voice or the lips thinned over his teeth. "The craziest things have been happening. Come into my chamber—"

"I thought you had just come out of it."

"A cocking room?" Her voice scaled upward. "Take William into a cocking room? Are you mad? Besides, I have not lain with a man in a cocking room for near ten years."

"Oxford *is* very crowded. If lust overcame you . . ."

"Lust *never* overcomes a whore," Magdalene spat, then looked up into his face and began to laugh. "You almost had me. Someday you are going to tease the wrong person and end up a head shorter."

Bell didn't acknowledge the remark, just asked, "Well what *were* you doing with Lord William in that room?"

His expression hadn't changed, but the teasing was gone from his eyes and his voice, and Magdalene realized that she had spoken the truth . . . but about the wrong thing. He almost *had* had her. He had almost made her believe that he could make a jest of his jealousy . . . and perhaps he could, but it was there as strong and hurtful as ever. She did not want another dead man, particularly Bell, on her soul.

"It is none of your business," she answered tartly, "but I will tell you anyway since it is all part of the craziness I mentioned." She looked around to make sure they were alone in the corridor and lowered her voice so it would not carry into the other curtained rooms. "We were in the cocking room, William and I, because Loveday of Otmoor is in my chamber and William wanted to speak to me where she could not hear."

"Who the devil is Loveday of Otmoor?"

Magdalene gave an exaggerated sigh. "Well, thank God that you, at least, do not want to marry her. It seems to me that every other man in and around Oxford does."

"A beauty to rival you?" Bell asked, and laughed.

"A rich orphan."

"Ah." Then he blinked and frowned. "A rich orphan? What is she doing in a whorehouse?"

"Now *you* had better join me in the cocking chamber."

"With all my . . . ah . . . heart." Bell grinned. "I missed you last night."

Magdalene lifted the curtain and went into the room. There was a chest against the back wall, and she sat down on it. Bell perched beside her. Magdalene sighed again.

"And you are like to miss me for several nights more since Loveday will be sleeping in the other bed in the room." She went on to tell him the whole story, which left him also shaking his head.

"You are right, of course," he said. "The whole tale stinks of bad fish. I can see someone like myself, who has no livelihood aside from what the bishop gives me, coming to blows with another in my condition over such a parcel of land, but the girl is in the king's ward. No one can seize her without Stephen's permission. No doubt Lord Waleran could obtain that permission, or Lord William—the girl's revenues could not be enough to make the king refuse her permission to marry—but neither would make a contest of it."

"William wouldn't, except that Niall is already neck-deep in the matter. Waleran might, for pride's sake. He cannot bear to be bested by William in anything."

But Bell was not listening to her; his mind was following its own path. "What I would like to know is who the clerk was. Likely what you said was true and he merely wanted to collect a reward from both Lord Waleran and Lord William. But what if he had another purpose? It might suit someone in the

Church to have those two at each other's throats and distracting the king."

"Oh, my God," Magdalene moaned. "Let us not mix the
Church into this stupid little matter of Loveday's marriage."

Bell shrugged. "Perhaps not directly to do with Loveday's
marriage, but if the clerk meant to embroil Lord William with
Lord Waleran, the Church is already involved."

"But why?"

"The dean is very worried by the feeling in the Court. I
know he, among others, has written to Salisbury to beg him
to come to this Council. He fears absence might be taken as
defiance. Could a battle between Meulan and Ypres make Salisbury's nonappearance less significant?"

"To the king, perhaps, but not to others. The common men-
at-arms are wagering with each other over whether Salisbury
will come, some saying he must to avoid the appearance of
treason, the others putting coin on his shutting himself up in
one of his castles, already stuffed and garnished for war when
Robert of Gloucester comes, and letting his treason come into
the open. Apparently no one thinks it worthwhile to wager
that Salisbury is not a traitor."

Bell stared at her, then said, "What?"

She repeated what Diccon had told her and Bell drew in his
breath, his mouth thinned to a hard slit.

"Then I need to be in Oxford today and tonight, not mewed
up in Wytham Abbey with a lot of monks who talk but know
nothing. I will go around the alehouses and listen, and a candlemark or so in the common room here might be useful too."
Then the grim look on his face faded into a smile. "Never has
duty and delight come together so well."

"Only duty, no delight, I fear. Remember Loveday is in the

other bed in my room. She is an innocent maiden, and you are a vigorous and noisy—if most enjoyable—lover."

"She will learn something then. If you won't give me a bed tonight, I won't have one."

"Oh, I'll share my bed. I just wanted to warn you that there will be a listener. You are often so coy about . . . ah . . . country matters."

He made a face. "Just how innocent is the maiden?"

"I believe she is still a virgin, but *she* says she's not innocent at all, after attending to the breeding needs of her manor for four years. But come and meet her yourself."

Bell rose without reluctance and they started for the door to Magdalene's chamber but were caught as they came out of the whore's room by a hard-eyed if pretty woman.

"You owe me," she said to Magdalene. "The man said you'd pay me for the use of my room."

"Yes, of course," Magdalene said, and then to Bell, "Give her a penny, please. I don't have my purse with me."

Without question Bell felt in his purse and drew out a silver penny, which he handed over. The woman smiled up at him. "I'm Geneva," she said. "If your lady here is too busy with Lord William, I'll be glad to make a place for you."

"That won't be necessary, I'm sure," Bell said coldly.

"One can never tell," the whore insisted, smiling more broadly. "Remember, I'm Geneva."

Magdalene was annoyed, not so much because Geneva had reminded Bell that Lord William had precedence—that was all to the good; Bell needed reminding—but because the interest in the whore's eyes was not wholly financial. A man attractive to a whore was *very* attractive. She found Bell so, but hadn't thought about other women. Cold washed over her. Could *she* be jealous? She was saved from having to answer that question by finding Loveday reading over two closely written pages and biting her lip uncertainly.

"I hope there are no lies in the writing that will be too easy to point out," Magdalene said with raised brows.

Loveday's glance flicked from her to Bell, and she looked angry. "Not another suitor!" she exclaimed.

Magdalene laughed. "No, no. You are growing spoiled. This one is mine . . . I think. His name is Sir Bellamy of Itchen."

"And I am not in the market for a wife," Bell said, and then asked, "Were you really reading that?"

"Yes, and I wrote it, too," Loveday snapped. "It is my complaint to the king about being threatened with a forged betrothal agreement when I was already betrothed. And an apology for not making clear to the clerk who made me the king's ward that I was betrothed. No one asked me, and I was so distraught over my father's and brothers' deaths that I did not think of it. Then Niall was away with Lord William and I was so busy learning to manage the estate that I forgot."

"Will it hold together?" Magdalene asked.

Loveday handed her the two sheets of parchment. "Read it over and see for yourself. I will have to buy more parchment for you. I used all you had."

Bell sat down on the stool across from Loveday and asked her a question about where her lands lay with respect to Oxford, and Magdalene also sat down and began to read. The document was very well put together and quite moving, when Loveday expressed her pain and grief over the death of her menfolk and her bewildered confusion as she tried to keep her lands from falling into disorder. She thanked the king most humbly for acting on the petition of her father's friend Reinhardt Hardel, the London wool merchant, to acknowledge her as her father's only heir and take her into ward to protect her. She explained her shock and terror when Aimery St. Cyr told her he had permission to marry her and she realized her terrible oversight in not telling the king's clerk of her prior betrothal to Sir Niall Arvagh of Murcot.

Bell was getting up when Magdalene put the sheets of parchment back on the table. He said he would go out and get dinner for the three of them. Magdalene suggested that he take Diccon along and buy an extra dinner, pointing out that the boy was a fount of information and could probably tell him which alehouses were frequented by which lord's meiny. When he had gone out, she turned to Loveday and smiled.

"If I did not know better, I would have believed you," she said. "Now we only need to tell Niall that he has been betrothed for at least four years and arrange that he have time enough to ride over to Murcot and tell his father."

They talked over the possibility of going to Noke themselves, possibly with Bell's escort, but Loveday was afraid that they would run afoul of St. Cyr with a whole troop. And the moment Loveday said it, Magdalene had a vision of Bell trying to fight a whole troop and lost her enthusiasm for leaving the city.

By the time Bell returned, they had settled on seeing if St. Friedesweide had any parchment to sell or would tell them where to go to buy some—more than two sheets, because copies were needed. When Magdalene had kept a house in Oxford, the archdeacon who taught her to read and write had provided parchment, which cost him nothing.

Bell kept Diccon so busy talking that the boy had hardly time to eat his meal and no time at all to learn anything about

Loveday except what Magdalene wanted him to know. He was told that her name was Maeve, that she was not a whore but, for private reasons of her own, had agreed to go with Magdalene to the Old Priory Guesthouse in Southwark. There she would be broached and relieved of her virginity by one particular man, who had paid well for the privilege.

Diccon accepted that without question or further interest. He was aware that to some men the broaching of a virgin was especially exciting and that they would pay well above the cost for an ordinary futtering; he was also aware that the same "virgin" might be broached several times and that the later "broachings" were often more ceremonious and costly than the first. In any case it had nothing to do with him and he concentrated on answering the questions of Mistress Magdalene's man, who promised to be a most excellent source of meals and money in exchange for information.

When the boy had been drained dry and they had all finished eating, Magdalene and Loveday veiled themselves and they all went out. The monks of St. Friedesweide had no parchment to sell, but the sacristan sent them to the archivist, who was able to tell them about a leatherworker by St. Michael's Church near the North Gate who often had small quantities of parchment for sale.

On coming out of St. Friedesweide, Magdalene and Loveday shed their veils. Nothing marked Magdalene as a whore, so Loveday did not need to hide her acquaintance with her and Loveday almost wished they would encounter St. Cyr. He would not dare try to seize her on a street in town, and if he did . . . there was something about Bell that implied Aimery would have even less luck with him than he had had with Niall.

For Magdalene the same reason applied for not needing to

keep her presence from contaminating Loveday. For herself, in
the company of another woman and a strong, armed man, it
was unlikely that anyone would accost her. However, Bell only
accompanied them along the Cornmarket to the first crossroad
on the right, which some called Market Street, where he entered an alehouse called The Broached Barrel.

"I will be back when I am back," he said to Magdalene.

"Any time will do," she replied, "a whorehouse is always
open. Just don't get so drunk that you spew."

He laughed and strode through the door. Magdalene and
Loveday continued on to St. Michael's Church by the North
Gate. Nestled close to the church wall was the leatherworker's
shop recommended by the archivist. The master came forward
bowing and smiling, prepared to offer worked leather for shoes
or pouches, belts or gloves, but his eyes opened in surprise
when Magdalene asked to see what parchment he had in stock.

To avoid a long argument about women having no need for
parchment, Magdalene told him it was a gift for her brother.
The doubt smoothed away from the merchant's face and he
brought out several boxes filled with sheets of differing quality.
He was disturbed again when Loveday and Magdalene discussed the stock too knowledgeably, sometimes freely disa-
greeing when he suggested this or that. However, as soon as
he saw the glint of their silver, he grew most accommodating
and their needs were rolled and tied and dropped into Magdalene's basket.

Idly, now, they strolled along in the market, looking at this
and at that and talking comfortably. For all that Magdalene
was almost ten years older than Loveday, the younger woman's
years of experience in managing her estate and ruling a substantial number of servants lent her a true maturity. They

passed another alehouse, The Wheat Sheaf, and two shops down found themselves in front of Perry Redding's mercery. Both stopped to look at the ribbons and embroidery yarn, Magdalene indifferently, just to see if anything new had been added, Loveday with a newly heightened attention.

"Would that shade of blue or green suit Niall?" she asked. "That hair of his . . . I could never use red."

"The green is closer to his eyes," Magdalene said. "And you are right, of course, about avoiding red, but if you are going to make his tunics of blue or green, brown or amber ribbons for neck and sleeves and then embroidery in the blues and greens—"

"Loveday!" a young man shouted, rushing from the doorway of The Wheat Sheaf to seize Loveday's arm.

"Let go of her, sir!" Magdalene snapped, her hand going to her knife hilt.

But even as her fingers closed around it she knew this was not Aimery St. Cyr nor any friend of his. Although he was a few finger widths taller than Loveday, this was a slender stripling with a wealth of tumbled curls—which could have been cleaner—large if somewhat bloodshot brown eyes, and a full, petulant mouth.

"Oh, Jules, do let go," Loveday said in an exasperated voice. "You silly boy, you are bruising my arm."

Magdalene relaxed her grip on her knife. It was quite apparent that Loveday knew the young man and had no fear of him.

"Where have you been?" he demanded, his voice high with excitement. "What happened to you? I heard the most horrible tale about some man claiming you were betrothed to him and trying to seize you. And your servants wouldn't open the gate for me!"

"There would have been no point in letting you in," Loveday said calmly, "since you were asking for me, no doubt, and I wasn't there. The tale was true, but the betrothal agreement was a forgery. Nonetheless, when my brother-by-marriage—"

"What brother-by-marriage?" Jules shouted.

As Loveday began to remind the young man of her eldest brother's marriage shortly before his death, Magdalene became aware of another man standing a few paces beyond Jules. He was staring at her and then glancing sidelong at Loveday. His mouth hung slightly open with surprise and indecision, and, with a sinking heart, Magdalene realized it was Lord Ormerod. She moved quickly to his side.

"She knows who and what I am," Magdalene said. "The brother-by-marriage of whom she speaks is one of William of Ypres' captains and it is he who placed her in my care to save her from being abducted and forced into marriage. He hopes to change his kinship to her from brother-by-marriage to husband so rumor of her whereabouts cannot hurt her."

Ormerod frowned. "Husband? Another suitor? Jules says she is promised to him."

Magdalene giggled. "By whom? From her manner to him, I would doubt that. Still, maybe you *should* tell him who I am and that Loveday is lodged in the Soft Nest with me. It would cool his ardour quickly enough."

"I am not so sure of that," Ormerod said, his lips twisting. "I suspect it is the lands Jules wants more than the lady. He was greatly overset at hearing of St. Cyr's having a betrothal agreement and confided in me that he had been a little too free-spending because he had been sure of a marriage that would cover all his debts."

"To you, too?" Magdalene asked.

Ormerod made a dismissive gesture. "Very little. A few pounds from when he came to the Council at Westminster to be confirmed heir to his father's estate. The old man died at the turn of the year. London is expensive; Jules ran short."

Magdalene had a feeling that Jules's debt to Lord Ormerod was a good deal higher than the few pounds Ormerod spoke of so lightly. She wondered whether, in fact, it was that debt that brought Ormerod to Oxford during the king's Council and whether Ormerod's purpose was to go before the king to lay a claim to this Jules's lands to satisfy that debt.

"He has managed to ruin himself with surprising speed if the estate only came into his hands at the turn of the year," Magdalene remarked.

"His father was the same kind."

The sour voice in which Ormerod spoke made Magdalene wonder whether the debt was Jules's or his father's, but it was really none of her business. At that moment she was distracted by the young man crying out, "What? He dared insult you that way? Why did you not tell him that you were pledged to me, Jules of Osney—"

"Oh Jules," Loveday sighed, "because it is not true. You have asked me to marry you, but you know that I have not accepted and I will not."

"I should think I am a better choice than this Aimery St. Cyr."

Loveday laughed. "A mowing ape would be better than him, but you must stop speaking of me as if I were promised to you, Jules. We were playmates as children but that time is long gone. Perhaps our fathers did think we might be suitable, but then my brother and his wife died and my father began to plan another arrangement—"

"I do not believe it! Why should he?"

Loveday's voice sharpened. "Perhaps because he heard certain things about debts that he didn't like. Perhaps because I protested that you and I were too much like brother and sister. I was not willing then and am not willing now."

"Nonsense! Of course you are willing." He watched her shake her head and saw her expression of pity, and went on, "Oh, I see, you are saying that because you fear for me. You need not, and you should send to me at once if that creature troubles you again. I will protect you."

"Do not be a fool!" Loveday exclaimed even more sharply. "St. Cyr is a practiced man-at-arms. He would kill you. I have enough protectors. Stay away from St. Cyr, Jules."

The young man's face flushed dark red. "Do you think me such a popinjay? Well, you need not. I have friends—" his eyes flicked sideways toward Ormerod "—who are eager to see us married and will support me in keeping St. Cyr from having you."

"Jules!" Loveday protested, but it was too late. The young man had rushed away from her back toward The Wheat Sheaf. She looked at Magdalene. "I hope he does not drink too much. He is of those who grow pot-valiant."

Magdalene looked up at Ormerod, who sighed. "I will make sure he does nothing dangerous." Then he grinned. "If anything happened to him and his estate went to the crown, I would never get my money back."

CHAPTER 7

21 June,
The Soft Nest, Oxford

The encounter with Jules of Osney having spoiled their taste for strolling slowly around the Cornmarket, Magdalene and Loveday returned to the Soft Nest. While Magdalene drew patterns for embroidery on the ribbons she had purchased the previous day, Loveday made two copies of her appeal to the king. One, she hoped, Lord William would present to the king, one she would keep, and the third would go to Niall at Noke so he would know what Loveday claimed.

They had spent the rest of the afternoon in what remained of the back yard, peacefully embroidering the patterns Magdalene had drawn. When the light began to fail, they carried in the stools on which they had been sitting and admired what they had wrought.

Diccon brought them an evening meal and told them that while running an errand, he had seen Bell in The Wheat Sheaf deep in conversation with men whose clothing was better than that of common men-at-arms.

"Drunk?" Magdalene asked.

The boy shrugged. "His face was red, but his eyes . . . no,

not drunk. Not yet, anyway. He's coming back here later, though. Does he hit when he's drunk?"

"Not me, anyway," Magdalene answered smiling. "I'm not sure I would trust him if a man crossed him. Get him into the back room as soon as possible."

"Sir Bellamy is going to sleep here?" Loveday asked.

"He has no other lodging. You need not be concerned. Drunk or sober, he will not trouble you."

That was true. Likely he did not even remember Loveday was in the other bed—to which she had repaired soon after dark, yawning most sincerely because she was accustomed to country hours. Magdalene, embroidering quietly by candle-light, which she often did far into the night in the Old Priory Guesthouse, was on hand to greet him. If not drunk, he was not wholly sober and needed help undoing his buckles and ties, but he did not giggle and jest over his clumsiness while she helped him as he usually did. His mouth was grim and he went to the bed almost without a word.

Magdalene expected that he would be asleep by the time she had put away her work and undressed herself, but he took her in his arms as soon as she slipped under the covers and held her tight against him.

"What you heard is not good news," she said softly.

He was silent for a time and then said, "You have often told me that most whores hate sex. Just so do most soldiers hate war."

He kissed her before she could ask a further question and began to stroke her body and caress her breasts. Magdalene gave herself to him with practiced warmth, but for once her mind was busy with other than the gratification of her senses. Bell, too, either because he remembered Loveday's presence or because his own mood was too dark, neither thrust nor cried out with his usual abandon. Still passion grew, and when the waves of satisfaction had lifted and cast them down, each was more at peace.

Resting quietly in the aftermath, Bell yawned and murmured, "I must go report to the dean early tomorrow. I may even have to ride down to Winchester to speak to the bishop." Then he laughed softly. " 'Tell Magdalene and feel better'," he said, recalling a maxim of Ella's, and detailed what he had gleaned from conversation with captains sworn to Warenne, Chester, Alain of Brittany, and several others, ending, "I do not know if there will be time, but Salisbury should be warned not to bring too many men into the city."

"Not bring too many men in? Will he be safer with fewer to defend him?"

"Did you not hear me? No one will attack the bishop himself. That would be unthinkable, even to Waleran de Meulan. The men will be used to make Salisbury appear guilty of an offense against the king. Something is planned—what, I could not find out; I think the men with whom I spoke did not know. Some breaking of the peace will occur and Salisbury will be blamed. If he does not have any men in the city other than the guard in attendance on him, they cannot break the peace and he cannot be blamed."

"Perhaps he would be better off claiming illness—he is an old man, he could be ill—and not coming at all."

"I suspect if he does that, the king will send a 'visitor' most anxious to inquire into his well-being—and into the condition of his keeps."

"William . . ." Magdalene whispered.

Bell stiffened and pulled free of her. "You have told me many times that I will not be your only lover, but I wish you would not cry for another man when lying in my arms."

"Do not be an idiot!" Magdalene spat. "I only meant that it would be William who would have to go to Salisbury, either to pry him out of his keep or to examine it inside and out. May I send him word of what you learned? His men are camped outside the city, but he could order some troops in to wander the market and maybe sit in the alehouses to prevent a riot from starting."

After a long silence, Bell sighed and drew Magdalene back to lie with her head on his shoulder. "You may tell him, of course, but I do not think . . ." He let his voice fade and said no more. Soon the ale he had drunk and the fatigue of his lovemaking had their way, and he slept.

Bell was gone by the time Magdalene woke in the morning. Loveday, awake with the first light of dawn as was her habit as the mistress of a well-run manor, told Magdalene she had been breaking her fast when he came from the sheltered side of the bed. She had offered him bread and ale, of which they now had ample supply, and he had eaten and drunk.

"And he will bring us or send us—if he must ride to Winchester—news of Noke."

Magdalene grinned and shook her head. "A woman after my own heart," she said. "You know how to make use of a man, but how did you turn Bell, who knows a thing or two about women, into your messenger boy?"

Loveday smiled back and explained that to be polite, she asked where he was going. And, of course, when he told her Wytham, it occurred to her that he would ride right by the lane to Noke. She shrugged. Since he already knew the whole story, she then explained that Niall was guarding the manor and that she was dying to know what had happened there and also wished Niall to know about her appeal.

"He is a good-humored man, and very kind," Loveday said. "He freely offered to ride the few extra miles to Noke and to bring the third copy of my appeal to Niall. I did not ask Sir Bellamy to tell Niall anything. I am sure Niall will realize he must send or take my letter to his father at Murcot."

Along with her amusement over how determined—and manipulative—Loveday was, Magdalene was relieved. Loveday's problem had slipped her mind, overlaid by anxiety about Salisbury's fate. But trust Loveday not to lose sight of her ends. Magdalene went out to use the privy smiling broadly.

On her way in, she saw Diccon and told him to bring in water for washing. When she was dressed, she and Loveday began to discuss what to do with the day that stretched long ahead of them. Both were women accustomed to being busy, but before their enforced idleness could drive them out, despite their concern about being recognized as they had been the previous day, Diccon was back.

"Man wants to see you, Mistress Magdalene," he said. "Said you knew him and that he's sorry to bother you so early but he has to ask you a favor."

"He didn't give a name?"

"No, but I think Florete will know. He's been here before."

"Very well, send him in. Loveday, you had better get back into the bed and draw the curtains. Too many people in this area know you."

The girl swept off the table any evidence of a second person having eaten and retreated behind her bedcurtains. Diccon scratched at the door and then opened it. To Magdalene's amazement, Sir Ferrau stood in the doorway.

"Yes, sir?" she asked.

"May I come in?" Magdalene hesitated and he added, "I promise that no insult will be offered you."

Magdalene bent her head. "Very well. Enter."

He closed the door behind him and cleared his throat uneasily. "I come on a very distasteful errand," he said. "I am sure you have not forgotten that stupid lout that Lord William nearly choked?"

"No, I have not forgotten."

"He fell into some quarrel with one of William of Ypres' men on the morning of the day he insulted you and was soundly thrashed, which is why he was all bruised. He claims that while he was unconscious, Lord William's man cut his purse."

"One of William's men cut Waleran's man-at-arms's purse?" Magdalene repeated, looking wide-eyed with surprise. Then she shook her head as if she could not believe it. "Forgive me," she said, "but what would such a man have in his purse to make it worth stealing? This sounds very unlikely, unless . . . unless there was something special in the purse?"

Ferrau sighed heavily. "There was a large sum of money. St. Cyr says he was robbed of nearly a pound in silver, and he is so angry he intended to go to Lord Waleran to complain. He claims there was another man with him at the manor who will swear he saw what happened."

"But what has this to do with me? Or you?"

He sighed again. "It is my misfortune to have met him in the street and have him invite himself to come here with me. You remember how he was put out. It seems when he came to himself he was bemused, and only late yesterday afternoon remembered what had happened. He came to Count Alain of

Brittany's lodging and bawled for me to accompany him to
Lord Waleran and bear witness when and how he discovered
his purse was missing. I took him to the Lively Hop instead
and calmed him. He left happy, but when I returned to my
lodging I discovered that my master, Count Alain, had heard
him."

"I hope you told that idiot St. Cyr that Lord Waleran is not
likely to concern himself over the loss of a purse of a common
man-at-arms?"

"Would he not if it was William of Ypres's man being accused?" Sir Ferrau asked pointedly.

"I see," Magdalene breathed.

Ferrau nodded. "Tensions are so high . . . I will not trouble
you with the cause—I am sure you are indifferent to it—but
Lord Waleran and Lord William are already at daggers drawn.
Count Alain is most eager that nothing disrupt the king's
Council. Although he knows none of this is my fault, he bade
me try to recover the purse to avoid another cause of anger
and resentment, however small."

"A most worthy purpose," Magdalene agreed, "but I do not
see why you come to me." She opened her eyes wide. "Surely
you do not suspect me of receiving stolen goods?"

"No! Good Lord, no. Lord William's woman would have no
need to. . . . No, it is your good services Count Alain hopes to
engage. That is, the count knows nothing of you but he told
me to be discreet. For me to go directly to Lord William . . .
ah . . . would not be . . ."

"Now I see." Magdalene smiled as witlessly as she knew how.
"You want me to ask William to tell his man to give up the
purse to you. But which man?"

"It would be best not to involve Lord William at all," Sir

Ferrau said. "Or me and through me Count Alain. St. Cyr says the man was Niall Arvagh. I hope you know him. I hope you can explain to him how much it would redound to his discredit if Lord William heard of what he had done. Count Alain desires that this not come to either Lord Waleran's or Lord William's attention."

"Then I suppose you do not want this Niall Arvagh to bring the purse to you . . . if he took it and is willing to return it."

"No, not to me. He would not want to admit to a knight that he cut a man's purse. That would make him more reluctant to give it up. Let him give it to you."

"I suppose I can find Niall Arvagh—the name is not so common—but I fear that if he cut the purse for the silver, the money will no longer be there."

Sir Ferrau stared for a moment too long at her, then nodded. "I, too, suppose the silver will be gone. I do not know what the count will wish to do about that. Possibly he will replace it to keep St. Cyr quiet; the money is nothing to him. That will be out of my hands. God knows I wish I had never met St. Cyr or taken pity on him because of the fight. But it is true he did not know the purse was gone until he had to pay Madame Florete—and then I was stuck for the price of the whore—" he bit his lip "—sorry."

"No need. That is what I am, a whore." Magdalene smiled slowly. "But I doubt many could afford my price." Then she frowned. "Well, I will do what I can. I certainly do not want William troubled with this matter, and I do know several of his captains. I will put out word about the 'lost' purse. If it should come into my hand . . ."

Ferrau shrugged. "Hold it, or since the money will be gone, you could leave it with Florete. I cannot imagine there would be anything else in it of interest to anyone. I will come by tonight and tomorrow. I do not know whether St. Cyr can be convinced to be patient longer than that."

"If the count is willing to pay him a few pence on account," Magdalene said, "St. Cyr will get himself too drunk to remember his outrage, and certainly too drunk to present any complaint to Lord Waleran."

Sir Ferrau laughed. "An excellent suggestion. And my thanks." He hesitated, then added tentatively, as if he were afraid to offend, "And since I will have my master's gratitude if this is done quietly, more than simple thanks will be forthcoming if you can help."

Although she kept her expression bland, Magdalene was amused. Ferrau was obviously uncertain as to what her true position was. If Lord William was her sole protector and she was all but his wife, which his ferocious protection of her implied, she was nearly a lady and must be treated like one. But here she was, lodged in a whorehouse rather than kept in private quarters. If she was merely a favorite whore, then she would expect to be paid for any service she performed.

"I will try," Magdalene said, with perfect calm but no intention of clarifying anything for him, as she stepped to the door and opened it.

Sir Ferrau said farewell and went out. Magdalene closed the door. She heard a soft sound and shook her head in a signal to Loveday to remain where she was. After a few moments more, she opened the door as if to come out. The corridor was empty. Florete's table was unoccupied, and the front door was closed. She watched a moment longer, then pulled her door shut.

Loveday slipped out from behind the bedcurtains, her

mouth set with anger. "Why did you speak as if Niall would steal that creature's money?"

"Hush! Because I wanted to find out if Ferrau knew that the forged betrothal agreement was also in the purse."

"Did you?"

Magdalene sighed. "No. There was nothing in his face or manner to say he knew. And his willingness to leave the purse with Florete implies that he believes, once the money is gone, that the purse has no value. Was there a pound of silver there?"

"Oh, I don't know! I was frightened to death and shaking all over. I don't really remember Niall giving me the purse. I know I didn't look into it. All I could think of was getting away from there before that monster came back with a full troop and killed Niall and raped me or killed me. I threw it . . . where did I throw it?" She wrung her hands, which were shaking with the memory. "Yes. I threw it into the strongbox when I took out money for living in Oxford."

"Then it is safe enough for now." But still Magdalene stood staring into nothing until she said, "You did see that agreement, did you not?"

"Yes. St. Cyr showed it to me the second time he came, the time he tried to rape me. Why?"

"I just wondered who had witnessed the document." She raised her brows. "Could the so-elevated, so-pious, so-proper Count Alain have put his signature and seal—"

"There was no seal at all on the document. I noticed that because I was looking for the royal seal. But why in the world should Count Alain witness my betrothal? I don't know him and I will swear neither did my father."

Magdalene sniffed. "He would not be the first high and mighty lord to put his sign and seal on a document for a price.

Could St. Cyr have been carrying a pound in silver to pay the count to use his seal? Well, you said there was no seal. So perhaps he had not yet paid to have the document sealed and thought if he could claim you by coupling with you he would not need to pay. Who were the witnesses?"

Loveday shook her head and looked miserable. "I don't know. I didn't look. I'd seen the part that said that I gave into the hands of my betrothed husband all my goods, servants, chattels, and so on, and that no provision was made for me at all. I saw there was no royal seal, and I thrust it back at him and said I would not sign. He laughed and said that was all taken care of, that I had signed already."

"Oh well," Magdalene shrugged, "it doesn't matter. It would just be something funny to tell William. He hates it when people with French-court ways look down their noses at him. If he knew that Alain was selling his seal and signature . . . oh, I know. When Niall brings the purse to return it to St. Cyr, he can bring the betrothal agreement too, and I can look at the names of the witnesses before we destroy it."

"Are we going to give back the money, too? A whole pound!"

"Loveday!" Magdalene sounded shocked, but her lips quivered. "Do you wish to steal the man's money?"

"Where would an animal like St. Cyr get so much silver? And who knows what he intended to do with it. Buy an application of the royal seal to bind me?" She made an angry moue and then said, "We will have to give it back. Otherwise he will claim that Niall stole it. And how will we tell Niall that he should bring the purse and the document?"

"I can ask Florete to let me know if one of William's men stops in. He will be able to arrange for a messenger or perhaps

Florete can. I certainly don't think we should try to ride out
to Noke ourselves. In fact, I am most reluctant even to go out
into the market today. The fewer people that see us together,
or you in Oxford, the better."

Although Magdalene could see Loveday was not happy with
the decision, the girl knew it was sensible and agreed. The
women spent the morning embroidering and had Diccon, who
had no real news, for company at dinner time. By early afternoon none of William's men had arrived and Magdalene was
about to leave the room to ask Florette about a messenger
when Bell forestalled her intention by calling through the door
and then walking in without waiting for a reply. It was a piece
of rudeness that made Magdalene lighthearted—a mark of trust
he didn't even know he had given. If the slightest suspicion
that she still plied her trade troubled his heart, he would never
have walked in and chanced finding her with a man.

Then Magdalene told herself not to be a fool. Doubtless he
had asked Florete if anyone was with her. Thus she moderated
the warmth with which she greeted him, which was just as
well. Too much gladness might have made him suspicious, particularly as he was in a foul mood himself. That was partly
because he had been caught in a nasty downpour and partly
because the dean did not feel the relation of gossip collected
at alehouses was sufficiently urgent for Bell to ride to Winchester.

He informed them of what he thought of that while he rid
himself of his wet cloak and wiped his face and hair with a
cloth Magdalene gave him. As he sat down to pull off his
boots, he finished with "He said that a messenger with a letter
to the bishop would be enough to describe the rumors. But
how can a letter convey the leashed-in excitement that some

of those men felt or the anxiety of others? Oh, I wrote of it, but if I told Winchester he would understand better."

"Likely," Magdalene agreed, "but what good would it do? Salisbury must be here by tomorrow if he wishes to avoid the appearance of contumacy. If Winchester wrote to Salisbury, his letter would never arrive in time."

"It certainly would not," Loveday put in. "It is near twenty leagues to Winchester and would take you a full day to ride there, even if you changed horses—a day and a half if you rode Monseigneur all the way. Salisbury will have left Malmsbury before you arrive in Winchester. And if the bishop of Winchester addresses his letter to Salisbury here—"

"That would not be wise." Magdalene's voice was flat. "And even if Winchester heard your news and felt it as strongly as you do, what can you expect him to do? He cannot ride the way you can, so it would be two or three days before he could arrive. Worse yet, it would be even less safe for him to come here than to send a letter. I know the bishop is a good and wise man, but consider the animosity between him and the king . . ."

"Oh, God," Bell sighed. "Of course he would stand up for Salisbury and perhaps be caught in the same trap."

"And if he stays quietly in Winchester and yet knows clearly what has happened and what the opinions of the men attending the Council are, perhaps he will be able to mend the harm or smooth it over. Salisbury cannot live forever; he is an old man already."

"If the king could be convinced of that . . ." Bell nodded and Magdalene could see his body relax. "So the dean was not so foolish as I thought for keeping me here to see and hear. Well he was right." Then suddenly he laughed. " 'Tell Magdalene and feel better.'" He laughed again. "Out of the mouths of babes."

"Do you have a child, Magdalene?" Loveday asked.

Now it was Magdalene's turn to laugh. "In a way. One of the women who serves in my house is . . . simple. She is not of those with round faces, narrow eyes, and slobbering lips. Perhaps she was born as you and I and some illness or accident befell her that robbed her of her wits. But she is like a five-year-old—" Magdalene grinned "—except for her love of fut-tering, which is as strong and insistent as some men's love for wine."

Bell shook his head in wonder. "Anyone, anytime, all the time. But she once told me when I was troubled . . ." His voice became slightly uneven as he thought of the mad miller whose throat he had cut, "that I should tell my troubles to Magdalene and she would make it all better."

Loveday smiled then sighed, turning to Magdalene. "Then I have a new piece of trouble to offer. I have just realized that we cannot simply send a messenger to ask Niall to bring the purse. He cannot get it out of my strongbox because I have the key with me."

"What purse?" Bell asked.

When they had told him the story, he glanced out a window and said, "I will go, but not now. It would be night before I arrived and—" his eyes flicked to Magdalene and he smiled "—I prefer a soft bed here to a pallet on the floor at Noke. It will make little difference in when you would get the document, since Niall could not ride back here by night. If you trust me, I will take the key with me, and depending on what has happened at Noke, either Niall or I will bring back purse and document."

"Thank you." Loveday smiled.

Very, very good, Magdalene thought cynically. She was almost sure that Loveday had remembered the key earlier when they were first talking about sending a messenger, but she only spoke of it when she had before her someone she knew to be trustworthy and too bemused by another woman to consider marriage to her no matter what he found in her strongbox. That thought made Magdalene wonder how much that strongbox held, how Loveday had concealed a good part of a rich income from the king, and whether Niall was making a marriage even better than he thought.

Her pleasure in that idea did not last long. If Niall no longer needed his employment with William, would he leave it? Would that deprive William of a strong, clever, and loyal captain at a critical time? Magdalene thought of Niall, of the lively eagerness of his face when he spoke of politics or war, his warm camaraderie with his fellow captains. She glanced once at Loveday, and recalled her absorption in her own affairs, her devotion to Noke.

No, Magdalene decided, Niall would stay with William as long as the heady excitement of conflict hung in the balance and his friends were involved in it. And Loveday was not the type to weep and wail of her loneliness and her need for a man to manage affairs for her.

Partly to keep Bell from recognizing how he had been handled and partly to hide her knowing grin, Magdalene rose and went to the shelves where she stored the tidbits she had bought. She collected a flask of wine and three cups. Another trip to the shelf produced a coarse cloth that when unrolled revealed another cloth, a set of chessmen, and four sets of differently dyed rounds of polished wood. The cloth inside was marked on one face with solid dark and light squares for playing chess and on the other with open interlaced squares for the three-in-a-row game often called Nine Man Merelles.

These anodynes to worry and boredom were greeted with enthusiasm and, since three could play at once and that made the game far more complex and interesting, Merelles was chosen quickly. While Magdalene poured the wine, Loveday brought a selection of dried fruit and sweetcakes to the table, and Bell handed out the wooden pieces.

Magdalene's single glance at Loveday, with eyes that flicked toward Bell and away, signed a conspiracy and they played together against him. He was so good-humored about being soundly drubbed, however, that Magdalene could not keep up the pretence. As he was about to lose one of the last three pieces remaining to him and be officially "beaten," she popped a particularly luscious piece of cake into his mouth, kissed him, and confessed.

Bell laughed heartily and admitted he had suspected the conspiracy, claiming he had not taxed them with their dishonesty just so he could demand some recompense. But before he could reveal what he intended to extract from them, the sharp crack of a sword hilt striking the door brought all three to staring attention.

"Who is there?" Magdalene called, while Loveday shook the pieces off the gaming board to hide how many had been playing and retreated toward the bed.

Bell stood up, taking his sword hilt in his right hand and holding the sheath where he had laid it handily near him on the table with his left. He could draw his weapon before anyone entering the door could reach him, and he knew Magdalene would take care not to be seized. However, the answer to Magdalene's question relieved them of any concern about attack.

"It is Giles de Milland, Magdalene. I'm sorry but I must come in at once."

"Come," Magdalene said, hurrying to open the door. "What is wrong? Is something the matter with William?"

"Not with my lord. Is Niall here?"

"No. He is at this lady's manor—" Magdalene gestured toward Loveday "—holding it against—"

"No, he is not!" Giles de Milland cut her off. "I was out there before midday. Your people would not let me in." He glared at Loveday. "But they swore that Niall Arvagh was not within the manor, that he had ridden away."

"Likely he had," Loveday said, looking puzzled. "I imagine he went to Murcot to . . . to see his father."

"Yes," Bell put in. "I saw him at Noke yesterday and I brought something that I think he would want to show his father. Perhaps he rode there."

"No, he did not. Lord William sent Leon there soon after prime."

"William sent a man to Niall's father?" Magdalene echoed. "But what does it matter where Niall is? Why do you need him so urgently?"

"Because Aimery St. Cyr was murdered last night and Manville d'Arras has accused Niall of the crime."

Soft Nest and Cornmarket, Oxford

"Murdered?" Magdalene cried. "Surely you mean that Niall killed St. Cyr in a fight to protect Noke."

"Murdered," Giles insisted. "St. Cyr was found behind a shed outside The Broached Barrel. He was stabbed in the back."

"No," Magdalene said indignantly. "Niall would not stab a man in the back!"

"Not in an ordinary way," Giles said, "but he had already shown he had no need to fear St. Cyr and could best him in a fair fight. If the man would not face him and was running away . . . he had sworn he would kill St. Cyr if he troubled Mistress Loveday—" he looked toward the girl and then back to Magdalene "—again. If he met St. Cyr and warned him away and the man made him angry . . . Niall's temper matches his hair."

"Not with me," Loveday said. "I can testify that he is not quick to anger and certainly would not strike out in such a way without thought or warning. Even in the heat of the fight at Noke, when I bade him not to kill St. Cyr he only struck him with the flat of his sword."

"Perhaps he regretted his forbearance," Giles said, frowning. "In fact, Lord William was of Magdalene's mind; that Niall would not stab a man in the back, which is why he sent me to Noke and Leon to Murcot. He wanted Niall to explain what had happened."

"Yes, but how did Lord William learn of St. Cyr's death in the first place?" Magdalene asked.

"A man from the sheriff came to us at our lodging in the armorer's house and asked for Niall, saying that a body had been identified by one Manville d'Arras as Aimery St. Cyr, and that this Arras had accused Niall of murder, saying he had heard Niall threaten St. Cyr."

"Come in and sit down, man," Bell said, gesturing toward the benches at the table.

Giles nodded and sat, breathing out a heavy sigh. "I have been riding or running from this place to that all day."

Magdalene got another cup and poured wine into it for him, pushing the remains of the cakes and dried fruit within easy reach. "But surely," she said, "you told the sheriff that Niall was no murderer."

"Of course, although what I said was that killing St. Cyr in a fair fight was not murder. Then the sheriff's man told us that a knife in the back was no sign of a fair fight. Naturally I protested that Niall would not stab a man in the back and asked for particulars."

"And those were?" Magdalene asked.

"That the Watch had found a body, dead of a knife wound in the back, behind a shed that belonged to The Broached Barrel alehouse. Those in the alehouse knew the corpse as Aimery St. Cyr, who was in service with Lord Waleran. When the sheriff sent a man to the lodging of Lord Waleran's men-at-arms, Manville d'Arras came forward at once, claiming to be St. Cyr's friend. He identified the body and then he told them the tale of St. Cyr's betrothal to Mistress Loveday and Niall's violation of that contract by driving St. Cyr away from Noke and by threatening to kill him if he returned there."

"It was a forged, false contract!" Loveday exclaimed furiously.

"But apparently St. Cyr did not go back to Noke," Bell remarked, brows raised. "He was killed here, in Oxford."

"Has anyone asked where this Manville d'Arras was when St. Cyr died?" Magdalene asked.

"Not yet, I think. The sheriff's man said that Arras was truly distraught and weeping when he saw St. Cyr dead."

Magdalene laughed. "If I had killed a man, I too would pretend to be distraught and weeping."

Bell glanced sidelong at her, and almost shuddered at the coldness that looked out of her half-lidded eyes and the way her softly curved lips had folded into a hard, cruel line.

"Truly I did not think so far ahead," Giles admitted, "only that Niall could not have done such a thing. And when I went to the keep and reported to Lord William what had happened, he said I had better bring Niall back here to answer the stupid charges, and then he remembered that Niall might have gone out to Murcot to his father's manor, so I went to Noke and Leon went to Murcot. But Niall was in neither place, and is not here, so we must assume that he has fled."

"Fled to where?" Loveday cried.

"Back to London or to Rochester, I suppose, where he would be safe from the sheriff of Oxford."

"Leaving me at the mercy of anyone who wished to take me?" Loveday sounded stunned.

"You're in no danger. St. Cyr is dead," Giles protested.

"And what of Lord William's men who were with Niall at Noke? Did he take them to London or to wherever too? Is the manor protected only by the servants?

Sir Giles de Milland looked at her with open eyes and open mouth. "Men? Lord William's men? Lord William's men were at Noke?"

"Yes," Magdalene put in. "Niall took ten men from his own troop with him to protect the manor."

Milland's expression darkened. "He must have taken the men with him or they would have let me in, no matter what the servants of Noke wanted." He sighed. "This is very bad."

"I want to go home," Loveday said. "I must go home at once and see what is happening."

"It is too late," Bell pointed out. "It would be full dark before we arrived, and the manor was peaceful this morning when Sir Giles rode out there. Since St. Cyr is dead, there can be no further threat to Noke."

"Bell is right, love," Magdalene said soothingly. "Why do we not go out to the market, since you now have nothing to fear, and find an evening meal at a cookshop? You will feel better for being out of this room and walking about."

"Yes," Bell agreed heartily, "and I will hie me off to The Broached Barrel. One alehouse is as good as another. I can ask about St. Cyr there as well as listen for the wagering about Salisbury."

"And I," Sir Giles said, "had better get back to Lord William." He smiled at Magdalene. "Shall I tell him that you do not believe Niall committed this crime and have set about finding out who did?"

"Twice was enough," Magdalene said, watching Bell collect

his boots and begin to pull them on. "I have no great urge to confront murderers. When my women and I were at risk, I did what I must. Of course if Bell finds an answer, I will let Lord William know, but I think Niall will be innocent or have a good reason for what he did."

They walked together to the Carfax where Sir Giles turned left on Castle Street. Bell, Magdalene, and Loveday walked straight ahead. The sun was just about to drop behind the hills to the west, but the market was as lively as ever with a long, light evening ahead and plenty of twilight for packing up goods on a midsummer day.

About midway along the street, across from Redding's mercery, Loveday pointed to a cookshop and said, "Let us eat there, Magdalene. Edmee and I often took a meal there, as it was close to the shop. It is a little more costly than the place at the end of the street, but that makes it a little quieter too. And I think it the cleanest."

"That last convinces me," Magdalene said. "The cleaner the cookshop, the less likely stomach gripes, I have found."

They crossed the street and Magdalene noted with approval that the benches seemed sturdy and the tables carried no more than recent spills. She told Loveday to order what she thought would be good, since she was familiar with the place, and then Bell touched her arm and she looked up.

"I assumed you would allow me to share your bed tonight," he said. "Was I right?"

"Do you still want to?" Magdalene asked. "I saw how you looked at me when I spoke of murder."

"It was not what you said, but how you looked," Bell said. "You are, I think, more intimately acquainted with killing than most." He looked down into her face, so lovely it made his chest hurt, into the misty blue eyes that met his steadily. "It is none of my business," he said. "If you will let me come, I will be grateful."

She smiled. "Remember Loveday will be there."

Bell wrinkled his nose. "That one knows men and knows how to use them. No sweet maiden, she. Loveday can stuff her ears if she does not wish to hear us. She may or may not be virgin, but I doubt anything we could do would shock her."

Magdalene giggled. "I fear you are right." Then she put her hand over his on her arm. "And thank you for finding out what you can about St. Cyr's death. William will be grateful if you can clear his man."

That brought nothing but a snort from Bell, who backed free of her light grasp and walked away up the street toward The Broached Barrel. Magdalene sighed. Sometimes Bell seemed ready to accept her relationship with William and other times he acted like a strutting cock. Well, it was his battle to fight; she had made clear her conditions.

She turned about and soon saw Loveday seated at a bench farthest from where she and Bell had been standing and went to join her. As Loveday had promised, the food was plentiful and very good. Having been together all day, they had run out of casual conversation and ate in companionable silence. Still, Magdalene was a little surprised by Loveday's hearty appetite. She thought that if she had been sworn to marry Bell and he had been accused of something as cowardly as stabbing a man in the back, she would be sorely troubled. Loveday was not. Was it because Loveday was yeoman stock rather than gentle born? Was it good or bad to be raised with notions of honor?

"Shall I step into the baker's and find a sweet to top off the meal?" Loveday asked, breaking into Magdalene's thoughts.

"Why not?" Magdalene agreed. "And I will walk across to The Lively Hop and get us some ale."

Their errands being completed at almost the same time, they met at their table, pushed aside the crusts left from the meal, and settled themselves together to eat sweet buns and drink their ale. Before they had even shared out the buns, a man past his middle years but still strong and active rushed across the road and seized Loveday by the arm.

"Come away!" he said to her. "You do not know with whom you are sharing food and drink."

"Master Reinhart," Loveday said, smiling at the man. "How surprised I am to see you." Then the smile disappeared and her eyes widened in distress. "Do not say you wrote to me and told me you were coming and I did not remember? Oh, how dreadful. You will have been turned away from Noke. Oh, I am so sorry."

"I was indeed turned away from Noke, but there is no cause for you to be sorry. I did not write in advance of my coming. It was a sudden decision. When I heard that the king was coming to Oxford and I realized that he might wish to examine and even end your wardship . . ." He looked at Magdalene, tightened his lips, and began to tug at Loveday. "Come away from this person. You must come with me."

Magdalene did not know whether to laugh or to curse. It seemed that Loveday not only knew too many people in Oxford and the surrounding neighborhood but extended her acquaintance to London as well. The man so horrified by seeing her and Loveday together was Master Reinhart Hardel, a wealthy and moderately powerful wool merchant from London who was a steady client of the Old Priory Guesthouse. He had been Sabina's client, but had happily transferred to Diot.

"Good sir," Magdalene said, as if she had never seen him before in her life, "I promise you that whatever I am I intend no harm to this young lady."

The man looked surprised, then satisfied. Nonetheless, he acted as if the words Magdalene had spoken had come out of unoccupied air and said to Loveday, "Come away, my dear. Even if she intends you no harm, to be seen with her is harm in itself. Come away."

"No, indeed," Loveday protested, pulling away. "You do not understand—"

"And that is just as well," Magdalene interrupted, giving Loveday a warning and admonitory glance which she hoped would be understood.

Until Niall's involvement in St. Cyr's death was resolved, it would be a mistake to confide too much in anyone. She rose, taking two of the sweet buns and one of the ale mugs.

"I will take another table so that you and this gentleman can talk at ease," she said. "Remember, you need to remain free to do anything you think best."

"Oh, my God," Master Reinhart said, as Magdalene walked away and settled at another empty table, "to what did you agree with her?"

"To nothing at all," Loveday said.

"Thank God! I am sorry to shock you, my dear, but the woman is—" He hesitated, apparently trying to think of a way to explain clearly without shocking or frightening Loveday, failed, and continued, "The woman is a whoremistress. She is beautiful, well dressed, and gently spoken, but a whoremistress she is, and likely as not she intended to recruit you to serve in her house in Southwark."

Loveday burst out laughing. "No, no, Master Reinhart. I swear she has no such intention and she told me at once when we first met several days ago that she kept a whorehouse and that I must not be seen with her. She was far more shocked than I when a common friend introduced us—"

"Common, indeed, if he introduced you to Magdalene," Reinhart remarked, his lips curling with distaste.

Loveday's brows shot up. "I see you know her quite as well as this 'common' friend does."

Reinhart looked shocked. "Loveday! A man's doings are between him and his priest, and no business of any woman."

"Of course," Loveday said, lowering her lids over her eyes.

She would not quarrel with Master Reinhart. It was he, when her father and brothers died and she was so dazed with grief that she hardly knew day from night, that went to King Stephen with a petition that she be acknowledged heir to her father's land and property and be taken into ward. Wardship cost; the king was supposed to receive all the profit a ward's property produced. But Stephen had been very busy and her estate small compared with most he took into wardship. The king had never appointed a warden, so Loveday managed on her own, each quarter sending to the exchequer a tidy sum . . . but not near as much as Otmoor produced. In addition, Master Reinhart bought large quantities of sheared wool and fleeces from her and could be trusted to give her an honest price with which she could compare other offers.

"I just meant that I was warned about Mistress Magdalene's . . . ah . . . business," Loveday went on softly. "I was not delivered unknowing into her hands, but I had little choice. She was the only one who could and would offer me a refuge when St. Cyr came with a forged betrothal agreement."

"I heard about the forged betrothal. I have been here two days, searching Oxford for you."

"Two days? But that was when I left Noke."

"Yes. I just missed you by a candlemark or so. When I arrived, your steward said he was commanded not to let any man or woman into Noke. He was most apologetic, saying that he was sure an exception would have been made in my case, but that no one knew I was coming. And then he told me that you had gone to Oxford with your brother-by-marriage, and about St. Cyr's attempt on you and his threats."

Loveday did not ask why Master Reinhart had not gone to Master Redding. He would not have known of her friendship with Edmee. There was hard feeling because Master Redding had married Edmee instead of Reinhart's daughter, so Loveday never mentioned Edmee to him.

"I have never been so frightened in my life," Loveday admitted. "Believe me, residence in a whorehouse was a cheap price to avoid being seized by St. Cyr. And Magdalene took great care that I not be recognized. I went veiled and was mostly confined to a private chamber so no one knows . . . well, except William of Ypres—"

"William of Ypres!" Reinhart exclaimed.

"He is Magdalene's . . . ah . . . protector—" Loveday began but was interrupted by a young man, who came over to the table, nodded at her, and drew Reinhart away.

Loveday had smiled warmly at Tirell Hardel, Reinhart's son. When she was a little girl, Tirell had sometimes come with his father on buying trips and they had played together. In recent years, when she had gone to London she had stayed with the Hardels and found Tirell amusing and brotherly. She knew he did not feel otherwise toward her. The way he would tell her she had a smudge on her nose or her veil was crooked or her hem, did not bespeak the admiration a man had for a woman.

Suddenly she frowned down at the bun she had not eaten. What was Tirell doing in Oxford with his father? He should be in London managing the business if Reinhart was traveling. They were not buying. It was too late in the year for buying wool. And Master Reinhart had said he had come to Oxford because he thought the king might wish to end her wardship. Usually a wardship ended when a young man came of age or a woman . . . married. Reinhart had made one successful petition to the king on her behalf; did he intend to petition again, to gain permission to marry her to Tirell?

No! The rejection burst into Loveday's mind with considerable force. She did not want to marry Tirell. To think of coupling with him made her queasy. Not that he was anything like St. Cyr. He was a fine young man, handsome, well-mannered, and clean, and he would be kind to her—but it would be like futtering a brother.

Moreover she knew he did not want her as a man wants a woman; he thought of her as a sister, which would just about guarantee he would spend good money on whores instead of enjoying what he had in his own bed. Even worse, he was trained to wool and to business and would want to stick his nose into every aspect of her estate. More, he would want to manage her lands as he saw fit.

Oh no. She had seen what she wanted. Niall's red hair and bright eyes, his broad shoulders and strong legs, the strength and skill at arms he had shown when he drove off St. Cyr. Oh yes, that was what she wanted. And if he had rid her permanently of St. Cyr by sticking a knife in his back? Well, it was surely a more certain way to remove the threat than petitions to the king, which might or might not be considered.

What he had done was not to save himself; there would be a good reason, not greed or cowardice. And she did not care. She wanted Niall Arvagh, who would breed his horses, breed children with her, and leave her wool trade and estate alone. He had laughed when he said she would manage the manor better than he because it meant so little to him. Yes, knife in the back of St. Cyr or not, she wanted Niall Arvagh.

She had been watching Tirell and his father with blind eyes while she thought about Master Reinhart's intentions, but a sharp gesture from the father broke into her musing. She almost smiled when she saw how unhappy Tirell looked; plainly he liked his father's plans no better than she did. And then Loveday did smile, quickly raising her ale cup to her mouth to hide it. Master Reinhart, who had been so intent on not knowing Magdalene, had not paid proper attention to where his son was taking him and had backed up almost into the table at which Magdalene was sitting. No doubt she had heard every word the two had said to each other.

Magdalene had indeed heard them. When Master Reinhart's back almost touched hers, Magdalene had intended to speak aloud to warn him. However, the younger man's first words made her lift her veil over her head to better hide her face and look down intently at the few crumbs remaining from the sweet buns she had eaten.

"I went looking for St. Cyr last night," Tirell Hardel said. "And I found him."

"To what purpose?" Master Reinhart asked sharply.

"Because, as I have told you before, father, I have no desire to marry Loveday." He shuddered slightly. "It will be like bedding my sister."

"Nonsense," the father said. "All cats look alike in the dark. Abed she will be soft and warm like any woman."

"That may be true, but if St. Cyr had not been a filthy and brutal animal, I would have let him have her. As it is from what I heard him say of her . . ." His voice faltered. "God knows what that beast would have done to her, how long she would even have survived in his keeping." He sighed.

"Tirell, where were you last night?" Reinhart asked, his voice now tinged with anger.

"You know where I was." Tirell's tone was bitter. "I could not bear the thought of that . . . creature . . . torturing poor Loveday, so . . . so I took care of the matter we spoke of. It is done. Over."

"I am sorry." Reinhart put a hand on his son's shoulder. "It was the best solution I could think of." He drew a deep breath. "Well, as you said, it is over. Go now and speak to Loveday."

"No," Tirell said, his voice thick. "My heart is too heavy with what I have done to bring to her now. Tomorrow or the next day I will go out to Noke and . . . and speak to her. Not now."

On the words, he pulled free of his father's hand and went out into the street heading north. Magdalene bit her lip. What in the world had Tirell Hardel done last night? Killed St. Cyr? But if he knew St. Cyr was dead and no longer a threat to Loveday, why did he still need to marry her?

Magdalene was so eager to know the answer to those questions that she would have pursued Tirell and drawn him into an alehouse, where a few jars of ale could have loosened his tongue. However, she could not move immediately without catching Master Reinhart's attention and once that was fixed on her she would not dare go after Tirell. So she waited, and in a moment Master Reinhart shrugged and marched in a determined way back toward Loveday.

As soon as he moved, Magdalene stood up and picked up the empty ale cup. With that in hand, she started to cross the street—ostensibly to return the cup, but actually so she could slip away and follow Tirell. However, when she glanced up the street, she could not see him anywhere and a moment later Loveday called out to her.

After the briefest hesitation, Magdalene turned to walk back to the girl. Tirell was gone, possibly into the nearest alehouse to drown his sorrows but equally likely to the nearest church to confess a mortal sin. Either way he had escaped her. It would be easier for Bell to find him and question him. Meanwhile she could try to discover whether Master Reinhart had any idea what his son meant.

Loveday had acknowledged her approach with a smile and a nod, and then looked up at Master Reinhart with a mixture of determination and pleading. "Please do not be angry with me, Master Reinhart," she said. "You know I could not reach Noke before dark, and with so many men-at-arms from different meinies abroad, it would not be safe for me to travel the roads after dark, even if you accompanied me. I swear I will be safer in the Soft Nest with Mistress Magdalene. You may come with us and see how quiet and private we are. And I promise I will return to Noke tomorrow morning."

"I would far rather you came to London with me, my dear. If one man tried to seize you, another may. You will not be truly safe until you are married, but you will be much safer in London where few know you."

"You are very kind, Master Reinhart," Loveday said, "but I cannot leave Noke for so long. At this time of year the flocks must be watched with care for illness, the first haying must be done, the hay dried, bound and stored. I cannot be away from my lands just now."

Magdalene had reached them and stood quietly beside Loveday. She cast a single, incurious glance in Master Reinhart's direction, and when Loveday had finished, said, "As you said, Loveday, the light is starting to fail. I think we would be best off returning to our lodging before it grows much darker."

"Very well, I am ready, but I would like to make known to you Master Reinhart, a dear friend of my father's and a very good friend to me also. It was Master Reinhart who had the good sense to petition the king for my right to Otmoor after my father and brothers died so suddenly. God knows what would have happened to me if he had not decided to help me."

"That was indeed a wise and kind action, Master Reinhart," Magdalene said, "and I understand that you are concerned for Loveday. I am not certain how you know what I am, but I am sorry you do not know me better. If you did, you would also know that I have a reputation for dealing honestly, and you would understand that I would never force or constrain a woman to serve me—especially not a maiden who has a good livelihood and no need to enter into the life my women lead."

Master Reinhart had the grace to flush. Magdalene pretended not to see that sign that he was, indeed, aware that she was known for her honesty, that her women were well paid, well cared for, and free to come and go as they pleased. She would not have bothered defending herself, guessing his reaction had been more one of shock at seeing Loveday in her company than of any real distrust of her motives, had she not wanted to show him that she would not betray how well she knew him to Loveday.

Since Reinhart was looking at Magdalene, Loveday took the chance to make a cheerful grimace behind his back. Magdalene swallowed hard to constrain an urge to laugh. It seemed that Loveday knew more about Master Reinhart than he thought she knew. Reinhart himself made a wordless noise that might have indicated acceptance.

So Magdalene continued without waiting for a more definite answer. "And as Loveday said, you are more than welcome to inspect our quarters."

"No, no," he said hastily, "I am sure Loveday will be safe. I hope that she will leave you and go back to Noke tomorrow, however."

"I will see her on her way as soon as she has broken her fast, I swear to you."

"Good. Good. I will be on my way then. Loveday, do not forget to veil yourself."

"No, I will not," Loveday said, pulling her veil around her face as she spoke.

Magdalene echoed her action and waited quietly as Master Reinhart took to the street in the direction of St. Martin's Church. Loveday waved until he had mingled completely with the crowd that was snatching at last-minute bargains or hurrying off home.

"But I thought that you and Bell were going to accompany me home," she said plaintively, as soon as Master Reinhart was lost to sight.

"Well, we are . . . if you want us. I just didn't want to say that in front of Master Reinhart, who might take a new alarm."

"Oh, dear. I hope you will forgive him . . . and me, too, Magdalene," Loveday said. "He knows you. I know he does. How could he act and speak as if you were going to . . . to . . .

do I don't know what? And does he think me such an idiot that I would remain in your clutches? What bait does he imagine you set for me that could make me willing to give up my lands to go and be a whore in London?"

"Southwark," Magdalene said, laughing as she fastened her veil more securely. "I don't even have the bait of the great, exciting city of London to offer you."

Loveday sighed. "I am glad you didn't take offense."

"I think Master Reinhart was just shocked to see you with me. Remember, he said he had been seeking you for two days. Then you suddenly appear in the company of an infamous whoremistress. I suppose he leapt to the conclusion that I had abducted you."

"Yes, and that we were cozily sitting at a table eating sweet buns, the abductee and the abductor." Loveday shook her head. "Oh, let it go. I will have to deal with him sooner or later because I think he wants me to marry Tirell—"

"Yes. I heard them talking about it."

Loveday made a dismissive gesture. "It is out of the question. First of all because I cannot think of Tirell as other than a brother, and secondly because he will want to manage Noke and Otmoor and I will not have it. I wish it were tomorrow already. I must find out what happened to Niall."

"Hmmm. Yes."

They crossed the street to return the cups to the alehouse and then started back toward the Soft Nest. After they had walked in silence as far as St. Friedesweide, Loveday said anxiously, "You will come to Noke with me, will you not?"

"Oh, yes," Magdalene replied much more positively than before. "There are some questions I want answered, like what has happened to William's men. Why didn't they insist the servants let Giles de Milland in? There are only two posible reasons I can think of. The first is that they did go off with Niall—but I can't imagine him taking William's men without permission—or else . . . Niall is hiding in Noke and told his men not to give him away to Giles."

"Do you think that is really so?" Loveday asked eagerly.

"Why? Are you so eager to see a man who stabbed another in the back?"

"Oh, pish tush." Loveday sniffed with disdain. "He did it for me. He cannot have had any other reason." She was silent for a moment then said, "I wonder if I could convince Father Herveus to marry us at once. Then if Niall did have to go to a safer place until this stupid matter of St. Cyr is settled—and once the king and all his useless nobles are gone I am certain I can deal with the sheriff of Oxford—I will not need to worry about—"

"Loveday," Magdalene protested, "have you forgotten you need the king's permission to marry?"

What Magdalene was thinking, however, was if Loveday married Niall atop the murder of St. Cyr—and it was still not at all clear why Waleran de Meulan should favor a low beast like St. Cyr with a sweet plum like Loveday—Waleran might be roused to serious anger. He would surely accuse William of complicity in both the murder and the marriage. And Magdalene remembered suddenly that the last thing William had said to her was that he was going to ask in the Court about St. Cyr. A cold knot formed under Magdalene's breastbone.

"So the king will fine me," Loveday said, a small smile curving her lips. "I can pay. And I will be married . . . and safe."

The cold spread across Magdalene's chest and up her back. It was she who had given Loveday shelter from St. Cyr. William would be livid with fury.

CHAPTER 9

23 June,
Soft Nest and Noke Manor

Although Magdalene tried in several ways to divert Loveday from the idea of instant marriage, and succeeded so far before Loveday retired to bed that she was willing to consider waiting, Magdalene was not at all happy. She was intensely relieved to hear Bell's rythmic tap on the door, and she told him her deduction and presented the problem to him in an undervoice as he came into the room. While she closed the door and dropped the bar across to lock it, he watched her, and when she turned to him, he looked down at her and grinned.

"Trying to put me off?"

His words were slightly slurred and he smelled of ale, but his voice was as low as hers had been. Magdalene saw at once that slurred words or not, his eyes were well focussed and clear. She shook her head and stepped forward into his arms. Bell's grin widened.

"I think that's the truth," he said, leading her around the bed so they were sheltered by it if Loveday should peer through her bedcurtains. "If you were playing with me, you would have thought of a bigger puzzle. And you are right. Niall is far more likely to be at Noke than have fled to London or Rochester. As for preventing the marriage, that is easy. You told me Niall was a good man and devoted to Lord William. All you have to do is tell him the trouble the marriage will cause and he will refuse to marry."

Magdalene sighed and turned her back to Bell who, without needing to be told, began to unlace her gown. "I thought of that myself, but you don't know Loveday as well as I. It may take more strength and cleverness than Niall has to outmaneuver her. She is the most redoubtable girl."

She pulled off the gown and untied the bows that held her undertunic closed at neck and wrists. Meanwhile Bell had unbelted his sword and propped it where he could reach it from the bed. Then he began to remove his clothing without assistance although more slowly than she, but that was because he would pause in what he was doing to caress her and murmur a litany of praise as he shed each garment. He seemed to forget he still had his shirt on when she was naked, and he might never have removed it at all, becoming instantly amorous after he pulled off his chausses and saw her, if she had not escaped from him and climbed into the bed.

Magdalene had intended to ask what he had discovered in the alehouse, but he had outsmarted her. All those kisses and touches, all those murmurs of praise and desire when she was half clothed had done their work. When he threw off the shirt and stood naked before her, his standing man as erect as it could get, red head bare and gleaming moistly in the light of the night candle, Magdalene simply pulled aside the light coverlet and held out her arms.

Later, she hoped that Loveday had been too soundly asleep

to be easily wakened. They had both forgotten her completely, and Bell's groans, which rose in climax almost to singing, had not been at all moderated. And then she chuckled softly and rubbed her head against his shoulder. No use blaming him. If Loveday had wakened, it was as likely her own cries that had done it.

"Can you talk?" she asked softly, "or shall we wait until morning?"

Bell yawned hugely. "No need to wait. I've little enough to tell you. The Broached Barrel was a total waste. No one had seen St. Cyr there last night and that was not because no one recognized him. He was fairly well known—not liked, but known. Apparently he was a quarrelsome drunk."

"And Niall? Did you ask about him?"

"Of course. He was not there last night either. The landlord and alewife both knew him, but he had not been in the house for several days."

"If neither murderer nor victim was seen at The Broached Barrel, why was St. Cyr's body found there?"

"*Because* neither had been seen there?" Bell asked doubtfully. "I even went out to look at the place where the body was found—I said I was curious and one of the servers took me out and showed me. I thought maybe the yard would have some feature that would make it peculiarly fitted for murder, but it was the same as the back yard of any inn or alehouse. Less fitted, really, because there are tables and benches there and anyone could come out of the alehouse at any time . . ." His voice faded and he yawned again.

"Never mind, love."

Magdalene patted the thigh against which her hand had been resting, felt his shaft stir slightly as her fingers grazed it, and hastily removed her hand. She enjoyed coupling with Bell more than with any other man she could remember, but enough was enough. She needed to think. Only he had drained her as thoroughly as she had drained him and she tightened her jaws against a yawn as large as his.

Her thoughts began with the notion that tables and benches might mean possible interruption, but they also might indicate a place people could meet without mistake: "At the table behind The Broached Barrel" would be a clear direction. But she could not grasp why that thought was so unpleasant, and, wondering about it, slept.

As so often happens, Magdalene knew at once upon being wakened why thinking of a meeting behind The Broached Barrel was distasteful. Loveday's voice not only brought her awake but made her think of Niall, and it leapt into her mind that if Niall had arranged to meet St. Cyr behind the alehouse, the murder was not a thoughtless act of fury but planned. Bell, too, had responded instantly to Loveday's voice and had probably been completely awake before her. He was just releasing his sword when Magdalene's sidelong glance caught him.

"Yes? What is it Loveday?" she asked.

"It is light. It is morning. When can we leave for Noke?"

Bell groaned and Magdalene giggled.

"I have set out bread and cheese and ale," Loveday said. "Should I run to the baker for sweet buns or get a quarter pasty at the cookshop?" She sounded a little aggrieved because at home her own kitchen would provide such extras.

"No, no," Magdalene assured her. "The bread and cheese will be enough." She poked Bell, who had sunk back onto the pillows with closed eyes and a deep frown. "You might as well get up," she said softly into his ear. "She will be at you every moment until you do. I told you she was a most redoubtable girl."

"She is a pain in the arse," he muttered. "If Niall is at Noke, he will not disappear like morning dew, and if he is gone the sooner or later that we arrive cannot matter."

"Were you never young and eager?"

"Not when my head ached from ale."

"Get up and I will give you something for it," Magdalene promised as she slid out of the bed.

She found clean undergarments in the chest and made a mental note to have the ones she had worn washed. It was not common to change or wash underclothes so frequently, but it was a habit from when she charged several times the price of a common whore. The crisp feel of the clean clothes, added to the sweet scent of the rose leaves and lavender with which they were stored, did much to let her clients forget how often the body under the clothing had been used. The freshness induced in them the illusion of an innocent new partner and that they were getting their money's worth.

Her riding dress was stained from the journey to Oxford, but it had been brushed free of dust, and more than that was not necessary. Behind her she could hear Bell's litany of curses as he struggled from the bed and also began to dress. She donned her gown quickly then went to the shelf where she had stored a cloth-wrapped bundle of medicinals. She was no great physician, although she knew the herbs that would flush out a woman's womb and a few other remedies. Among those the one most often used was the potion to soothe men who had drunk too much, and she had taken an adequate supply of the ingredients in case William should need them.

She mixed it for Bell and he drank it, waving irritably at

Loveday to be quiet when she asked if she should get one of
Florete's men to saddle the horses for them. Wincing and peering at her from one half-open eye, Bell told her not to be a
fool. Early morning was one of the quiet times for a whorehouse; the men would be asleep.

"Well, I can saddle my own mare and likely Magdalene's
gelding, too, but your destrier is beyond me—"

"Sit down and shut up!" Bell snarled, placing his elbows on
the table and supporting his head in his hands.

"Why does he drink so much if he knows he will feel this
way the next day?" Loveday whispered impatiently.

Magdalene, who had quietly been eating her bread and
cheese and sipping her ale, put on a reproving face. "He was
doing his civic duty," she said as soberly as she could, although
her voice quivered slightly. "You cannot get men to talk freely
in an alehouse without buying them drink, and if you do not
drink with them, they are likely to become suspicious and not
talk anyway."

Loveday did not look convinced. After sitting a while longer
until Magdalene finished her bread and cheese, she slid out
from behind the bench and stood up. "I will go saddle my
mare and your gelding," she said. "That will save some time."

"Remember your veil," Magdalene urged softly. "There are
men leaving at this time of day. You remember you need to
go out the front door and then around through the alley at
the side of the house to the back."

Loveday nodded and went out. Bell groaned softly again and
sat up. "If Niall did kill St. Cyr, we should let him marry that
girl. It will be punishment enough."

Although she smiled broadly, Magdalene made no reply.
She knew how long it took for the hot spices she had mixed

with the ale to calm a roiling belly and the leachings of willow
bark to ease a pounding head. Well within that time, and before Loveday had saddled both horses and come in to voice
her impatience again, Bell reached for the jack of ale, refilled
his cup, emptied it, opened and closed his eyes several times,
then sighed and stood up.

"I will survive if we go now," he admitted.

Nonetheless the first part of the ride to Noke was accomplished in near silence until, a league and a half out of Oxford,
the sun disappeared, clouds gathered, and rain began to spatter
down. Fortunately Loveday was acquainted with every foot of
the way, and she led them to shelter in a pleasant barn. By the
time the downpour was over, Loveday was more impatient than
ever, and she rode somewhat ahead, as if she could draw the
others into a faster pace by keeping a distance between them.

When they first set out Bell had uttered an occasional grunt
when Monseigneur's gait jarred him. While they waited for the
rain to end, the exercise having sweated the drink out of him,
he told Magdalene that those who had wagered that Salisbury
would not come to the Council at all were gloating over the
winnings they would soon collect. It was not good news, but
Magdalene only shook her head. At the moment she was more
concerned with a personal advantage that might arise from the
problem.

They had turned from the main road north onto the side
lane that led to Noke before she broke a long silence to ask,
"What shall we advise Niall to do if we find him at Noke?"

"Find a good excuse for what he did," Bell responded dryly,
"although I cannot really think of any good reason to stab a
man in the back."

"I was afraid you would say that," Magdalene said. "So, if

there is no good excuse and if Niall did go off to London or Rochester, do you think in all the fuss over Salisbury failing to come to the king's summons the murder of a nobody could slip by unnoticed?"

Bell turned his head to look at her. "You are very eager to get Niall away from Oxford and very hot against an immediate marriage to Loveday. Is it possible you have a personal reason to prevent the marriage?"

Magdalene, who had been watching Loveday, now looked at Bell. He met her eyes at first, then looked away. She said, "It is none of your business if I do." Her voice was thin with fury. "I am a whore. It is my calling. It is none of your business who shares my bed when you are not in it. But if one hint of that jealous lie comes to Loveday's ears, you can seek another lodging in Oxford . . . and in Southwark too."

Bell opened his mouth and then closed it, swallowing joy and an intense relief. If Magdalene did not want Loveday to hear his suspicion that Niall was futtering her, then she did want Loveday and Niall to marry and did not care in any special way for Niall. Nonetheless the thought of that young, strong body entwined with Magdalene's, as his had been only a few hours past, lit a fire in his belly.

"I do not like your being a whore," he said sullenly.

"Well, it is ten or twelve years too late to consider *that*." Magdalene laughed, good humor restored. "I was a whore long before we met and nothing will change it."

"If you swore—"

"It would make no difference."

"I would believe you."

She stared at him, then smiled. "Until I bought a new gown or wore a pair of earrings that you did not recognize. Then you would want to know for whom I was dressing or who gave me the earrings. You might not even tax me with infidelity, but you would eat yourself up . . . as you are doing now." She sighed and shook her head, but Bell could sense the anger under her resignation. "I am no different. I will never be different. No matter what man I entertain before or after, what I give to you is all yours, no part of it tainted with what I give to others . . . if I give to others. When I am with you, I think only of you. What tortures you choose to inflict on yourself are your doing, not mine."

It was all true, Bell thought, furious with her and himself. But it had been so sweet, the way she welcomed him, the joy they had found together, the pillow talk. . . . He wanted that for himself alone. When they lay together in the Old Priory Guesthouse, he knew that Magdalene—except perhaps in the few moments when she came to climax—listened with one ear for any sound of disturbance in her domain. It was her business, not another man, with whom he shared her. Here she was not responsible for anyone and she had given herself to him completely.

He glanced sidelong at her face and it was only an exquisite mask, drained of the laughter and friendliness, the intelligent animation she usually offered him. He stared out between Monseigneur's ears, wondering how he could still have been such a fool, wondering how he could redeem the easy bond that had existed between them.

Bell did not give a single thought to breaking the bond completely, to leaving Magdalene and finding another woman. He knew what that was like during the time he lived at Winchester with the bishop or was sent to other places on the bishop's business. With or without another woman, all he did was think about Magdalene, wonder what she was doing, make comparisons—always unflattering—to whatever woman was with him, and suffer agonies of jealousy. He was at peace only when he was with her; even their quarreling gave him joy.

Suddenly, what he was *not* seeing between Monseigneur's ears pierced his self-absorption. "Loveday!" he roared, kicking his stallion hard in the ribs. The horse leapt forward and thundered down the lane, around a curve to the right and a sharper one toward the left . . . and Loveday was there, surrounded by four rough-looking men bearing axes. Bell drew his sword and shouted for Loveday to ride away.

"No!" she shrieked. "These are my people."

Bell made no attempt to sheathe his sword or rein in his horse. What Loveday said could be the truth or the result of her fear. However, although the men had closed in on her and the axes were lifted in readiness, none struck at him and when he pulled Monseigneur to a stop and turned back, Loveday spoke sharply to them in English and they quickly melted into the woods bordering the road.

When they were gone, Bell sheathed his sword, which was not much good against bowmen anyway—not that he had seen any bows—and the quick response to Loveday's order virtually proved they were her people.

"You should not have ridden so far ahead," he snarled at her and then, remembering Magdalene, kicked Monseigneur into action again and rode back.

He was not really worried though. Atop her gelding, Magdalene would have had plenty of time to scream for help if she had been attacked, and the animal had a fair turn of speed. She could have ridden away from any threat. And, indeed, he found her safe, waiting just past the sharp left turn in the road where she could not be seen or be used as another target. They rode back to Loveday together, but instead of looking chastened, the girl looked smug.

"It is just as well that I did ride ahead," she said as soon as they were in easy earshot. "Those were my woodsmen. When they saw Bell, they were afraid that I had been taken by the man who threatened me and they determined to try to bring him down and capture him."

"Oh, indeed. How?"

"I'm afraid they intended to kill Monseigneur." She was smiling slightly.

Bell's expression froze and then he smiled. "I hope you cleared their minds of that notion. Between us my father, mother, and I paid near seven pounds of silver for Monseigneur. I would need to take all four of them and their whole families to sell as slaves before the price was made up. And I am rather fond of Monseigneur."

"Seven pounds!" Loveday was horrified. "He is only a horse. I have bought a stallion, fatted for servicing mares too, for less than one pound."

"But not trained for war, not unafraid of horns calling and the crack of siege machines and the smell of blood. Not for a horse ready on command to charge directly at a line of men or other horses. No, he is worth what we paid."

Loveday sighed. "I will issue a special warning about Monseigneur." Then she looked alarmed. "Will Niall need to buy such a horse if he leaves Lord William's service?"

"How should I know?" Bell laughed. "Ask him."

"I will indeed," Loveday said, turning her mare's head down the path, and starting forward again.

"She is already calculating how to make up the sum," Magdalene said softly.

Holding his breath at Magdalene's amused and intimate tone and seizing the hope that she had forgiven him, he murmured, "Maybe the punishment of marrying her is too great, even for stabbing a man in the back."

Magdalene looked startled, then pursed her lips in pretended disapproval, and they both laughed. However, they had barely exchanged a few more bantering remarks at Loveday's expense when they were at the gates of Noke. Those were closed, and when Bell looked up at the wall he could see what looked like a field serf with a pitchfork in his hand on a watchtower. There was no sign of armed guardsmen.

The lookout had obviously already called a warning about them. Before Bell could try to see who, if anyone, was on the hoardings, the gates were pulled open and the steward came out crying a welcome. And right beside him, red hair blazing in the newly bright sun and smiling almost as brightly, was Niall Arvagh.

Loveday slid off her mare into Niall's willing arms. "Niall!" she exclaimed. "What if someone sees you?"

"What do I care for that?" he said, giving her a squeeze with one arm while he caught her mount's reins with an experienced hand.

The steward took the reins from him and then stood aside politely to allow Bell and Magdalene to ride past him. They dismounted in the small inner bailey, grooms running from the stable to take their animals. Bell shook his head at the boy reaching for Monseigneur's reins and said to Magdalene, "Get those two fools into the house where we can talk more privately while I care for Monseigneur."

Bell was not the only one who perceived the advantage of privacy. Loveday was already hurrying Niall toward the manor, so Magdalene had no more to do than follow behind. Once inside, when she saw that the hall was empty except for a few servants, she drew close. Loveday had flung her arms around Niall's neck and was thanking him passionately for protecting her from St. Cyr.

Niall frowned. "Yes, but I haven't, Loveday. And you know William's men cannot stay here forever."

"But—" Loveday began.

Magdalene didn't want to begin an argument about the rights and wrongs of murder until Bell was with them. Niall might too easily dismiss her warnings of the danger to Lord William of what he had done. He would listen to Bell.

So she interrupted Loveday to ask sharply, "Niall, where *are* William's men?"

"I didn't want them walking the hoardings for anyone to see. We would have had all of Loveday's neighbors here, asking questions, so I ordered that one of Loveday's serfs be set to watch for St. Cyr."

"Yes, but where are the men?" Magdalene looked around the hall where men-at-arms usually lounged when they had no other duty.

Niall grinned from ear to ear. "Making themselves useful. According to the steward, it is not Mistress Loveday's custom for anyone lodging in the manor to be idle." To Magdalene's amusement he looked down at Loveday with considerable admiration. "Three are mending harness, two are working with horses, two more—"

"Never mind. I believe you, but I am amazed at their docility," Magdalene said.

"They are my men," Niall replied, his voice suddenly hard, but then he smiled again. "Well, they were bored, too. They spent the first day lying on the hoardings ready to jump up and defend the manor, but no one came. Then after they realized how small the place was, compared with the keeps we are usually set to guard, they complained about being sent to the hoardings, which I admit could not be comfortable, when they could run up to them in plenty of time, given a lookout's warning. So, when the steward said that if they were not guarding the manor they would have to work in it and they saw I agreed . . ." He shrugged.

"Very right. You did just right," Loveday said with enthusiasm.

"Murder in such a manner is not right." Bell's voice from the doorway was firm, exasperated.

"Murder?" Niall echoed, turning to face Bell. "Oh, Bell, thank you for seeing Loveday home safe. Of course murder is not right . . . if it was murder."

Bell's lips thinned. "A man stabbed in the back is scarcely a light jest."

Niall blinked. "No. That is murder."

"It depends on the circumstances," Loveday said firmly.

"Loveday?" Niall's voice was uncertain and his frown, as he turned his gaze on her, was anxious.

Magdalene had to choke back a giggle. It seemed that Niall was in no doubt at all about the character of his chosen bride. But then the humor became ugly. Magdalene knew that Loveday had not killed St. Cyr. Was Niall trying to thrust the blame for murder onto her?

"Hmmm." Bell made a thoughtful noise. "I never thought that the killer might be a woman. A knife in the back is easy enough to understand. A woman would not want to chance facing him and being seized."

"Him? Who?" Niall asked.

"St. Cyr," Bell replied, looking surprised. "Who else?"

"It wasn't Loveday," Magdalene put in quickly. "She was in my keeping and I will swear she never left our chamber. You know it, Bell. You were there."

"I was fuddled with ale and . . . er . . . tired out. I doubt an army marching through the door would have waked me."

Magdalene knew that to be untrue. Any hostile sound would have brought Bell instantly awake, his sword in his hand. But he was unlikely to think of the creaking of bed leathers as hostile. Loveday could have got out of the bed . . . yes, but not out of the room. Bell would have responded quickly to the sound of the bar being withdrawn and the door latch being lifted. And it was silly to be thinking about it anyway because she herself would have been alerted by Loveday trying to leave.

"Loveday? Of course not," Niall said, his fair skin beginning to redden again with temper. "How dare you accuse Loveday? If it was St. Cyr who was killed, half the people in Oxford probably have cause."

"You seemed to think Loveday not perfectly innocent yourself, just a moment ago," Magdalene remarked, her lips twitching.

"No one is accusing Loveday of murder," Bell said, soothingly. "But Manville d'Arras has brought an accusation against *you* to the sheriff, Niall."

"Me?" Although he was a grown man, Niall's voice squeaked.

"It doesn't matter," Loveday exclaimed, stepping closer to Niall and putting an arm around his waist. "You did it for me, and I will find a way to—"

"I didn't do it at all!" Niall bellowed. "Who the devil is this Manville d'Arras who says he saw me stab St. Cyr in the back? I won't even bother stabbing him. I'll choke his lies out of him with my bare hands."

"He didn't say he saw you stab St. Cyr," Magdalene offered in an attempt to soothe him. "He said he heard you threaten to kill St. Cyr if he ever came back to Noke."

"So I did." Niall's green-blue eyes glittered in his scarlet face. "And I would have killed him that first day, except that Loveday forbade it."

"And you were right," Loveday said. "I am very sorry I didn't let you kill him then. I was afraid you would get into trouble, and all I have accomplished is to get you into far worse trouble."

"Loveday!" Niall exclaimed, seizing her by her upper arms and shaking her gently. "Are you saying that you believe I would stab a man—even such a man as St. Cyr—in the back?"

"Well, it was for me . . ."

"I'll kill anyone you want dead, Loveday, and that's the truth, but not by stabbing in the back." He drew himself up indignantly. "God, I nearly killed St. Cyr with the flat of my blade. What need had I to sneak up behind him to stick a knife in him?"

"I never could understand that," Bell admitted. "I don't know you very long, I admit, but I could hardly believe you would kill that way."

"Then why *did* you believe it?"

Niall was so angry, staring aggressively at Bell, that Magdalene felt it was time to intervene. "We didn't believe it when Giles first told us, but when he said he had come here yesterday to ask you to come back and explain Arras's accusation

against you to William, and the servants wouldn't let him in
and said you were not here . . . we thought you had fled, taking
William's men—"

"Taking my lord's men? Without his leave? I've done stupid
things in my life, but not so stupid as that!"

"Yes, I realized that after a while. That's when I also realized
that you must still be here and the men wouldn't force Loveday's servants to let Giles in because they were helping you
hide—"

"I wasn't hiding," Niall roared. "I had no reason to hide,
except from Waleran learning that Lord William had sent men
to protect this property." He took a breath. "I did tell the men
that no one must know they were here. Of course they should
have told Loveday's steward to let Giles in, but you know how
blindly men-at-arms tend to obey orders."

Bell nodded, but Magdalene asked, "Then where were you
when Giles arrived?"

"Likely on my way to Murcot. Soon as Father Herveus read
Loveday's appeal to me, I realized my father had to know all
the details so he could support . . ." He stopped abruptly before
he said 'Loveday's lies'; Magdalene nodded, and he finished
somewhat lamely, "It was four years ago. My father might well
have forgotten just what was arranged."

"But Giles told us that Leon Blound rode to Murcot and you
weren't there either," Bell remarked.

"Likely because I hadn't yet arrived! In any case, what does
it matter where I was—unless St. Cyr was killed between Prime
and Sext yesterday?"

"No," Bell said. "He was killed on the night of the twenty-
first, but his body was not found until the morning of the
twenty-second."

"Then it does not matter if I claim I was up in a tree trying to fly yesterday. I could not have killed St. Cyr on the night of the twenty-first because I was here, right here in Loveday's hall, and every servant in the place can speak for me . . . oh, and Father Herveus, too. He heard the news about St. Cyr and came to see if he could be of help to Loveday. By the time I had explained what had happened and where you were—and no, Loveday, I did not tell him you were lodged in a whorehouse; I am not an idiot—it was dark, so I offered him a bed for the night. Father Herveus shared my evening meal and we played chess until quite late."

"Good for you, man!" Bell exclaimed, swatting Niall on the shoulder.

"I am very glad," Magdalene said.

Loveday threw her arms around Niall's neck again. "I forgave you for anything you did for me, dear heart, but this is much better. I will not have to bribe the sheriff or—"

"Loveday!" Niall said. "We all know it is done, but it is better if you do not speak so openly about it."

Loveday smiled at him and then at Magdalene and Bell. "Oh, I would not, in general, but we are among friends," she said.

Bell looked a little sour, but even he had to laugh, acknowledging that none of them ever had any intention of allowing Niall to suffer for the crime if he had killed St. Cyr.

CHAPTER 10

23 June,
Noke and the Soft Nest

But if Niall did not kill St. Cyr, who did?" Magdalene asked somewhat later.

Loveday had moved smoothly from fugitive to mistress of the manor, ordering dinner and swiftly solving those problems of household management that had arisen while she was gone. The question of Niall's innocence being settled, the men had quickly shifted to political matters and the pros and cons of Salisbury's absence had been worked over while they ate.

Magdalene's attention had drifted. Although she was concerned in a general way about a rift between the king and his chief ministers, political turmoil would have little effect on her whorehouse—unless William was killed in the fighting. She shuddered and jerked her mind away from such an eventuality. She told herself not to be ridiculous. William had been fighting one war or another since he was fifteen or sixteen years old. But she saw again the gray in his hair, the way he blinked to clear his vision. He was not so young, so quick . . . The need to think about something else prompted her question about St. Cyr's killer.

"I don't know and I don't care," Bell said emphatically. "The man deserved killing and I am not in the least tempted to hunt down his murderer."

"No, I suppose not." Magdalene sighed. "I suppose I am just curious."

"There are better things to be curious about," Bell said sharply.

"Most likely it was simply a drunken brawl," Loveday offered, peacemaking. "I would not be too surprised if it happened at one of the other alehouses and they dropped the body by The Broached Barrel to save themselves and make trouble for a rival. Better forget about it."

"We can't forget about it completely," Niall said, frowning. "I must ride back to Oxford and clear myself of Arras's accusation."

"No," Loveday protested. "The sheriff's men might take you, and you know how they are when they think they have an answer. They do not want to hear any evidence against it."

Magdalene nodded. "Loveday has a point. I think we had better tell William that you are innocent and can bring proof of it and ask how he wants this done. I mean, if the sheriff takes you and William orders your release, even if he brings proof of your innocence with him, there are bound to be rumors of undue influence. If he brings the proof of your innocence before you are taken, the sheriff will never arrest you."

"Yes, which means the proof will need to be written," Bell put in. "Lord William cannot go to the sheriff with Father Herveus and all the servants of Noke trailing along. Magdalene and I will ride back to Oxford while you and Loveday see that Father Herveus writes a testament and also writes down under oath what the servants have to say."

Niall looked troubled. "Are you all sure I should not ride back to Oxford at once and report to Lord William myself?"

There was a little silence and then Magdalene nodded. "Yes. Honestly, I believe that will cause the least trouble. And I will send a message to William as soon as I arrive. That will give him the news just as quickly as you could bring it. If he still wants you to come to Oxford, he can send for you."

"I hope he will not do that," Loveday said. "If Niall goes, who will protect me?"

"St. Cyr is dead. From whom do you need protection?" Bell asked, fighting the corners of his mouth.

"If one man came to seize me, others might come also." Bell might be tempted to laugh, but Loveday was not amused. "Lord Waleran will have heard by now that his attempt to marry me to his man has failed. Will not he send another?"

"It is possible," Niall said. "Then if you do not think I am honor bound to return to Oxford, Bell, I will stay here and guard Loveday." He turned his head toward Magdalene. "I thank you for offering to be go-between. Please be sure to ask Lord William what I am to do about the men. There is no longer any reason for them to stay here and give Waleran cause for complaint, if he hears about them."

Soon after that decision was made, Magdalene and Bell were ready to leave, but they had to wait out another fierce downpour. A third caught them when they were on the road and drove them to take shelter in a tiny village. That storm lasted so long that they did not arrive at the Soft Nest until late in the afternoon. Magdalene went in at once to find Diccon so she could send her message to William, and Bell took the horses to the back to be unsaddled and curried free of drying mud.

Diccon came eagerly into Magdalene's chamber where, as he no doubt expected, she gave him a handful of sweetmeats to nibble while she wrote. In the end, she indited two brief letters. One said simply "I miss you, love. Do come as soon as you can." The other read "There is good proof that Niall did not kill St. Cyr. If you come, I can explain fully."

"You are to hide this message out of sight," she said to Diccon, handing him the second message. "This," she waited while he tucked the small folded piece of parchment away and then handed him the first, "you can carry in your hand. If you are stopped and questioned, give over the first message—with a becoming appearance of reluctance—but do not mention the second unless you are threatened with harm. You need not try to be a hero. There is nothing written here that can cause me any trouble. It would merely give someone we fear to be an enemy warning that one of his plans has gone awry."

"Same place?" Diccon asked. "The armorer's house?"

"Yes and try to give the messages—you can hand over both—to the same man as last time, Sir Giles de Milland. If he is not there, ask for Sir Leon Blound."

Diccon nodded and Magdalene walked to the door of the chamber with him to let him out. She stood there a moment, amused as she heard the boy declare loftily that he had other herring to salt when one of the whores told him to fetch her some ale. Magdalene shook her head though, hoping Diccon would not suffer for his sauciness when she was gone.

A brief notion of taking him back to the Old Priory Guesthouse flitted through her mind, but she dismissed it. Diccon knew every street, every hidden alley, and the lodging of nearly all the important people in Oxford. In Southwark and London, the boy would be lost, of no use to her and frightened and ashamed of himself. It would be cruel to uproot him, and she was afraid he was already too practiced a thief to trust.

She stepped back, about to close the door, when Bell walked in the front. He paused to nod at Florete's bully boys. At that moment, the curtain sealing the whore Geneva's room was pulled aside and a man Magdalene recognized stepped out. He was busy tying a last point and did not notice her or Bell. For a moment she could not think what to do and then it was too late, for he had lifted his head.

Raoul de Samur, one of Waleran de Meulan's captains—the one she and Sabina had rendered unconscious and she and Bell had delivered to the untender mercies of William of Ypres—straightened up. He was turned away from her, but he and Bell saw each other simultaneously. Bell went for his knife. At the gesture, both of Florete's enforcers reached for their cudgels and stood up. Raoul de Samur raised both empty hands, palm out toward Bell.

"Peace," he said. "I've no quarrel with you, Bell of Itchen. You may have meant me harm, but you did me a good turn and I'm willing to call it all bygones."

By that time, Magdalene remembered that William had told her Waleran's men as well as his used the Soft Nest. She stepped farther back into the doorway and gestured to Bell to come in and, if he could, bring Samur with him. She could not tell whether he had seen her and understood, although he took his hand away from his knife. Florete's men sat down again.

Still wary, Bell said, "I am glad of it. Actually I didn't mean you any harm. All I wanted was to be sure that you would not trouble the Old Priory Guesthouse again."

Samur laughed loudly. "Don't trouble them now. They're

glad to see me. I pay my pennies like any other customer. Stop in whenever I'm in London. And I'm glad to have met you because I've got a word of advice for a common acquaintance. You can save me the trouble of trying to find him."

"Glad to be of use," Bell began, and then a party of three men came in the door, filling the passageway behind him. He looked toward the common room, then moved slowly toward Raoul, his hands away from his weapons. "For giving advice it would be well to have some privacy. My friend has rented the room at the back. We can talk there."

Magdalene had backed out of the doorway, and Samur turned and walked ahead of Bell into her chamber. He nodded at her without any great warmth as she closed the door behind Bell. It was true that Samur had come to the Old Priory Guesthouse. Ella had taken him once and Letice another time, but his purpose was to leave messages for William. These Magdalene had written down, using a symbol that had meaning only to her and William to identify the messenger, and sent off with the first of William's men to stop in so there was no direct line of contact between William and his spy.

"Got only one thing to say about Lord Waleran," Raoul said. "Lord William's seen more of him than I have the last week. Only thing . . . he's neck deep in something with the Count of Brittany. Got no idea what. And he's jumpy, real worried about Salisbury. Something big's building, so I want you to say to Lord William that this is no time to tweak Lord Waleran's nose."

"What do you mean, tweak his nose?" Bell asked.

"The girl wasn't worth murdering Waleran's man. Don't think he's heard about it yet, but when he hears that Lord William's man did it—"

"But he didn't," Magdalene said. "Niall Arvagh, the man Arras accused, has about seven or eight witnesses, one of them a priest, who will swear that he was leagues away from Oxford when St. Cyr was killed. What was this all about, Raoul? Did Waleran send the lowest, filthiest creature he could find to marry Loveday just so William's man would be outraged and drive him away?"

Samur's low brow creased in a puzzled frown. "Don't think so. He hasn't said much about Lord William since we got to Oxford. Usually he curses him out whenever the king won't jump high as he wants, but it's like he's got something going more important than Lord William this time."

"Then how did you hear about Loveday and St. Cyr?"

"From that idiot Manville d'Arras, of course. He and St. Cyr were in my troop. Well, Arras still is. He has the loosest mouth I know. He babbles everything. I didn't believe him this time so I asked St. Cyr. I couldn't believe . . ." He shrugged. "I suppose Lord Waleran had his reasons."

"Yes, but what *were* they?" Magdalene asked. "What reason could he have for giving a creature like St. Cyr so sweet a plum?"

"Don't know, but St. Cyr had other highborn friends. Maybe they put in a word for him. And it was a done thing. When I first asked about the girl he told me how glad she would be to have such a fine man to manage her lands. But when she threw him out—he'd been boasting to others and everyone roasted him over that—he only laughed and said he would have a betrothal agreement before nightfall and marry her the next day. How he got her to put her mark on it when she'd just had him thrown out of the manor, I don't know."

"She didn't," Magdalene said. "The document was false, and

useless, too, because Loveday was already betrothed to Niall Arvagh of Murcot. Murcot is only a few leagues from Noke and the agreement had been made a long time ago."

Raoul obviously wasn't interested in Loveday's betrothal but he whistled softly and said, "Got a false document, did he? And a highborn friend who would lay down the silver for it? St. Cyr couldn't, I know that. Must've called in a big favor . . . or pushed real hard." He hesitated, staring sightlessly ahead for a moment, and then added, "If Lord William's man didn't kill him, I wonder if his fine friend did? Doubt he's the kind to like being pushed."

"Who was this friend?" Magdalene asked eagerly.

Samur frowned again. "Don't know, not for sure. Didn't care. How'd I know he was going to be murdered?"

Bell laughed. "I can hardly think of anyone more likely to meet that fate. Think, man, you noticed he had a high-born friend. What drew your attention to it?"

"Seeing him in The Wheat Sheaf. Never would have noticed because him and his 'friend' were off in a corner on the same side of the wall as the door, but some young drunk—Osney, Jules of Osney, a young loudmouth I've seen around town— was being dragged out of the place by a friend and he was yelling and pointing, so I looked. And there was St. Cyr with this well-dressed person. Didn't try to see who he was. Like I said, did I know St. Cyr was going to get murdered?" He narrowed his eyes. "Dark hair, knight's cut, but longer than yours . . . that's all I remember."

"Would you recognize him if you saw him again?" Magdalene asked.

Samur pursed his lips. "Doubt it, but the next day when the

count of Brittany came to speak to Lord Waleran, St. Cyr had
one of *his* men off in a corner."

"One of Alain of Brittany's men?" Bell repeated as if he could
not believe what Samur had said. "Didn't think one of them
would spit on the likes of St. Cyr. Did you know him?"

"No, but I think I'd be able to pick him out. There was something odd about the way he held his shoulders and moved . . .
but maybe that was only because he was annoyed with St. Cyr."

Magdalene sighed. "Well, keep a good watch for both of
them. Lord William would be grateful to anyone who helped
identify the murderer and put to death all and any doubts
about his own involvement in St. Cyr's death."

"His *own* involvement?" Samur's eyes were suddenly intent.

Magdalene went cold. What a stupid thing to say! Raoul de
Samur could not be trusted at all. She forced a tiny smile to
curve her lips and shook her head. "You should know Lord
William better than to think he would have anything to do
with that kind of murder. It is only that he is a good master.
Because of what Sir Niall told him, Lord William wanted to
know more about St. Cyr, and he asked about him in Court,
that was all."

Samur again whistled softly between his teeth. "That might
be enough." But then he nodded. "You may be sure I will keep
a good watch." He twisted a heavy gold ring on his left hand,
and Magdalene was reminded that most mercenaries saved
what they could in jewelry, which they could carry with them
wherever they went and sell if they needed money. His next
words confirmed the thought. "Lord William's rewards are very
useful," Samur remarked.

"He can be generous when he is pleased," Magdalene agreed, and went to open the door.

When he was gone she said to Bell, "My tongue does not usually slip that way."

Bell grinned. "If I had ever doubted Lord William's innocence in this matter, I would no longer. Had he the smallest involvement, that word would never have passed your lips. Don't let it worry you, Magdalene. If Samur tries to ride that horse, he won't get far."

"He could start an unpleasant rumor."

"More than are already circulating after Niall was accused? Besides, I am quite sure Samur avoids even the slightest hint that he knows anything about Lord William. He may not be the keenest-witted of men—although I think him much cleverer than he seems, clever enough for Lord Waleran to send him on a special mission to your house and clever enough for Lord William to *want* him as an informer—but clever or not, he cannot be such a fool as to let his name be linked with that of William of Ypres."

Magdalene sighed. "I think you are only trying to comfort me, but thank you. And maybe the sinking I feel in my middle is because my belly thinks my mouth has forgotten it. It's a long time since dinner."

"Let's go out an get an evening meal. That place Loveday took us to yesterday was very good."

"So it was, but I cannot go with you." She sighed. "I have a feeling that William will either come himself or send one of his men for the details of Niall's proof of innocence. I had better be here to satisfy those questions. You can get food for both of us and bring it back, or if you want to sample more of the talk in the alehouses, you can take Diccon along and let him bring the food back."

Bell froze. "You expect Lord William?"

Magdalene shrugged. "It will depend on what appointments he has and whether St. Cyr's murder is important enough for him to cancel them." She hesitated, then added, "William will not mind meeting you here. If you mind meeting him, that is your problem, not mine."

"It is, indeed," Bell snapped. "I'll send Diccon back with a meal for you."

After he was gone—Magdalene was glad he had not slammed the door on his way out—she sat down at the table and sank her head into her hands. She knew she should break off her relationship with Bell. It was gaining too tight a grip on her, and he did not seem to be gaining acceptance for what she was, not even of her relationship with William. That was dangerous. Magdalene wiped her cheeks on the heels of her hands, shuddered, hugged her arms around herself. Bell's jealousy was dangerous to both men! Despite what she had said to Samur, William could easily arrange Bell's death. On the other hand, William would not expect harm from Bell, and . . .

Nonsense! Bell was not the kind to creep up behind a man and stab him. If he were jealous enough, he would simply leave her. It was not as if she had pledged herself to him as did a wife. Then it was as much a matter of pride as of desire to have a woman faithful. And Bell was not a wild boy like that idiot Samur was talking about, who had made a scene with Loveday in the street . . . Jules of Osney. Bell would just go away and find another woman he could mold to his desire.

The thought was painful but oddly less so than she expected. It seemed as if some other idea obscured the full weight of the misery that planning to do without Bell usually inflicted on her. Because she had been thinking at the same time of someone who could not simply find another woman . . . oh, yes, how silly. Jules of Osney needed Loveday's estate more than he needed Loveday. Now who had told her that? Loveday?

Someone kicked the door and Magdalene called out, asking who was there. Diccon's voice replied. She went to open the door, laughing as the boy staggered in loaded with cookshop containers. He set those on the table, breathing out heavily in relief at having delivered all of it intact.

"What in the world is this?" Magdalene asked. "Even you will not be able to make serious inroads on this supply. Whatever was Bell thinking?"

Even as she asked, she knew the answer and a mingled relief and pleasure made her laugh again. Bell was . . . what? Apologizing for his bad temper by providing food enough for William, and even perhaps some of his men? Hinting that he would be back to share the food with her and William? She hoped not the latter. Having them together always made her chest tight with anxiety. William was never jealous of her body, but he might not take so lightly any indication that more than her body was involved with Bell; and Bell was like a dog with his hackles up, just waiting for a sign to attack.

"Said most of it would be just as good cold," Diccon said. "Hope you've got some bowls. I've got to bring these back soon."

Magdalene was grateful to have her thoughts interrupted. She said vaguely, "Yes, of course." And then realizing that she was not at home and had virtually nothing, added quickly, "Ah, no. Run out and ask Florete if she has anything I can use."

While the boy was out, Magdalene got out the half loaf of bread that remained from the previous day and cut three substantial slices to make trenchers. On those she laid slices of roast pork and pieces of the roast chicken, which she tore apart. She covered the heaped trenchers with a piece of cloth just as Diccon came in with two bowls and a clean chamber pot. Magdalene laughed heartily when she saw that vessel, but she only stopped to smell it carefully and wipe it again with a clean cloth before she dumped into it a large amount of stew. Into one of the other bowls she put the boiled greens and into the last the sweet pudding. Finally she gestured to Diccon.

"Eat," she said, "but quickly. Soon as you are done, you can take the cookshop's vessels to the pump and wash them. Then bring them back."

Diccon nodded and ran out but was back again before Magdalene could even seat herself. He brought his own bowl and a spoon. Magdalene nodded for him to help himself, which he did, and started eating. Magdalene sat down with him and ladled some of the stew into a smaller bowl. She divided up what was left of the bread and handed Diccon a piece just as the door flew open.

"What do you mean Niall did not kill St. Cyr? How do you know? Where is he?"

Diccon had jumped to his feet as soon as the door opened, clutched his bowl and bread to his chest, and began to sidle to the door. Magdalene nodded at him and then said calmly, "Would you like something to eat, William? I can make the story very short or tell you all the details, which will make it long enough for you to have a meal."

"He is innocent?" William insisted. "There can be no doubt?"

"None at all. He was at Noke the night St. Cyr was killed

and not only all the servants and your men-at-arms will swear
to it but the local priest, a Father Herveus. The priest had
come to comfort Loveday, but stayed to play chess with Niall,
had the evening meal with him, and spent the whole night."

William's small blue eyes grew even smaller as he thought
hard. Then he drew up the chair and sat himself at the table.
Magdalene immediately reached over and pulled one of the
trenchers out to set before him. He took a chicken leg and
began to bite chunks off it. Magdalene got up and got her
other bowl and spoon—brought for just this eventuality—
which she filled with stew, laying a few of the greens on one
side. She set the bowl near the trencher.

"So, from the beginning," William said between bites.

Magdalene told him, virtually move by move and conversation by conversation, beginning with Giles de Milland's arrival the previous day. He cocked his head when she described
the conversation Reinhart Hardel had with his son, Tirell, but
did not stop chewing a mouthful of stew. He stopped her twice
to ask questions when she described Loveday's intention of
marrying Niall without leave from the king and simply paying
the fine, but he looked more thoughtful than angry, blinking
slowly. When she described in detail the servants' and men-at-
arms' assurances of Niall's continual presence in full sight of
them all the afternoon, evening, and night of the twenty-first
of June, he breathed a satisfied sigh, and finished the meat on
the trencher.

"Niall and Loveday will have a written statement from the
priest about his presence in Noke that night also, and sworn
testimony from all the Noke servants signed and sealed by the
priest. I thought it wiser not to take evidence from your men.
It would not add much and might be thought to be tainted.

Niall wanted to come back to Oxford to report to you yesterday, but we all agreed—"

"Who are all?"

"Sir Bellamy, myself, and Loveday. We all felt that it would
be better to publish the proof of Niall's innocence before he
arrived . . . or if you prefer, he could come to the town carrying
the proof that he could not have attacked St. Cyr. I felt that
if the sheriff first arrested Niall, there would be unpleasant
words said about your influence, even if you went with proof
to free him."

After a moment, William nodded. "Likely you are right
about that. Ordinarily I would not care or might even prefer
that it be thought my influence was so strong as to free a
murderer, but not here and now."

He bent over his bowl of stew, reaching absently for the
bread Magdalene put near his hand, but she did not think he
was much aware of eating, guessing that soldiers' habit drove
him. Still, she quickly emptied her bowl and wiped it clean,
finally adding a little water from the jug on the shelf and drying it. She cleaned the spoon too, then put a helping of the
sweet pudding in the bowl and brought it to the table. William
was using the last of the bread to scour his bowl.

"Will you have some sweet?" she asked.

He looked up and at the bowl she was proffering as if he
had never seen such a thing before and said, "I was fool enough
yesterday to ask two or three if they knew of St. Cyr. I am
more cautious usually, but it was so strange that Waleran
should have chosen such a man that I grew curious. I wonder
if . . . no, that is too convoluted even for Waleran."

Magdalene put the bowl of pudding down on the table.

"There is a chance that this has nothing to do with you, William."

"No?" He reached for the bowl and put a spoonful of pudding into his mouth.

"It seems that Aimery St. Cyr knew a number of highborn men and that he may have coerced one of them to get the forged betrothal agreement he presented to Loveday. If that 'friend' grew impatient or frightened, could he not have killed St. Cyr?"

"Perhaps, but how did you learn this?"

"There was no message for you left with Florete from Raoul de Samur?"

"No, there was not."

"Oh, then it was just for the woman he came, and possibly to make his future visits here seem ordinary."

"Who came?" He took another spoonful. "Magdalene, your mind is wandering."

"Sorry. That happens when I try to think of more than one thing at a time. Raoul de Samur was here not long before you came. He was with a woman—by accident I even know her name; it is Geneva. He came out of the cocking chamber just as I was sending Diccon off with my message to you. He said since he had seen me he would not need to look for you, but he had no real message to leave. He just warned you not to tweak Waleran's nose. He said Waleran was too busy about something that involves the count of Brittany to be bothered about you just now—"

"Yes, I know that! And Stephen is also extending himself to show favor to the count. What I don't know is why, or what Waleran is busy with."

"Samur doesn't know either. Maybe that's why he didn't

want to leave a direct message. He said he couldn't get near Waleran, that you'd seen more of him this last week than he had."

"Likely that is true too. Meulan spends all his time in court whispering in this ear and that about Salisbury." William's lips thinned. "And if the bishop does not show up tomorrow, I will join the whispering. But none of this explains how Raoul came to tell you about St. Cyr's friends."

"That was because I told him that the betrothal agreement was a forgery and that Niall had nothing to do with St. Cyr's death and had many witnesses to being outside of Oxford that night. Samur then said he knew St. Cyr could not have afforded to pay for the forged document and wondered if one of his grand friends had laid down the silver. Naturally I asked who those friends were."

"Good girl." William put down the bowl and pushed it away.

"Do you want some wine? I have—"

"Gahh. Not the stuff they serve here. Send the boy out to the wine merchant and get some decent wine. Meanwhile, ale will do." Magdalene went to fetch her two cups and the flagon. "So, about those friends of St. Cyr's?"

Magdalene filled the cups. "Samur said he did not know who they were." She giggled. "He was *very* annoyed. Said he hadn't paid attention because he hadn't known St. Cyr would be murdered, had he? He said he had seen only a back view both times; once in a dark corner of The Wheat Sheaf, and once when Count Alain was visiting Waleran, he noticed St. Cyr was talking to one of the count's men."

"They are not known much for mixing with other men's troops," William said thoughtfully.

"I think that was what drew Samur's attention. In any case,

I told him to keep a watch out. I made bold to say that you would be pleased with him if he recognized either man and discovered who he was."

William grinned at her over his ale cup. "Well, I see you have the investigation well in hand already."

"Investigation? No. I was not intending to seek out St. Cyr's murderer."

"No? Giles told me that your Bell was out asking questions in the alehouses about what they had seen and heard."

"But that was when we thought Niall had done it and that *you* might be blamed."

William put down the ale cup, still grinning. "I doubt Sir Bellamy worries overmuch about my being blamed for this or that."

Magdalene laughed. "Well, no, but I do."

"And Sir Bellamy is still so besotted he does your bidding even against his own interest?"

"It is not against his interest. What you and I have together has nothing to do with Bell." Magdalene put her hand on William's arm.

He covered her hand with his own. "He is young, Chick. Be patient with him. He is useful, too . . . especially now, because I might well be blamed for this crime even if it is proven that Niall did not do it."

"Why should you be blamed?"

"The armorer's house where my men lodge backs on a lane that goes right to the Cornmarket and comes out near The Wheat Sheaf. Some of the men use that lane to get to the alehouse. I can prove Niall did not kill St. Cyr. What of the others?"

"But no other had any cause," Magdalene protested.

"Except to fulfill my will."

Her eyes widened. "But why? Why should you care?"

William grimaced and shrugged. "To have a man I could trust close to Oxford? Who knows what reasons may be found by anyone who simply wishes to blacken me? The reason will not be important. What will be important is that my men were close and—" his mouth twisted bitterly "—it will be said it was not the first time."

Magdalene made no reply, except to cover William's hand with hers again. She knew that William felt he had been deprived of the rule of Ypres because he was blamed for the murder of Charles, count of Flanders, through the instrumentality of the provost of Bruges. Whether William was directly guilty, in that he had actively planned that murder with the provost, or whether he was indirectly guilty, merely by allowing those who could accomplish it to know he desired Charles' death, was a moot point.

He looked down at their hands, blinking, and then up. "I need the true criminal to be exposed so there is no doubt of his guilt, Magdalene. Will you do it?"

"If I can, William." Tears stood in her eyes. "I have not the resources here that I have in London, but I will do my very best."

He stood up, knocking over the chair, and dragged her up and into his arms. "There's my Chick! Don't say you don't have the resources." He pulled a heavy purse from his belt and dropped it on the table. "Florete will serve your purposes." He pulled her closer, and kissed her. "Will you serve mine?"

CHAPTER 11

Angry as he was at Magdalene's seemingly indifferent reminder of her relationship with William of Ypres, Bell remembered to stick his head into the common room of the Soft Nest and snarl at Diccon to come with him. The boy hesitated as Bell turned away, and then ran after him. Bell hardly noticed him at first, but by the time he had reached the end of the street, his fury was dulling into angry resignation. He felt like a fool too, for having exposed his resentment against William of Ypres. Resentment was stupid. It was as if a woman he married to breed him sons should be angry and blame him over the love he bore Magdalene for years before he ever met that wife.

In any case, he thought, Ypres plainly had not summoned Magdalene for the use of her body and she certainly did not lust after Ypres. Jealous as he was, Bell knew that as surely as he knew she *did* want him. He gnawed at his lower lip. Fool that he was, he would drive her into fighting that desire if he did not curb his jealousy.

A scrape and stumble close behind him made him whirl with

his hand on his knife and then curse softly as he saw the boy from the whorehouse pick himself up. He had forgotten about the child, who had tripped over his overlarge shoes—Bell wondered distractedly from which dead man they had been stolen—while trying to keep up with the pace he had set.

"Sorry, Diccon," he said. "Sometimes women can drive a man to—"

"Drink, murder, blasphemy, war . . . Don't have to tell me, Sir Bellamy. I got to live with twenty or thirty of 'em. And what one wants, the other don't. And what's too early for one's too late for another." He snorted heavily. "Don't tell me about women."

Bell grinned at the boy's too-old cynicism, and because Diccon's world-weary manner had lifted his spirits, he continued the game. "Well, I have just annoyed the one to whom I am bound. What would you say is the best remedy?"

The answer, with twisted lips and lifted brows, came without the slightest hesitation. "Buy her a present."

"Ah, but this lady doesn't want money from me and I am not rich enough to buy her such a jewel. . . ." He grimaced. "No. That would make things worse."

Suddenly Diccon smiled. "She's a one, that Mistress Magdalene. Never seen her kind before. Even Florete thinks she walks on water."

Bell laughed. "I wouldn't say that. She has her faults. But I do need to make amends."

"For what?"

Bell scowled. "Jealousy."

The boy was silent, then shook his head. "Most of 'em don't get mad for that. Think it's a compliment, most do. If she

don't—" he hesitated, then shrugged "—show you didn't mean
it?"

That was more a question than a statement, but Bell thought
the boy had hit the right idea. He could go back and say he
was sorry. No, he could not. He might meet Ypres and . . .
and he did not know how he would react. Besides, he had said
he was sorry too often already and apology grew stale if it
brought no amendment.

What a fool he was to beat a dead horse. Magdalene had
been a whore for much longer than he had known her. Little
as he liked it, she could never undo that past—and had told
him again and again that she would not if she could, that he
must take her as she was or leave her. Bell sighed. Since he
could not leave her . . . he must show her the flash of jealousy
was meaningless. Somehow he must show that he would endure Ypres, even welcome—

"Did you want me for something?" Diccon asked sharply,
interrupting Bell's thoughts. "I'm getting tired and it's nearly
time for the evening meal." Now there was a distinct whine in
the child's voice. "If I'm not there, no one will leave anything
for me."

"Evening meal!" Bell repeated, and smote himself gently on
the head. "I was supposed to buy an evening meal for Magdalene and send you back with it. Don't worry, there will be
plenty and Magdalene won't stint you."

He had to turn back to reach the cookshop across from
Master Redding's mercery because he had passed it. That was
all to the good. By the time he walked up to the counter, the
three ideas had come together. The boy needed to eat. William of Ypres—if he came—would probably arrive in time for
the evening meal. He had said to Diccon there would be

plenty. Bell nodded to himself. If he sent food enough for three or four, Magdalene would very well understand that he was inviting Ypres to dine with them or, in other words, telling her he understood that Ypres must be made welcome.

Bell grinned as he ordered a dozen slices of roast pork, a fat roast chicken, a meat pasty, a dozen ladlesful of stew, boiled greens, and sweet pudding. The whole cost less than a night in Magdalene's bed . . . not that he had ever paid her. A feeling of warmth suffused him as he felt in his purse for the coins to give the cookshop owner. He had just realized that he was the *only* man who did not pay her. Even William of Ypres paid, and a good round sum, too, for his comfort and his men's, and the men never touched Magdalene.

His grin had probably broadened to an expression of total idiocy when he caught a look at the cook's face. The anger in it made his hand drop to his knife hilt, and then the cook asked what he was going to carry the food in.

"Stew kind of runs through the fingers," he said caustically. "Why are you wasting my time?"

"Good Lord," Bell muttered and then laughed and explained that he had been so angry when he left to buy the food that he had forgotten containers.

As soon as he offered to pay a farthing for the loan of what was necessary until the boy could bring everything to the Soft Nest, the cook was all smiles. Mention of the whorehouse seemed to seal the bargain.

When he had paid and seen Diccon start off for the Soft Nest, Bell himself walked north along the road until he came to The Broached Barrel. The landlord remembered him as the bishop of Winchester's knight who had been asking questions about the slain man the previous day. He looked apprehensive until Bell assured him he only wanted to know where the body had been taken and who, if anyone, was investigating the death.

The landlord grimaced and said the Watch had taken the body but he didn't know where—and didn't care. Then he admitted that the sheriff's deputy had come to inquire about the killing but had not stayed long.

"Did he look out back?" Bell asked, blandly curious.

"Don't know. Think I want to be accused of spying on the sheriff's man? Kept on about my own business, didn't I?"

The voice was sullen, the words possibly a warning, but Bell did not allow his expression to change. "Right, but in a way this *is* my business. Still, there's no reason for you to be troubled about it. Where do I find the sheriff or his deputy?"

For a moment Bell thought he would receive no answer, but, even as he turned away, the landlord said that the town Watch was managed from one of the buildings in St. Martin's church-yard west of the Carfax, and the sheriff had an office there too. Bell sighed and retraced his steps through the Cornmarket and then west on the road that went to the castle.

St. Martin's was on the right not more than a hundred paces from the meeting of the roads. It was an imposing church, set well back from the road and divided from it by a large, bustling churchyard in which there were, as the landlord had implied, several buildings. The closest to the gate, built right against the wall, was long and low. It looked like a barracks.

Bell's guess was confirmed when several armed men passed him and went inside. He assumed it was a place where the sheriff's men and the Watch were housed when on duty or mustered if they were needed on special call. He walked to the door, only to be stopped by a guard, but not before he noticed that the single room inside, which ran the full length and width of the building, held a large group of men clustered together. There was an aura of tense excitement about the men, who seemed to be listening to orders from a leader in the center of the group.

Bell asked for the captain of the Watch and the guard shook his head. "Busy, sir," he said. "Don't think—"

At that moment men began to come out of the building, forcing Bell and the guard apart. Bell scanned the group and stepped into the path of the last man to emerge.

"Captain," he said. "I have one very short question. Can you tell me where the Watch took the body of the man who was slain behind The Broached Barrel the day before yesterday?"

The captain waved toward the church. "St. Martin's. They've a chapel for the dead."

He took in Bell's clothing, the war belt ornamented with gold wire, the long knight's sword, the gem in the pommel of his shorter knife, and added politely that the sheriff was looking into the killing. Bell then asked where he could find the sheriff. The captain told him briskly that the sheriff's house was about midway between the barracks and the church, but that the sheriff was not there.

"He's rid out toward Lechlade," he said. "And taken most of his men with him." He took another long look at Bell, grinned, and said in a low, confidential voice, "Had word yesterday that the bishop of Salisbury's left Malmsbury. He should be here tomorrow."

Bell's eyes widened and then he grinned back. "I am happy to say I had no wagers on the bishop's decision, but thank you for giving me warning." While he spoke, his fingers had found his purse and he put a silver penny into the Watch captain's hand.

The man nodded his thanks, but his mouth twisted. "My men've got to clear out the house right opposite the castle. Salisbury paid for the place, but when he didn't show up the landlord got greedy and took other lodgers. Now they've got to go. The sheriff's out doing the polite, and like always, we get the dirty work."

"Sorry for your trouble," Bell said. "Believe me, I understand. My lord owns property in Southwark and I get to evict the ones who don't keep up their rents."

The captain found a rueful smile for a fellow sufferer. "It's really not a bad place, Oxford. Quiet enough, except for the students, and the trouble they make is mostly mischief, drunkenness. Not real fighters, they aren't. A couple of taps with the cudgel quiets them down."

Bell laughed. "Not too quiet these last few weeks with the king here."

He got a shrug and a laugh in answer to that. "Not our kettle of fish. The sheriff told us not to try to manage the men-at-arms. He knows my men ain't fit for that. Let their own captains do it, the sheriff said, and there hasn't been much trouble. . . ." His expression changed. "Only that one killed the other day."

"Did your people find him?"

"Not mine, thank God," the captain said. "That would have been Wessel's men. He's on street duty now. If you want him, he should be back here to report to the sheriff—" he pointed, and now that the men were out of the way Bell could see a small but well-built house backed against the wall of the church "—at Vespers."

"Will the deputy be there now?" Bell asked.

"Should be." The captain shrugged. "But he's a gentleman and don't need to show his face according to the hour."

Bell made no reply to that, merely lifting a hand in farewell. He walked away uncertain of whether he wanted to see the body first or talk to the sheriff's deputy. A faint taint of foulness in the air, perhaps from some merchant's midden, reminded him of what the body would be like after two days at the end of June. He turned toward the sheriff's office.

The door was open, and he could see several men; one sat behind a good, solid table, the others on benches along the wall, talking idly or working over leather or weapons. Bell walked up to the table.

Having asked if he addressed the sheriff's deputy and received a brusque nod in return, Bell continued, "My name is Sir Bellamy of Itchen, and I am looking into the murder of the man called Aimery St. Cyr. His body was found behind The Broached Barrel yesterday morning."

Bell had not claimed authority as the bishop of Winchester's officer. He thought it unwise to associate himself with any bishop at the moment and he did not want to involve his master, or imply that Winchester had any interest at all in the proceedings in Oxford.

"Looking into it? Why?"

The man behind the table looked at him almost blankly for a moment. He was portly and heavy-featured, dressed in a sober brown tunic. His shirt, decently white but not as bright as Bell's—for which Bell paid extra to his laundress—was open at the throat. His voice was flat, neither aggressive nor inviting, but his eyes, glinting past half-closed lids, were surprisingly bright.

"Mostly because I am a friend of Niall Arvagh's."

That got a reaction. The deputy sat up straight and began to push back his stool. "Where the hell is he?"

"At Noke, where he has been with twenty witnesses, including the priest who will swear he was in their sight since Sext on Wednesday except for the time it took to piss and shit. He is not the man you want for the crime."

The sheriff's deputy relaxed back into his seat and sighed. "I should have known it would not be so easy, especially when that looby was so sure." Then his eyes opened all the way and he stared hard at Bell. "You did say you were looking into the killing, not that you came to provide vindication for Arvagh. If your friend is free and clear as you say, why do you care who killed St. Cyr?"

"Because the accusation was made and Niall Arvagh will never be clear until the true killer is found."

"Why should he care? He will leave here with William of Ypres—"

"No," Bell interrupted, then temporized. "He may well go with Ypres, but he will be marrying Loveday of Otmoor soon and thus be often in Oxford." Having said that truth, Bell cleared his throat. He felt his color rise, but went on doggedly. "He has been betrothed to Loveday for a long time, but she was very young and in the king's ward while he was rising among Ypres' men. It seemed reasonable to wait."

The deputy was sitting more upright again. His face, enlivened with interest, did not seem so heavy-featured. "If she was already betrothed, how come St. Cyr thought he could marry her?"

Bell shrugged and cleared his throat again; he hated to lie. "Niall has no idea about that. It is true that no big ceremony was made of their betrothal. His sister had aforetime been married to Loveday's brother, but they both died. The fathers still wished to bind the families, but this rebonding brought back too many sad memories for a large or joyous celebration."

After a moment to think that over, the deputy shook his head. "Well, if Arvagh did not do it, I cannot see how you will find the true killer. St. Cyr could have been killed by anyone."

"That is why I want to see St. Cyr's body. It may well tell me some interesting things."

The deputy drew back a little, his eyes averted. "You are going to . . . to ask the corpse to speak? To name his murderer?"

Bell laughed. "No, of course not. I am not a witch, an idiot, or a fanatic. But if I look at the wound, I will know what kind of knife was used, mayhap how hard the blow was." He shrugged. "Who knows what I may learn? Was he robbed? Was any blow struck other than the stab wound?"

"Do you know how that body will smell?"

Bell sighed. "I have been a soldier for fifteen years and have been on more than one battlefield. I do, indeed, know and do not look forward to it. All I can say is that I am glad I have not eaten." He sighed again. "Where is it? The quicker there the quicker done."

"You really mean to do it? To find the killer?"

Bell lifted his brows. "I suppose once Niall was proven innocent, the sheriff would have preferred to forget about the murder. St. Cyr was only a common man-at-arms. And Niall, although a knight, was scarcely important enough for the sheriff to worry about his reputation."

"You'd think so, wouldn't you? But he won't be let forget it, it seems. Here you are nosing around, and that lunatic Manville d'Arras was in again this morning asking whether we had yet taken Arvagh." He gestured with his head toward the men on the benches. "Peter and William told me that Arras had been in the alehouses, crying that the sheriff wouldn't seek his friend's killer." The deputy stood up. "My name is Sir Rolf de Dowch. I will take you to the body. I am interested in what you think it can tell you."

It was a short distance to the church of St. Martin and Sir Rolf led Bell around to the right, toward a dark arch closed by a heavy door. Outside was a stand of torches and a clay pot holding some ashed-over coals. Sir Rolf plunged one of the torches into the pot of coals, and it hissed to life. Bell took a second torch and lit it from the first. Both men took deep breaths, and Sir Rolf opened the door.

The chamber was small and had no windows, and the odor in it was heavy and sweetly putrid. However, it did not carry the stench of the befoulment of death, which usually added a final sickening effect. Doubtless someone had washed the corpse; that annoyed Bell because he would not be able to judge whether St. Cyr had been standing or already fallen when he was stabbed—unless the stains on his clothing could tell the tale. He glanced around and saw with satisfaction the pile of garments by the body's feet.

At least the washing had kept the air breathable—if barely. Bell put his torch into one of the holders on the wall. Then, lips set, he went up to the shrouded body and uncovered it.

Sir Rolf made an indistinguishable sound, perhaps of protest when Bell uncovered the corpse. After a moment, however, Rolf drew closer, holding his torch over the bier as Bell seized the right shoulder and lifted. It was not easy. The body was flaccid, the rigidity of death gone completely. Bell was not surprised. Although he had known the stiffness to linger as long as two days, it came and went faster in warm weather, and it had been warm.

The knife wound, as Bell had expected, was to the right of the backbone, where it should be if a right-handed man had stabbed St. Cyr from behind. He looked at the wound and the area surrounding it. The body had been lying on its back for some time and the flesh was very dark, as dead flesh always was on whatever part was lowest. Even so Bell could see that the edges of the wound were smooth, and he could make out two bruises alongside the wound where something protruding from the hilt of the knife had struck the flesh hard—quillons, downturned toward the blade.

"You see that?" he said to Sir Rolf. "The blade is ordinary but very well honed, a straight blade about like mine or yours, and it had quillons that point down." He leaned closer, holding his breath and gesturing to Sir Rolf to bring the torch closer. "Rounded quillons, or maybe part of a double guard, one curve up and one down."

"How the hell do you know that?" Sir Rolf asked, sounding annoyed.

"That the knife was very sharp, because the flesh around the wound is smooth. About the quillons being rounded, because the skin was badly bruised but not broken. A square guard or a pointed one might have broken the skin or left a sharp line at the core of the bruise."

Sir Rolf looked at him suspiciously. "You've done this before."

"Often enough," Bell agreed absently, looking carefully at the back of the corpse's head. After a moment he braced the

head with one hand and ran the other over it. "No one struck
him on the head." He eased the body down flat and looked
carefully at the forehead and nose. "Didn't fall on his face either . . . but the stab wound was clean, so he didn't try to pull
away when the knife went in. Why?"

"Too shocked? And sometimes it hardly feels like anything
at first. It takes a while to feel a stab wound from a sharp knife."

"Yes, I agree, but remember the quillons hit St. Cyr hard
enough to bruise him. He should have staggered forward, away
from his attacker, maybe even have had time to cry out. He
did not."

"We don't know that. Doubtless they were noisy enough in
the alehouse to drown any cry."

Bell nodded. "A good point, but with the knife in him why
didn't he fall forward? Wait, maybe he did." Bell walked along
the bier and took first one hand of the corpse and then the
other. The palms of both were clean and without bruises. "I
will have to discover who prepared the corpse and ask whether
his hands were dirtied from trying to stop a fall."

Bell walked back toward the head again and examined the
face even more minutely. He shook his head. "No, he didn't
fall on his face," he repeated. Then suddenly he bent closer
and gestured for Sir Rolf to lower the torch. "Look," he said.
"What are those marks on his neck and under his chin? Did
the murderer first try to strangle him?"

"The mark is too wide for a cord," Rolf said. "Wait, it might
have been a belt with a design carved in the leather."

"The carving must have been very deep and the leather very
hard. Look how clean the edges of the bruises are. I don't
remember . . . oh, fool that I am, that's the mark of chain mail."

"But how would a man get bruises from chain mail on the

front of his neck? You mean he was wearing his hauberk with the hood raised and someone tried to strangle him or struck him in the neck? No. Impossible. How would the knife go in so smooth and deep? Surely the mail would have stopped it."

Bell had been silent, staring down at the gray bruises on the corpse-white skin. Suddenly he turned away, walked quickly behind Sir Rolf, put his left arm around the man's neck, and jerked him upright. The knight cried out, flailed backward with the torch. Bell released him and jumped out of the way, laughing.

"Like that," he said, before Sir Rolf could drop the torch and go for his sword. "It was not St. Cyr who was wearing mail but whoever killed him. He came up behind St. Cyr, put his left arm around the man's neck—which would hold him still and also prevent him from crying out—and then he used his right hand to stab."

Sir Rolf was not amused. He glowered at Bell, who sobered and apologized, adding, "Forgive me. I could not resist trying to see if it would work, and it does. St. Cyr's attacker might have been waiting in ambush, but it is equally possible that St. Cyr knew the attacker was there and simply did not expect to be attacked."

"Very well, I can accept everything you say, although I am not certain I agree completely. But I do not see that it brings us any closer to the murderer."

Bell looked at him in surprise then said, "Wait. Let me finish looking at this body. Then we can go outside and talk."

There was nothing much else to see, however. Some faint marks indicated how the body had been lying behind the shed, but since it had clearly been moved to that place—there was not room enough behind the shed for St. Cyr to have been stabbed there—those bruises were not significant. With a sigh of relief, Bell drew the worn cloth over the still figure, turned away, and removed his torch from the wall holder. Sir Rolf waited no longer but preceded him out of the chamber and doused his torch in the sand in which the unused torches were set. Bell followed his example.

Outside the church both breathed deeply several times to rid themselves of the odor of death. A moment later Sir Rolf shook his head and said, "I can still taste it. Let's go over to The Lively Hop where we can drown the corpse smell in some wine."

"Done," Bell agreed.

When they had their mugs in hand, Bell sent the serving boy to the nearest cookshop for a pork pasty. By the time it arrived, he had swilled out his mouth, spitting the first mouthful of wine onto the stained earth by his feet, and taken a good second swallow. Sir Rolf did the same.

"What is there to talk about?" he asked. "The Watchman said St. Cyr had been stabbed in the back and he was. Now you know he was stabbed with a sharp knife with downturned, rounded quillons . . . so what?"

Bell had broken off a piece of the pasty, but he held it in his hand instead of putting it in his mouth. "So what? So I know a good deal about St. Cyr's killer now that I didn't know before."

"You are going to search every man's belt knife for downturned quillons?" Sir Rolf asked, his lips twisted. "There are a lot of men in Oxford right now."

"I don't need to look at *every* man. I know St. Cyr's killer was a knight, not one of his fellow men-at-arms nor a common thief who came upon him by accident. Men-at-arms and thieves do not wear mail. I know that either St. Cyr was sitting when he was attacked or the man was taller—"

"Taller? How can you know that?"

"Because the mail marked not only his throat but the bottom of his chin. But St. Cyr may have been sitting, waiting for someone. There were tables and benches out in the back of The Broached Barrel. And I know that because I went to look."

Sir Rolf cleared his throat. "You are thinking that we were careless, but the sheriff has been very busy, as you can imagine, and it isn't as if we could have caught and questioned witnesses if we arrived promptly. It was clear that the man had been dead for hours. The landlord and servers at the inn were not going anywhere. I spoke to them and every one swore they had not seen St. Cyr in the place the previous night."

"So he didn't meet whoever it was *in* the alehouse. I wonder whose idea that was?"

"Well, but if he wasn't in the alehouse, the landlord and servers couldn't have seen him killed, and they hadn't heard anyone cry out—I did ask that. So what was the point in asking more? So I went back to the sheriff's office and not a candlemark later in came Arras saying he knew who had killed St. Cyr. Surely the most reasonable thing after that was to question Niall Arvagh?"

"Yes," Bell said, smiling as he swallowed his second large bite of the pasty.

Bell was thoroughly annoyed with the man who clearly did not have the smallest interest in who had killed St. Cyr, but there was no sense pursuing the subject and exasperating the sheriff's deputy further. Sir Rolf might be too lazy to take a proper interest in his work, but he had not been obstructive— and if angered he might become so. Thus, Bell dropped the subject of St. Cyr's death and asked about Salisbury's expected arrival.

He was surprised to receive not only a repetition of the information the captain of the Watch had given him, but a fulsome litany of praise of Salisbury's efficiency as justiciar and an indignant rejection of the assumption that Salisbury had any rebel intentions. Bell made no attempt to argue against any of Sir Rolf's claims and in the end they parted pleasantly. As Bell turned north toward The Broached Barrel, Sir Rolf commented that he found Bell's insights very interesting and it was a shame they could not have been made in a more worthy cause.

This opinion was close enough to Bell's own that he wondered as he stepped into The Broached Barrel why he was pursuing St. Cyr's killer. But he knew the answer . . . both answers. First, murder, even of such a cur as St. Cyr, was wrong. Killing him would not have been wrong, even if it were the result of forcing a quarrel on him and cutting him down in a fair, if uneven, fight. But to creep up behind a man and stab him without warning . . . no. A man who did that once was all too likely to do it again, and possibly to someone who deserved killing less. The murderer had to be exposed and punished. And second, of course, because Magdalene wanted the killer found.

Bell sighed as he took his tankard of ale from the landlord and dropped a farthing on the barrel beside him. Magdalene wanted Lord William cleared of any suspicion of involvement in St. Cyr's death. Bell himself thought it a waste of time. What was one more suspected killing attached to Lord William's name? Well, possibly at this time, uneasy as the political situation was, Magdalene was right.

As he made the grudging concession, Bell looked around at

the tables. Before he had decided where he wanted to seek a place, he was hailed by name. At first in the dim light he did not recognize the man whose hand was raised in greeting, but in another moment he recalled the disputed farm and the seller who was trying to extort more money from the buyer.

"Lord Ormerod," he said, making his way to the table and sliding onto the end of the bench. "So, did you find Sir Bruno, and was he able to arrange an appeal to the king?"

"I did find him. I was fortunate enough to run into Sir Ferrau—you remember, the gentleman who fled our company so suddenly in fear that I would ask him to intercede with his overlord for me?"

"Yes, I remember." Bell chuckled. "I gather he was more cooperative in introducing you to Sir Bruno."

"Yes, he was—at least, he pointed Sir Bruno out to me and would have introduced us but he was called away by a most haughty and elegant gentleman . . ."

"Likely his overlord, Count Alain."

"Hmmm. I can see why Ferrau was not eager to present my problem to him. But fortunately Sir Bruno is very easy to know. I walked over and introduced myself and he was most welcoming. He said he would try to accommodate me, since I had come a long way, but warned me that this was a bad time, that the king's mind was elsewhere. He offered to arrange for an audience when the king is in Westminster, which he expects will be in only a few months—"

"Who's this Ormerod?"

The voice was still high with youth, the words definitely slurred with drink. Bell looked up at the young man weaving past the table beside them. When he reached them he steadied himself on Ormerod's shoulder. Bell saw Ormerod stiffen, rather more than what was necessary to steady the slight younger man's weight; an expression of exasperation crossed Ormerod's face, but his voice was even when he spoke.

"This is Sir Bellamy of Itchen, Jules. He is the bishop of Winchester's knight and has been most helpful to me in that matter of the farm near Thorpe. And this is my host, Sir Jules of Osney, Bell."

"Are you buying drinks?" Jules asked.

Bell raised his eyebrows. "I think you've had enough, Sir Jules—"

"*Ahhh!* Another old woman! I'm shell—celebrating! We're rid of St. Cyr and I'll sh—settle with Loveday tomorrow or th' next day. Then Osney'll be free and clear and m'sister'll be betrothed to Ormerod's brother . . ." He waved wildly at a barmaid, nearly hitting her. "Bring's some wine here."

Ormerod rose and pushed Sir Jules down on the bench opposite where Bell was sitting, for which Bell was grateful. He suspected that the young man would not be able to hold much more wine than he had already consumed and preferred not to be sitting next to him if he were going to spew. Nonetheless he had not missed the references to Loveday and St. Cyr.

"I think the world as a whole is better off without St. Cyr," Bell said mildly. "Did you know that it was here that he was killed?"

"Wash it?"

Sir Jules leered drunkenly, bracing himself upright, his arms folded on the table before him. Bell suddenly found himself wondering whether the expression of satisfaction he wore was only owing to the drink and St. Cyr's death or whether it was an expression of satisfaction over duping everyone. Could St. Cyr have been killed elsewhere? By Sir Jules? Bell was tempted to go out back and look for signs of the murder, but he knew there could be none. The earth, table, and benches were too stained and weatherworn to show any mark of the blood that had been shed—and it was possible that very little blood had actually been spilled.

It addition, Sir Jules hardly seemed the type to walk around wearing mail. Still, he must have armor because he had been belted a knight. And if he expected to face St. Cyr, who was larger and stronger, he might well have donned mail as an insurance—and might equally well have lost his nerve and crept up and stabbed St. Cyr from behind.

"Yes, it was here," Bell replied to Sir Jules' question, watching him carefully. "Out in the back, probably not long after dark." He smiled as if he were going to make a joke and asked, "And where were you on the night of the twenty-first?"

"Here," Jules said. He hiccupped. "Right here." He giggled weakly. "I could have done it." And then his head dropped to his folded arms on the table.

Bell shook his head. "Will you have to carry him home?" he asked Ormerod.

"It will not be the first time." There was distaste in Ormerod's voice. "He was a charming page when I was senior squire at Lord Haricot's, although he was never much of a fighter." He shrugged. "But many are not and he was then as he is now, slight boned. Some gain heft over the years. Jules did not, but I was knighted and left Lord Haricot's service to oversee my father's lands before he was advanced to squire, so I do not know how he came to be knighted."

"He sounds as if he was a much indulged son. Perhaps his father . . ."

"Perhaps."

Ormerod's tone of voice did not encourage further talk on that subject and Bell said, "I assume either he was not here at all or he could not have killed St. Cyr despite his joy in the man's death?"

"He was here, all right, since I found him here." Ormerod's lips twisted. "That was one of the nights I had to tie him to his horse to get him home."

"And that night he was dressed as he is now?"

Ormerod's eyes narrowed. "Does it matter? I think he wore a mail shirt. His sister begged him to put it on when he said he would ride into Oxford after dinner. I urged it too, knowing he wished to warn St. Cyr away from Mistress Loveday." He stared at Bell for a moment and then went on hastily. "I could not *swear* he did not kill St. Cyr before I found him, but I cannot believe it. To speak the truth, I do not believe he has the courage even to creep up behind a man and stab him."

"Are you sure you want him for a brother-by-marriage?" Bell asked with raised brows.

Ormerod sighed. "No, but the girl is nothing like him, except in looks. She is sweet and modest, not stupid, and has a rich farm for dowery. My brother would be happy with her, I think." He sighed again. "Jules wants the marriage, but he cannot afford to part with the farm just now. He is arse over ears in debt."

"And marrying Mistress Loveday will cure that problem?"

"It would cure all of Jules's problems. She would pay off the debts, manage the property for him, and keep him on so tight a rein that he would have no chance to drink or to gamble." Ormerod laughed. "Of course, Jules doesn't realize the last is as true as the first."

"I am almost sorry there is no hope of it," Bell said. "Mistress

Loveday has long been betrothed to Niall Arvagh, William of
Ypres's man. Neither was in a hurry to marry so they made no
parade of the matter, but now that this trouble has begun,
Mistress Loveday has written a declaration of the betrothal to
the king and Niall is with her at Noke."

Ormerod stared at Bell, paling. "Betrothed?" he asked, and
when Bell nodded soberly, he snarled, "I thought Niall Arvagh
was only another suitor! Jules swore to me that once St. Cyr
was gone Mistress Loveday was his for the taking. He said
they were not wed only because he wished to keep his freedom." He swung a leg over the bench on which he had been
sitting and rose.

Bell looked up at him and raised a questioning brow.

"I am sorry for his sister," Ormerod said, pulling Sir Jules
roughly to his feet. His face was rigid with anger as he muttered, "And it may be that I have gone too far to go back." He
grimaced and shook the slight young man into a vague consciousness. "Mayhap I should leave him here. It would be a
good thing for poor Marguerite if an accident took him before
he got home."

Despite the words, Ormerod supported the staggering Sir
Jules out of the door. Bell sat a little longer, turning his ale
tankard between his hands. Then he got to his feet and started
down the street toward The Wheat Sheaf.

CHAPTER 12

23 June,
Soft Nest

Magdalene heard William shout for his men as the door closed, and she slid out of the bed at once. She was annoyed with herself as she hastily pulled her clothing back on. William had been more relaxed than usual, less brutal, less in a hurry. She could have enjoyed him honestly instead of feigning a satisfaction she had not felt, if she had not been so sure Bell would walk in on them.

The thought made her shudder and she turned to look at the bed. Before she considered what she was doing, she began to straighten the tumbled bedclothes, then stopped and drew back her hands. Perhaps she should leave the bed just as it was to make unmistakably clear that she and William had coupled. If Bell flew into a rage . . . but was that fair? She herself would not like to get into an unmade bed that had hosted other coupling bodies.

It was doubly unfair after Bell had made a noble gesture in buying all that food. Magdalene compromised by straightening the bedclothes so they did not shout of what had passed there, but she was uneasy about what she had done until her eyes noted William's purse lying on the table. What a fool she was to be wasting time worrying about what Bell would think and feel when she had a murder to solve and virtually no hope of doing it.

She bit her lip and took a deep breath. That was not true. Bell was out learning what he could, Bell . . . she jerked her mind away from him to William, who had reminded her that Florete had many of the opportunities to garner information in Oxford that Magdalene herself had in London. Not quite the same; Florete's clients did not have the kind of trust in her that Magdalene's did. They would not sit beside the fire with Florete and tell her all sorts of tales they should not, but men did talk to whores and what they said could be bought.

Magdalene took a half dozen silver pennies out of the purse William had left and dropped them into her pocket before she put the purse safely away. Then she covered the remaining food that needed to be protected, cleaned the bowls out of which she and William had eaten, and put their trenchers aside to carry to St. Friedesweide's for the beggars. Nothing now gave any obvious hint of the service she had done William. She wondered again if she should make the bed, and then whether she wanted to spare Bell pain or feared too much to lose her lover.

Such weakness was very wrong in her, putting another man's life at risk. Turning away from the bed, she went briskly to the door and out. The corridor was empty fortunately, and she made her way to where Florete sat.

"I need to talk," she said.

Florete frowned. "This is a busy time, and—"

As if to give proof of her words, an altercation broke out behind one of the curtained doorways. Florete cocked her head, listening, heard a smack of flesh against flesh, and said, "Rand, go see what that is."

He took his cudgel and rose, but Magdalene smiled at Florete. "There's no need for secrecy about this. We can talk right here, and there's money in it for you and possibly for your women."

"I always listen when money is mentioned," Florete said, smiling.

The man who had gone to the curtain where the argument was taking place had pulled it aside and stuck his head in. Magdalene did not hear what he said, but he pulled out a moment later, came back and sat down.

"Nothing," he said to Florete. "Hertha said it was all right. He's drunk and slapped a little too hard."

The other man laughed. "She'll make him pay for that."

Florete looked from the men to Magdalene, but Magdalene shook her head. "As I said, this is no secret. Your men are welcome to listen, and if they have information I will pay them as well as the women."

Both men made interested noises, and Magdalene smiled at them.

"I assume you all know about that clod St. Cyr being murdered and that Lord William of Ypres's man, Niall Arvagh, was accused of the crime," she continued. "Well, it turns out that Niall could not have done it. He has a dozen or more witnesses, including a priest, that he was more than a league distant that night. Unfortunately, for another reason entirely, Lord William was asking questions about St. Cyr and now there are whispers in the Court that he is somehow involved. Thus, Lord William wants the real killer discovered and exposed."

Florete began to shake her head as soon as Magdalene began her final sentence. "I myself will not bear false witness," she said. "No matter who I accuse will have friends and such a reputation—"

"No, no," Magdalene interrupted. "Neither William nor I is interested in simply accusing someone to make an innocent man seem guilty. It would never serve any purpose and, if the truth were exposed, it would make William's situation far worse. No. What I desire is that your men and your women keep their ears open for any mention of St. Cyr—not necessarily his murder, but anything about him—and bring me what they hear. I will pay for any news—" Magdalene's mouth twisted wryly "—any that I think is true and not made up for the purpose of chousing me of farthings—and that is all the pay will be for rumor and gossip, farthings. However, if what I am told leads to taking the killer, then I will pay what that news was worth to Lord William. And for your trouble and spreading the word among your women . . ."

Magdalene reached into her pocket and laid three of the silver pennies on the table before Florete and one each in front of each man. She warned them again about wanting to hear only information that seemed likely to be true. As she rose, Rand said, "When Florete went out to the privy there was one man who spoke of St. Cyr. It was while you were with Lord William."

She turned to him eagerly. "What did he say?"

"That he wanted to lie with the whore that St. Cyr usually used."

"Usually used?" Magdalene echoed, glancing at Florete. "But I thought the night that he accosted me was his first time here."

"Whatever gave you that idea?" Florete asked. "He was not

a regular client from Oxford, but he had been here before that night. He first came soon after Lord Waleran's men arrived. He was here . . ." She looked up at the ceiling, pursing her lips, thinking. "Oh, three or four times."

Magdalene shook her head. "How odd. I was sure he was a stranger." She shrugged. "Maybe because of the way he behaved." She turned back to Rand. "Did the man say why he wanted the woman St. Cyr had used?"

"Yes, but I'm not sure I believed it. He said he was St. Cyr's friend, and using his whore was like a farewell to him." He made a face.

"Oh. I remember him," the other man said. "It might even be true. He's a looby. He talks funny, like his tongue is too big for his mouth."

"Shut up, Ogden," Rand said. "It's my story."

Magdalene laughed. "No, Ogden, don't shut up. Tell what you remember and I'll pay you both." She laughed again. "It's Lord William's money and he can afford a couple of farthings."

"Got nothing more to say," Ogden admitted. "Rand asked the whores who were free which of them had served St. Cyr and I went to look in on the big room to be sure all was quiet."

"Do either of you remember which of the women it was?"

"Hertha," Rand said immediately. "When you started to ask about St. Cyr, I remembered."

Magdalene found two farthings for each man and passed them over. Probably it was too much, atop the penny she had already given them, but she wanted them alert to any new incident and trying to remember anything else from the past.

"Will it be all right for me to talk to Hertha when her man leaves?" Magdalene asked Florete.

"I'll see to it," Florete assured her, but this one is in for the night. You might as well go to bed yourself."

The words seemed to unlock Magdalene's tight-wound body, and fatigue flooded over her. It had been a long, long day, full of tension and anxiety. She put a hand on the table to steady herself, nodded at Florete, and then, suddenly, yawned.

"I'll do that," Magdalene agreed. "And don't wake Hertha especially early to talk to me."

"Should I turn your young man away?" Florete asked, then grinned and added, "Or offer him other entertainment to leave you in peace?"

For one moment Magdalene was so racked with jealousy that her voice failed. Then she managed to force a laugh. "No, send him in. We are old friends and my bed is as much to give him a lodging as to give him pleasure. He won't wake me if he finds me sound asleep."

Glad of the excuse Florete had inadvertently provided, Magdalene hurried to her chamber, closed the door carefully, and then rushed to the bed. As soon as she reached it and stretched a hand to straighten the bedclothes, she began to laugh and called herself ten times a fool. Loveday had wakened them at first light, they had ridden the distance to Noke, had an exciting discussion and a full meal, ridden back. She then had worried about reaching William, talked to Raoul de Samur, explained everything to William and coupled with him. Mary have mercy on her for an idiot. Why was she worrying about the state of the bed, when the most natural thing in the world would be for her to be in it and fast asleep when Bell arrived?

She continued yawning as she lit the night candle and then set a torchette near the door so that Bell would not run into the table, but she left the remainder of the food where it was. Bell would know William had come and had eaten; he could make what he wanted of that. As she had told him many times, what she did when he was not with her was none of his business.

24 June, the Soft Nest

Magdalene never learned whether Bell had even noticed the proof that William had been with her or how he had reacted to it, if he had noticed. In fact, she never knew when he arrived. Possibly she had been half aware of his joining her sometime during the night, but he had not tried to wake her to make love and she slept on, obscurely comforted by his warmth and solidity beside her, until she woke naturally and found him.

She lay for a very little while, enjoying his presence, thinking idly that what she felt was common to a wife in a happy marriage. But the word sent a faint chill through her, and she slid carefully out of the bed to be shocked by the angle of the sunshine through the window, which told her she had slept far into the morning. Then she shrugged, dropped the curtain behind her, sought the chamber pot, and used it.

Her unruly thoughts were not diverted by how long she had slept. What came to her mind as she pushed the chamber pot back under the bed was that there were far too few happy marriages. Her shift and undertunic lay on the chest near the wall, and she pulled them on, then turned to sit on the chest to put on her stockings.

Unwelcome memories came. Certainly there had been no

contentment in waking beside Brogan. For herself as a wife she remembered only her distaste, her care in moving away from him and escaping from the bed before he could notice her and use her to assuage his morning lust.

Was her satisfaction based on Bell himself or only because he was so responsive and considerate a lover? And would he remain responsive and considerate if she should become his wife? Magdalene snorted softly. Not likely. As long as she did not belong to him, he would try to keep her satisfied so she would not look abroad for other men. Once she was bound, why should he trouble himself?

Yet they had not made love in the night and the pleasure in his being beside her was just as strong. She sighed softly, slowly slipped on one shoe and then the other. There was no possibility of discovering any answer to her doubts. A whore cannot make a happy marriage. The room grew dim.

She rose from the chest laughing silently and took a heavy linen gown from a peg. Not sadness but a cloud covered the sun. The light from the window was now dull and gray and the room was damply cool. It would rain again, she thought, just as a soft rustle betrayed the movement of the bed curtains and Bell's voice asked, "Are my clothes dry? I was soaked coming here from the Carfax. What a downpour!"

"Dry enough to wear, but a bit rough and wrinkled. I see your head is all right this morning, so you did not drink too deep. Were you late last night? I was so tired from Loveday waking us at dawn and all that exercise and excitement about Niall that I went to sleep soon after dark."

He made no direct reply to that, but got out of bed and walked around it to use the chamber pot. Finished, he drew on chausses and braies but no shirt, saying he needed to wash.

His shoes were not yet dry and he grunted and let them sit, padding over to the table while he drew a twig from his purse and began to chew the end of it to clean his teeth. Magdalene nodded at his remark about washing and went out to find Diccon to bring in some water.

When he came with it, she bade him empty the chamber pot and the boy made a face, but took it and went out. She rather regretted having dressed so completely because she had not bathed or washed well for several days, but she had more important things to do than undress and set ideas into Bell's too easily inflamed mind. She made do with pushing up her sleeves and loosening her undertunic so she could wash face, neck, and arms.

Bell did a more thorough job, then pulled on his shirt and sat down at the table. As he reached for the leftover food, he said, "I learned some very interesting things yesterday."

Magdalene went to get two cups and what remained in the jack of ale. She filled the cups and sat down across the corner of the table from Bell.

"That's just as well. William has asked me to expose the killer if it is possible."

Bell frowned. "Why should he care? His man is well free and clear of any suspicion."

Magdalene's lips twisted. "Niall is not William's only man. The armorer's house, where his captains are lodged, is only across a back alley from The Wheat Sheaf. Any one of William's men could have lain in wait there unseen for St. Cyr to come out, gone with him to The Broached Barrel, and killed him. Worse yet, because he could not understand why Waleran should offer Loveday to such a man, William was asking questions in Court about St. Cyr."

Bell whistled softly between his teeth, took a swallow of the ale, and began to eat a chunk of the pasty. Magdalene pointed out that it was nearly time for dinner, but he shrugged and said he was hungry and that he would be able to eat dinner too. Then, dismissing the subject of food, he told her, "Then one of the things I learned is not so good. St. Cyr was killed by a man wearing mail, which might throw more suspicion on Lord William's men."

"How in the world did you discover that?"

So he told her about examining the corpse in the presence of the sheriff's deputy and the lack of interest the man had shown for discovering St. Cyr's killer.

"Then we can't look for much help from the sheriff," Magdalene said. "On the other hand, he is not likely to interfere against us, either—unless you think he was willing to accept Niall as guilty because he is Waleran's supporter?"

"Not that. From what Sir Rolf said, the sheriff only desires all of us to be gone: king, Lord Waleran, Lord William, and the whole Court. If he is any man's man, it is the bishop of Salisbury that holds his loyalty. Oh, Lord! I forgot. Salisbury will most likely be here today. The sheriff had gone out to meet him on his way from Malmsbury."

"There will be a lot of unhappy wager-makers," Magdalene said, grinning, but then she sighed. "There will also be trouble, Bell. I feel it in my bones and being a whoremistress has honed those bones into a sharp appreciation of trouble."

Bell nodded. "I think so too." He glanced out of the window into a gray dimness. "If the weather were bright and dry, it would matter less." He shrugged. "Well, it may be that Salisbury has sense enough to have his men pitch tents outside the walls. If so, all may still go well."

"William thinks Waleran and the king are looking for some cause of dissatisfaction."

"Likely he is right." Having finished the pasty, Bell fished a slice of roast pork out of the bottom of a bowl, where it had been kept soft in its own dripping. Folding it over and leaning well forward, so the meat would not drip on his shirt, he took a bite, saying indistinctly through the food, "I cannot see what I can do about it. And I must say that now I am glad Winchester did not come. He would have had to try to stop the king, which would just set him and Waleran more bitterly against each other. Maybe if he is not involved at this time he can mend matters later."

Magdalene had torn a chunk of bread from the half loaf left and was scooping cold stew out of the chamber pot and eating it. Bell stared at the pot for a moment and then began to laugh.

"Well," she said, trying to sound indignant, "Florete has no kitchen as we do at the Old Priory Guesthouse. I had to take what basins and bowls were available, and nothing was large enough for the amount of stew you sent, except this."

"I hope it was well cleaned," Bell said, still laughing, but he broke off some of the bread and also helped himself to the stew. Abruptly, as some thought came to him, he stopped laughing and began to frown, but after a few moments he shook his head and said, "No one I can reach knows what is being planned. Some time today I must ride out to Wytham Abbey and warn the dean, but there is no urgency in it. He knows without my telling. And mayhap I *can* do something about St. Cyr's death. I traced his movements that last night and discovered a number of men with whom he spent time."

He explained about meeting Lord Ormerod and Sir Jules in The Broached Barrel and repeated what Ormerod had said. "So

Jules was wearing mail because his sister insisted." He stopped speaking and cocked his head. "I wonder if Ormerod was mail-clad too—he didn't say." He shook his head and continued with what he had been saying. "As for Jules, I am not sure he is strong enough to have made the marks on St. Cyr's neck and chin, but some who look slight have a wiry strength. Later, I learned he had already quarreled with St. Cyr."

"In The Broached Barrel? But I thought—"

"No. That was in The Wheat Sheaf, but I am giving you his movements backward. Let me tell you of the day in order. St. Cyr seems to have been on duty in the morning; he was one of the men guarding Lord Waleran's lodging. And by the by, Lord Waleran is not lodged in the castle like Lord William."

"Now *that* is strange," Magdalene muttered. "Why is he willing to allow William to be closer to the king than he?"

"Because he and the king are agreed on something he must do in greater private than he can find in the castle," Bell said with a grimace. "I would give a great deal to be a fly on the wall in that house." He sighed. "However, to get back to St. Cyr. He ate with the other men, and Jean Kaleau, with whom I spoke at The Lively Hop, said he was in remarkably good spirits for a man who had been soundly beaten the previous day and lost a chance at a rich marriage."

"Ah, but did he believe he had lost it? Had he been assured that a lost forged betrothal agreement could be forged again? I am sure he told whoever made the arrangement that he had lost the document. But it is not really so easy to forge such a parchment. And likely that person feared he would be forever at St. Cyr's beck and call. Would he not agree to do as St. Cyr wanted and later kill him?"

"So I think also, but Jean Kaleau certainly has neither the

wealth nor the influence to provide such a document. I think we can exonerate all Waleran's men-at-arms on the same grounds."

"The captains too?"

Bell sighed. "I think so," he said slowly. "You must remember that his own captain, Raoul de Samur, did not speak well of him. But he spoke with contempt, not fear or hatred, and the others I spoke to in the alehouses did not seem to know St. Cyr at all."

Magdalene nodded acceptance, and Bell continued, "After the meal he seems to have disappeared for some hours, but he must have been somewhere around the lodging because he was later seen leaving it with Manville d'Arras, the man who accused Niall. They went to a cookshop between The Lively Hop and The Wheat Sheaf and they ate there. I spoke to the cook, who said that they seemed to be on good terms."

"Probably they were. Did not Giles, or maybe one of William's other men, say that this Manville was distraught when he brought his accusation?" She shook her head. "A looby and a cur . . . appropriate friends."

"A looby?" Bell frowned. "Yes, come to think of it, Sir Rolf called Niall's accuser a lunatic. Possibly St. Cyr could only take so much of his company. The cook said they went out together but I know they must have soon parted because St. Cyr appeared in The Lively Hop alone and it is only a few steps away. There he went to drink with two men, also from one of Lord Waleran's troops—Jean Kaleau, from whom I learned what St. Cyr was doing earlier in the day, and another, Peter Arnason, with whom I have not yet spoken."

"Since they are unlikely to have killed him—I imagine neither has a mail shirt or the influence St. Cyr wanted—you can leave Arnason to himself for a while."

"Well, the next man is not likely to have a mail shirt either, but he did approach St. Cyr and offer to pay for his ale. They spoke together for some time, St. Cyr laughing and sneering and the other growing more and more withdrawn or angry until, at last, he pushed his cup of ale away and left the ale-house scowling."

"Why do you say he is unlikely to have a mail shirt?"

"Oh, sorry. Because the landlord of The Lively Hop was sure he was a merchant, both by his dress and by some words he heard spoken between him and a mercer from farther along the market. However, it was a busy time and the landlord was not paying much attention. Maybe we can learn more from the girl who served them."

"I'll do that," Magdalene offered.

Bell looked at her and smiled slowly, and she shook her head at him and laughed.

"No love, I'm not trying to keep you away from other women. I just think I'm better at extracting information from them than a man would be." But even as she said it, she wondered how true it was. An alehouse server often served more than ale and would certainly try to win a few more farthings from a handsome young man who questioned her.

Bell sighed as if his heart was broken, made his eyes large and sorrowful, and said, "And I thought you were trying to protect me from evil influences."

"You are too far gone for that!" Magdalene snapped, and then giggled. "Did St. Cyr leave then?"

"No, there was one more man he spoke with—off in a corner. The landlord said the other man was richly dressed and

wore no house badge. An independent lord, like Ormerod perhaps? We will need to get more information from the server
about that. All the landlord could tell me was that they seemed
in close agreement, and that St. Cyr left with him."

"That sounds almost as if we have found a good suspect.
Did the landlord know whether the man wore mail? And they
left together. He could have killed St. Cyr then or walked him
to The Broached Barrel—"

"No. He certainly didn't kill St. Cyr because St. Cyr appeared in The Wheat Sheaf not long after, safe and sound. But
if that man is one of the two Samur mentioned, and he is
lodged with Alain of Brittany, he could have gone to his lodging, put on mail, and caught St. Cyr before he came out of
The Wheat Sheaf because St. Cyr was there for some time."

"Ah, yes. You said he met Sir Jules there and they quarreled?"

"I am not sure quarrel is the right world. It seems as if St.
Cyr came into some money between the time he left the well-
dressed man from The Lively Hop and the time he entered
The Wheat Sheaf. It's impossible to be certain, of course, but
I got the feeling that more time passed between St. Cyr leaving
the Lively Hop and his entering the Wheat Sheaf than he
would have taken to walk from one to the other. I think he
and his well-dressed companion stood and talked for a while,
and the companion gave St. Cyr money."

Magdalene cocked her head looking puzzled, but then nodded with satisfaction. "Yes, because St. Cyr was looking for
others to buy his ale at The Lively Hop but offered a round
to the house soon after he came into The Wheat Sheaf."

"Right. And that is when he and Sir Jules had a difference
of opinion. It seems that Sir Jules took the cup, but when St.

Cyr said he wished to drink to his coming marriage to Mistress Loveday of Otmoor, Sir Jules poured the ale on the floor, said he'd see St. Cyr dead first, and rushed out of the place."

"Hmmm. I am surprised that St. Cyr did not react to that. I wonder—"

She stopped and turned her head to the door as someone scratched at it. A moment later Giles de Milland's voice called, "Magdalene, may I come in?"

"Yes, come," she responded.

He came in and shut the door, but did not advance toward the table. "Only a message," he said. "Lord William would like you to ride out to Noke and tell Niall to return to Oxford by midmorning tomorrow, bringing the documents that clear him of murder."

"Is Lord William suddenly so short of men that he cannot find a messenger to send?" Bell asked sharply. "It is dangerous for a woman alone to ride abroad with so many men-at-arms wandering loose."

Giles grinned. "Lord William said that he was sure Magdalene could find a Churchly escort. He does not want to send any of his own people because he desires no connection with Noke or Loveday of Otmoor until the matter of the accusation against Niall is settled."

"Do not be so silly, Bell," Magdalene said. "William does not take me for a fool and he knows I would find some escort through Florete if it was impossible for you to accompany me. He would make good the price of the escort, too. Is there anything else, Giles?"

"Lord William says it seems certain that Salisbury will arrive some time today and present himself to the king either at or after dinner. Lord William wants to see how that goes but thinks the first meeting will go well. He wants to clear Niall of suspicion in St. Cyr's death before dinner tomorrow." He shrugged and grimaced. "Before anything happens that will draw attention away from Lord William's proof of innocence and the false accusation of his man."

Bell raised his brows. "A very good sense of timing. I hope everything moves according to Lord William's plan."

"Good planning makes for less hoping," Giles said and lifted a hand in farewell.

CHAPTER 13

23 June,
Cornmarket

Sir Giles went out and Bell and Magdalene looked at each other in silence for a moment. Then Magdalene said, "If you want to be here in Oxford so you can report to the dean about the first meeting between Salisbury and the king, I can hire—"

"No, there are half a dozen young priests and several friars, all of whom have no connection to Winchester who will gladly carry the news. In fact, the dean insisted that I be at Wytham Abbey when Salisbury arrives so it cannot be said that I went to greet him or to bring him any message. I'll ride out to Noke with you."

"Yes, but not immediately," Magdalene said. "Niall doesn't need to be in Oxford until tomorrow morning so we can have dinner first and talk to the serving people in the alehouses. No, let's talk to them right away, before dinner. The morning should be a quieter time for them, and we've just broken our fast so we can eat later."

Bell finished his ale and agreed, but before they could decide whether to take cloaks in case it began to rain, there was a second scratch on the door.

"Who?" Magdalene called.

"Hertha. Florete said you wanted to talk to me."

"Hertha . . ." Magdalene muttered, trying to remember, and then, gesturing at Bell to make himself less in evidence, "Oh, yes. Come in Hertha." And when the door opened, Magdalene asked, "You are the woman who lay with the man asking for Aimery St. Cyr's woman?"

"I was not that, thank God, but he did lie with me twice, complaining bitterly about the price and demanding I suck his filthy rod and stick my fingers in . . ." Her lips turned down. "He stank, too. I told Florete that I would not take him again. Oh, was that why he made trouble for you? I am sorry, but—"

"No, no. It is nothing to do with that. You know St. Cyr was murdered?" Hertha nodded and Magdalene continued, "Someone I know might be blamed for the murder so I am trying to find out who was truly guilty. I just wanted to know why St. Cyr's friend wished to be with St. Cyr's woman."

Hertha frowned. "I didn't know you would be interested, so to tell the truth I didn't listen. It's boring enough to have to lie there with some fool pounding away on you; listening to what they say is too much. And that one! He was the stupidest man I've ever had. I mean, they're all stupid, but this one could hardly talk."

Hertha was not a whore who would ever make more than a penny, Magdalene thought, and as soon as she lost her looks she would be in the farthing room. She was pretty now and clean enough, but plainly she never tried to make a man feel welcome and important. That was what brought a client back, what drew from him an extra coin. Magdalene suddenly had to bite her lip to cover a bitter smile. There was something to be said for the painful way she had learned to please Brogan;

that training plus her beauty had made her a very successful whore.

She took a farthing from her purse and showed it in her open palm. "Do you remember anything about St. Cyr?"

"I remember that St. Cyr told me not to worry about his being married—as if losing him as a customer would worry me. He said he'd be a better client than ever because he'd have more money to spend. I was annoyed so I asked him what if I told his future wife, and he said it didn't matter. He had a highborn friend who would arrange that the girl be betrothed and married to him, will she nill she." Hertha was silent for a moment and then said, "If I'd thought she'd listen to me, I'd've warned her."

"She knew. She was in hiding from him." Magdalene put the farthing in Hertha's hand. "The man who wanted to lie with you in St. Cyr's name, can you guess whether he was glad or sorry about St. Cyr's death?"

"Oh, I think he was sorry about that . . . which was another reason I thought him addle-witted. He cried when he talked about St. Cyr, only he called him Aimery. Said he knew him for years, that he taught Aimery to fight, but Aimery—he called him something else then, too—Carl, I think. Anyway, it was Aimery who got him a place in Lord Waleran's troop, which was better pay and less real work than what he'd been doing before."

"Cried, did he? But for grief or guilt, Hertha?"

The woman thought for a moment and then said, "It's hard to believe, but real grief, I think. He said he asked for me because he was Aimery's heir so it was right he should use me instead of his usual girl." She shook her head. "Stupid."

Magdalene laughed but gave Hertha another farthing. "I

doubt it means anything, but I'm glad to know St. Cyr had an heir. It wouldn't be the first time an heir collected a bit early . . . and even felt bad about collecting."

Hertha took the second farthing. "Not this one, I think. I don't know why but I . . . I almost liked him."

"I have a feeling you're right about him, but if you remember anything else either that St. Cyr said or this other man, come and tell me. I don't promise to pay, but if what you say is worth thinking about, I will."

When the woman was gone, Bell came around from the hidden side of the bed where he had been sitting quietly on Magdalene's clothing chest. "Manville d'Arras?" he asked.

"It must be," Magdalene agreed. "I wonder if we will find him in any of the alehouses? I would like very much to talk to him, but not quite enough to go to Waleran's barracks and ask for him."

Bell nodded agreement, glanced out the window again and took his cloak, which he had left hanging with Magdalene's when he rushed out in a rage the previous afternoon. Magdalene followed his lead and they went out, deciding as they walked toward the Carfax to reverse Bell's order of investigation and start with The Lively Hop. They were just about to go in the door, when Magdalene, glancing idly down the street, saw Sir Ferrau in the cookshop where Diccon usually bought food for the women of the Soft Nest.

"Lord have mercy," she said to Bell. "There's Sir Ferrau at the cookshop. Did I tell you about his asking me to get the purse Niall cut from St. Cyr's belt?"

"Of course. Loveday maneuvered me into saying I would fetch it, but it went right out of my head when we all decided to ride to Noke to discover what had happened to Niall. And then in the excitement of learning that Niall was innocent, I forgot all about it while we were there."

"Me too," Magdalene admitted. "And I don't suppose it matters any more, since St. Cyr is dead and can't bring any complaint. Still, I did say I would try to get it for Sir Ferrau, so I suppose I should step over there and ask him if he still wants it."

She had no chance to do that, nor any doubt about the answer to her question because as soon as they started in his direction, Sir Ferrau noticed them, stood up, and met them halfway.

"Have you brought the purse?" he asked eagerly.

"No," Magdalene replied, feeling considerably surprised by his eagerness. "I am sorry, but after I heard St. Cyr was dead and could make no complaint to Lord Waleran or anyone else, I am afraid I put it out of my mind. I did go to Noke, but I forgot to ask for it."

"Good Lord," Ferrau said, looking quite put out. "I must have it!"

"But why do you want the purse of a common man-at-arms?" Bell asked.

Ferrau made an ugly grimace. "I have no idea," he admitted. "Count Alain wants it and charged me with the duty of retrieving it. How am I to do that now? I cannot ride out to Noke and ask for it. For one thing, I do not know where the accursed place is, and for another I greatly fear that Sir Niall will deny ever taking the purse if I ask for it."

"But surely now that St. Cyr is dead—" Bell began, then hesitated and asked, "Are you sure Count Alain knows the man is dead?"

"Oh yes," Ferrau said bitterly. "When he sent for me this

morning and asked for the purse, I immediately told him that St. Cyr was dead and would make no trouble." He shrugged. "If he heard me, he gave no sign of it, merely asked again when I would have the purse." He grimaced again. "One does not ask questions of Count Alain."

"It is possible," Magdalene put in, "that it is the pound of silver in the purse that Count Alain wants." But a small smile curved the corners of her lips upward and inner laughter lightened her misty blue eyes almost to silver.

Bell looked astounded. "Pound of silver? Where would St. Cyr have come by a pound in silver? I heard the captain of his troop say he knew him unable to pay for—for something he wanted badly."

Magdalene now had control of her mouth, but her eyes were still bright with amusement. "It does not matter," she said. "I believe the money now belongs to Manville d'Arras."

"Manville d'Arras?" Ferrau repeated. "Who is that, and why should the contents of St. Cyr's purse belong to him?"

"I am not certain, but a whore in the Soft Nest with whom this Manville lay told me that he told her that he was St. Cyr's heir." Magdalene laughed and shook her head. "He is not a very clever man, this Arras. He seemed to think that he had inherited St. Cyr's whore with the rest of his goods. She was quite annoyed, not having been particularly fond of St. Cyr."

"Who can believe the word of a whore!" Ferrau exclaimed, and then drew a sharp breath, recalling to whom he was talking, and made a gesture of apology.

"What you say may be true," Magdalene replied calmly, nodding acceptance of the apology, "but usually even a whore needs a reason to tell a lie, and I cannot imagine why she should lie over something so silly."

"In any case," Bell said, his voice a good deal colder than Magdalene's had been, "we will need to determine whether the whore spoke the truth and Arras is truly St. Cyr's heir—I mean legally—before we hand over this purse. If Arras is St. Cyr's legal heir, there can be no contest; the purse and its contents belong to him."

"A common man-at-arms . . ." Ferrau's mouth turned down. "His claim cannot come before that of Count Alain of Brittany, legal or not. If you will get the purse for me, Count Alain will make all smooth, I am sure . . . unless, does this Manville d'Arras know the contents of the purse?"

Magdalene shrugged. "I don't know. He didn't say anything about that to the whore . . . or, wait, perhaps he did hint that he would have more money in the future? No, that was what St. Cyr said to her, and he was referring to his marriage to Loveday, not to the contents of his purse."

"Look," Sir Ferrau said, appealing to Bell, "my master wants that purse. I have not the faintest notion why. But if I obtain it, I will have his favor; if I do not he might even turn me away. He is not the easiest master in the world, but there are many advantages to serving him. For old times' sake . . ."

Bell got a funny look on his face, but then nodded. "I cannot promise that the silver will still be in the purse. Niall would not have touched it, but who knows what has happened since he took it or before he took it? But he is coming to Oxford early tomorrow and we can ask him to bring the purse. Once it is here, we can determine the rightful owner. Likely Arras would be willing enough to let Count Alain have it if you, as the count's representative and St. Cyr's friend, asked him for it."

"Good God, don't call me St. Cyr's friend. I am almost grate-

ful to whoever did away with him! He was nothing but trouble."

Bell grinned. "However did you come to know the man?"

Ferrau sighed. "I knew him in the village from which I came,
oh, years ago. He used to deliver . . . I forget what to the
manor house. He was some tradesman's son. He remembered
me, accosted me. I saw that he had been beaten and, fool that
I was, I was sorry for him. I bought him a drink." He shook
his head. "If I had known the trouble that one drink would
cause me, I would have stuck a knife in him then and there
and saved his murderer the trouble." He shrugged. "In any case,
I will thank you for the purse if you can get it for me." He
sighed again, smiled weakly, and added, "I had better finish
my dinner before the cook takes it away."

Magdalene and Bell turned back toward the Lively Hop, but
when they were out of earshot, just before they entered the
alehouse, Bell asked, "What the devil were you grinning about
when you said Count Alain might want the pound of silver? A
pound of silver is no light thing, even to a man of the count's
wealth."

"I wasn't grinning," Magdalene said, now smiling broadly.
"And it's quite true that a pound is a pound's worth even to a
man like Count Alain, but I do not think it is equal in weight
to his dignity, and that is what the contents of the purse might
cost him."

"What is that supposed to mean?"

"The forged betrothal, Bell, the forged betrothal. Is it not
possible that that pound in silver paid for Count Alain's name
on that document? Remember Gervase de Genlis?"

Bell, who had been about to step in the door of the alehouse, stopped and stared down at Magdalene. Gervase de

Genlis had been the father of Mainard the Saddler's first wife
Bertrild. In the course of discovering who had murdered her,
Bell and Magdalene had discovered that Gervase had, for a
price, witnessed many false documents—and then blackmailed
their owners.

"But Gervase was in every way the scum of the earth," he
said. "Count Alain—"

"Not scum. Say rather the cream above the milk. But do you
think he cares any more for the rights of others than Gervase
did? His wealth is great, but the expense at which he lives for
pride's sake might put a strain even on his income. Who knows
whether he has added to that income now and again by wit-
nessing a document or two that . . . ah . . . he had no way of
knowing was not perfectly legitimate?"

Magdalene was grinning again, but Bell was not. He drew
her to the side where a bench flanked the open door and
signed her to sit, sitting beside her. "If it is so," he said softly,
"the document in that purse is more dangerous than the charge
of a full battle of armed knights. Can you not imagine what a
man of such pride will do to prevent such an exposure? When
we go to Noke, we must examine the forged betrothal and if
his name appears, we must deface the document so that Loveday's name and her properties are no longer listed on it. Then
it must be returned."

Magdalene wrinkled her nose but then sighed and nodded.
"Yes," she agreed, "but not until William sees it."

"Good God, no!" Bell exclaimed, voice still not above a murmur but eyes wide with horror. "The trail from Lord William
to you is far too short."

"Oh, William would not use the knowledge—without proof
it would be far too dangerous and blacken his name as much

as the count's. It is only for his delectation and amusement. He is so irritated by the way Count Alain and Lord Hervey have their noses in the air. It would be a little warm hearth inside him whenever he must suffer their cold courtesy."

"You will tell him no matter what I say, I suppose." Bell's voice grated. "Despite how well you know him. Despite knowing that if it suits his purposes, he will use the knowledge no matter what the danger to you."

"Why should Count Alain even think of me? It was Niall who took the purse. It was Niall's betrothed who was threatened by the false document. Niall is William's man. Surely it will be assumed that Niall told William, even that he offered him the document, and William magnanimously returned it to Count Alain." She fell silent, then hmmm'd and nodded. "Is that not a good thought?"

"Count Alain will think of you because Ferrau will tell him that you were supposed to get the purse for him and instead you passed it to Lord William," Bell said, lips tight.

Magdalene laughed shortly. "Oh, but if William gives Count Alain the document, Ferrau will not come into it at all, and even if Count Alain asks why the document fell into William's hands, do you think Ferrau will admit he asked a whore to get it for him? He will likely say that Niall had sent the purse to William before he was ordered to retrieve it. That will save him from blame as much as he can be saved."

Bell sighed. "I am not overmuch concerned about saving Ferrau from blame. I would not wish to do him harm—he did me a good turn when he forced reality into my dreams—but he is skilled at looking out for himself, and lucky, too. Fortune smiled on him with an offer from Count Alain just before turmoil broke out in Lord Sutton's household. Not that Ferrau was suspected of being in any way involved with the death of Sutton's daughter, but Count Alain would not have touched a man who came from a household in which murder had been done."

"That tale touches so many that are connected to this business about Loveday," Magdalene said thoughtfully. "Lord Ormerod was to be betrothed to Lord Sutton's daughter. Sir Jules was a long-time playmate. Sir Ferrau knew her as the daughter of his overlord. Did you know her too, Bell?"

"I must have, but I have no memory of the girl . . . Well, maybe a dim memory of *a* girl. I went to Culham a few times and Lord Sutton may have brought her with him to the abbey. But I was not of an age to be interested in girls—"

"Oh you liar!" Magdalene laughed. "At twelve? thirteen? I cannot believe you were still innocent."

Bell laughed too. "Well, I was, cloistered as I was in the abbey. Maybe I had some dreams, but they would not have been of a girl near my own age. If I dreamt, it was of full-breasted, full-hipped women. Come to think of it one of the dairy maids who collected milk from the abbey's herd . . ."

Magdalene poked him hard in the ribs and rose, still laughing. He got up too and followed her into the alehouse. There she patted him on the shoulder and walked away to a table in a corner while Bell walked up to the broached tun where the landlord sat. He paid for a mug of ale, shook his head at the landlord's glance toward Magdalene, and took his drink to the other side of the alehouse where he too sat down with his back to the wall.

Meanwhile Magdalene had beckoned to a serving girl, who cast a quick glance at Bell and came to Magdalene with a definite flounce to her step.

"Too cheap to buy you a drink?" she said to Magdalene in English.

"No," Magdalene replied in the same language. "I told him to go away. We are old friends." She took a farthing from her purse and laid it on the bench beside her. "You can bring me a small ale, but I have come to ask questions about a man called Aimery St. Cyr—"

"He was the one who was murdered some days ago," the girl said, beginning to back away. "That was at The Broached Barrel. We at The Lively Hop have nothing to do with that. We don't know anything about the killing."

Magdalene pushed the farthing a little closer to where the girl was standing. "No one thinks you have anything to do with St. Cyr's death. Indeed, Bell—" she gestured with her head at Bell, who was talking to the only male server in the alehouse "—has already discovered that St. Cyr was killed by a man wearing mail." She smiled at the girl. "I doubt if you could even carry a chain-mail shirt, much less wear it."

The girl giggled faintly and came closer again. She looked down at the farthing. "No one in this place has a mail shirt or has ever worn one."

"I believe that, my dear." Magdalene looked around but she and Bell and one old man, close to where the landlord sat, were the only ones in the alehouse. "I see that you are not busy now, so will you not sit down with me, perhaps share a cup of ale or of wine if you are permitted, and answer my questions? I promise they will not be about any who work in The Lively Hop."

"Oh, well, in that case . . ." The girl went to get the drinks, said a few words to the landlord, and returned to seat herself beside Magdalene on the bench, but on the side where the farthing lay.

Magdalene began by asking the girl's name, and when she was told it was Mayde, went on to describe St. Cyr with his greasy black hair, bruised eye, cut and swollen mouth, and slurred speech. The girl nodded and said she knew him, and that he had been a frequent visitor since early in June when Lord Waleran had arrived in Oxford.

"The landlord told Bell that St. Cyr was here on the night that he died," Magdalene said, watching with satisfaction as Mayde relaxed even more; clearly as if the girl had said it, Magdalene understood Mayde thought that if the landlord had already spoken to Bell about St. Cyr, she would not be blamed for doing the same. "I want to know to whom St. Cyr spoke and, if you know it, I would pay to know what they said to each other."

Mayde frowned. "He was here quite a while. Thomas there—" she gestured with her head to the server to whom Bell was speaking "—was serving the two men he was sitting with. He knew them well. He often drank with them, but I'm not sure he had a drink in hand that night. I think those men were from his troop."

That accorded well with the assumption that St. Cyr had little or no money until later, when he appeared in The Wheat Sheaf. Magdalene nodded. "They were. Bell has already spoken to one of them." She smiled at the girl, and pushed the farthing a little closer to her, but kept a finger on it.

"I don't know what they said to each other," Mayde said, rather resentfully, thinking the farthing might be withheld and she would have done better to make something up. Then, how-ever, she relaxed into a smile because Magdalene pushed the farthing right up to her and removed her finger from it.

"I want the truth," Magdalene said, "even if it tells me nothing." She took another farthing from her purse.

Mayde nodded with enthusiasm. "What I saw was after a while, a well-dressed fellow—dark, sober clothes, like a merchant—went over there and tapped St. Cyr on the shoulder. St. Cyr got up and walked away with the merchant-looking man and he called to me and told me to bring ale for both of them. I didn't hear what they said at first because I had to get the drinks, but when I came back, the merchant man was looking black as a summer storm, and St. Cyr was laughing and saying something about his being a fool if he thought women didn't need to be well-schooled. I heard the merchant man say he had hoped for better. Then I was called away and the next I knew the merchant man had pushed his ale aside and jumped up with a raised fist. Thomas came running over because he looked as if he were going to hit St. Cyr, but then he just turned his back and went out. Looked to me as if he was going to cry."

Magdalene handed over the second farthing.

The girl took it and then shrugged. "That's all I know. St. Cyr sat there for a while, laughing to himself. He finished his ale and the merchant man's too, but he didn't call me to bring any more and after a while I stopped looking over at him. Later, though, I saw he was gone from that place and wondered if he'd left. He—" she made a moue of distaste "—sometimes wanted to go out in the back with me, and he liked to hit. So I was glad he was gone, and when I saw him with the other man, I let Mary bring him an ale."

"Did you see the other man?"

Mayde shook her head reluctantly. "Not really. It was so

dark there, I wouldn't have noticed St. Cyr, except his face was so broken. Maybe Mary could tell you more."

"Send her over if you will," Magdalene said, and gave Mayde a third farthing. "This is for thinking and for telling the truth. If you remember anything more, or if something happens among any of the men you saw with St. Cyr, you can find me at the Soft Nest. I am renting the back room there; I do not work in the house. My name is Magdalene."

After Mayde's bright interest, Mary was a sad disappointment. She was an older woman, much harder, her skimpy hair wound into a tight knot, her lips thin and downturned, and her eyes dull. When Magdalene made the same advances to her that she had to Mayde, the woman snatched at the farthing and shook her head.

"Didn't know 'em, either on 'em," she said. "Didn' hear nothin' neither. Who looks at 'em anyway?"

A second farthing, this one displayed briefly and then held in Magdalene's closed fist, elicited a little more information. When reminded, Mary recalled St. Cyr's bruised face and the fact that the man with him had his hair cut shorter in the back than at the sides. The color? "Not blond," Mary said at once and then shook her head and insisted it was too dark to see more; perhaps his hair had been brown. A knight's cut, Magdalene thought with a stir of excitement.

Unfortunately that was the end of Mary's information. First she could remember nothing about the man's face, and then when Magdalene handed over the second farthing, she remembered quite well far too much. Magdalene discounted nearly everything she said, except that the man's clothing had been very fine, rich even. That went with the haircut of a man who wore a knight's helm and if the clothing were rich . . . Magdalene wondered if St. Cyr's companion could have been more than one of the hired knights, like one of Waleran's captains. Perhaps he was a landed knight, even a baron.

She also found herself believing it when Mary said neither man had raised his voice and they seemed to be dealing amicably together. One thing more might have been true: Mary claimed she heard St. Cyr laugh and thank the other man for his generosity. So was the richly dressed man the one who had given St. Cyr money? If Mary was right, he did not seem to mind. Then, Mary said, they were gone. She had served someone else and when she looked back both men had left. Possibly together. But Magdalene asked for no speculations on Mary's part, offered no more money, and when Bell glanced her way, she waved Mary away and got up to join him.

They walked slowly to The Wheat Sheaf, exchanging information, not that Bell had much more to tell than he had told her that morning. Thomas, the server, had confirmed what he and Magdalene suspected, that St. Cyr, having lost his purse and whatever was in it, had no money and his troop companions, knowing him too well, had declined to pay for his ale.

"But that means," Magdalene said, "that he had only the ale the merchant bought him—if he was a merchant. Bell, I wonder if that was Tirell Hardel. Remember, I told you what I overheard when Loveday and I were in the cookshop. But that was before St. Cyr was killed . . . No. It was just after we *knew* he was dead." She hesitated, then added, "Good God, could it have been Tirell that killed him? He did say something about having taken care of the matter he and his father had discussed. That it was done. Over."

"Done. Over. That *could* have referred to killing St. Cyr. To take him from behind would not take any armed skill, but this

Tirell Hardel was not wearing mail and I doubt would have a way to borrow a mail shirt."

"And he said he was sick at heart over what he had done." Magdalene frowned. "Is there nothing else that could have made the marks you saw on St. Cyr?"

Bell shrugged. "I don't—" he began, then stopped in his tracks and stared into space. "Net," he said. "A small-mesh net. I remember when I sailed as a merchant's mercenary I saw nets like that. But I would think the marks on St. Cyr would not be so sharp and clear if they were made by cord. And where or why would a wool merchant be carrying . . ."

"A cargo net?" Magdalene suggested. "A strange thing for a man to carry about, and he did not have it with him in the alehouse, but perhaps he went somewhere to get it. The merchant-looking man left The Lively Hop quite a time before St. Cyr left."

"Not a cargo net," Bell said slowly. "Those are thick rope with large holes, but a kind of mesh bag for smaller, more valuable items."

"And a merchant might well use something like that to carry things on a journey," Magdalene remarked, "but I cannot see how he could use it in killing a man."

Bell slowly shook his head. "Nor me neither. But of course, I think of killing in terms of ordinary weapons, a knife, a sword, because I am trained in their use. If I were not a fighter . . ."

"Well, well, let us not hang the man on the grounds of a few words overheard. It *might* have been something else he meant. After all, is it likely that Reinhart Hardel would have been discussing murder with his son?"

Bell chuckled. "Is it? You must know Reinhart better than I. Since he seems to have known you, doubtless he is a client. I don't think he has ever dealt with the bishop, so likely I've never met the man."

Magdalene flicked her fingers at him in amused irritation, and since they were near The Wheat Sheaf's door and the subject was hardly important, Bell abandoned it. They were not as lucky in The Wheat Sheaf as they had been in The Lively Hop; early diners were coming in with their bread, cheese, and slabs of meat or bowls of stew or soup from the cookshops to eat with their ale, and others were fetching ale from the landlord to take out to the cookshops with them. Still, a silver penny that Magdalene held between her fingers induced the landlord to invite her to stand beside him and to talk to her between customers.

He remembered St. Cyr and that night clearly because of the murder and because Bell had already questioned him, and he repeated the tale of St. Cyr buying a round of drinks for the entire house—and said that would have been unusual enough to stick in his mind even if St. Cyr had not been killed. And, yes, St. Cyr had said the largesse was to salute his new prosperity in finding a most generous friend and as the husband of an heiress, Loveday of Otmoor. At which point Jules of Osney being, as he often was, well-watered, stood up and said . . .

The landlord paused to pour a jack and a tankard full of ale; when he turned back to Magdalene he added that Sir Jules had dumped his ale on the floor and swore that he'd see St. Cyr dead before he'd let him have Loveday.

"A real threat?" Magdalene asked. "After all, St. Cyr did die."

"*Eech!*" The landlord sounded disgusted. "Even with St. Cyr dead, I never gave Sir Jules a second thought. Pot-valiant, that one. He was always saying . . ." His voice drifted off, and then he added, "Now that's queer."

"What is?" Magdalene urged. "I don't care if it doesn't seem to have anything to do with St. Cyr."

"Well, it doesn't. It has to do with Sir Jules. His sister often sent a servant to watch him and help him home, but this last few days he's been with a well-dressed man, a knight or maybe even a lord. He don't mix much, sits quiet with his wine unless Sir Jules starts to make trouble, and then he takes him away. But that night, he didn't."

Lord Ormerod, Magdalene thought, but she didn't say his name, only asked, "Didn't take Sir Jules away? Didn't come with him?"

"Didn't take him away. He came in with him . . . I *think* he did. But he didn't try to stop Sir Jules pouring out his ale or yelling insults at St. Cyr. It was my server who urged Sir Jules out the door."

"Could Sir Jules's companion have been at the privy?"

The landlord shrugged. "Wouldn't he have come in and asked for St. Jules if he'd been at the necessary?"

"Likely," Magdalene agreed. "And that was the end of it, when your server got Sir Jules out of the house?"

"Yea, it was, for a miracle. When Sir Jules spilled the ale and said he'd not see Mistress Loveday married to a cur like St. Cyr, I thought St. Cyr would go for him. He was a nasty drunk and strong with it. My server was looking for his cudgel. But St. Cyr wasn't drunk. Oh, he'd had a few ales from the smell of him, but he only laughed at Sir Jules and called him a little crowing cock. Anyway, after that St. Cyr went round the place having a few words with this one and that one and a couple of more drinks. But from what I heard he was only getting good wishes, and then he went out."

"Was he befuddled enough to have invited a footpad to attack him?"

"Nay. He wasn't unsteady on his feet nor fumbling. I don't think he was drunk, and he said he was going to meet a friend."

"At The Broached Barrel?" Magdalene asked.

The landlord shrugged. "Didn't say that."

CHAPTER 14

Magdalene handed over the penny and thanked the landlord, who she was pretty sure had told the truth. On the way
to The Broached Barrel, Bell agreed. He had spoken to the
server—in between customers—and got about the same story
except that the server had not noticed Lord Ormerod's presence or absence, but it was more the landlord's business to
keep a general eye on the place.

The Broached Barrel was even busier than The Wheat Sheaf
had been, and Bell and Magdalene decided there was little
sense in trying to talk to anyone just then. St. Cyr had not
been seen there the night he died, and without him as a point
of reference it was difficult to ask questions about people for
whom they had no names. Bell suggested that he get dinner
for them from a cookshop. They could eat at the table and
bench in the back—unless Magdalene objected to eating
where a dead man had lain.

She laughed at that and said if she had feared to make use
of what the dead had touched, she would not have a single
bed in the Old Priory Guesthouse. And then she put her fin-

gers to her lips and swore that if he let that slip to Ella she
would murder him. He laughed heartily, but swore the rack
would not make him divulge the secret to Ella; he no more
than she wanted to hear the shrieks and wails such news would
bring forth. Whereupon Magdalene laughed too and said she
would get the ale and meet him in the back yard.

She pulled up her veil before she entered the alehouse but
looked around over it as she made her way to the landlord
sitting among his broached barrels. The house was smaller than
The Lively Hop and had no female servers she could try to
befriend. A shrill voice drew her eyes and she saw Sir Jules,
but Lord Ormerod was not with him. So, she thought as she
carried the ale out to the back, Lord Ormerod did not *always*
accompany his young host, and his absence the night St. Cyr
died might not be significant.

Magdalene was relieved to find the back premises empty of
other company. Likely, she thought, others were not as indifferent to the fact that a dead man had rested on the rough-
hewn table only a few days before. For a moment she was
concerned that people might wonder why she did not fear the
dead as others did, then realized that she had never been to
The Broached Barrel before. Most likely if anyone noticed they
would think she was a stranger and did not know St. Cyr had
been killed there.

That concern shed, a bitter smile curved her lips. If the dead
were able to haunt the living, Brogan would surely have driven
her mad long before now. But after his death Brogan had never
been more than an unpleasant memory. Her terrors were all
natural, about being blamed for the killing, about how she
would live if she escaped that. She never had had any fear of

Brogan's spirit—not even right after that knife had slipped into him.

She pushed the memory away and set the ale tankards down on the table. It was a pleasant place, shaded by a large tree that grew in an adjoining yard, the privy in the far corner distant enough that the smell did not offend in this spot. She was tired, she realized, despite sleeping far longer than usual— perhaps *because* she had wakened so late or perhaps because she had been anxious while she was questioning the two women in The Lively Hop and the landlord in The Wheat Sheaf.

Magdalene closed her eyes and slumped forward, an arm protectively around the ale tankards. A few moments later, she became vaguely aware of two men's voices, both slightly familiar, rising over the general noise from within the alehouse, one urging the other not to be such a fool and to go out and use the privy. She didn't bother to open her eyes until she heard a kind of horrified, choked gobbling—the kind of sound one makes in an extremity of terror when the voice won't work. She jerked up, wondering what could have caused such fear, only to meet Sir Jules's eyes.

Thinking that he might suspect she was a masked robber, she lifted a hand to remove her veil, but he croaked, "No!" and bepissed himself in his fear just as Bell came out the alehouse door. He was carrying two heels of stale bread hollowed out and filled with stew and two thick trenchers, one covered with slices of pork and the other with lamb or mutton. He could do nothing but watch, mouth open, as Sir Jules crumpled to the ground in a faint.

"Well," Magdalene remarked, "that's the first time I've caused *that* reaction in a man."

Bell stepped over Sir Jules's body and put his burden down

on the table, Magdalene holding the stew-filled bread upright. He turned to look at Sir Jules. "What did you say to him?" he asked Magdalene.

"Not a word. I was tired. I was just resting my head on my arms and waiting for you. I heard someone telling him not to be a fool and to go out to use the privy if he needed to piss, and then . . ."

Bell started to laugh and bent to lift up Sir Jules, who was starting to stir and moan softly. "With that veil over your head, he must have thought you were the ghost of St. Cyr's corpse." As he seized Sir Jules under the arms to haul him upright, he wrinkled his nose. "Well, he doesn't need to use the privy any more."

"What a fool!" Magdalene said, but then her eyes opened wider. "But it was only your supposition that St. Cyr was sitting at the table when he was killed because of the marks on his neck and chin. Unless you told too many people, all that most *know* is that St. Cyr was found hidden behind that shed. So why should Sir Jules have been frightened by me resting on the table? Doesn't that mean that he saw the body before it was hidden behind the shed?"

"I didn't kill him! I didn't!"

Sir Jules twisted in Bell's grip in an attempt to break free, like a kitten trying to escape a lion. Bell merely tightened his hold, ignoring Sir Jules's yelp of pain, and propelled him toward the table, where he ordered, "Step over the bench and sit."

"You have no right to hold me here!" Sir Jules whined.

"I have witnesses who will swear that you said you would see St. Cyr dead before you would permit him to marry Loveday," Bell snapped. "And I told no one of my supposition that

St. Cyr was sitting when he was killed other than Sir Rolf, the deputy sheriff, and Mistress Magdalene here."

Sir Jules's lips twisted into a sneer. "You told a whore? Well, then, it's no surprise if the whole city knows."

"But the whole city does not know," Magdalene said. "Shall I bring out a few men and ask them what they know about St. Cyr's death? Or should Bell tell the landlord to send some out to us, if you think I will tell them what to answer?"

Bell cuffed Jules lightly. "Oh, do not waste our time. You did not cry out that you did not kill him and bepiss yourself and faint for no reason. You saw St. Cyr dead, lying across the table with a knife in his back—"

"No!" Jules whispered. "There was no knife in his back. Do you think I could have seen a dead man and walked back inside the alehouse and gone on drinking without saying a word?"

Bell and Magdalene exchanged glances. Magdalene shook her head, indicating that Jules probably would have screamed his head off if he'd known he'd seen a corpse. Bell nodded.

"I will accept that. What else did you see?"

"Nothing. Nothing."

Bell stared at him hard.

"Maybe a shadow moving toward the privy . . ." Sir Jules's voice trembled. "But there was no one there when I went in." Then his voice rose, shrill with protest. "Why should I have looked with care or been suspicious? I did not know the man was dead!"

"But there was a moon that night," Bell said. "You could have seen who killed him."

"No one was there, I tell you, and I did not know he was dead! All I thought I saw was a drunk lying across the table. I saw nothing but that. Nothing."

"Then why are you so sure the figure lying across the table *was* St. Cyr?" Magdalene asked softly. "It could have been a drunk who later went away."

"It . . . Later, the next day, after I learned St. Cyr had been killed, it came to me that no one lies as that body lay." He swallowed hard.

"Lay how?" Bell's voice was also soft, encouraging.

"The–the arm hung straight down. The face was turned away from me, but it was flat on the table. Not like Mistress Magdalene; she used her arm to protect her skin from the rough wood." He swallowed again. "It was foolish to be so shocked. I–I . . ."

"You actually saw quite a lot, didn't you, Sir Jules?" Bell remarked. Jules shook his head nervously, but his eyes would not meet Bell's, and Bell continued, "Maybe you saw too much. If the killer recognized you, might he believe that you noticed even more than you were willing to tell us? I see you are not wearing mail today and Lord Ormerod is not with you. You would be safer if you just went home now and if you didn't drink any more."

"Ormerod." Jules sneered. "He just doesn't want me to spend any more money or have any fun gambling, but it won't matter once I marry Loveday."

"You are not likely to marry Loveday," Magdalene said sharply. "And if you think you saw something and can fill your pinched purse by extortion, remember St. Cyr. Sir Bellamy and I think that was what killed him."

"That man Arvagh, who wants Loveday, killed him," Jules said sullenly. "Ypres bribed or threatened the priest and the servants to say he was at Noke—"

Quick as a snake, Magdalene's free hand flashed out and

struck his cheek. "That is a lie, you nasty little viper!" She folded her lips together for a moment, then said, "We have done our best for you. If you tell us—or Bell only, if you do not trust me—what you saw, you will be safe, for it would be too late for killing you to do any good. If you do not . . . on your own head be it. In any case, go away. I do not need to have my stomach soured by your presence while I eat my dinner."

"You whore! You cannot tell me—"

Bell rose and lifted Jules up with one powerful hand around his neck. He shook the smaller man like a rat, and just before Jules's eyes began to bulge out, set him down on his feet and gave him a powerful shove in the direction of the alehouse's back door.

"She can tell you or any other man anything she likes," he said. "Get out!"

Jules picked himself up, his wet tunic and braies now mottled with dirt, twigs, and dried leaves so there could be no doubt of the accident that had befallen him. He cast one furious and terrified glance over his shoulder at Bell and scuttled toward the door. Bell watched him, his fair skin reddened, his eyes intent. Magdalene had hastily propped the stew-filled bread against the tankards of ale and come around the table. Now she put a hand on Bell's arm. When he looked down at her, she shook her head.

"Sit down and eat, love." Her lips twitched. "I have been too long one to mind the name." Then she leaned against him for a moment. "Fifteen years ago . . . ah, then the word cut like a knife. But no one cared then." She sniffed, hugged him tight, and then pulled away, smiling. "We do not need cold stew atop the foul smell that one left. Come, sit down and eat."

He raised a hand to touch her cheek, then bent his head over hers. "What I would not give to wipe away those years!"

She raised her head and let their lips touch briefly. "Fifteen years ago I would have destroyed you . . . and had another burden on my soul." She shuddered, then smiled and took his hand to turn him toward the bench. "Sit. Eat. What was cannot be changed—and I want to know whether you still think Jules could have killed St. Cyr."

He sat silent, not answering, jaw set, staring at the bread bowls as if he could not recognize them, but then he took one and bit into the side, sucking at the juice of the stew as it ran over. Magdalene did the same, eyes lowered, thinking that if she had married such a man as Bell her life would have been so different . . . or would it? She could not imagine Bell being as mean-spirited or cruel as Brogan, but as a young man, hot-tempered, with a more than beautiful wife . . . There would have been little peace in their household. Oh, no. Whore she might be, but she was better off, *femme seul*, needing to be obedient to none, owing no man an explanation for what she did.

"No," Bell said suddenly, startling her. "I cannot believe Jules murdered St. Cyr, can you?"

She gathered her wits, briefly amused that she was still thinking of him while he had dismissed thoughts of her in favor of their problem. "That ninny?" she said. "No. Too bad. He was certainly in the right place at the right time." Then she frowned. "Were we wise, Bell, to let him go like that? He saw something, and I fear he intends to use it."

"Not until he is sure Loveday is beyond his grasp. We have told him so, but that is a young man accustomed to having what he wants handed to him on a silver platter. I think he is unable to believe she will not fall into his hand when he

stretches it for her. I hope he will not use what he knows until
he is desperate."

"So I hope also. And I hope he will not blab too much when
he has had a cup too much of wine."

Bell shrugged. "He did not talk last night, and he was too
full to walk on his own. I think Ormerod tried and just got
tired of trying to wet-nurse him. We had better finish our meal
because we need to start for Noke soon. We need to get there
in time for the priest to write his statement, if he has not
already done so. And remember we have to go back to the
Soft Nest to get the horses."

"Could Ormerod have killed St. Cyr?" Magdalene asked.

"For what? To save Sir Jules? I cannot believe it. He does
not like to lose money, but he is also an honorable man. If he
is committed beyond retreat to Sir Jules's sister, I think he will
find some small property for the girl and his brother to live
on. Perhaps he would try to wrest the farm that is the girl's
dower-right away from Sir Jules and save it from ruin, but I
cannot believe he would kill so Sir Jules could ruin Loveday's
estate as well as his own."

"Ah, but perhaps he would not ruin it?" Magdalene pointed
out as she drew her eating knife and speared a slice of mutton.
She alternated bites of that, praising its succulence, with nib-
bling at the stew while she thought. Then she said, "Did you
not tell me that Ormerod said Loveday would manage her
lands, Osney, and Sir Jules himself, so that he would have no
opportunity to do more damage? Might Ormerod not think he
was not only saving himself and the girl—oh, yes, her name
was Marguerite—but saving Sir Jules, too? And he is fond of
Sir Jules."

Bell looked uneasy while he chewed alternately a bite of the

stew-gravy soaked bread and a bite of pork. "But murder?" he
protested. "Admittedly Ormerod might think in that fashion,
but as an excuse for *murder*? Stabbing a man in the back? Ormerod might not be able to match me in a fight, but I believe
he could have killed St. Cyr."

Magdalene looked dissatisfied too. "But would he want
openly to kill St. Cyr? A knight against a common man-at-
arms?" She shrugged and shook her head. "Let us finish eating
and be off," she said. "I want to ask Loveday if she had never
met Niall or been pressed to marry, whether she would eventually have accepted Sir Jules."

23 June, Noke

Bell and Magdalene arrived at Noke well before sunset,
even though they had lingered in Oxford long enough to hear
from William, via Leon Blound, that Salisbury had arrived soon
after dinner and had been greeted civilly by the king. Magdalene had made a cynical mouth over the civility of Stephen's
greeting because William was so sure that the king had decided
on confrontation. Blound had assured them that William believed nothing more would happen that day. Claiming ex-
haustion, Salisbury had begged permission to retire to his
lodging, and leave had been given.

Bell and Magdalene had left at once and kept their horses
to a good pace because they wanted to arrive while there was
still enough light for the priest to write his declaration that
Niall had been at Noke on the night of St. Cyr's death. It
would not have mattered if they had arrived after dark, however. There was no need for light. The priest's declaration was

all signed and sealed, as were the statements of all of Loveday's servants.

Magdalene laughed to herself when Niall praised Loveday's harrying of priest and servants until the documents were complete. She should have known, she thought, that Loveday would not permit neglect of her own interests. In fact, Niall and Loveday were ready to ride back to Oxford before it grew too dark to present the proofs of Niall's innocence to the sheriff. However, Magdalene told them that Lord William did not want Niall in Oxford until just before dinnertime the next day.

"He wishes to present you and the evidence that you are innocent to the king himself right after dinner and before any political disaster can take place that will wash away the effect of disproving the accusation against you."

Loveday nodded decisively. "Very clever, your Lord William. He does not look it, but he is remarkably subtle, and absolving Niall that way will be very good for us, too." She squeezed Niall's hand. "As soon as the king accepts your proof of innocence, you can tell him that you are nonetheless guilty of a fault of oversight. You can tell him about our betrothal and say, with truth, that you hardly knew me at the time and never heard I had been taken into the king's ward. Moreover, you were rising in Lord William's estimation and had no desire to tie yourself to a wife and a small estate. Thus, you put the matter out of your mind and did not tell Lord William either."

"But then the fault for not telling the king's clerk about it will fall upon you! I cannot—"

"Ah, but I understand that the king is soft to women. It is all in my letter, how I was mazed with grief over the death of my father and brothers and half mad trying to save the estate after the plague. The last thing in my mind was marriage. No,

I will come away scot-free, meek and trembling and apologetic as I will seem."

"Loveday! You would deliberately deceive the king?"

She smiled at him. "It is best, my dearling, and we will be hurting no one."

Niall sighed and Magdalene hid a grin. What Loveday said was true, but it skirted close to the bounds of what was honorable. Magdalene suspected that Niall would do a lot of sighing over the years, and then had to turn a laugh into a cough. No, he would not. As she grew older and came to better understand the nuances of his knightly honor, Loveday would become a past master at keeping from him everything that could cause such sighs. Niall would go through life comfortably assured of his stainless honor and grow richer and more powerful by Loveday's quiet manipulations.

Bell now said that he really must ride on to Wytham Abbey to report to the dean and Niall assured him that he would bring Loveday and Magdalene safely to Oxford between Tierce and Sext. Bell stood for a moment irresolute and then said, "Wait for me until Tierce."

Niall raised his brows. "You think me incapable of—"

"No," Bell said, but frowning. "Something is niggling at me. Something someone . . . Ah!" He hit himself gently on the side of the head. "The purse! Sir Ferrau told us that Alain of Brittany wants the purse you took from St. Cyr."

"Alain of Brittany?" Niall sounded stunned. "What does that haughty gentleman want with a common man-at-arms's purse?"

"Why do we not get it and see," Magdalene said, and looked at Loveday.

She shrugged and laughed. "I must admit, I forgot all about it once St. Cyr was dead and Niall proven innocent." She pulled at the light chain with which her household keys were fastened around her waist and went out of the Hall and into a chamber beyond. When she returned a few moments later she was carrying a worn-looking purse closed with a leather tie and with another pair of leather ties showing clean cut ends. By common consent they went to the benches that flanked the empty hearth. Loveday pulled forward a stool, opened the purse, and laid its contents there.

There were a few pennies and about ten farthings, two arrowheads, a strong black cord with a strong wooden peg attached to each end, a few supple leather lengths to be used as ties, and a folded parchment. Magdalene and Loveday, who could both read, reached for the document simultaneously. Loveday nodded and pulled back her hand. Magdalene picked up the parchment and unfolded it.

She read aloud rapidly over the first part which, as Loveday had told them in the Soft Nest, released into the hands of her betrothed all control of her property to administer during his lifetime and leave as he wished at his death. The shock of seeing that had been too much for Loveday, apparently, because she had stopped reading at that point. Actually her welfare had not, as she had said, been totally neglected. Indeed, it could not have been without putting the whole document into question. A brief paragraph stated that it was Mistress Loveday's intention, if she outlived her husband, to take the veil, and a parcel of land was named that would go with her to the cloister she chose.

Loveday made a loud and very rude noise. "Love you, I do," she said to Niall, "but if I outlive you, I tell you now that I have no intention of taking the veil."

Niall grinned. "Since you will doubtless have a dozen quar-

reling children by then, I would think it very unwise to re-
nounce the world. They will need your steady hand on them
to quell the riot my demise will set loose."

She laughed aloud. "A dozen! Well then, you need not
worry about my remarriage. A dozen should serve to keep me
busy."

Magdalene had been reading quietly during this exchange
and looked up after Loveday's remark to say, "That is a relief.
There is nothing here but the usual provisions for any estate.
I half expected that there would be another named to share
with St. Cyr. In that case, we might have had a fight over the
authenticity of the document."

"Nonsense!" Loveday exclaimed. "It is a forgery. Why should
I sign with an X when I can write my name? Why should I
agree to such unreasonable conditions? In any case, why should
we not destroy the parchment at once?"

"All for the same reason," Magdalene said, lips thinned with
anger and contempt. "You would have been thought to agree
out of fear and respect for those that signed this document as
witnesses, and presumably urged it upon you."

"Who?" Bell asked eagerly.

"Alain, count of Brittany and earl of Richmond, and Lord
Hervey . . . with a string of French titles that have no meaning
to me."

"Who are *they*?" Loveday asked indignantly. "Why should I
fear them?"

"They are noblemen who think very well of themselves,"
Magdalene said. "Their manner is such as to induce fear in
most folk like yeomen and merchants. And the reason why *you*
should fear them, and why we simply cannot destroy this doc-

ument, is because they are at present very much in favor with the king."

"Then destruction seems even more reasonable," Loveday insisted. "To show that to the king with his favorites' names on it might make him refuse to honor my betrothal to Niall."

"I did not say you should show it. Niall must take it to William of Ypres, as he would take any other spoil of war. William will decide what is best to do on much better grounds than I have or you or Niall."

"But St. Cyr was Waleran de Meulan's man," Bell protested. "Why is not Waleran's name on that document if he wished to give Loveday to St. Cyr? Or the names of his men? Why not Raoul de Samur, who was captain of St. Cyr's troop? He would be the person to witness his man's betrothal."

The other three sat looking at Bell in silence. Finally Magdalene said, "There can be only two reasons that I can see. First, Lord Waleran does not want to be connected with this betrothal—and that would mean this whole thing was a deliberate plan to damage William of Ypres and involved the king himself through his clerk—"

"My God!" Niall breathed. "I would not have believed—"

Magdalene gestured at him to be quiet. "I do not believe it either," she said briskly, "and for very good reasons. Raoul de Samur told us that Waleran is giving not the smallest thought to William—even allowing that William is quartered in the castle near the king while Waleran himself is staying in the town—because he is neck-deep in something involving Count Alain of Brittany. Moreover, William is sure he is safe from any attack by Waleran's men because it may be necessary to take Salisbury's castles by war, and Waleran would prefer that William do that dirty work and earn the enmity of the Church rather than that the king assign him to the task."

Niall breathed out a heavy sigh of relief and nodded. "True enough. It would be stupid to involve Lord William and perhaps have him dismissed when the king might need him."

"You said two reasons," Bell remarked, smiling at Magdalene. "What is the second, since you deny the first?"

"The simplest in the world—that Lord Waleran knows nothing at all about St. Cyr's plan to marry Loveday."

Now all three sat silent, looking at *her.*

Magdalene smiled sweetly at them. "I doubt the king's clerk thought that the matter of a minor heiress available for marriage was a deep secret. In fact, we know he carried the tale to at least two men: Lord Waleran and Lord William, and garnered a prize from both. Perhaps he told even more. In any case it is likely that he simply told Lord Waleran about the matter in his Hall. A Great Hall is never really empty. There are servants, guards, idling men-at-arms . . . all sorts of people about. Why could not St. Cyr have overheard the clerk's message himself or had it relayed to him? Being bolder and more inventive—and mayhap because he did have a friend in high places—"

"Yes," Bell interrupted. "Do I not remember Samur saying that he noticed St. Cyr off in a corner with one of Alain of Brittany's men?"

"You are right. I remember that, too," Magdalene agreed. "Perhaps St. Cyr appealed to his friend to get the document, possibly offering payment or repayment from the coffers of Noke. That might be why Count Alain's name and that of his guest Lord Hervey appear on the document."

Loveday nodded. "There was no pound of silver in the purse. If there ever was, it went elsewhere."

"Then why did St. Cyr go crying to Sir Ferrau about his loss?" Niall asked indignantly.

"I do not think that much of a problem," Magdalene replied. "It is barely possible that he was so muddled, given Niall's beating, drunkenness, and William's throttling him, not to mention what Florete's men may have done before they dumped him, that he honestly forgot he had paid for the document with it. A far more likely reason is that he thought he could pressure Niall into paying something to silence him."

Bell nodded. "And Count Alain, having heard St. Cyr demanding Ferrau's help in getting the purse back from Niall and fearing the betrothal was in it, bade Ferrau to retrieve it." He stood up. "I must leave for Wytham now, but I would like you to wait for me to return to Oxford with you. I do not know whether Ferrau will have gone to the count, but he may well tell him that Niall will be bringing the purse tomorrow. Count Alain will understand at once that Niall is more likely to take it to Lord William than give it to Ferrau."

"Do you think it likely he will set an ambush to take it from me?" Niall asked.

Bell pursed and pulled back his lips. "Not likely, but why take a chance? If there are two of us . . ."

A brief conflict showed in Niall's face. Pride bade him say he could take care of himself, but his service with Lord William had taught him caution. Any man could be taken down by an arrow that struck just right; such a hit on two men would be near a miracle. Instead of refusing Bell's offer, he said, "What of the women? Is it best we leave them here in Noke?"

"No!" Magdalene exclaimed. "I must go back to Oxford to warn William that it is entirely possible Lord Waleran knew nothing of this."

"And I must go to present my petition to the king," Loveday insisted. "It is my best chance to reach King Stephen himself. If Lord William is going to bring Niall to him to prove his innocence, he might as well also present the cause of the quarrel—me."

Bell looked from one to the other and shook his head, but he said nothing until he had risen to his feet and belted on his sword. Then he looked at Niall.

"I leave to you the dubious pleasure of convincing them that you can give the warning to Lord William and present Loveday's petition. I will see you between Prime and Tierce tomorrow, and depending on the dean's instruction may also see you at Court."

Magdalene, lips thinned with determination, rose to accompany him to the door, but they both stopped to listen to a mild disturbance in the bailey. A moment later, Loveday's steward hurried in, an anxious frown on his face.

"There is an armed man at the gate, Mistress Loveday. He says his name is Manville d'Arras and that he is heir to Aimery St. Cyr. He said he wishes to speak to you about your betrothal."

CHAPTER 15

23 June,
Noke Manor

Niall leapt to his feet. "Just keep him at the gate until I pull on my armor," he said to the steward, who hurried out. To Loveday, his face red with rage, he said, "I will see him away from the gate and off these lands in a way that will convince him the only thing being St. Cyr's heir will get him is a sound beating."

Loveday also got to her feet, biting her lip, but Magdalene hurried back to Niall and laid a hand on his arm. "Yes, go and arm," she said, "but don't drive him away before I can speak to him. I have heard from several sources that the man is a half-wit. Still, he was much in St. Cyr's company and it may be that he can tell us who St. Cyr's high-born friends are. Since that is the man most likely to have killed St. Cyr—"

"Who? Why?" Loveday and Niall asked in chorus.

"Go and arm," Bell said to Niall. "Magdalene will tell you the whole tale of what we have discovered after we have questioned Arras. She is right. It is important to find out what he knows."

"Then I will go to the gate and invite him in—" Loveday said.

"No! Wait until I am armed," Niall exclaimed, hurrying toward the back of the Hall, where a rough framework had been built to support his armor.

Since speed was necessary, Niall did not bother to remove his good tunic and don his gambeson. Bell followed to help him slide into the heavy metal shirt, and as soon as it was seated on his shoulders, Loveday went out. Magdalene watched from the doorway, holding up a hand to discourage the men from showing themselves.

"The servants are all around her," she said softly, "and he is threatening no violence." Then she added urgently, "Back! Into the privy chamber. Loveday is bringing him into the Hall."

The three of them hurriedly passed up the length of the Hall to a partitioned-off chamber where Loveday's bed stood next to a table holding heaps of tally sticks and a box of rolled parchments. There they all huddled in the doorway, hoping Arras would not notice them.

Loveday brought Arras to the benches near the hearth and gestured for him to sit—with his back to the partitioned-off room. "You cannot inherit people," she was saying, "except, of course, slaves, and you know I am no slave."

"But the will says everything."

The tone was puzzled, not aggressive or argumentative; the voice was thick, the words oddly slurred. Magdalene remembered that the whore Hertha had said he spoke as if his tongue was too large for his mouth. It was a good description. Behind her, Magdalene could feel the tension ooze out of the watching men, although they pressed closer to hear.

"I have it written," Manville d'Arras said plaintively, fumbling in his purse and bringing out a parchment, which he offered to Loveday. "I have his horse and his armor and his clothing . . ." His lower lip trembled. "I do not want them. I want . . . I want Carl—no, I mean Aimery—I want Aimery back. He—" the man swallowed hard "—he talked to me all the time. Sometimes I didn't understand him, but he never yelled at me for that. He only laughed and said it was good to talk to me. No one else ever said that."

There were tears in Loveday's eyes, and she leaned forward and patted Arras comfortingly on the arm. "It is hard to lose a friend. I know too well what it is to lose those I loved, but your friend Aimery was deceived. The betrothal document offered to him was false and worthless. You see, I had been previously betrothed, and you know the Church does not permit the marriage of a betrothed person."

Arras nodded. "Yes, I know that. But—but the betrothal was not offered to Aimery. He thought of that himself and had to find someone to write it for him."

"But then how did Aimery find out about me?"

A big grin split Arras' face. "Oh, he was clever, that Aimery. He found—" He stopped speaking suddenly and frowned. "No. I promised I wouldn't tell anyone."

"And you didn't," Loveday said, smiling at him and patting his arm again. "That was right while Aimery was alive, of course, but now that he's dead, you want to explain how clever he was so that he will be well remembered. The promise you made must have ended with his life so you can be free to praise your friend."

Behind her, Magdalene heard Niall draw in a hissing breath, and she jabbed backward with an elbow to keep him silent.

"That's true." Arras was frowning. "But Aimery said if I told, it would be his death. I never did tell, never . . . but he's dead anyway."

"Yes, but it was not your fault, and nothing can hurt Aimery now. Nothing can hurt him ever again, so you can tell me how clever he was."

"He found a place—" the grin was back "—up in the attic over Lord Waleran's solar. I'm not sure where it was, maybe near the chimney hole—where he could hear all the lord's privy conversations. It was there that he heard the king's clerk tell Lord Waleran about an orphan with a good property who was not rich enough for a king's man but might be suitable for one of Lord Waleran's men. Well, Aimery was one of Lord Waleran's men, so why shouldn't he have the orphan?"

Magdalene had clapped both hands over her mouth to hold back a gasp, and her eyes were as wide as they could get. If Raoul could find that place, William would soon know most of Waleran's secrets. Arras was still extolling his friend's cleverness, making it quite clear that he had no idea that what Aimery had done was wrong, and Magdalene took the chance of glancing back at Niall and Bell. Both wore almost identical expressions of mingled horror and speculation.

Meanwhile Arras had wandered from his adulation of Aimery to anger at the man who had robbed him of his friend.

"But it was not Niall Arvagh who did that," Loveday said. "He was here, at Noke, when your friend was killed. Indeed he was. I am telling you the truth."

"But who else could it have been?" Arras said pitifully. "No one else wanted Aimery dead. Everyone liked him. He told me so."

"I do not know," Loveday said, choking a little over the idea of St. Cyr as a general favorite. "Perhaps it was the person who wrote the false betrothal document for him. It was false, you know. I did not sign it. I can write my name and would not use an X, and besides that, I knew I was already betrothed—although I did make a mistake and not tell the king's clerk of my arranged marriage. But it is wrong to write a document you know is false, so that person may not be a good person. He might have feared Aimery would tell someone about the false document and killed him to ensure his silence. Do you know who that person was?"

"No!" Arras cried, looking shocked. "Aimery talked about his friend who had found a high place, but he never named him and I never saw them together. And I do not believe that someone would kill over a silly piece of parchment. I *heard* Niall Arvagh say he would kill Aimery."

"Only if he ever came here and troubled me again, and he never did, so Niall had no cause to kill him. And Niall was here, at Noke, when Aimery was killed in Oxford. You need not believe me. Indeed, I was not at Noke that night, but the priest was here. Why do you not go down to the village and seek out Father Herveus? You know a priest would not lie. He will tell you that Niall was here, playing chess with him that night, and could not have killed your friend."

"Will he?" Instead of looking stubborn or doubtful, Arras looked relieved. "I will be glad if it is true. I would have had to fight Sir Niall if he killed Aimery. I am a strong fighter." He shook his head. "But I do not think I could have won that fight." He uttered a long sigh. "I will go to the village and speak to the priest. If he tells me Sir Niall is innocent, I will look for the man who gave Aimery the false document and ask him where he was the night Aimery died."

"Be careful," Loveday said, rising as Arras did to see him to the door. "Such a man is dangerous. Be on your guard. If he killed Aimery, he might wish to harm you also."

Arras smiled at her. "Oh, I am not afraid of anyone who writes. I was a much better fighter than Aimery. I taught him to use a sword and he was big and strong, but he never wanted to practice enough. He was cleverer than me, but I was the better man-at-arms."

His voice faded as he went out of the Hall. Loveday, who had gone with him to the door, stood watching as he mounted his horse and rode out. The steward closed the gate after him. Meanwhile, Bell helped Niall shed his mail shirt and then followed Magdalene into the Hall. Sure the house was secure again, Loveday had returned and stood near the benches, wringing her hands.

"The poor thing," she said, and tears stood in her eyes. "Should I have tried to stop him from searching further into St. Cyr's death? He may be a good fighter, as he said, but that will not save him from someone who will creep up and stab him in the back."

Niall put an arm around her and kissed her forehead. "You cannot order everyone's life to protect them, Loveday. You might have convinced him not to ask one kind of question, but he would not have understood the general idea and would have asked another."

"True enough," Magdalene said, "and I am very much afraid that poor Arras was not long for this world in any case. Did you have enough time to look at that parchment, Loveday? Was it really a will signed by St. Cyr? Who witnessed it?"

"What do you mean he was not long for this world in any case? And yes, I had time to read the will," Loveday replied. "It was very simple; it just said that everything in St. Cyr's

possession was willed to Manville d'Arras. It was written by
Peter, priest of Sutton, and witnessed by a mercer and a
butcher of the village."

Magdalene nodded in a satisfied way. "What will any of you
wager that Arras has something—some small property or an
income from his family—and that there is an identical will
leaving everything Arras owned to St. Cyr?"

Bell laughed. "I do not wager on sure things." Then his lips
turned down. "And I fear that what Magdalene did not say was
true also—that when it suited St. Cyr, Arras would have had
a fatal accident or died in some action that Lord Waleran's
troops fought." He shrugged. "I really must go or I will not
reach Wytham until after dark."

Magdalene walked with him to the door and across the bailey to the stable. "Can there actually be any danger for Loveday and me in riding to Oxford?" she asked. "I really must
go. Raoul de Samur must hear about this listening place at
once. If he can discover what Waleran and Alain are planning
we could—" She stopped, aware of her mistake.

"Could what?" Bell made a sound of disgust. "Doubtless if
one ploy fails, another will be tried." He shrugged, then said,
"Arrows can go anywhere and either you or Loveday might be
seized as a hostage and threatened so that Niall will give up
the purse. Why take the chance? I can seek out Raoul—" He
laughed harshly as he saw the expression on her face. "Very
well. I suspect you will ride alone if I deny you. All you can
think about is your precious William's benefit once his spy has
this news."

Magdalene shook her head, although Bell had sensed the
truth. The thought of how much Raoul's information could
benefit William if he could find St. Cyr's hiding place made

her want to ride to Oxford at once, but she dared not say that and incite more jealousy in Bell. Beside that, she was afraid to foul William's plans by bringing Niall into the city too early. So she only squeezed Bell's arm and said that if the danger were not acute, it would be better for Loveday to come too because she would be more likely to receive a sympathetic hearing from the king.

Bell sighed, caught her to him for a hard kiss that expressed mingled frustration and amusement, and went into the stable. Magdalene, returning to the house, heard an echo of her own statement coming from Loveday's lips.

"But my love," she was saying, "it will have an entirely different effect if *I*, weeping and trembling, present my letter and my petition to be pardoned for forgetting to mention my betrothal, than if you simply give them to Lord William, who will give them to a clerk. Why, the king, in the great press of business that falls upon him, might never get to see them. Whereas if I am there, complaining of the forged betrothal and then I beg him to honor my true betrothal—"

"I have just spoken to Bell," Magdalene interrupted, fearing that she would have to listen to Loveday repeat the same message, although in different words, until they actually left the next day, "and he admits he does not think an ambush very likely, just wishes to be sure. Let the matter rest for now, because I think Niall should know what Bell discovered about St. Cyr's death."

Niall was only too happy to fall in with this proposal and Loveday was also well satisfied. She had had the last word on the matter and felt her reasoning might have more effect if she did not nag. Both listened eagerly to Magdalene's explanation of why Bell was almost certain St. Cyr had been killed by a knight.

"But who?" Niall protested. "What knight would so soil himself when he could have easily found cause in the man's drunken insolence to cut him down?"

Magdalene frowned suddenly, thinking of a knight who had worn mail but was unlikely to be capable of cutting down St. Cyr. "Sir Jules of Osney?" she suggested.

Loveday giggled. "Not Jules," she said. "I do not think he has donned his mail for a year."

"But he was wearing it that night. Lord Ormerod told Bell that Sir Jules had been ranting about how he would make St. Cyr leave you in peace. His sister, knowing him to be pot-valiant, took fright and begged him into his mail shirt."

"Marguerite is sweet and clever," Loveday said, with a rather fond smile. "Her fault is that she loves her idiot brother too much to deny him what he desires—and thereby does him great harm. Oh well, she is young yet. I hope she learns better before he destroys Osney completely."

Magdalene cocked her head. "If Niall did not exist and this stupid business with St. Cyr had not catapulted you into the need for an immediate marriage, would you eventually have accepted Sir Jules?"

Loveday's lips turned down with distaste. "I might have if nothing better appeared or I was threatened with a worse marriage. I know I could manage him—one way or another—and Osney is, or was, a good estate. Perhaps it could be brought back to a decent yield. My children would have been gentlefolk . . ." She shrugged, then turned to look at Niall and smiled. "Thank God and all His saints I have that and more—a real

man to take to my bed and father my children and teach my
sons to be men."

Niall, who had been looking distressed while Loveday answered Magdalene's question, now grinned at her. "You may
rest assured I will see to fathering the children and raising my
sons as men. And your children will be gentlefolk." He took
her hand. "I am sorry I will bring almost nothing else to our
marriage."

"Do not be so silly," Loveday said. "You will bring William
of Ypres's favor, which will be worth more in the long run
than a ruined estate that might drain Noke and Otmoor in my
attempts to save it. Your father will help us set up to breed
horses—I know just where they can be grazed." She squeezed
his hand. "And you bring yourself, a man willing to let me do
what I love to do, see to my lands and my flocks. Which is
why I was never willing to marry Tirell Hardel, even though
he is a good man, I owe his father much, and I knew Master
Reinhart desired our marriage."

Reminded by the name, Magdalene then recounted her talk
with Mayde, the server in The Wheat Sheaf, and repeated her
description of the merchant-looking man.

Loveday nodded. "That might well have been Tirell. Master
Reinhart told me that he had gone to seek out St. Cyr to see
what kind of man he was and try to come to some arrangement
with him to forego the betrothal, since I was clearly unwilling
and would fight to be free."

"I doubt he was successful," Magdalene said. "Mayde told
me that he looked as if he were about to strike St. Cyr but
then left the alehouse. It is fortunate that he is most unlikely
to have a mail shirt—"

"But Tirell does have mail," Loveday said. "When he was a

boy, he used to tell me all the time how he dreamed of being a knight and wanted to learn how to fight. Knighthood was only a dream, but Master Reinhart indulged him with some lessons in fighting and Tirell kept them up even after he became truly interested in the wool trade. And as he grew into a man, he showed so much skill and promise in arms that it occurred to Master Reinhart that his own son would make the most reliable leader possible for the guards he hires to protect his pack trains against thieves and outlaws. And then, of course, he bought him the best armor that could be obtained. Master Reinhart does not lack for money, and he loves his son, so mail it was."

"How would he match up against a trained man-at-arms?" Magdalene asked.

"I have no idea," Loveday said, laughing, but then sobered suddenly. "You think he would not trust himself in a fight against St. Cyr and that he crept up behind him and killed him?"

"I don't know the man, and I heard him say to his father that he had taken care of the business they had spoken about and that it was finished. Over."

Loveday shook her head. "No. No, I cannot believe Tirell would do such a thing. And why should he? He had no cause. Tirell certainly did not want to marry me, as I had no desire to marry him. Oh, we are fond, as brother and sister are fond. Perhaps if I had been married to St. Cyr and he had mistreated me, then Tirell might have killed him, but not to become my husband, not murder."

Magdalene nodded, although she was not truly convinced. St. Cyr had been a disgusting creature and considering what most merchants thought about men-at-arms, Tirell might easily

have felt the world would be a better place without him. And
if Reinhart had convinced his son that Loveday's estate was
essential to them, Tirell could have nerved himself to kill.
Sister-like or not, Loveday was pretty enough and well made,
and Noke and Otmoor was a profitable estate. For the sake of
his inheritance Tirell might have put aside his doubts and killed
St. Cyr only later to regret the bond he must make.

The discussion had taken them near to Vespers and they all
walked down to the village to hear the service and then back
to eat a leisurely evening meal. Magdalene gave them the news
of the bishop of Salisbury's arrival and then answered the few
questions they still had about the murder. But now that Niall
was proven innocent, that subject was growing less and less
important to them.

Soon Magdalene was listening indulgently to Loveday and
Niall planning the future and discussing what should go into
the formal betrothal agreement that must be written even
though they intended to marry as soon as possible. Softly,
Magdalene sighed, hoping that the plans Waleran was making
would not cause war, and that plague or any other misfortune
would not bring sorrow instead of the planned joys. And then
the talk of betrothal brought her mind back to St. Cyr and
she remembered Raoul saying that he had made no secret of
his intention of marrying Loveday.

Suddenly Magdalene was aware of a possibility she had not
considered before—that Waleran de Meulan had ordered St.
Cyr's death. The more she thought about it, the more likely
it seemed. Was it possible that Lord Waleran could have remained totally ignorant of what St. Cyr was saying? Would
not gossip among his men have carried to him the news that
such a creature as St. Cyr was claiming he would take an heir-

ess to wife? If Arras was right, the priest had told Waleran about Loveday not in the Hall but in his private solar. So, if Waleran had not chosen St. Cyr for Loveday, might he not have suspected that St. Cyr had found some way to spy on him?

That would have been enough to sign St. Cyr's death warrant. Waleran was not the man to bother seeking proof, from what Magdalene knew of him. He would simply order St. Cyr killed. Another thing to tell William, Magdalene thought. But a faltering in the talk drew her eyes to Niall and Loveday. Magdalene saw him stroking her arm and the way she was leaning toward him. Suppressing a grin, she yawned widely and shook her head.

"Sit up and talk if you will, children," she said, "but I am not so young and strong. We must be up and on the road early tomorrow, so I am off to bed."

With the words she rose and made her way to the chamber at the back. Well away from the two lovers, she let herself chuckle softly. Since she was sharing Loveday's bed, they would be saved from any physical excesses all the talk of their forthcoming marriage might have stimulated in them. Not that it was important, really, but it would be best if Loveday could swear that she was a maiden still.

More tired than she had realized, Magdalene fell asleep as soon as she had gotten herself into bed and slept so soundly that she was totally unaware when Loveday joined her. She rested well, however, so that when Loveday rose, she woke also. The chamber was still very dark and she called out to ask if anything were wrong.

"No." She heard the smile in Loveday's voice. "It is morning

and time to rise, but the shutters are closed. We will have a
wet ride, I fear."

Magdalene groaned, but got out of bed and found the wash-
basin by the light of the night candle. When she had washed
and dressed, she followed Loveday out into the Hall, where
servants were already setting up a trestle table for a more substantial fast breaking than usual since they would be riding out.
Niall was also awake, wearing shirt and hose with his gambeson laid ready near his mail shirt.

Halfway through the meal of porridge, cold pasty, bread,
and cheese, they heard a hail at the gate. Niall went out and
came back with a soaked and furious Bell, but his rage was
somewhat abated when Magdalene hurried to him with a drying cloth and Loveday drew another stool to the table.

"I had forgotten," Magdalene said with a sigh, "how unreli-
able the weather is in the spring. Yesterday and the day before
were so fine."

"And neither of you two madwomen will consider remaining
here warm and dry? Niall and I must go. He to Lord William's
command and I because the dean desires that I present a petition from the priest of Lothbury, near the Jewery in London,
for the closing on Sunday of the houses of Change near the
church. It seems they close on Friday afternoon and remain
closed on Saturday, but open again on Sunday so that church-
goers are distracted."

"Would not addressing the mayor of London be more to the
purpose?" Magdalene asked.

Bell grinned sourly. "It is a reason for me to be there that
has nothing at all to do with the bishop of Winchester, and
not too transparent an excuse because Stephen is always interested in anything to do with London. Londoners were the

first to welcome and acknowledge him king and they have always supported him."

Whereupon he addressed himself to his breakfast with strong devotion, mumbling as he ate that the meals provided by the brothers of Wytham Abbey to the residents of their guesthouse were somewhat less lavish than those to which he was accustomed. However, his efforts to make up for past deprivation had a second good result. By the time he was finished and Loveday packed for her stay in Oxford, the rain had eased off somewhat.

The heavy rain earlier may also have been an advantage, although they would never know. All they knew was that they rode safely; there was no ambush. Whether that was because there never had been any such plan, or because the attackers were driven off by the rain or felt their prey would wait for better weather, no one could guess. In any case, they arrived safely, wet but not soaked, at the Soft Nest near to Tierce. Bell rode on toward the castle and Niall took Loveday with him to the armorer's house from whence he would send a message to William of Ypres asking for orders.

Magdalene found herself looking forward to a quiet day on her own. She felt as if she had been rushing around from place to place and problem to problem ever since she had arrived in Oxford. She was thinking about the half-finished ribbon of embroidery meant for Ella's hair, planning the next row of flowers, as she stepped in the door and swung her wet cloak off her shoulders.

"Wait," Florete called, jumping to her feet and holding up a hand to keep Magdalene from coming down the corridor.

Magdalene stopped and caught her breath. Florete hurried up to her and murmured in her ear. "There is a man waiting for you—and not for service. I have never seen him before, and I did not like the way he looked."

"Did he give a name?"

"That, yes. Lord Ormerod, he said."

CHAPTER 16

Magdalene breathed a sigh of relief. "I know him," she said. "And I do not think he means me harm—"

But even as she said the words, she remembered that Lord Ormerod was deeply involved with Sir Jules and not too happy about it, because Sir Jules's solution for paying his debts and giving his sister a dowry was marriage to Loveday. And St. Cyr had stood in the path of that marriage. Still, she had nothing to do with that.

"What do you mean you did not like the way he looked?" she asked Florete.

"As if he had not slept. As if . . . as if he were desperate."

Magdalene stood staring at Florete, biting her lip as she tried to decide what to do. Could Lord Ormerod have killed St. Cyr? Was that why Sir Jules would not name the man he saw behind The Broached Barrel? But why should Ormerod come to her? Not about the murder. She *knew* no more ill of him than of any other man.

What did she know? He had been uneasy when he spoke to Bell about his involvement with Sir Jules. Bell thought he might have come to get money, a loan that had not been repaid, from Sir Jules. But according to Loveday, Jules never had a penny. Florete said Ormerod was desperate. Was *he* short of money? He knew the Old Priory Guesthouse made money and he might even have guessed that William had summoned and was paying her well . . .

Her eyes narrowed as she remembered William's purse hidden in the chest. She could give Ormerod something, enough to carry him back to his own estates anyway. She nodded at Florete.

"Thank you for the warning, love." She wrinkled her nose. "As I said, I know him and I do not think he means me harm. It will be better if I see him. But I will leave the door of my room a little open and appreciate it if you listen for loud voices or a call for help."

Florete nodded and walked the few steps to where her table partially blocked the opening into the common room. She bypassed the table to enter the room, while Magdalene stopped at the table. She could see Florete standing before a man whose head was sunk into his hands, supported by his elbows on his knees. As the whoremistress spoke, he looked up, then started to his feet as he saw Magdalene.

"Where the devil have you been?" he asked, brushing by Florete and coming around the table to stand by Magdalene.

"How could that be of interest to you?" Magdalene asked.

He made a dismissive gesture and said, even more urgently, "Where is Jules?"

"Sir Jules?" she echoed. It was not money Ormerod wanted— at least not from her.

"Yes. Where is he?"

"How could I know?"

"I hoped he had told you where he was going when you talked to him out in the back of The Broached Barrel."

"But that was yesterday, before Sext."

"Before Sext? So early?"

Ormerod looked past her, but it was obvious that he did not see the curtains of the cocking chambers behind her. She had not been cold while riding, even though she was damp, but standing in the corridor with the door open behind her, she was getting chilled, and she shivered.

"I am wet and cold," she said. "Come into my chamber so I can change my clothes."

She waved him down the corridor, unlocked the door of the back chamber, and waved him through ahead of her, leaving the door open until she could get some light. He did not care. He walked as far as the table, and turned to face her.

"He's disappeared! He never came home last night! I am at my wits' end."

Magdalene shook her head, then walked past him to light candles on the table and past again to partially shut the door. Then she went for dry clothing. As she gathered her things she said, "Why? I know Sir Jules is a fool, but he *is* a man grown. Why should you be responsible for him?"

Ormerod shrugged then disappeared from her view as she stepped behind the bed, where she was shielded from his sight by the bedcurtains. She could hear his voice clearly enough.

"Because I have committed my brother Edward to his sister," he said, "and we quarreled bitterly the night before last over the condition to which he has brought his estate. I . . . I said some things I did not mean—really I am very fond of Jules— and when he went out yesterday morning, he would not accept my company. And I . . . I do not deny that I was not sorry. In fact, I went to look over his lands, more particularly the farm that will go to Edward with Marguerite."

"That seems reasonable enough to me. I cannot see why it should make you feel uneasy."

"Not that." A stool scritched against the rough floorboards as Ormerod seated himself. Magdalene dropped her wet clothes and pulled on a dry shift. "But I was sorry for what I said, and Marguerite had sent his servant to Oxford around Nones, only the servant could not find Jules, so when she begged me to find him and bring him home, I went."

Magdalene's lips thinned with irritation even while her brow creased with uneasiness. She pulled on her tunic and gown hastily, saying a sentence each time her head was free. "He should have arrived at home soon after dinner, before Nones anyway. Bell told him, rather forcefully, that he should go home and stay there just before we ate our meal."

"Oh, Lord! Don't tell me he was fighting or insulting drunk so early."

"No. He had had a few; I could smell him. But he was not drunk—well, maybe a little because he was frightened when he saw me dozing on the table while Bell fetched dinner for us from a cookshop. My veil was over my head and I fear he thought me another dead body."

"But St. Cyr was found behind the shed," Ormerod said, drawing in a sharp breath as Magdalene came back around the bed where she could see him. "Why should he think you were *another* dead body?"

That sounded to Magdalene as if Ormerod had not overheard the conversation at the back of the Broached Barrel. She raised her brows and admitted, "I asked him what he had seen in the yard to give him such a shock, but he insisted he had seen nothing, that it was dark and he had been drunk. Bell pointed out to him that even if he had seen nothing suspicious, simply having been out there that night was dangerous and that he should go home and stay there."

"But he didn't." Ormerod's shoulders slumped. "He got fresh clothing from the landlord." He grimaced. "Jules often had little accidents from drinking too much and the people at the alehouses regularly lent him clothing. When he was clean, he asked the landlord to send a boy to fetch his horse from the stable and to bring him another cup of wine. Before the boy could leave, a man the landlord said looked like a merchant offered to pay for the wine. Jules seemed surprised, but the man said something about Loveday and Jules immediately told the boy not to bother with the horse. He went with the merchant to a bench at the side of the room. A little later, they left together."

"Did you find the merchant?" Magdalene asked eagerly.

"Yes. Before I even tried to find him, I walked to the other alehouses, thinking that Jules might have been rolled into a corner and left for the night. A girl at The Lively Hop knew Jules—they all know him—and told me she saw him walking down past The Wheat Sheaf with a companion. She was so surprised that Jules didn't go into The Wheat Sheaf that she noticed the door they did enter."

"Who was this merchant? What did he say?"

"He was home, nursing a sore head." Ormerod snorted. "Not an unusual thing when one has been in Jules's company, but he didn't know what happened to Jules either. They had had one or two more cups of wine at The Broached Barrel and then, wanting to make some plans—although to tell the truth

I think they were both too besotted to plan anything—Hardel—"

"Tirell or Reinhart?"

Ormerod stared at her suspiciously. "Tirell. Why, do you know him?"

Magdalene swallowed the impulse to say that Tirell had a mail shirt, reminding herself that Ormerod had a mail shirt too and did not know that the man who had killed St. Cyr had been wearing mail when he committed the crime.

"No, but Loveday does," she said. "They are father and son and the father desires that the son marry Loveday."

Ormerod shrugged. "Well, they were not quarreling over her, according to Master Woller, the mercer in whose house Hardel is lodging. I spoke to him after I spoke to Hardel and realized he could remember little of what happened. He said he had invited Jules to his lodging because he had heard a rumor that Jules would marry Loveday, and he wanted the truth of it."

"And was what he told you the truth?"

Ormerod grimaced. "As much of it as he knew himself. He was in no case to think out elaborate lies. He was drink-sick. All he said was that he and Jules sat drinking and talking for some time. Then they heard the bells for Nones and Jules said he must go. Hardel thinks he begged Jules to stay and eat something and sleep off the worst of the wine, but he cannot be sure."

"So Jules left Hardel's lodging staggering drunk?"

"Yes. Actually Woller told me more than that. He had been lending half an ear, fearing there would be trouble, because he realized they were drinking their dinner. He even crept up and opened the door a little, but from what he heard Woller thought they were companionable, commiserating with each other about some woman, which fits. Eventually he heard Hardel saying that Jules was drunk and offering to send for some food and let him sleep off the wine, but Jules would not accept. He left—the landlord saw him go—and Hardel stood on the landing watching and then went into the solar again.

Magdalene sighed. "I think you should hire some men and boys and have all the alleyways between the Lively Hop and the Broached Barrel searched, particularly around The Wheat Sheaf. If I have read Jules's character aright, whatever he meant to do when he left Hardel's place, he might well have ended up in the nearest alehouse."

"No, because his horse was gone from the stable."

"The horse was gone," Magdalene repeated, her voice now faint and her eyes large with sudden anxiety. "When? When was it gone?"

"When I came to Oxford to look for Jules yesterday. I saw the horse was not in the stable, so I called myself a fool, thinking I had passed Jules along the way because he had stopped to piss or some such thing. I rode back to Osney, but he was not there. I was furious, but Marguerite was beside herself, so I gathered up some servants and we searched the woods along the road, thinking he might have fallen off or simply taken the horse into the wood so he could sleep. We didn't find him and by then it was getting dark, so we returned to Osney and went to bed. But the horse returned in the night."

"Oh." Magdalene felt herself pale. "That is not good news at all."

"There was no blood! I examined the saddle and the beast itself almost hair by hair. No blood. No sign of strain or scuffing on the stirrups." He took a deep breath. "That was when

I came back to Oxford and began to try to find where he had gone. And after asking all those questions and learning so little, I cursed myself for a fool and thought the likeliest place he would go would be to a whorehouse. It would even explain the horse, if he left it tied in front and it ̄got loose. So I came here—Jules had mentioned the place—and once I was here I asked the whoremistress for you because I remembered the landlord had said you spoke to Jules at The Broached Barrel."

"He did not come here, apparently. Florete knew him and would have . . . no, she might not if he paid her to . . ."

Magdalene gestured for Ormerod to stay put and went out the door to speak to the whoremistress. When she returned she shook her head at Ormerod.

"I thought he might have paid Florete to say he was not here. When I spoke to him, he sounded resentful of his sister's watchful care. But Florete would not lie to me. Jules was not here last night, and neither was I. Bell and I went to Noke to fetch back Niall Arvagh and Mistress Loveday for an audience with the king."

There was a silence. Then Ormerod said, "He had no money . . . I mean above a few pence in farthings to pay for his drink. Where could he have gone? No, he went nowhere because the horse came back alone." Another silence followed before Ormerod asked, very softly, "Do you think he is dead, Magdalene?"

She bit her lip and tears came into her eyes. "We should not have asked what he saw that night. The back door of the alehouse was open. But he said again and again that he saw nothing, and it was noisy inside, and we were not shouting. Oh, I am so sorry if any hurt befell him. But Bell *warned* him and I warned him, too, to go right home."

She remembered that neither she nor Bell had believed completely what Jules said and wondered if it had been his expression that betrayed him, which no one in the alehouse could have seen, or something in his body or voice. If his tone had betrayed him, a listener might have taken alarm. Magdalene put a hand across her lips to still their trembling and sniffed.

"No. Let us not believe the worst, not yet. What did the stableman say? Did Jules himself take his horse? Was he too drunk to ride? Could he have fallen right near the stable and then crawled away to sleep in a corner?"

"Of course he took his own . . . no, I don't know. When I was with him, I dragged him with me to the stable so he could walk off the drink a little, but now I remember that the landlord of The Broached Barrel was going to send a boy to get Jules's horse. I didn't speak to the stableman. I saw the horse was not in its usual stall and rode out again. It was a different man this morning. He hadn't seen Jules."

"A different man?" Magdalene said faintly, then shook herself. "No. I will not think horrors. Come, Lord Ormerod, I will go to the stable with you—"

"You? What do you know about horses or saddling or how to talk to stablemen?" He stood up and looked down at her. "Besides, if what I fear is true then what happened to Jules is likely your fault. What business is it of yours to be interfering with the law and hunting a murderer? Is your life so clean? Or were you trying to warn the killer? Who knows what a whore will do for money?"

Magdalene was so shocked by the sudden attack from a man who had always been civil to her, despite being well aware of what she was, that she simply sat staring at him as he whirled away from her and flung himself out of the room, slamming the door behind him. Then a wave of fury hit her, and she rose to her feet stiffly, feeling for her pocket. She had a sudden impulse to pay Rand and Ogden to follow Ormerod to the stable and lesson him to mind his tongue.

She sank back down on the stool before she touched the coins. How stupid! Rand and Ogden were doubtless known to the sheriff, and beating a nobleman could only get Florete in trouble. Then she blinked, recognizing the reason for her own fury; had she not been missaid far worse before? She was angry because she felt guilty for any harm that came to Sir Jules, and Lord Ormerod's fury was not really directed at her at all but at himself for not having been with Jules, of whom he was truly fond.

Yes, likely he was, Magdalene thought, but even so, would not Lord Ormerod's guilt and thus his fury be even more intense if he was half-hoping that Jules was lying dead somewhere? That would surely make Marguerite the heir to the entire Osney estate and a real prize for his brother. And if Ormerod had already killed St. Cyr so that Jules could marry Loveday, would it not be that much easier to kill again?

Magdalene shook herself like a dog ridding its fur of something unpleasant. Nonsense. She had known Lord Ormerod for nearly five years, from the time he was a blushing boy, and she knew him for a good-hearted man. She sighed. But he did love his lands and held what was his in a tight grip. If he felt Jules was misusing his land and thus robbing his brother of what would rightfully be his . . . No, she told herself, surely she was making this all up in her head. Surely Jules would turn up none the worse for his absence except for his aching head and empty gut.

She went to fetch her sewing basket from the shelf and drew out the ribbon she was embroidering for Ella, fixing her mind on trying to recall what she had decided about the next row of flowers. Having remembered and planned the pattern, she chose a yellow thread to do the knots that would be the heart of the flower, but put it down again at the scratch on her door.

"Come," she called, then grabbed for the scissors from the basket, fearing that it was Ormerod returning to tell her Jules was dead and attack her to punish her. She had welcomed him once, and Florete would never think to have her men stop him.

Even as the thought came, she dropped the scissors and laughed. A man bent on beating a woman does not scratch politely on the door. And when the door opened, it was the whore Hertha who poked her head in. Geneva followed close on her heels.

"You said you wanted to hear anything even faintly connected to St. Cyr?"

"Yes," Magdalene said, and gestured to the other stools near the table.

The two women seated themselves and Hertha said, "The looby was in again yesterday, late. It would have been near Vespers." Then she shrugged. "He didn't mention St. Cyr, though. All he kept talking about was how good his memory is and how he remembered—"

"Yes he did," Geneva said. "It was when he was standing by Florete's table. He was arranging to have you at the same time each day—"

Hertha nodded and groaned, then almost smiled. "He isn't so bad. He's in and out in no time and he doesn't hit. If he didn't smell so bad . . ." Then she giggled. "I wonder if he *can* remember the way he said. I told him he should take a bath and he blinked at me, stupid as an owl, but he said he would. If he's clean when he comes tomorrow—"

"What did he say about St. Cyr?" Magdalene asked, but she could not help smiling at the women and hoping that Manville d'Arras would take a bath.

"He said that Aimery—he always calls him Aimery, not St. Cyr—was cleverer than he, but that when Aimery needed something remembered, like where he had left something to be repaired, it was he, Arras, who remembered."

"Interesting," Magdalene remarked, feeling in her pocket for farthings, "but I don't see it gets us any further toward who murdered St. Cyr. What else did Arras talk about?"

"Nothing to do with St. Cyr, not even his will, which he was so full of the last time he came. This time he was going on and on about where the bishop of Salisbury's men were lodged. He seemed to think it was very funny that they were in St. Peter's churchyard out in the rain because the church isn't big enough to hold them all."

"He thought that was funny?" Magdalene asked.

"Yes, because there were some half-empty lodgings just across the road." Hertha shrugged. "Oh, yes, it was St. Cyr who told him that and when I asked Arras why it made him laugh, he said that Aimery had laughed when he told him that might happen. Sorry. That was another time he mentioned St. Cyr."

"There was something else," Geneva said, "which is why I stuck myself in here. His voice is very loud and after he talked about the empty lodging, he laughed and said, 'I've got you. I've got you.' Likely it doesn't mean anything, but when I asked Hertha about it, she said she remembered him calling out but he was just about to spill his seed, and she thought it was that

that made him cry out. But it didn't sound like that to me,"
Geneva added, a bit defensively, as if she were afraid Magdalene wouldn't credit her tale. "Usually he just chokes and gur-
gles, and you did say 'anything,' so I thought I'd come and tell
you."

Magdalene laid the two farthings she had removed from her
pocket on the table. "I don't know what it means, if anything,
but I'm glad you came to me. For one thing, I'm glad the man
is alive and well. Yesterday at Noke Manor he was swearing
that he would find St. Cyr's killer and be avenged for the loss
of his friend. It is a relief to me that his mind is fixed on
something else now. I doubt that finding the plight of Salisbury's men amusing will get him into any more serious trouble
than a beating."

"One more thing was a little odd," Hertha said. "He paid
Florete to be sure I would be free tomorrow, then a man left
Chloris's room; that's the one right near the outside door. Arras
watched his back—the way one does sometimes watch someone moving away—then he said to me he'd see me tomorrow.
But his face . . . his mind moves so slowly you can almost see
him thinking. Anyway, he didn't even finish his sentence, but
went out the door."

Magdalene frowned. "Did you recognize Chloris's client?"

"No," Hertha said, and there was nothing in her manner that
hinted to Magdalene that she was lying to protect the man.

"Never really saw him," Geneva agreed. "Just a glimpse of
dark hair and a shoulder in a red cloak going out the door."

Red cloak. Half the men she knew, including Bell, wore red
cloaks. Magdalene dismissed that. "Do you think Arras was
following the man who had left Chloris?"

Both whores pursed their lips thoughtfully. "I don't think he was," Geneva said. "It was as if he remembered something and intended to take care of it."

"You only say that because you heard him say he remembered things." Hertha was clearly annoyed. "What were you doing there anyway?"

"I had come out to—"

"To see if you could snatch a customer from me," Hertha snapped.

"Well, the way you groan and complain every time he shows up, I thought you would be glad to be rid of him."

Geneva snatched up her farthing, got to her feet, and walked out. Hertha said angrily, "She wouldn't leave the rest of us a single man if she could. I told her not to come with me. You've just wasted a farthing on her."

"Maybe so." Magdalene smiled. "But it isn't my farthing, so it is easier to part with. And to speak the truth, I don't know what will be useful. Nothing I've heard today, I suspect. Still . . . I am still ready to pay for anything Arras says, or if anyone asks about St. Cyr."

"I will listen," Hertha said, also picking up her farthing and going out.

Magdalene worked on Ella's ribbon for a time, thinking over what the women had told her. She hoped Geneva had been wrong about Arras's exclamation, just trying to earn another farthing. She also hoped his sudden departure had nothing to do with the man he had seen leaving—she must ask Chloris if she knew the man. It was some comfort to her that Arras had talked about nothing except the lodging of the bishop of Salisbury's men. Probably he could hold no more than one idea in his head at a time.

She began to feel hungry and put aside her embroidery to

tell Diccon to go out and get her a meal, but she heard the
rain pouring down so she picked up the embroidery again.
Most of the time she was grateful for the almost mindless quality of the work, which permitted her to listen while hiding her
expression from impatient clients. But today she wished it held
her thoughts better to exclude Arras and Sir Jules.

Eventually the rain eased off and she stepped out to give
Diccon her order. She found that Rand was going as well as
the boy. None of the whores wanted to go out in the rain and
Florete had collected a sum that would cover meals for everyone. Magdalene gladly contributed her portion, then added
four more farthings and asked to have three meals brought to
her.

"The men are supposed to feed you!" Florete remarked dryly,
"Not you them."

Magdalene laughed. "It is not a matter of money with Bell.
You saw the meal he sent in the other day. And William . . .
well, he pays me generously enough so that I would be
ashamed to charge him for a meal here and there. Anyway, it
is just to be sure. I doubt either of them will come today—
they are both tied up at Court—but Bell will probably spend
the night." She grinned, wrinkling her nose. "Likely Diccon
will eat very well this afternoon and tomorrow morning."

Since the rain had discouraged custom, the Soft Nest was
quiet and Magdalene sat down beside Florete to gossip, as she
had been longing to do since she arrived.

"I hope I did no wrong in sending Hertha and Geneva to
you," the whoremistress said. "I was afraid they were just spin-
ning tales to winkle out another farthing or two from you, but
you did say you wanted to hear anything about the looby—"
Florete grinned suddenly "—and I figured you were old enough

and wise enough to be rid of them if they had nothing to tell you."

Magdalene grinned back. "And you have to deal with them day by day, so it is better for me, who will soon be gone from Oxford, to disappoint them than for you to try to keep them away from me."

"Exactly!" Florete said, giggling. Then her eyes filled suddenly with tears. "Oh, Magdalene, it is so good to talk to someone who understands and has no bitterness. How? How do you keep your spirit so light?"

"Because God, or perhaps the Merciful Mother, has been very good to me."

"To make you a whore?"

Magdalene put her hand over Florete's. "If you knew from what I fled to whoredom, you would agree. And beyond that, I have William to protect me—"

"And a handsome young lover to make up for any lacks in your great patron's looks and ability." Florete glanced sidelong at Magdalene.

"It is more than that with Bell," Magdalene admitted. "We laugh at the same things and we think about many things the same way; we have the same kind of curiosity, too. Bell will worry away at St. Cyr's death until he finds the truth . . . and so will I."

Florete shuddered. "While I would be only too glad to forget it, no matter who did it. Which brings me back to the looby. Did he say anything that might be useful to you?"

"No, he seems to have been distracted from his friend's death to the problem of lodging the bishop of Salisbury's men—in which, thank God and all His saints, I have no interest at all. I thought he was going to make trouble about . . . ah . . . that girl's betrothal—"

Magdalene's voice checked suddenly and she caught her breath. Loveday's betrothal! How St. Cyr had learned that Loveday was an heiress! Heaven help her, she had forgotten that she must tell Raoul de Samur at once about the hidey hole in Waleran's house. Or should she tell William first? No, Niall would tell William; he probably had told him already. She glanced out the door and saw that the rain was little more than a fine mist now.

"I have just remembered that I must speak with Raoul de Samur. He is one of Lord Waleran's captains."

If Florete was surprised by Magdalene's truncated first remark and the non sequitur that followed it, she gave no sign of it. All she said was, "As soon as he returns, Diccon can carry a message to Samur."

"No. No. I do not want anyone in Waleran's lodging to know Samur received a message. Can one of your girls go, perhaps acting as if she were just seeking custom? Geneva. She was the one who lay with Samur a few days ago, so she need not say she is from the Soft Nest or that I wish to speak to him. He will guess. Let her name another whorehouse if anyone might hear her invite him to come back with her. I will pay, of course." Then Magdalene snorted lightly and grinned. "Perhaps she should pay me. From what I hear, she is always seeking customers. She may find a few more in that lodging."

Florete looked toward the closed curtain of the cocking chamber. "She is with someone right now, but will find a way to be rid of him, I am sure, when Rand gets back with the meal. You can talk to her then."

So Magdalene asked for Chloris, but when Ogden fetched

her out, she could remember nothing about the man who had
gone into the corridor when Arras was there. In fact, she was
not at all sure which day or which man Magdalene wanted her
to remember, until Magdalene mentioned the red cloak. Then
she nodded recognition but she could still say little. He had
offended her by asking about the other whores while he was
futtering her, and he might have been a gentleman from his
speech because his English was halting. His face? Chloris
shrugged. Who looked at them? It was a face. He had dark
hair . . . or maybe it was only wet with sweat.

Magdalene sighed, but she had not expected much more.
Still, she gave Chloris a farthing and told her to come to her
if she remembered more. By then Geneva was finished with
her man, but when Magdalene made her request, the first thing
she did was ask Florete where Rand was, and why he was
taking so long.

"I am starved," she said, "and I paid for my food." She
glanced at Magdalene. "Your errand will have to wait."

"There's no hurry," Magdalene responded, knowing that to
show her impatience would increase Geneva's price, but when
the whore had taken the half-pence she offered and gone to
the door to look out, Magdalene frowned at Florete. "It is taking Rand a long time to walk a few streets."

"He is going a little farther than our usual place," Florette
admitted. "Across the alley from The Broached Barrel there is
a cookshop that does large quantities at reduced prices and
throws in a couple of loaves of bread and a jack of ale, too.
And the food is still good," she said, defending herself.

"I am a little concerned because the men-at-arms will be
eating now and likely Samur will be there, but if Geneva comes

much later, he may well be gone about some other duty or his own business. Will she wait to speak to him?"

"In a house full of men?" Florete laughed. "Unless she cannot find even one who will make an idle hour profitable for her she will wait. If not, do not trouble your head. Geneva knows on which side of her bread the dripping has fallen. You pay, and she wishes to please you. She will find a way to bring your man here."

"He is no man of mine—" Magdalene began, only to be cut short by the door bursting open to admit Rand and Diccon.

"Dead!" Diccon piped, his eyes open wide with excitement. "There's another one dead!"

CHAPTER 17

24 June
The Soft Nest

W"hat? Who is dead? Where?" Florete cried, leaping to her feet.

Rand deposited his burden on Florete's table and smacked Diccon alongside the head as soon as his hands were free. "Nothing for us to fear, Mistress," he said to Florete. "The dead man was found at the stable in that lane near The Broached Barrel. You know it. It's on the same side of the street as the cookshop, except the cookshop is on Cornmarket Street itself and the stable is in the lane."

"Who is dead? Do you know?" Magdalene asked faintly.

"Not one of yours," Florete said, putting her hand over Magdalene's, which was clenched hard. "Lord William's horses would not be in that stable and your Bell—"

"No," Magdalene said, drawing a deep shuddering breath. "It is not for them I fear." She looked up at Rand. "Did you hear anything beyond that a man was dead in the stable?"

"Not in the stable," Diccon said brightly, and skipped out of Rand's reach. "He was out in the yard under a pile of straw. Some lord came asking for a friend, oh, just before it began to rain very hard again. He saw that the horses were acting funny, all huddled together on one side when there was a pile of hay on the other side, so he looked. It was his friend under the hay. Made a terrible fuss, he did. All kinds of threats against the stablemen."

Magdalene closed her eyes. "My fault," she whispered.

"Oh God," Florete murmured. "Don't tell me that men have been fighting over you again."

"No. This time my face is not to blame but my stupid curiosity."

She told Florete about her meeting with Sir Jules in the backyard of The Broached Barrel, and of her fear that the man who had murdered St. Cyr had been watching and listening and decided to do away with Sir Jules, who might have seen something incriminating.

"But maybe it isn't him," Florete said.

"It must be," Magdalene sighed. "The man who made the fuss must be Lord Ormerod. You remember how he rushed out. He had been looking for Sir Jules all over—he asked you if Jules had come here and I asked again. Then I reminded him that he had seen Jules's horse was gone from the stable but never looked for Sir Jules himself there, where he might have fallen down drunk. So he rushed out to look."

"An accident?" Florete asked. "He curled up to sleep and pulled the hay over him . . ."

"Not after he bashed in his own head," Rand said with a coarse laugh. "Wasn't enough of his brains left to know he was cold and wanted the hay to cover him."

"It still could have been an accident," Florete insisted. "He was drunk. He could have fallen down in the yard and something startled the horses so that they kicked him in the head."

Diccon opened his mouth, but Magdalene shook her head at him and directed him to take two of the dinners into her chamber. She picked up the third portion for which she had paid and said she would send Diccon out again with bowls for the stew—a spicy fish concoction today—which was in a large kettle. When the boy came back, she shut the door behind him and gestured for him to sit, take some bread, and a bowl of stew.

"Now, what did you see and hear? I want everything, from the beginning."

The beginning was the crowd of people in the alley, which distracted Rand from his errand. Diccon, being small, had been able to worm his way through the lane right up to the stable where he had heard the gentleman who had been in the Soft Nest bellowing at one of the stablemen—the night man, who was still knuckling sleep from his eyes. Essentially Diccon had little more to tell than Rand had already told Florete—except one thing.

"It wasn't the horses. The cudgel he was hit with was in the hay with him."

"A real cudgel, not just a piece of wood?"

Diccon swallowed a mouthful. "Yeah, a real cudgel. A bullyboy's cudgel. From The Broached Barrel, it was. I didn't hear it myself, but the people was saying that the sheriff's man was in the alehouse trying to find out who used the cudgel."

"The sheriff's man? The sheriff was taking an interest?"

The boy laughed. "With a lord shouting his head off at the stable and it being a knight who was killed, and with a common man's cudgel? Sure the sheriff will take an interest."

"But I don't think a common man killed him," Magdalene murmured, putting a hand to her head. "Oh, I wish I could reach Bell before they blame the people at The Broached Barrel."

"Do you want me to look for him?" Diccon asked, but his voice was reluctant and his eyes were on his food.

"No. I doubt you could get to him. He was going to Court to bring a petition to the king."

Diccon shrugged. "Might get in. Might not. Depends on the guards. If I say I'm running a message, sometimes they let me pass."

"Well, finish your dinner first and then go seek out Bell. You can say that I sent you, but not that he must come here. Tell him about Sir Jules's death, tell him what you saw and heard at the stable, and tell him it is most unlikely that the killer was the bullyboy from The Broached Barrel, although the sheriff's man was questioning him. Lord Ormerod discovered that Sir Jules left the alehouse in perfect health with Tirell Hardel and was in Hardel's lodging until at least Nones. Can you remember all that?"

"I can remember, but I might as well finish eating. They'll be setting up for dinner, or eating it at the castle. The guards won't let me in while there's food on the tables. They figure I'll be begging or trying to steal."

Magdalene nodded acceptance of that, broke off a piece of bread, and dipped it in the stew. It was good stew, with chunks of tender fish in it. But it was cooling a little now, and she had lost her appetite. She ate slowly, her mind on Sir Jules's death. He had left Tirell at Nones and Master Woller said that Tirell had gone back to his chamber. But how long had Woller watched? Could Tirell have slipped out?

He, at least, knew that Sir Jules was headed for the stable. Ormerod had said Woller heard Jules tell Tirell he was going home, and to do that he needed to get his horse.

The man who had been listening—if there was such a man—could not have known Sir Jules would go to the stable. Yes, he could have known if he had heard Bell warn Jules to go home. But then would he have gone ahead—the stable was just around the corner and across the lane from the alehouse— or would he have waited to follow Jules? If he had waited to follow, he would have heard Jules ask for his horse, then stop the boy, and drink and go with Tirell.

He must have been very desperate if he waited outside Woller's shop until Jules came out. And he could not have known that Tirell would not accompany Jules. Why should he be in such a hurry to kill? Ah! Possibly the fact that Jules had gone with Tirell fixed in the killer's mind that Jules *did* know who he was. If Jules had not known of whom to be afraid, would he have trusted an utter stranger after he had been warned of his danger?

Diccon finished his meal and Magdalene roused herself to give him three farthings: one for him and two for bribery if necessary. The boy ran off, returned to bring back the cleaned bowl from which he had eaten, and went off again. Magdalene finished her stew but found she did not want anything more. She rose and rinsed her bowl, opened a shutter to throw out the wash water and then, because it was not raining hard, left the shutter open. Still thinking of Jules's death, she covered the three slices of pork pasty and the remains of the bread—not nearly as generous a dinner as she usually took, but enough for tidbits if Bell came later.

That hope lightened her heart a little, but not for long. It occurred to her, as she again took up the ribbon she was embroidering for Ella, that she had too easily dismissed Tirell as

the murderer. Just because Loveday said he would not kill . . .
No, there was also Woller's evidence that Tirell had not left
after Jules did, and Woller seemed reasonably vigilant if he
crept up to listen and make sure the young men were not
quarreling.

That left only Ormerod and the "friend in a high place"
mentioned by Arras. Magdalene continued to create delicate
flowers while she considered Manville d'Arras and his statements. Could he have desired Loveday for himself and, having
St. Cyr's will, stabbed his friend in the back? Magdalene shook
her head. She simply could not believe it and, in addition, she
doubted Arras had a mail shirt. So the friend . . . good Lord,
could it be Ferrau?

Ferrau was a knight. Ferrau was in Alain of Brittany's Household and could have been in Waleran de Meulan's lodging
when, St. Cyr had backed one of Alain's men into a corner.
To Arras, would a knight in service like Ferrau be a friend in
a high place? And even if Ferrau was the friend, was St. Cyr's
approach in Waleran's lodging and several other minor em-
barrassments enough to kill over?

Not Ferrau's embarrassment, that was not enough, but Count
Alain was *very* proud. What if he threatened to dismiss Ferrau
from his service if he did not cut his connection with St. Cyr?
Magdalene nodded slowly to herself. Ferrau would have rid
himself of St. Cyr for that, she thought, but then realized that
Count Alain could not have threatened dismissal because he
had instructed Ferrau to retrieve St. Cyr's purse, which carried
the betrothal agreement. But that was after St. Cyr was dead
and not contaminating the atmosphere any longer.

Well, it was something to ask Bell about. He knew Sir Ferrau
and might either know how he would react or be able to find

out if Count Alain had objected to the relationship. Of course, it would be easier for William . . .

A loud crash of thunder, then another, then the sound of rushing rain. Magdalene jumped up and ran to close the shutters on the window. She was just in time. Two of the three candles on the table were blown out. She relit the two from the one still flickering and then went to get torchettes from the shelf. Although with the sky black and the shutters closed so she couldn't hear the bells of St. Friedesweide over the rain, she had no idea what time it was; still, it did seem unlikely that the day would become any brighter. The torchettes would not blow out so easily either.

The room was less dim, and Magdalene felt somewhat better and was about to settle herself to her embroidery again when the corridor outside her door rang with full-throated obscenities. She dropped her embroidery on the table and ran to open the door.

"William," she exclaimed, "you are soaked! Come in and I will dry you off."

"Damn me if I ever go out on such a day again only to give a friend some good news," he bellowed, swinging off his cloak and spattering Florete and her two men with water.

His guardsmen, following him in, were a bit more careful and, as they turned into the common room, Magdalene saw Florete say a few words to her men and go off. Magdalene hoped the whoremistress was going to get some cloths with which to dry William's men, but she did not linger to see. She ran ahead of William into her room to fetch her own drying cloths. He hesitated in the doorway for just a moment, then came in praising her for lighting the place decently.

He threw his cloak on the table, barely missing the ribbon

on which Magdalene had been working, but she did not try to snatch it to safety. The drying cloth lay atop the chest and she dried William's hair and face, then the hands he held out to her. He unbuckled his swordbelt. Dropping the cloth on to a stool, she began to unlace his tunic.

"Sit down, love," she said. "You are too tall for me to pull it off." He sat as she said and let her remove his tunic and spread it on the other end of the table. She *tskd* over the shirt, which was also damp. "I am sorry, love, I never thought to bring any of your shirts or hose. You will have to make do with a blanket—"

"What?" he growled, half laughing and half hurt. "Am I not enough to you for you to lend me one of your Bell's shirts?"

Magdalene gave him a rough hug. "You are enough to me to lend you one of *God's* shirts, if only I had one. Bell has some clothing at the Old Priory Guesthouse because, when Winchester is in London, he lodges with me to act as bullyboy—which *you* suggested, dear William—but he is not my responsibility. I do not think of him when I pack. I should have thought of you."

It was true, Magdalene thought, as she dropped a kiss on William's thinning hair and went to get a blanket in which to wrap him. Bell was her equal and she expected him to see to his own needs. William, so much more powerful, was somehow like a child and incapable of everyday foresight. Nonsense, it was not that William was childlike; he was so accustomed to being served that he no longer bothered to think of such needs as clean shirts. Still, it was rather like caring for a child.

She returned with the blanket, which she draped over his shoulders. "Did you dine, William? Shall I send out for a meal?"

"I dined, but not well." He was grinning fit to split his head.

"Stephen kept me beside him and so busy in talk I hardly had time to fill my mouth and chew."

Magdalene drew a sharp, hopeful breath. "He has quarreled with Waleran? Seen what he truly is?"

William grimaced. "No, not that, unfortunately, but I am certainly in favor today. Of course, I do not know how long it will last, but let me tell this story right side up."

Nodding, Magdalene cleared away her sewing and pushed the slices of pasty and a jack of ale almost under William's hand. Absently he took several swallows of the ale and lifted one of the pasty slices to his mouth.

"Thank God the first thing Niall did was tell me you were all reasonably sure Waleran had nothing to do with forcing that creature—"

"Aimery St. Cyr," Magdalene offered.

William chewed and nodded. "St. Cyr on Loveday." He laughed, seeing that Magdalene's lips had parted to offer the name. "Oh, one does not forget Mistress Loveday. So, not being a fool, I left Niall and his lady and the documents in a corner and went to seek out Waleran. Lady Fortuna had her finger on my shoulder today; he was standing with the king."

He chuckled deeply and Magdalene laughed with him. "What did you say to him?"

"I begged his pardon, humbly and with downcast eyes."

"What?"

William's full laugh bellowed out. "That was just what Waleran said." He stopped laughing and a frown formed between his brows. "He looked quite alarmed, too, as if he did not want to offend me and feared one of his allies had done so without telling him. Hmmm. I must keep my eyes and ears more open than ever. But that has nothing to do with today. I answered him literally, begging his pardon again for thinking ill of him and believing he would set such a man as St. Cyr on a decent woman."

"Did he understand you?"

"No. I will swear he did not. He did not recognize St. Cyr's name nor Loveday's neither. He looked at me as if I had grown a second head and asked why I should think he would meddle in the marriage of some yeoman woman. So then I told him what St. Cyr said to Loveday that first day."

"Did you mention that greedy clerk?"

"No." William laughed again, took another huge bite of pasty and washed it down with more ale. "First, how do I know I will not wish to squeeze that clerk for information some day in the future? I know who he is and I have a hook in him now. And second, since they spoke in private, I did not want Waleran to start wondering how St. Cyr had discovered who and where Loveday was. I quickly diverted him from that idea by apologizing again for not informing him about Loveday's prior betrothal."

"Did he not wonder why you *should* have informed him?" Magdalene sputtered. "I know it must be like a stroke of lightning to him that you should come and apologize for anything, but still . . . It is as if his thinking powers are missing or muddled."

The look of glee faded somewhat from William's face. "No, just so fixed on some purpose he has that he cannot spare a thought for anything else. That may mean grief in the future, but it was of immense benefit today. Anyway, by then I think he had remembered the clerk and Loveday and he swore that he had done nothing about her, she being the king's ward."

"So then I was able to turn to the king, who had been lis-

tening to every word, and confess, again with apologies, that
Niall had mentioned the betrothal to me some four years ago
but that I did not think it important. After all Loveday was not
a great enough heiress to merit special attention and had been
taken into the king's ward, which would keep her safe. Niall
was in no hurry to marry and was necessary to me just then,
so I just put the matter aside and then, of course, forgot it
completely."

Snatching bites between words, William had finished the
second slice of pasty and emptied the ale. Magdalene took the
empty jack away and pushed another into its place.

"And then," William continued, "Dame Fortune touched me
again and made Stephen ask about Niall: why, if he already
had the lady in hand, had he killed St. Cyr? So I was able to
say he had not and could not have and summon him forward
to present the priest's and servants' statement's."

"The king received them well? He had no doubts? No ob-
jections?"

"The king received them with relief and joy . . ." William's
voice faded, and he looked hard at Magdalene. "Why was he
so glad? And Waleran, too? I swear he was delighted that no
shadow with regard to the killing should fall upon me." His
lips thinned. "You know what that means? That means fighting." He sat silent for a moment and Magdalene put her hand
over his. He looked down at their hands. "Well, it is no surprise! It will come when it comes. Meanwhile, your task is over.
It no longer matters who stepped on the louse, St. Cyr."

"But it does, William," Magdalene said. "The man who
stabbed St. Cyr has killed again."

"Killed again? Who?

"A rather worthless young man called Sir Jules of Osney. Sir

Jules seems to have gone out to use the privy in The Broached Barrel just when the killer stuck the knife in St. Cyr's back or a few minutes later. He claimed to have seen nothing, but Bell and I both had our doubts about the truth of that. We warned him to go home where he would be safe, but he did not, and he was found dead under a heap of straw in a pen in the stable yard with his head bashed in."

"But that has nothing to do with me! I never heard of Sir Jules of Osney."

Magdalene looked down at the table. "No, of course not. Niall was still at Noke the day Sir Jules was killed, and since Niall cannot have killed St. Cyr he cannot have had any reason to kill Sir Jules, nor could you have."

"As long as that is understood."

Magdalene nodded rather sadly. William did not care for simple justice or about stopping the murderer. His ends were satisfied and he wanted no further connection to the crime, not even that of solving it. Worse he might even tell her not to look further into St. Cyr's and Sir Jules's deaths. Magdalene sought a diversion.

"What of Loveday's petition?" she asked. "Did she get to present it to the king?"

The frown that had been gathering on William's brow dissipated and he began to laugh. "Yes she did. In fact I could not have stopped her if I wanted to. What she did was to come right up to the king in Niall's shadow. She waited while he was presenting the evidence to clear himself, and then, the betrothal having been mentioned, simply stepped in front of him, weeping . . . Oh, just a little, and very prettily, and began to beg the king's pardon for all the trouble she had caused."

Magdalene nodded. "That is what she said she would do. A most redoubtable girl."

William was still laughing and shaking his head. "She is a one, that one! I wish I could hire her to present cases for me. The king was wrapped and tied in half a candlemark. We all went together, Waleran included, so he could not say he meant her for another at some later time, into Stephen's private closet so he could call a clerk, approve her appeal, and approve her marriage." William laughed again. "I was sincerely glad she did not ask for the crown; he might have handed it to her."

"Thank God that is finished." Magdalene sighed. "Is Niall recalled to duty?"

"I am not so cruel," William chortled. "I sent them both back to Noke to plan their wedding." His grin widened. "Not that keeping him here would have benefitted me in any way. Until he has her fast and has bedded her, I would not get any work out of him anyway."

He looked at the table, empty except for his cloak and tunic and Magdalene's sewing basket, and blinked his eyes. "I seem to have eaten your dinner."

Now Magdalene laughed. "I am not so improvident. I ordered extra food because I thought Loveday might return here. And I think I have some sweetcakes to finish off the meal, if you would like them."

"With wine," William said. "I drank that damned ale because it was by my hand, but no more, at least not with sweetcakes."

Magdalene went to fetch the cakes and wine, and when she had put them on the table said, "I hope you destroyed that betrothal agreement. It was false, of course, but if it came into the hands of someone who wished ill to Niall or Loveday it could be used to make trouble. Do you have any idea why

Count Alain and Lord Hervey should have signed it?"

"They did not do so. I knew the hand was not Count Alain's. I have seen his signature elsewhere." William made a face, and Magdalene thought he must have witnessed that signature on some recent grant. "I thought a long time before I decided what to do, but finally I cut out Loveday's name and all that pertained to her estate and brought the parchment to Count Alain." He showed his teeth in what was not a smile. "It was a pleasure to see the look on his face, but he told me it was not Hervey's signature either." He sighed. "I had sort of hoped that Hervey had forged Alain's signature. Still, he will be look- ing cross-eyed at his Household, wondering who took his name in vain."

Magdalene could have told him that, but she said nothing. If Count Alain had not signed the forged betrothal, he would never have told Ferrau to retrieve it from Niall; in fact, he would not have known the document existed. So it must have been Ferrau himself who had the forgery made. Of course. He would not ask Count Alain to sign the betrothal of a common man-at-arms to a yeoman's daughter. She wondered whom he had got to sign such august names.

So that was why St. Cyr was killed! No, that couldn't be the cause. If Ferrau intended to kill St. Cyr over the betrothal, he would have killed him before the document was prepared. And if Count Alain knew nothing about the forged document, that eliminated the only other cause Ferrau had to be rid of St. Cyr—that Count Alain would dismiss him for associating with the creature.

Hardly realizing what she was doing, she leaned forward to refill William's cup of wine, and was somewhat surprised to be seized and pulled from her seat into his lap and into a rather passionate kiss. William hardly ever kissed when having sex.

"Will you put a cap of pleasure on this singularly pleasant day?" he asked, when he released her lips. "The rain is stopping, but I will not be wanted until after Nones." He chuckled. "And I am half undressed already."

"Very gladly," Magdalene agreed, although a slight pall of anxiety passed over her like a chill.

She had told Diccon to tell Bell she did not expect him to come, but he might do so. No matter. Florete would tell him that William was with her and Bell would go away. He would be angry. Then he was a fool!

Magdalene held out her hand and smiled. This was the second time William had *asked* if she would serve him. Usually he simply grabbed at her. He was pleased and relaxed. She had spoiled her own pleasure the last time they had coupled and was determined not to do it again. William was aware that the satisfaction she simulated was false coin and usually did not care, but he had been different since she had arrived in Oxford. If she possibly could, this time she would repay him in true gold.

CHAPTER 18

24 June,
The Soft Nest

Magdalene looked down at the heavy gold ring in her hand. It was worth a month's earnings from the Old Priory Guest-house, but she still rather wished William had not given it to her. It had been very good between them, a warm comfort that built slowly into passion and fulfillment. And they had been able to rest quietly in each other's arms until the languor of love had passed. Even then, when he said he had to go, he had not offered an extra purse, but said only, "You are good to me and for me, Chick."

Perhaps it was her own fault. She had trod amiss after he was dressed and just ready to leave the room, blinking less than usual and smiling back at her. She had run after him and caught at him. His eyes had widened and his face was soft and surprised. Magdalene bit her lip. How could she have been so stupid? She now realized he had been expecting her to ask him to stay or to say . . . she loved him. Which she did! But she had not said it.

She had said, "Good Lord, I almost forgot. Niall told you about the hiding place in Waleran's attic, I am sure. I've sent for Raoul de Samur. Shall I tell him? Do you trust him enough to carry honestly what he hears to you?"

William had become instantly tense and alert, all softness gone from his expression, but not all pleasure. "Samur!" he exclaimed, grinning broadly. "Bless you, Chick! God in heaven, my wits have gone to seed. I had forgotten all about Samur. Yes, yes indeed, tell him. He is just the man for dirty work like that. As to bringing me the news honestly, I do not believe he knows what honest is. You know, he seems actually to take pleasure in telling me what he learns in Waleran's Household. I pay him well, of course, and praise him . . ."

"He admires you, William," Magdalene said, smiling.

"Admires me?"

Magdalene went up on tiptoe to kiss William of Ypres's nose. "Yes, he does, I have heard it in the way he speaks about you. But even so, you had better consider carefully anything he tells you. The man is a snake. He might take a perverted pleasure in bringing down someone he admires."

"Teaching your grandfather to suck eggs again?" he asked grinning. Then, acknowledging her warning, he said, "You wiggle a bit snakelike yourself, both mind and body," and pulled off the ring and pressed it into her hand.

Magdalene sighed. Yes, it had been her own fault, but she had not hurt William. He had been doubly assured of her care and loyalty. It was only she, herself, who was hurt by being reminded that William thought her loyalty could only be bought or reinforced with gold. Then she tossed the ring up and down in her hand and grinned. She would be loyal to William if he never paid her another penny, but it was just as well he didn't know that—and much more profitable.

She had barely had time to put the ring away before the

door was scratched. She hurried away from the chest—there was no need for Florete or any other whore to know she had just put a treasure away—and when she reached the table called, "Come."

Raoul de Samur stuck his head around the door, stepped in, and shut it tight. "Why the devil did you send for me when Lord William was here? I barely had time to grab one of the common girls to pretend . . . What if word gets back?"

"He was not here when I sent for you. And unless you opened your mouth, no one should know you were coming here. The girl was told to name another whorehouse, if she had to give a name. As for Lord William, he came to give me news of two friends, Niall Arvagh and Mistress Loveday, to tell me they are, as we all hoped, to be married and have gone out of Oxford to Noke. Nothing to do with you."

"Then why did you send for me?"

"I have learned a secret that might be very profitable to you. You remember Aimery St. Cyr?"

"Of course I remember him," Samur growled, grimacing. "The lout was in my troop, and more trouble than he was worth, I assure you."

"St. Cyr found a place in the attic of Lord Waleran's lodging above the solar where one can hear clearly whatever is said below."

Samur stood staring at her. "And was killed for it?"

Magdalene did not answer, remembering that she had wondered whether Waleran had found out about St. Cyr and ordered his death.

After a moment Samur shook his head. "No. I swear no order was given to remove St. Cyr. I do not believe Lord Waleran knew he existed." His eyes narrowed. "And there have been no workmen around the lodging. I cannot imagine that Lord Waleran would leave open such a crack in his privacy."

"Neither can I. Which means Lord Waleran is still unaware that there is a place in which his private councils can be over-heard. If you can find the place and listen—" Magdalene reached out and gently touched the gold ring that Raoul de Samur had hinted he had bought with what William had paid him for information "—it might be very profitable."

"Why are you telling me this? Are you planning to betray me? Or do you want a share of what Lord William will give me?"

Magdalene laughed. "A share would not be amiss, but that is the least of my reasons. When Lord William is satisfied and happy, it is greatly to my profit. When he is harried—" she shrugged and mentally apologized to William who had never taken out his ill humors on her, except for a bellow or two "—I suffer for it. The more he knows, the more he prospers, the more do I."

Samur nodded curtly. "Mayhap I will. Mayhap I will not use this information. It may be too dangerous."

"Do what you think best," Magdalene said shortly, stepping around Samur and opening the door.

She had not liked the speculative look in his eyes, as if he might ask her to convince him with her body to serve William. Likely enough he did not expect her to agree; he merely wanted to be able to tell William that she did not think his safety and profit worth ten minutes on her back. He opened his mouth, she suspected to ask anyway, and she thought nas-tily that two could play his game. She smiled sweetly at him but kept her voice very low.

"I asked Lord William's permission to tell you," she said, "and he approved."

"Bitch," Raoul remarked, but there was little heat in the word. "You're as clever as they say."

She kept her sweet smile, trying to look idiotic. "It is a wise man who thinks so, anyway."

Samur lifted a lip at her and then went out the door. Magdalene could see that the rain was coming down again, although not with the rush that had soaked William when he came in. But he must be safe back in the castle by now.

The corridor was quiet and Florete smiled invitingly, but Magdalene was aware of being in her bedgown and, mindful of the trouble she had caused by being caught in that attire previously, she retreated to her chamber. She stood for a while listening to the rain and hoping that William had not gotten wet again. Then she chuckled at her fond foolishness; if he did, there would be a bevy of servants to take away the wet clothing and supply dry.

She considered changing into a gown, but dismissed the thought. She would not be going out in the rain, and in any case it must be well after Nones now, possibly near Vespers. Vespers. Surely the king was no longer holding Court. And then she wondered where Diccon was and whether he had ever found Bell.

That question answered itself before she had set another row of stitches in Ella's ribbon when Bell simply opened the door and walked in. She did not bother to protest. Florete had seen her go back into the room alone and would have told him it was safe. He was wet but not soaked, and he dropped a blanket, smelling strongly of horse, that had shielded him half on a stool where it slipped to the floor.

"You went to the stable where Jules was killed?" she asked.

"That was what you wanted me to do, was it not?" He came and lifted her face and kissed her.

"Did you discover anything?"

"Some things, but not who killed him, I am sorry to say." He pulled the stool William had been sitting on closer and dropped down on it, stretching his long legs. "And I do not like what I learned. Ormerod was behaving as if he had lost his father and his only brother in one blow. His grief and desire for revenge seem a bit overblown to me. Do you realize that he stood to profit substantially from St. Cyr's death and does profit enormously from Sir Jules's?"

"Yes. Once St. Cyr was dead, Ormerod believed Jules would get Loveday. Then Jules could have repaid his debt to Ormerod and given the promised farm to his sister." She hesitated and then went on slowly, "And with Jules dead, the sister gets everything and Jules could not continue to destroy the property."

"Yes." Bell did not sound happy.

"But I could swear he was not that kind of man," Magdalene protested weakly, then sighed. "Of course, he did not come frequently to the Old Priory Guesthouse and I do not think I have seen him since his father died. Mostly I remember him as an awkward, blushing boy. He could have changed, grown more grasping."

Bell sighed. "I would have said the same as you. On the other hand, I did not know him before his father died. It was afterward that there was trouble about the farm his father had bought and he came to the bishop for help. I was surprised by his insistence that the price was fully paid. The sum in question was not large." He rubbed his arms. "Of course he may simply have objected to being thought a fool and easily cheated."

"Why don't you take off those wet clothes?" Magdalene suggested, although she suspected it was more his distaste for
suspecting Ormerod than the dampness that had chilled him.

He nodded, removed his swordbelt and propped it where
he could reach the weapon easily, and she rose to help him
with ties and laces. When he was rid of his tunic, she laid it
on the other bed carefully so it would not wrinkle as it dried,
then found places for the rest of his clothing. Finally she
handed him the blanket that William had cast away when he
caught her to him.

"Had other company, have you?" he asked, but he was smiling.

Magdalene ignored the question. "Did you see the body?
How did Sir Jules die?"

"Quickly. I doubt he felt more than the single blow that
felled him, and drunk as he was, I suspect he did not even feel
that." Bell's lips thinned. "But whoever hit him was a vicious
man, or had come to hate him. He continued to strike him
until . . . well, long after he was dead."

"How did he dare—out in an open pen? And the stable is
a busy place."

"Mostly in the early morning when people come into the
city to do business and in the late afternoon, near Vespers,
when people ride home again. During the day there are far
fewer customers. I was quite alone when I spoke to the stableman. I could have killed him easily, with no one the wiser, by
just walking him farther back where it is dark.

"Then Sir Jules wasn't killed in the pen."

"No. He was killed in the back of the stable. I found the
place because the stableman mentioned that the horses would

not go there. One cannot see much on packed earth on which horses have been urinating and defecating for years, but when I pushed aside the bedding straw, there was a dark stain in the earth. I *think* it smelled of blood, but between horse piss and manure I could not be sure. But I did try to lead a horse there— a sorry old nag, not in the least fractious, and it jibbed."

"Then he was carried to the yard?"

"Likely wrapped in a blanket. And hiding him in the pen was easy. It would have looked like a man forking hay."

"But even if no one else was there, the stableman—"

"He says he ran out because something startled the horses in the pen, had a sack thrown over his head, was gagged so he could not call out, and his hands bound—"

"That was not what he told Ormerod, or the sheriff's man."

Bell laughed. "Would you have told Ormerod or the sheriff's man that you allowed yourself to be pushed into a corner and told to stand there—and obeyed? He said if he had known of the murder, he would have called for the Watch, but when he was released, he ran first to look at the horses, and all were there, safe. And then he looked at the tack, and that was untouched. In fact, he could see nothing disturbed at all. He says he began to think it was some jest that he did not understand. I think that was true enough, but there was something else he was not telling me."

"Bribed to be silent about the murder?" Magdalene asked.

"Not that. I think he was all but foundered when the body was discovered. I suspect he was paid to run an errand and is afraid to admit it."

"After he was released? Released," Magdalene repeated, frowning. "You said he had been released. How could that be done without him seeing the man who tied him?"

"I did not take to the idea very easily either," Bell admitted
with a shrug. "But when he described what was done . . . What
he said was that the rope, or whatever held the sack into his
mouth was untied, then the rope was loosed from his hands,
very swiftly, and then as the sack was pulled off his head, he
was thrust violently forward so that he fell face down. By the
time he scrambled to his feet, whoever had seized him was
gone."

"He did not look to see who had done it?"

"I think he was afraid at first." Bell was slightly contemptu-
ous, but not much; the stableman was a poor common creature.
"Likely he gave himself the excuse that if he did his duty by
looking after the horses and the tack he would not be blamed.
And then when he saw nothing was missing or damaged, I
think he was ashamed of not having resisted the 'jest' played
on him. And then he was distracted. I think someone came
into the stable and sent him on an errand."

Magdalene's eyes widened. "The killer?"

"Not impossible. The man is clever. Possibly he wanted time
to look around and cover any traces he had left."

"And once the body was well hidden, who could say when
Sir Jules died? How soon would it have been found?"

"Who knows? Possibly not until someone smelled it in two
or three days' time." Bell grimaced and then looked thoughtful
and rather pleased. "But if that was the murderer's purpose,
then Ormerod is not the killer since he made all the fuss that
caused the body to be discovered."

Magdalene nodded slowly. "I suppose so, and yet there is
no one else who profits so much from Sir Jules's death. And
he told me he had ridden into Oxford yesterday, even that he
had stopped at the stable. He said he had seen that Jules's

horse was gone, concluded he had missed Jules somewhere on the road, and had ridden back to Osney. So if he was seen here . . ."

"What do we do, confront him?" Bell asked. "Perhaps if Lord William—"

Magdalene shook her head hard, then looked down at her fingers, knotting and unknotting in her lap. "William says all this has nothing to do with him." She shivered, and added almost bitterly, "He does not care if the killer goes scot-free or goes on killing and killing . . ."

"Good Lord," Bell said softly, dropping the blanket and getting up from the stool to embrace her. "You think that if the killer heard Jules say he had been in the back yard of The Broached Barrel, then he must know it was you to whom Jules was talking." He hugged her tight. "Not to worry, dearling. I am here now, and if I have to leave, I will just warn Florete's men not to let anyone in here."

"I'm not frightened," Magdalene assured him, hugging him back. "I'm . . ." She was going to say disappointed in William, but she would never say that to Bell, and it wasn't true; she knew what William was. She shrugged. "I don't know. William would act quickly enough if I told him I was in danger, but I'm not, not really. And I don't know whom to tell him to act against. Jules didn't tell me anything. If I were concerned it would be for Tirell Hardel, with whom Jules spent everal candlemarks yesterday."

"The merchant who has a mail shirt?"

"Yes. Instead of going home from The Broached Barrel, Jules went with Tirell to his lodging." She then repeated the story Ormerod had told her.

"So this Tirell knew where Jules was going," Bell said. "If he killed St. Cyr to keep Loveday safe and feared Jules had seen him, he could have followed Jules and killed him."

"Master Woller told Ormerod that Tirell didn't leave."

"Then. I would have to look at the shop to see if he could have come down and crept out without Woller's knowledge a little later. We don't know whether Jules actually went directly to the stable."

"And what happened to Jules's horse? Ormerod said it came home by itself during the night, which means someone set it free on a road it knew."

"Came home during the night? The stableman said a servant from Osney paid for stalling it and took it . . . Lord, that killer is a clever beast. He took the horse away so if he somehow missed Jules, Jules would berate the stableman and send him to look for the servant. Meanwhile, Jules would wait or, more likely, go to The Broached Barrel. Whoever killed Jules has the devil's own luck because he didn't even have to fetch Jules out of The Broached Barrel. He must have found him right in the stable."

"Perhaps even asleep. Ormerod said Tirell told him Jules was, as usual, drunk when he left his lodging."

Bell dropped a kiss on Magdalene's head. "I don't think I can do anything more this evening, so I think I'll just step out and tell Diccon to bring us an evening meal."

"Not like that, you won't," Magdalene said, laughing. "I know this is a whorehouse, but it is not the men who usually wander around naked." She grinned at him. "You might shock the poor girls. I'll go."

She rose as she spoke, remembering as she picked up and handed back his blanket that she had told Florete that Lord Ormerod was known to her and meant her no harm. It would be better, she thought, if she made clear that that was no longer true and that Rand and Ogden should not allow *anyone* to walk into her room unannounced except William or Bell. And it was just as well that Bell not know she had been so careless. He was worried enough—and trying to hide it so he would not frighten her.

She grinned as she finished making the situation clear to Florette and turned toward her room. Bell was extraordinarily body-shy for a man; he must have been really distracted to say he would go and speak to anyone wearing nothing. His concern worried her a little. She did not actually feel at all afraid, certain that when the murderer heard her speaking to Jules he must have realized that she did not know anything dangerous. Could Bell know something he was not telling her? Or was he just being a man—certain that a woman was helpless and needed protection?

When she entered the room, Bell was looking out past a shutter he had partly opened. It was raining very hard again—enough excuse for him to turn and say, "I'm not leaving—unless you put me out by force."

Magdalene smiled at him. "No reason for you to leave. I don't think anyone else will come today. William has been and gone and Raoul de Samur, too. He now has the information Arras let slip, about the hidey hole in Lord Waleran's lodging, but he thinks it might be too dangerous to use."

"It might at that." He came back and sat down again.

"Oh," Magdalene said, "speaking of Arras, he was here yesterday, alive and well. He seems either not to have found St. Cyr's friend, or the friend was not the murderer. Besides he seems to have put the question of St. Cyr's death aside. When he was here, he only talked about the lodging for Salisbury's men and another lodging nearby they could have had because it was half-empty. Hertha did not make it very clear and I could not see that it was important. At least that interest should not alarm the killer."

"Now why does that tale make me feel uneasy? It is very odd that Salisbury's men would not be accommodated in a lodging that was too large for those now in it."

Magdalene dismissed his concern. "As I said to Hertha, I thank God and all His saints that that is no business of mine. The murder is enough. Now what . . . oh, Lord, I almost forgot." And she related to Bell the fact that neither Count Alain nor Lord Hervey had signed the forged betrothal. "So why did Ferrau go to such lengths to get it back? Could he be the 'friend' St. Cyr was boasting about?"

Bell suddenly looked very tired. "I don't know," he sighed. "And right now I cannot think of any way to find out. Can we talk about something else, Magdalene? This is a weight on my soul, yet there is nothing more I can do today, and tomorrow I *must* attend Court again. Salisbury did not come today; he sent word he was not well and needed to rest. But he will be there tomorrow and I must report to the dean what his reception is and whether the king gives him a private interview. Fortunately my business was not finished yesterday, so I can return as a plaintiff for the diocese of London and Winchester will not be involved."

"Ah, yes. Speaking of the Court reminds me: I hope you won't starve before Diccon can go out and fetch food because William ate everything in sight. He was in tearing good spirits, said the king kept him so busy talking he had no time to eat. Did you see him and what happened?"

"I saw him," Bell said; his harassed expression disappeared

and was replaced with a smile that was very nearly smug, "but he didn't choose to see me."

"William would not acknowledge you?" Magdalene asked, her heart sinking.

Clearly that smile meant Bell thought William was jealous of him and was deliberately ignoring him. Bell was an over-confident fool if he thought he could win any contest with William of Ypres, who could command a whole army. No, Magdalene thought, Bell must be mistaken. William was never jealous . . . but he had been different since she came to Oxford. And he *had* made that remark about her being unwilling to lend him Bell's shirt.

Bell was still smiling very slightly. "Well, we are not total strangers and I was right near him when he walked over to Lord Waleran. I did not speak to him, but as I said, he looked at me and didn't choose to see me."

See him. William's vision was erratic, Magdalene had dis-covered—although William would never admit it. Perhaps he really had not seen Bell. Or, fixated as he was on his meeting with Waleran, perhaps William really had not noticed Bell. After all, to William Bell was a bare acquaintance and not a very important one at that. But that was not a thing she could say to Bell. Magdalene began to feel better. Let Bell have his little triumph. William would never know and it would keep Bell's temper sweet . . . at least for a while.

"Yes, perhaps," she said in reply to Bell's remark that William had chosen not to see him, "but what happened when William spoke to Waleran?"

Bell chuckled. "You never saw a man more surprised or, after he understood what William was saying about Loveday and St. Cyr, more indignant. The king was indignant too, and asked Waleran why he had tried to give a decent yeoman's daughter to a common man-at-arms. And Waleran swore he had done no such thing, that he had barely given Loveday a thought beyond a vague idea that she would do for one of his captains . . ."

"What is it?" Magdalene asked as Bell's voice faded and he looked past her into nothing.

"It was the way he looked at the king when he said he had been too busy to bother with Loveday. Something passed between them without words and then Waleran swallowed whatever indignation he had felt and accepted William's apology in the most gracious manner. And both he and the king almost leapt with joy when Niall brought forward his proof that he could not have killed St. Cyr. It was clear that neither wished to involve Lord William in the murder and could not care less who had killed St. Cyr."

Magdalene nodded. "William told me that too. He says it means they—the king and Waleran—expect that there will be fighting and he will have to do it." Bell looked concerned— not about William, Magdalene was sure, but about the situation. She shrugged. "I do not like the idea of William going to war. I know, I know. He has told me often enough that he has been fighting since he was fifteen, but he is *not* fifteen any longer, and I worry—"

She stopped abruptly and glanced sidelong at Bell, expecting him to show the thinned lips and flared nostrils of jealousy, but he looked calm, less anxious than he usually did when she spoke of William. Because she had called William old, Magdalene thought, not in so many words, perhaps, but she had implied it. Did he think that would make her care less for William? Did he never think of growing old himself?

However, she was in no mood for argument, so she only said, "There is nothing we can do about what the king and Waleran are planning. Let us lay this killer by the heels and leave the management of the realm to the mighty."

"If you are afraid, Magdalene, go back to London."

She looked at him as if he had sprouted a second head. "Go back to London, when God alone knows what political lunacies will erupt any day and to whom William will need to speak in private? I was called here to provide that privacy. I cannot go back to London."

Bell's mouth opened to make some protest, but a scratch on the door heralded Diccon, who said that the rain had abated and looked like it would stop, at least for a while, and he was ready to go out and fetch an evening meal. Magdalene ordered generously, since Bell would surely break his fast with her and William might be back during the day, and she included two farthings for the cost of borrowing until the next day any dishes or pots.

Bell's expression grew slightly darker as he realized how much of the food was of the kind that could be stored and eaten cold, and remembered what she had last said. However, he said nothing about that in Diccon's hearing, and even when the boy was gone only remarked on the terrible weather and hoped Diccon and their evening meal would not be drowned before he could return. Then Magdalene wondered whether Niall and Loveday had arrived safe at Noke, and Bell, laughing, said doubtless she had spoken firmly to the Lord and his angels and arranged to suspend any downpour until they were under shelter.

The rain came down again, and Magdalene sighed at her lack of influence with the holy powers, and then Diccon was there, looking just like a drowned rat because he had used the blanket Florete had given him to cover himself to protect the food, instead. Such nobility deserved a reward, although Magdalene was well aware that he had done it apurpose to win her sympathy—and his presence would keep all serious topics in abeyance—so Magdalene invited him to share the meal with them. She even went out and asked Florete for some dry clothing for the boy, and made him so happy that he chattered like a magpie.

Neither she nor Bell listened closely. Both had had a busy day and were glad to eat the good, warm meal and let the boy talk. It was not until much later, when the torchettes had been extinguished and they were lying close and warm in Magdalene's bed that she said, "Did I hear Diccon aright? Have they still found no better place for Salisbury's men than St. Peter's churchyard? When they arrived, it did not matter because the weather was mostly fine and warm—"

"It rained several times," Bell mumbled, then yawned. "And Salisbury is in a house a few doors down from the church. I suppose it was the best place to put them so they could come to him quickly at need." He yawned again and snuggled Magdalene closer to him; the day-long rain had made the room chilly and damp. "But I pity those men. I remember too well the misery of needing to camp in the open when there were days of rain, even if the tents did not fail, which they sometimes do."

"I hope it will be better tomorrow," Magdalene breathed.

Bell uttered a sleepy laugh. "For my own sake as well as theirs. I must be out and about tomorrow."

CHAPTER 19

Bell was as good as his word and was gone by the time Magdalene woke. She had only a faint memory of his leaving and was mildly surprised at the soundness of her sleep. Then she rose, smiling, to clean her teeth and wash. She was not responsible for anything here; noises or movements in the night were Florete's problem, not hers.

Magdalene broke her own fast with good appetite, noting that Bell had helped himself liberally, and when she was finished went to check on how much wine and ale remained. The sweetcakes were gone as was all the candied fruit. She took off her bedrobe, gowned herself, and made sure her purse was well filled, frowning as she considered what beside food and drink she would need to buy. There was enough, she thought, to ask Diccon to accompany her and, after a glance at the still-gray sky, she drew a heavy veil over her head.

Then she went out to shop and arrange for a well-stocked larder. She was in no hurry, and when her basket and Diccon's arms were full she sent him back to the Soft Nest while she idled about, talking to merchants and craftsmen. She had just

sent Diccon off for the second time when she noticed a mercery beyond the baker and on the opposite side of the street
from Redding's shop. That mercer had not been there when
she lived in Oxford. Magdalene went across to the place
briskly to look at the goods displayed on the outside counter
and saw a young man seated disconsolately on a stool just
inside the door. He looked familiar. In a moment she recognized Master Reinhart's son, Tirell Hardel.

Beyond Hardel was a counter on which were bolts of cloth.
Magdalene beckoned to the apprentice who was minding the
counter and asked if she could go in to examine one of the
bolts that attracted her. He glanced at her gown, possibly remembered her sending off a boy with an armful of packages,
and made way for her, bowing slightly.

Inside Magdalene walked right past Tirell Hardel, her eyes
fixed on the cloth, which she lifted and examined. Turning
with it in her hands, as if to examine it more carefully closer
to the light, she uttered an exclamation of surprise.

"Master Hardel. How nice to see you." And then, allowing
a look of concern to come into her face, "Is something wrong?
You do not look at all well. I hope there is nothing the matter
with your father!"

Tirell jumped to his feet as if the stool had taken fire. "Ah . . .
no. No. My father is . . . is very well. He has ridden out to
Noke to speak to Mistress Loveday. Ah . . . do you want that
cloth?"

"No. It is the wrong shade when in the light."

Footsteps approached from beyond the counter, and Magdalene realized there must be a workroom behind it in the
back. If Woller had gone back there, Tirell could easily have
come softly down the stair and . . . but there was a bell on the

door that would ring if it were opened. On the inside of the
door. A man could reach up and, if he were careful, seize the
bell in his hand so that it did not ring. But when he closed
the door? Ah, but in the summer the door would be open. Had
Ormerod questioned the apprentice about whether Tirell had
left the house? Probably not. He had not questioned the stableman.

Suddenly Tirell pulled the cloth from her grip, tossed it back
on the counter, seized her wrist and pulled her out of the shop.
Except for her initial start of surprise, Magdalene did not resist.

"Perhaps you would like to buy me a cup of ale," she said
as they passed the apprentice, and when they were out of
earshot, laughing, "Even whores must buy cloth for gowns, you
know. Nor do I think Master Woller would object to taking
my coin."

He ignored her remark and asked angrily, "How do you
know my father?" His eyes were circled with dark rings as if
he had not slept, and he looked over his shoulder toward the
north of the Cornmarket in a harried way. Then he said, "Yes,
yes, I would be delighted to buy you a cup of ale. Come in
here."

Tensed to resist, Magdalene saw he was leading her toward
The Lively Hop and relaxed. She slipped a hand into her
pocket and fingered out two farthings. Those would go to
Mayde, who would come if she signaled or cried out. Tirell
looked north again and quickened his pace to hurry her off
the street.

For two heartbeats Magdalene had to fight the temptation
to tell him his father was a long-time client. Her lips twisted
a little with disgust at the way Reinhart Hardel pretended a
virtue he did not have. To the public at large, that was rea-

sonable, but to his son it could only be because he wished to control the boy's—no, the man's—behavior. But her commitment to her business was more important than Reinhart's relationship with his son, so she assumed an expression of surprise.

"I know your father because Mistress Loveday named us to each other a few days past." She swallowed a giggle; a hint, a very small hint that could be understood if Tirell were clever enough, would not hurt. "Master Hardel seemed to think I had a nefarious purpose in offering Loveday shelter, but truly it was at the behest of one of my patrons' captains. The man is betrothed to Loveday and knows I would never force any woman into my trade."

"Oh," he said, reddening and seeming at a loss, and then added stiffly, "It seems very strange that Loveday would seek shelter with you."

As they entered the alehouse, Magdalene raised a hand and beckoned to Mayde. She looked significantly at the girl and nodded slightly. Mayde hurried over. "I will take a cup of ale," Magdalene said and slipped the farthings into the girl's hand.

Then to Tirell she said, "Mistress Loveday intended to stay with a friend."

"Edmee," Tirell said, "but she is in London."

Magdalene was surprised, remembering what Loveday had told her about Reinhart's rage when Redding married Edmee instead of his daughter.

"Yes," she said. "Loveday could not go back to Noke for fear of St. Cyr and could not stay here alone for fear of Sir Jules . . ." She sat down on the bench, looked up at Tirell, and added, "But she does not need to fear him any longer, does she?"

Even in the dim light at the back of the alehouse, Magdalene could see that Tirell had paled. She was safe enough, she decided, to take a wild chance. "Why did you pretend to remain in your lodging but then follow Sir Jules to the stable?" she asked, her voice soft.

"I did not!" he exclaimed. "I did not follow Jules. I never saw him again after he left my lodging." But then he sat down suddenly as if his knees had given way and dropped his head into his hands. "But I am to blame for his death." His voice was muffled and thick. "I cannot put it out of my mind. I knew he was drunk. I should have gone with him. Instead I left him to stagger about in the street, an open invitation to anyone to beat and rob."

"From what I have heard," Magdalene said, "Sir Jules has been staggering about in the street for years. And what was done to him was no chance, too-strong blow from a thief. It was deliberate murder."

He shuddered and whispered, "But Jules was not there and his horse was gone. I spoke to the stableman and sent him . . . that does not matter; it has nothing to do with Jules."

Mayde appeared with two cups of ale, which she set down. Tirell paid and she backed away, looking at Magdalene, who gave an infinitesmal shake of the head.

Jules was already dead, Magdalene thought. *Or had Tirell seen him asleep somewhere and determined to kill him?* Magdalene asked, "But if Jules was going to the stable and you were too, why in heaven *didn't* you accompany him?" *Because you didn't want to be seen with him?*

"I didn't want—" He set down the cup he had lifted without drinking and made as if to rise. "It is none of your business. I told you it had nothing to do with Jules."

Magdalene caught his arm. "But it is very much my business," Magdalene said, her voice hard. "I was among the last to speak to Jules—and I am a whore. Whores are always guilty. I need to know who killed Jules. I swear that if what you tell me has nothing to do with Jules it will be kept secret. If you will not answer me, I will pass this to someone who has the right to question you."

"Do not tell my father!" Tirell swallowed. "I will tell him myself when the contract is signed. Otherwise he will make trouble, and it is not his right. I am of age. I have a right to marry whom I will."

"Marry? You cannot marry Loveday. She is already betrothed."

"Not Loveday!" Tirell smiled. Now that his secret was exposed, he relaxed. "That is my father's fixation. I never wished to marry Loveday, although I would have done so to save her from St. Cyr. I . . . it is Edmee Redding's sister, Mary. She is not as rich as Loveday, but she has a good dowry. My father would have been delighted with my choice if Redding had not married Edmee instead of my sister. Then he took a spite to the family." He sighed. "I told you it was nothing to do with Jules."

"Something must have had to do with Jules," Magdalene said. "You invited him to your lodging. For what?"

Tirell sighed again, but he looked even less worried. "I had told Mary's father I would not be making contract when I thought I would have to marry Loveday. I wanted to be sure Jules still planned to marry Loveday before I went back to Mary's father. The stableman carried the message that I would come to him after dinner today. That was what I asked Jules in the alehouse, and he began a tale of woe that I could not stem so I invited him to my lodging. There he told me of Loveday's prior betrothal. I could hardly believe it, much as we had seen of each other over those four years, that she had not told me."

"Could she have been hiding it from your father for fear he would be less willing to help her?" Or perhaps a fear that she would be abducted and married by force? Magdalene wondered.

"Certainly not!" Tirell exclaimed, but he looked uncomfortable. Then he stood up and said, "There is no need for you to return to Master Woller's. My father is not there. I do not know when he will return."

That, Magdalene thought, barely restraining a laugh, *is a damned lie. It is your father for whom you were watching when you looked north, so you expect him soon.* And then she had to swallow and swallow again and finally begin to cough. It seemed that Master Reinhart Hardel had not really managed to keep his image perfect in his son's sight. Still Tirell was making a noble effort to protect the older man. She kept her lips from curving and opened her eyes to their widest.

"Your father? What in the world would I want with your father? I only spoke a few words to him about Loveday." She shook her head. "You mistake me, Master Hardel. I was not looking for your father in Master Woller's shop. I was interested in that length of cloth and I recognized you."

"I am glad to hear it, but I cannot see why you spoke to me. I, no more than my father—"

"I do not solicit custom, Master Hardel," Magdalene snapped. "My motive was not so innocent. Lord Ormerod had told a friend, who told me, that you had been with Jules not long before he died. Since I had spoken to him only perhaps a tenth candlemark before you did and he had told me he was going home, I wondered why he went instead with you. Even more important to me, you are a witness that Jules left me alive and well."

Tirell glared down at her. "And Master Woller will testify that he left me alive and well also—and the stableman will warrant that Jules and I did not meet in the stable."

Unless you first knocked him down and then sent him away, Magdalene thought, as Tirell walked out. Mayde was at her side as soon as Tirell cleared the door. "He was the one," she said. "Sir Jules went out with him that day, before he was killed."

"Thank you, Mayde," Magdalene said, giving her another farthing. "And thank you for watching out for me."

"Did he do it?" the server asked eagerly.

Magdalene smiled. "I have no idea. He could have done it, yes, but there is something in his manner, little as I like it, that makes me believe him innocent."

But is his father equally innocent? Magdalene wondered, lifting her cup to screen her expression. Could Tirell's distaste have had less to do with Mary than with arranging a meeting between Reinhart and St. Cyr? He said he had spoken to St. Cyr and that he must not have Loveday. Was he urging his father to buy St. Cyr off so he could marry Mary? Had Reinhart thought of a less expensive way to accomplish his purpose? But it was Tirell who had the mail shirt. So what? Mail was not fitted to the figure like a tight-laced gown. It was not impossible that Reinhart had once guarded his own caravans and knew well how to don and carry mail.

It was a good reason for the attack from behind. Reinhart was older and if he had ever borne arms, long out of practice with them. He could never have fought St. Cyr on even terms.

She took a last drink from her cup. No. It was simply too far out of reason that Reinhart would *kill*, either to save Loveday from St. Cyr or to get her for his son.

She handed Mayde the now empty cup, rose to her feet, thanked the girl again, and urged her to come to the Soft Nest and let her know if she heard or saw anything that might connect with either St. Cyr's death or that of Sir Jules.

Diccon found her soon after she left the alehouse, complaining that he had been up and down the street looking for her and didn't she feel that it was about to begin raining again? Magdalene glanced up at the clouds, lower and grayer than they had been earlier, and sighed. Well, better confined than soaked. So she bought dinner for herself and Diccon and returned.

The Soft Nest was very busy. Every curtain in the corridor was closed and men's voices filled the common room behind Florete's table, not quite drowning out the grunts and moans from the fully occupied pallets in the dormitory. Magdalene hurried into her room, but before she could close the door, Florete called aloud for Diccon. Magdalene had to turn back to take the stew-filled bread from him, juggling them into a stable position against the two slabs of bread that were holding slices of meat between them. Just as she paused to assure him she would save his meal for him (unless William showed up, which she did not expect), she saw a familiar figure come out of Hertha's room and head for the door.

Diccon reached around her to open her door and Magdalene went inside, shutting it with her heel. She was grinning when she set down the half loaves and propped them against the candleholder so they would not spill the stew. It seemed that, looby or not, Manville d'Arras had told the truth about

remembering things. He had been pink with hard scrubbing
in a bathhouse, so he had washed, as he promised he would.
And he had been smiling broadly and idiotically, so he was no
longer worried and angry about St. Cyr's death.

Magdalene rid herself of her veil and sat down to eat, wondering idly if Arras was really as stupid as he acted or only
had a speech impediment. If he were clever enough to pretend
to be stupid, he might have killed St. Cyr for private reasons.
And if he had gotten blood splattered on him from killing Sir
Jules, he would have a better reason to wash than simply remembering he had promised Hertha that he would.

Then Magdalene shook her head. Clever enough to act stupid? He would have needed to be brilliant—and Samur, his
captain, had called him an idiot. Surely he would not have
been pretending stupidity for years.

Still the doubt made Magdalene wonder what he had said,
if anything, to Hertha. However, from the look of the common
room and the fact that men had been entering even as Magdalene shut her door, she was sure it would be some time
before the whore would be able to come to speak with her.
And if Arras was clever, he would have said nothing pertinent.
But that, too, might be revealing. If he pretended to have forgotten—Magdalene giggled; no, he would not have admitted
to forgetting, but would just say he had found another way to
satisfy his sense of obligation to his friend.

A candlemark later it was pouring again. Diccon had come
and had his meal before it started and gone out again. The
Soft Nest was still crowded, but mostly with men waiting for
the rain to abate before leaving. They were growing short of
temper, so Ogden and Rand were wandering around, cudgels

in hand. One of them shepherded Hertha into to Magdalene's room.

"I knew you would want me to come, but I've little to say. He was still on about that lodging. Apparently he actually tried to tell Salisbury's men about it—or tried to tell them it wasn't a good place to go, even if there was room for them, I don't know. I couldn't make him out. Merciful Mother, trying to understand him is nearly impossible when he talks as if he has a mouthful of pebbles and he is bending over to undo his shoes at the same time."

Magdalene laughed. "But I bet he didn't stink. I saw him going out and he was shiny with scrubbing."

Hertha laughed too and her expression grew softer. "Yes, he does remember. And he pays without argument, too. I should blame you, not him, for my troubles. If you didn't ask me to listen to him, I wouldn't have to strain my ears trying to understand one word in ten and wouldn't care about those."

"Did he mention St. Cyr at all?"

"Only once, and it was nothing to do with his death or the will. He said that he was getting almost as clever as St. Cyr, although it had taken him two days to figure 'it' out. And I haven't a guess whether what had taken him two days to figure out had to do with the lodging of Salisbury's men or had to do with him wanting me to handle him. I think St. Cyr must once have told him that he should ask whether such handling costs extra."

"Did you charge him extra?" Magdalene asked, chuckling.

"You know, I didn't." Hertha shrugged. "You would think I was past any sympathy for a man, but he is so . . . innocent. And he was so clean and pleased with himself for remembering. Oh well, even a whore can be a fool now and again."

"I am glad," Magdalene said. "It is good to be a fool some-times and give another pleasure. I will make it up to you so you do not regret it." And she took two farthings from her purse and handed them to Hertha.

The whore looked at them, then slipped one through the slit in her skirt into her pocket and tucked the other into a fold of her girdle. "I will not refuse it," she said, "for some day that farthing may be all that stands between me and starving. But I will keep it separate to remember—and pray I can afford to do so forever."

When she went out, Magdalene shivered once. She did not think it likely that she would ever be in any danger of starving, but she had come close once and catastrophes did happen. To drive away the dismal thoughts, she lit candles and torchettes and then sat down to embroider another row or two of flowers onto Ella's ribbon.

The rain continued to pour down, but the crowd in the Soft Nest diminished as men grew impatient and went out into the wet, cursing heartily. Magdalene wondered whether the tum-bledown shed in which she had stabled the horse and mule when she had first returned from Noke was still standing and keeping out the worst of the weather. If not, she would have the men repair it when the rain eased off; somehow she had the feeling they had not seen the last of the bad weather.

It was nearly dark before Bell arrived, damp and irritable, but relieved because a novice had been sent to Wytham Abbey with news so Bell himself would not need to ride out tonight, just to report that nothing had happened, and ride back to-morrow morning. The rain had prevented Salisbury from ap-pearing at the Court session as he had promised.

The king, Bell said, grimacing as he pulled off his tunic and

shirt, had been rather unpleasant about it, saying that if the
bishop was too old to come out in a little rain, perhaps he was
too old to be justiciar of the realm. And as for the castles
Salisbury held from the Crown, and even those Salisbury had
built himself, it seemed unsafe to leave the defense of them to
one who feared a wetting. He looked at Magdalene blankly.

"I cannot imagine who will manage this realm if Salisbury
and his kin are driven out," he said.

"If you want the truth, neither can William, who pointed
out to me that nearly all the sheriffs who rule the shires were
appointed by Salisbury and are loyal to him." She sighed. "I
thank God by day and by night that I live under the bishop
of Winchester's protection."

"If even he is safe."

"Not his own brother!"

"He stole the archbishopric from him."

Magdalene shook her head. "Winchester is the legate now.
The pope is his overlord. Even Waleran is not bold enough to
urge the king to offend the pope." Then she took a deep
breath. "Let us discuss murder. Even that is more pleasant than
thinking about the chaos I envision."

She told him about her meeting with Tirell and her doubts
about Master Reinhart and even Arras. When she was done,
Bell sighed heavily. "Magdalene, you are more of an idiot than
Arras. Are you *trying* to make yourself a target for the killer?
And I *must* be in Court again tomorrow. I am now accredited
and recognized as a servant of the diocese of London . . . not
that it is much of a disguise. After all, the king knows that
Winchester is managing the London diocese until a new
bishop is appointed."

"But I do not *believe* it of the Hardels, and my doubts about Arras are ridiculous."

Bell sighed. "And Ormerod? And Ferrau?"

She laughed. "I must admit, I cannot believe Ormerod would kill just so Sir Jules could marry Loveday. That is ridiculous. Nor do I believe him *that* avaricious or that needy of repayment of a loan. And Ferrau's reasons are even more far-fetched."

He sighed again and reached out to take her hand in his. "Magdalene, I love you very much. Will you do one small thing for me for the sake of that love?"

"What small thing?" she asked eyeing him warily.

"Will you stay within tomorrow? Just for the one day. Or if you must go out, will you take Rand or Ogden with you? You 'do not believe,' but there is a strong likelihood that one of those men is a clever and cruel killer. I am bound to my duty, but if you were harmed because I was standing about in Court waiting for the king to insult the bishop of Salisbury, I could never forget, never."

His eyes were shadowed with fear, not only for her but for adding another burden to his soul, like the killing of the mad miller. Magdalene turned her hand in his and squeezed it, smiling.

"I can sacrifice one day of boredom to your peace of mind, love. Yes, I promise I will stay within tomorrow, or take Ogden or Rand with me if I go out."

CHAPTER 20

26 June,
St. Friedesweide's Church

The day was every bit as boring as Magdalene had fore-
seen, although William sent Sir Giles to tell her he might want
to meet friends in her room about the time of the evening
meal. Magdalene checked over her supplies and decided they
were sufficient and congratulated herself on having purchased
six rather nice glazed earthenware cups large enough for ale
or watered wine. It would be serious political business William
and his guests would be discussing; they would not be drinking
straight wine to get drunk.

Magdalene was somewhat surprised at how eager she was
for the meeting. She had been at many—she could not count
how many since William had first sent a man he should not
know to her house. He had warned her what would happen
to her if anyone ever discovered he had been in the house at
the same time, but of course no one ever did know. And over
the years he had come to trust her utterly so that he allowed
her to serve tidbits to nibble and wine and ale to drink even
while the talk went forward.

Sometimes she had been frightened, sometimes saddened,

sometimes disgusted, sometimes overjoyed by what she heard, but she had permitted no reflection of her emotions to show on her face and never by word or act implied she was not deaf as a stone to what had been said. Now, sometimes, William even asked her what she thought after the others were gone and they were safe in her bed. She smiled. Sometimes she even told him the truth.

Bell had appeared at dinnertime bringing food and stayed to eat with her to ease her sense of confinement. Fortunately, before she confessed that William would be coming for the evening meal, he told her he would have to ride to Wytham after the king dismissed the Court.

"Salisbury will come today," he said, lips tight and grim, "even if it *is* sun one moment and spitting rain the next. Doubtless he has been told what the king said yesterday. The dean will want more than a novice's message, and there is enough to tell him about the feelings of the Court."

"Ride safe," Magdalene told him, kissing him as he left. She smiled at him. "And I promise I will not go out alone."

She kept her promise, but it was sorely tried when Sir Giles returned to say the meeting that evening was canceled. "After all that harsh talk yesterday, the king was sweet as new milk when Salisbury, Lincoln, and Ely appeared today. He greeted them with sweet words, ordered stools for them to sit upon, and actually presented business, questions about two wardships for minors that had been contested. On one he approved of the warden appointed by Salisbury; on another he suggested a change and Salisbury agreed without argument."

"And Lord Waleran? Was he there? How did he take the king's mildness?"

Sir Giles snorted. "With smiles." They looked at each other

silently and Sir Giles went on, "Something stinks, but I cannot tell from where the stench is coming." And then he bowed slightly and went out.

Magdalene could do nothing but swallow her disappointment. It had been so perfect, William choosing a night when Bell had to be at the abbey. Now she might have to tell Bell not to come. She bit her lip. Was that not for the best? She was growing far too attached, too accustomed to Bell's strong warmth beside her at night, to his pleasant masculine grumbling in the morning. Yes, and to feeling guilty if something did not please him, which was not so pleasant. She was *not* a wife. She would never be a wife and did not wish to be what amounted to a slave to a man's will.

For some reason the words made her think of Loveday. She giggled and her spirits lifted. Wife or no wife, Loveday was not likely to be any man's slave . . . and neither now would she herself be, Magdalene thought. She had been so young and totally ignorant when Brogan married her. She had been learning, though, about husbandry and the serfs. Brogan was no lover, but she had endured his demands, until he went mad with jealousy.

Magdalene sighed and wrenched her mind away from the bloody past, but she could not find a pleasant topic to dwell upon and she had half a mind to go out and sit with Florete, even if it made trouble, when Ogden called through the door that there was a woman to see Magdalene.

A woman? Loveday? Trouble already? But it was not Loveday who waited under Ogden's watchful eye; it was Mayde.

"He's in St. Friedesweide's infirmary," the girl said, her eyes big in a pale face. "He won't live, they say."

"Who?" Magdalene asked through stiff lips.

"I don't know his name," Mayde said. Her voice trembled.

"The tall, fair man with whom I first came to The Lively Hop?" Magdalene's voice was trembling also.

"No, no, the looby."

Relief and horror coursed through Magdalene, and she pulled Mayde into her room. "Poor Manville," she whispered, crossing herself. "God help him."

"Wait here?" Ogden asked before she shut the door.

"No . . . or, wait." She turned to Mayde. "You said you didn't think he would live, didn't you?" The girl nodded. "Then he's alive now?"

"Was when they took him to St. Friedesweide's."

"You don't need to wait now," Magdalene said to Ogden. "Mayde will not harm me, but I may have to go out to St. Friedesweide's soon. Will you or Rand be able to accompany me?"

"I'll ask Florete."

He turned away and Magdalene shut the door and looked at Mayde. "You are so pale." She went to the shelves and poured two half cups of wine. One she drank herself, the other she handed to the girl. "Here, drink this, and tell me what happened."

"I found him." Mayde swallowed hard and took a tiny sip of the wine, as if she feared she would not be able to keep it down. Then she took another larger sip, and said, "He was by the privy, half in and half out, lying on the ground. I didn't think nothing of it. Lots of them make it to the privy and then can't go no farther, but when I bent down to see if I could drag him a little out of the way, I saw the blood."

She put down the cup hastily and uttered a sob; Magdalene put an arm around her.

"It was still coming out, red and wet, and I screamed and Jack—the landlord—came running out. I–I don't remember what happened next. Maybe I swooned. Someone must of carried me back into the alehouse. Then when I came to my senses, I heard someone tell Jack they would take him to St. Friedesweide. I started to get up to serve, but I was dizzy and shaking so Jack told me to lay down on a bench. I did for a bit, but then I heard he was like to die and I remembered you wanted to know about these people, so I ran here."

Magdalene nodded and pulled a whole silver penny from her purse. "I must go and see if Arras is still alive and can tell me who attacked him. It must be the same man who killed St. Cyr and Sir Jules. Here." She gave Mayde the penny. "This is for being clever and faithful. If you still feel weak, finish your wine here. When you feel able, go back to the alehouse. Try to remember who was there tonight and who talked to Arras— that is the . . . the looby's name." Magdalene blinked hard, forcing back tears. She hated to call him that now.

"I'm better," Mayde said, staring at the silver coin in her hand for a moment before she tucked it away carefully. "I'd rather go back where there are a lot of people talking than stay here alone."

"Very well," Magdalene agreed. "But be careful." She shook her head at Mayde. "Don't be a fool. Likely the man who struck down Arras is long gone, but you don't want him to think you could recognize him. He might go for you next. If anyone asks you what you saw when you screamed, you say you only screamed when you saw the blood, that before that you just thought the man was drunk. You saw nothing unusual, only a drunk lying on the ground."

Mayde nodded. "But I'll think about it, about who could have gone out to the privy before the looby did. About who he talked to . . . Oh, I can tell you now that he talked to the man you were with yesterday, him and an older man that looked a bit like him. The looby went over to ask them something and they told him to go away. He answered loud and sharp that it would be better to tell him the truth, but then he went away. I don't remember what they said; don't think I really heard. There was a crowd because it was in the middle of a rain squall."

It was all Mayde had to tell at the moment, although she promised again to think about whom Arras had been with. They went out together, Magdalene locking her room behind her. When they passed Florete's table, Rand stood up. "Going to St. Friedesweide?" he asked. Magdalene nodded.

Florete said, "Is Rand all right? Ogden had to go and see about a girl who went home with a client and never came back. Or you could wait for Ogden."

"No, I can't wait," Magdalene said. "The man to whom I must speak is badly wounded and might die. Can you let Rand come with me? You have no one else here."

"Ogden will be back soon. This has happened before with this girl." Florete made a face. "When she realizes she will not be queen of the household, just another maid—only doing double service—she is glad enough to return."

Rand nodded at Magdalene. "Go ahead," he said. "I'll just get my sword and be after you in a few minutes."

"I will be going to the infirmary," Magdalene said. "I'll meet you there."

Getting into the infirmary, however, was not so easy, and Magdalene forgot all about mentioning Rand. The monks were not pleased at having a woman intrude into their monastery and did not wish to admit her. She insisted, telling the infirmarian that Manville d'Arras had no male relatives in Oxford, no other relative but herself.

That she knew his name and the name of the captain under whom he served convinced the infirmarian that the tale was true. Other marks in her favor were her decent clothing, her discretion in veiling her face, and her obvious and sincere concern about the wounded man. A final inducement to make an exception was Arras's very grave condition. The infirmarian, a kind and gentle man, did not wish his patient to die without human comfort, even though he had been taught that God's comfort should be sufficient.

"He is not clever," Magdalene said as the brother led her through the dim room toward a cot lit by a single candle, "but he is a good man. I am an embroideress in a good way of trade. If there is any comfort he desires, will you see that it is given him? I will pay."

The infirmarian shook his head. "I do not think he will be with us long enough to desire any further comforts. He is bleeding deep inside, and I have no way to stop it. What you bring, your care and your kindness, will provide all the comfort he will need."

Magdalene choked back a sob and brought out five pence from her purse. "For whatever purpose can bring him the greatest ease," she said, pressing the coins into the hand of the infirmarian.

He looked down at the silver and sighed. "We will pray for his soul," he said but he went away to fetch a stool, which he set beside the cot so she could sit in comfort and stay longer. "I will leave you with him. If you sit for a while, he may wake. He drifts in and out of sleep because of his weakness. Also we have dosed him for the pain."

He left her then, disappearing into the shadows at the end of
the long chamber, where Magdalene could barely make out the
oblong deeper shadow of a doorway. She sat down beside
the cot, loosening her veil so her masked face would not startle
the wounded man.

"Manville," she said softly, "can you hear me and speak?"

At first there was no response, but at a second repetition,
his eyelids fluttered and then his eyes opened. He stared at
her for a few moments and then asked, "Are you an angel?"

"No," she said, smiling although tears stung in her eyes. "I
am a friend of Hertha's. She could not come, but she sent me
to tell you how sorry she was that you were hurt. She is very
angry also, that anyone should hurt you. She asked me to come
because I have a strong, brave friend who will avenge your
hurt—if you can tell me who did this."

"Hertha likes me?" he asked in a small, wondering voice.

"Yes, she does, and she wishes to see you avenged. Who
wounded you, Manville?"

"Didn't see," he said. "Pissing. Heard someone at the door.
I moved aside to make room . . ." His brow wrinkled in puzzlement. "He hit me. Why did he hit me? I was moving out
of the way."

"He is an evil man. I think he is the man who killed St. Cyr.
Do you know who did that?"

"Yes." He smiled a little. "Know who. Make . . . make trouble
for him. Spoil . . . spoil game."

"But who is it? My friend will punish him for what he has
done to you and to St. Cyr."

"Aimery." Tears came into his eyes, ran down his face. Magdalene found a cloth on a little table near the cot and wiped
his face. He said, "Thirsty."

She saw a covered pitcher and a cup and assumed since it was there that he was allowed drink. She poured a little into the cup and lifted his head. He drank. His eyes fluttered shut. Magdalene laid his head on the pillow again.

"Knew Carl when he was . . . butcher's son . . . Culham," he whispered. "Long ago. Not me. From Sutton. Never saw him. Never knew name. Carl, no Aimery . . . Aimery recognized him. Saw him go in . . ."

His voice faded and his eyes closed again. Magdalene bit her lip and waited. After a little while she said, "Manville, can you tell me nothing about this man? How will my friend find him?"

His eyes opened again. "Aimery knew him. He said . . . he had come up in the world."

"What did he look like, Manville?"

"Look like?" His head moved a fraction to and fro on the pillow. His brow furrowed. "Could show . . . if I saw."

He looked distressed because he was unable to satisfy her. Magdalene said, "Never mind," abandoning any hope of a description. Instead she asked, "But why should he attack you?" hoping that Arras would give her some clue.

He tried to smile again. "Figured . . . what Aimery meant. Tell them not to go . . . there. Spoil . . ."

"Surely he wouldn't try to kill you for that. Did Aimery tell you anything else he knew about that evil man, not about the lodging?"

"Told me, long ago . . ." His eyes opened wider but his voice was weaker. "Long ago, Carl saw . . . girl killed. Carl had . . . maid . . . Late to meet mistress. Carl . . . no, Aimery . . . must call him Aimery. Followed . . . saw . . . dead girl. Then . . .

killed maid too. Carl was afraid. Hid . . . Then he . . . became
my friend. Wanted . . . learn to fight."

"No, not long ago, Manville. Something that happened here,
in Oxford," Magdalene said urgently.

His eyes had closed again, now they opened only to slits
and closed again. "Met again . . . Oxford. Lodging . . ." It was
a thread of a whisper and tears glittered in the slit his eyes
were open. "Tried . . ."

The last word was more a movement of his lips than a spoken sound. Magdalene took his hand and squeezed it. "You
did very well, Manville. Very well. You did everything right.
You remembered."

His lips twitched; perhaps he meant to smile at the praise.
Magdalene would have said more, but tears choked her voice
as she sought for new words of comfort. She was angry with
herself for having plagued the dying man, but if he was to be
avenged she had to discover whom to be avenged upon. Perhaps if she let him rest a while, he would regain some strength
and be able to tell her more.

His broad, coarse-featured face was smoothed now of the
worried frown he wore most of the time. Poor man. He had
spent his life puzzled, trying to understand, trying to please.
And she was planning to make his last moments as miserable
as the rest of his life. Tears filled Magdalene's eyes and she
had to look away from his peaceful face.

Fighting her pity and guilt, she glanced around the room,
back to where she had seen some shelves when she came in.
She could not see the shelves now, only an irregularity in the
darkness that shifted as she watched. She looked more intently,
but all was still. Had a shadow moved beside the shelves or
was it only the wavering light of the candle?

The room was really dark now and her vision impaired by the lighted area in which she sat. She turned her head away from the light and closed her eyes to allow them to adjust. When she opened them again, she stared purposefully at the place where she had sensed movement. No movement now, but was there a darker shadow there?

Suddenly Magdalene remembered Bell calling her a fool for drawing the murderer's attention with her questions. She swallowed. This interview with Manville was worse. If someone was watching, he would have heard her questions but not Manville's faint replies. Now she also remembered her promise not to go out alone. Rand was supposed to have followed her. Where was he?

Trying to control her breathing so she would not appear panic-stricken, she looked down and then, keeping her head bent toward Arras but letting her eyes glance around the room she said, "Manville, Manville, wake up." And gasped, rising to her feet, as a shadow detached itself from the wall and came deliberately toward her.

She reached for the pitcher to use as a weapon, but before she could decide whether to throw it or strike with it, Brother Infirmarian came into the light. Relief turned her knees to water so that she sat down on the stool again. Doubtless the infirmarian had been waiting politely out of earshot until he saw that the wounded man could not respond. His actions confirmed her supposition. With his eyes carefully averted from her face, he went to the cot and bent over it.

"I do not think you will be able to rouse him again," he said gently.

"I must have exhausted him," Magdalene admitted guiltily.

"I am so sorry. I hoped he could tell me who had attacked him."

The infirmarian straightened up but still did not look at her. "We asked him also, but he could not or would not tell us. I do not understand this. He did not seem like a person who could arouse a stronger feeling than irritation, yet apparently this stabbing was not the result of a brawl. He seems to have been attacked, and with intent to kill, while using the privy. He would have been dead at once—the knife was well placed—but he was wearing boiled leather armor so the blade did not go quite deep enough. Did he expect to be attacked? Do you know why he was attacked?"

Magdalene bent forward to squeeze Manville's hand one more time, then placed his arm by his side and stood up. "There have been two other killings, Brother. I do not know whether you have heard about them. One was Manville's friend Aimery St. Cyr, and the other was Sir Jules of Osney. I am much afraid that the killer believed Manville knew something about those deaths and tried to silence him."

"That is dreadful. Was he able to tell you anything?"

"He was wandering. If some fact was mixed in with all the memories of which he spoke, I will need to winnow it out. If I come back tomorrow . . ."

The infirmarian bent over the cot again, touched the wounded man's cheek, moved his fingers to the base of his throat and then under his ear. His lips thinned and he straightened up. "You can try, but I cannot hold out much hope that he will be able to speak to you—that he will even live out the night."

Magdalene nodded and used the edge of her veil to wipe away a few tears. Seeing how flaccid Manville's features were, she too had little hope that he would wake again, or be able to tell her more than he had. She sighed.

"I know he is not penniless," she said. "He had some small income, but he never told me from where it came. It was willed to his friend St. Cyr, but St. Cyr was killed two or three days ago. There should be enough to bury him decently. I know he was a man-at-arms in a troop captained by Raoul de Samur, one of Waleran de Meulan's men. He should have more information than I, since this was the first time I had seen Manville in many years."

"Thank you. I will send a lay brother to ask about the burial. Would you like a lay brother to see you home? It is quite dark."

Magdalene's lips parted to accept the offer and then she closed them together tightly. That shadow she had seen was only the infirmarian, and she did not want anyone at St. Friedesweide to know that she was lodged at the Soft Nest, a whorehouse. Men sometimes made miraculous recoveries. If Manville became able to speak again, she did not want to be denied the opportunity to question him further.

"I thank you, but I have only a little way to go beyond the churchyard. I am sure I will be safe."

She drew her veil over her head and across her face and the infirmarian uttered a little sigh. "Then you will want the north door of the church," he said. "It is shortest to go across the cloister, and since you are veiled and we will not linger, I am sure that will be best."

He set out briskly, assuring her as they went that he had earlier sent for a lay brother who would sit with the wounded man now that she was gone. Magdalene breathed a sigh of relief. That explained the shadow much better than that it belonged to the infirmarian. The door to which he had gone and doubtless come back from was not near enough to the wall where the shelves were for the movement to have been his. But if a lay brother had come in without her noticing and had waited by the shelves . . .

They entered the church by the door that connected to the monastery. It was almost black inside, and only the faint reflection of the altar lamp on the columns along the aisle saved Magdalene from crashing into one. Sensing her start, the infirmarian slowed his pace while they made their way across the nave, both crossing themselves and genuflecting as they passed the altar.

"Careful, there are more columns," the infirmarian murmured as they reached the north aisle.

Magdalene sensed him stepping to the side and peered right and left to pick a path. Something moved, and her heart seemed to leap into her throat. Then she saw it was the infirmarian, gesturing past the columns to a rectangle that was a paler gray against the black, and she breathed again.

"There is the door," he said. "I will leave you here. It is lighter outside and I must get back to my patient."

"Thank you," Magdalene said, and he was gone, passing swiftly through the darkness with the ease and confidence of long familiarity.

She stood still, staring into the dark, and caught what she thought was a single glimpse of him as he crossed in front of the altar light. Then she heard the scritch of leather on stone. With an indrawn breath, she rushed toward the open door, only to strike one shoulder against a column. Pushing herself away from it, she ran headlong for the rectangle of gray light. Something caught her veil; she yanked it free, stumbled out the door and almost fell down the two broad steps of the porch, her body twisting as she bent and staggered, trying to regain her balance.

Something whistled past her head, and she thought she heard a man's angry shout. Magdalene gasped, too frightened to scream, and leapt forward, tugging at her eating knife. Someone was behind her. She could almost feel the heat of his body, sense a motion that was a threat. She grabbed the sheath of her knife to free it more easily, but before it came loose, a hand seized her and pushed her hard. She fell, rolled, freed her knife, and drew breath to scream for help. But no one was near her now, and a man's heavy steps pounded past her and up the church porch. Rand? Magdalene rolled over, and sensing no threat managed to sit up.

There was light enough to see, at least light enough at the end of the long twilight of summer for her to see a tombstone nearby. She knew she should run, try to reach the safety of Blue Boar Lane, but her legs shook and she thought she would fall if she tried to walk so she sat down on the tombstone to catch her breath. What a fool she was! She should have gone out the east door into the South Way, where there would have been others in the street. She shivered. That was no protection. He could have come up behind her . . .

Stop it, she said to herself. *Stop imagining horrors that did not happen. Nothing happened. You are safe.* But was she? What if the killer cut down Rand? She clutched her eating knife and tried again to stand.

A dark figure appeared on the porch. Once more Magdalene drew breath to scream for help.

"Sorry, Mistress Magdalene," Rand said as he started down the porch steps. "It's black as pitch in that church and I ran into one of the columns." He rubbed his head ruefully. "He got clean away, and I never caught a glimpse of him."

"That's too bad," she said, laughing tremulously, "but you did save my life by shouting, so I cannot complain too much."

"Shouldn't have come to that." Rand hawked and spat. "I should've been with you, but the monks wouldn't let me in to the infirmary. I *told* them I wasn't the one who stuck the knife in Arras, but all they said was that he was too far gone for company. I figured you'd be safe with the brothers, so I thought I'd wait in the church. Then it got too dark to see in there, so I went out to stand by the door, but . . . but I had to piss."

"It doesn't matter," Magdalene said soothingly.

"Well, I would've got him if I'd been by the door. I saw you come running out and then a man, and he lifted up a weapon— couldn't see whether it was a sword or a cudgel—and I yelled and started to run. I pushed you out of the way, but . . . but if I was gonna fight, I had to tie my braies or they would've been down around my ankles and I would've fallen on my face."

Magdalene began to giggle and the trembling inside her stopped. "That was very sensible," she said, finally able to get to her feet. "I mean, if you had fallen he would have had time to kill me."

He laughed too. "Or I would've fallen on top of you and squashed you dead."

They began to walk through the churchyard toward the narrow alley between the alehouse and the whorehouse that led to Blue Boar Lane and the entrance to the Soft Nest.

"We'll keep good watch, Ogden and me," he said, his voice hard now. "Sir Bellamy, he warned us, but maybe we didn't take him serious enough because . . . well, it's clear how he feels about you. But you can bet we'll watch." He sighed. " 'Cause if anything happened to you, after Sir Bellamy was through with us, Lord William'd skin us alive."

CHAPTER 21

27 June,
The Soft Nest

Despite Rand's and Ogden's assurances, Magdalene had a rather sleepless night, waking at every sound and shivering in her bed, aching for Bell's presence . . . or William's. She had the comfort of neither and very early could sleep no more. Waking both Ogden and Rand—she had been very generous with her reward and neither of them protested—she went to St. Friedesweide, hoping to speak to Arras again but also to warn the monks of the attack on her and to urge them to protect the wounded man, but her effort was wasted. Arras had died during the night without ever regaining consciousness more than to mumble a general confession.

Magdalene went back to the Soft Nest in a somber mood. She had known Arras was dying, but had still hoped he would live long enough to answer some further questions. It had occurred to her during one of her wakeful periods in the night that she had never offered him the names of any of the suspects. Of course she was not sure that he knew any of the men, but she should have asked. Perhaps he would have been able to say that this one or that had never been to the lodging that persisted so strongly in his mind.

She and her escort went home the long way, making a detour to buy breakfast at the nearest cookshop. While she waited for the cook to wrap the fried fish and vegetables, she looked up the street. Could the lodging Arras kept on about be the room above Woller's shop? That seemed highly unlikely.

Back in her room, she ate with little appetite, finally drawing a cloth over the crisp tidbits and simply staring out of the unshuttered window. The light grew stronger and then nearly disappeared as the clouds cleared away from the sun and then obscured it again. Thinking of anything but the murder, she hoped the weather would improve. It would not lift her spirits to have another day of solid rain. There had been several little spitting showers while she was in St. Friedesweide and the cookshop, but it was getting so dark now it seemed as if a cloudburst was imminent.

Rand's scratch on her door was a welcome distraction, and when she heard Bell's voice, she ran to open the door for him with an enormous sense of relief. Bell would help her discover who the killer was and thus who had attacked her.

When he stepped into the room, however, and tossed a canvas-wrapped bundle on the table, she saw they would not get to that problem immediately. His face was red, and he burst out, "Did I not tell you not to go out alone? Did I not? God in heaven, what madness made you to rush out at night to comfort a dying idiot who did not even know you?"

Magdalene was immediately furious—and much more cheerful. "I am glad if I gave him comfort, poor creature," she snapped, "but that was not my purpose. Does it not occur to you that the man who attacked him must be the same who killed St. Cyr and Sir Jules?"

"Did it not occur to me?" he roared. "Of course it did, you beautiful lackwit! Why did you think I told you to sit still and safe within?"

"Ridiculous!" Magdalene exclaimed. "Do you not see that it would be much better to discover who the killer was and be rid of him?"

"And did you?" he asked acidly.

Magdalene sighed. "No, Arras never saw the man who attacked him, but—"

"But! But me no buts. Did you not think that the monks would ask that question? You were nearly killed yourself. The killer is now hunting *you*, and I cannot stay to protect you. I must be in Court after dinner to hear whether the petition of the priest of Lothbury for closing the houses of exchange near his church will be granted."

"Well, of course you must," Magdalene said.

Bell grimaced. "It is more than just duty. I think the king favors keeping the exchanges in the Jewery open because he gets a tithe of their profits, but instead of simply giving that judgment, I fear he intends to present the case to Salisbury, hoping Salisbury will take the priest's side."

"That seems a very small point of conflict. Surely—"

"Who knows what will be sufficient cause for the king to act against Salisbury? Who knows but that Stephen may even be right to do so?" He rubbed his forehead, pushing his fingers under his mail hood. "Yesterday afternoon all was sweetness and light, but underneath . . ."

Magdalene nodded. "Giles de Milland came with a message from William—he had expected to bring guests but because all went so smoothly he decided against it—Giles said he could smell a stink but did not know from where it came."

Bell sighed. "I *must* be there. I might be able to withdraw the priest's petition or add to it something Salisbury could not approve . . ." Then he scowled at her. "But I cannot dance attendance on you! And, curse me, I cannot even give my mind to a national disaster if I can think of nothing but whether you are safe."

Magdalene came and took his hand. "Come, shed that wet armor. Have you broken your fast? I will lay odds you did not, for you must have ridden out of Wytham Abbey before Prime to arrive here so early."

While she spoke she had unlaced his mail hood. Sighing, he bent double. When she had freed his head from the hood and coif, she seized the sleeves and tugged the shirt forward. After the tails cleared his buttocks, he bent even farther forward and with very little more pulling, the shirt slid off into Magdalene's arms. She clutched it to her, staggering a little under the weight, but got it laid out across one end of the table.

"There was so little time. I had to try to discover what Arras knew before he died," she said apologetically as Bell straightened up and ran his hands through his disordered hair. "Sit, love—" she hooked a stool closer with her foot and uncovered the food "—and have something to eat. You will feel better."

His face twisted with exasperation. "You think a full stomach will make my visions of you with a slit throat more palatable? I knew. I knew when I rode out to Wytham after Court that I should have stopped in here and either nailed you to the floor myself or told Florete to have you tied hand and foot so you could not get out of the house." Then he laughed. "And the only reason I did not was that I was sure even those drastic devices would not control you."

"Probably not," Magdalene admitted, smiling but with a crease between her brows. "But when the murderer is caught and hanged you will not need to worry about me any more. And Arras did tell me some things that I am sure will lead to who he is—if only we can make head or tail of them."

Bell was alternating a fingerling of fish with a clump of fried vegetables and made an inquiring noise around the mouthful. Magdalene pushed her half-full cup of ale nearer.

"He was very weak but he kept talking about the lodging as if it was a matter of prime importance, and I could not imagine why any lodging should matter until I remembered what he told Hertha—that Salisbury's men were lodged in the church-yard of St. Peter's and that there was a lodging across the road that was far too large for the men occupying it."

Bell took a swallow of ale and said, "I can see that if Salis-bury's men hear of so suitable a lodging—one as near to their master as the churchyard—they might try to move in, but what that has to do with the murder is beyond me."

"Arras said the murderer stayed in that lodging and that was how he knew who the murderer was—"

"But you told me he said he did not see the man who at-tacked him."

"He thought he knew who the murderer was before he was attacked. He said he planned to spoil the murderer's game."

"He knew who the murderer was but would not tell you?"

"He did not know the man's name and—you know what he was—he could not describe the man to me."

Bell wiped his greasy fingers on his gambeson and ran them

through his hair again. "I cannot see that this is of any help at all."

"Yes, because if Arras was right, it clears Tirell. We know where the Hardels are lodging, and that is certainly not across from St. Peter's Church."

Bell frowned and then nodded. "And it clears Ormerod, too, because he is not lodging in Oxford at all."

"Unfortunately not," Magdalene said. "Ormerod might easily visit another nobleman lodged in Oxford and might visit frequently enough, since he no longer needs to watch over Sir Jules, that Arras might have thought the place his own lodging. That could not be true of the Hardels. They might go once to talk business—if that nobleman grazed a large herd of sheep—but they would not go in and out as if they lodged in the place."

"I see that." Bell put the last piece of fish in his mouth and chewed. "And it might be the place where Ferrau lodged." He sighed. "I think I had better walk down to St. Peter's and see what houses are across from the church and who is lodged in them."

"Not without me," Magdalene said.

"Oh, nearly being killed once was not sufficient for you? You feel the need to flaunt yourself under the murderer's eyes again?"

She laughed uncertainly. "Perhaps that is not such a foolish notion. If he attacked me again, we would have him." Bell's complexion flushed hotly, making his blue eyes sparkle dangerously. Magdalene laughed again, more easily. "No, honestly that was not in my mind at all. I would not go alone, but I will be safe with you. And I just feel that I am overlooking something. Arras was trying to tell me something, something about that lodging . . ."

Bell got up and untied the bundle wrapped in oiled leather he had dropped on the table when he first came in. Inside was a yellow shirt, liberally embroidered around the cuffs and neck, and a deep green tunic. Magdalene rose to undo the ties of the gambeson. When he pulled it off, she could see that his chausses were a light red, cross-gartered with the dark green of the tunic.

"I could not wear mail to Court," he said, but the words were almost drowned in a sudden rush of wind and rain.

Magdalene ran to close the shutters, and sighed. "If this continues long, we will have no time to go to St. Peter's before you must get to Court."

Bell followed her and slightly reopened the shutter she had closed to peer out. "I do not think this heavy rain will last long," he said. "If I can borrow a cloak from Rand or Ogden, we will be able to go. I must admit I have a very strong desire to know who has enough influence and can afford to pay for a lodging only half full."

Enough influence. Magdalene knew that was important, but so many had "influence." God knew the king was not difficult to bend this way and that. In those terms the man who had the most influence was Waleran de Meulan, but the lodging in question could not be his because Arras lived there himself and certainly knew any among Waleran's men who had "come up in the world." And then she remembered William complaining about being told to dance attendance . . .

The thought was deflected by Bell's irritable voice asking if Arras had spoken of nothing but that accursed lodging.

"Almost nothing, but he was wandering in the past, too, talking about a girl that was killed—"

"Lord Sutton's daughter?" Bell interrupted sharply, abruptly turning away from the window to face her.

"Sutton? Sutton? Arras said . . . I think he said he was *from* Sutton, which was why he did not know the man who killed the girl. The girl was killed in Culham."

"That would be Lord Sutton!" Bell exclaimed. "His seat is now at Culham. It may once have been at Sutton and he still has a manor there—oh, that does not matter. If the girl was killed at Culham, it was Lord Sutton's daughter and the last I heard he was still stubbornly hunting the killer—he was inordinately fond of the girl."

"St. Cyr saw the murder . . . Of course! That was why St. Cyr had to die. He must have threatened to tell Lord Sutton what he had seen."

"Four years later? Why didn't he go to Lord Sutton at once?"

"Ah! Another piece has fallen into place. Arras said that St. Cyr was then a person called Carl, a butcher's son. He was not then a man-at-arms. Arras said Carl was afraid of the murderer and after he had seen the man kill the girl and her maid—this Carl had apparently been futtering the maid when she should have been waiting for her mistress so she arrived too late to prevent the murder and was herself killed—he ran to Sutton and befriended Arras so Arras would teach him to fight."

"And then his path did not cross that of the killer again until St. Cyr saw the man here in Oxford," Bell mused. "And now, thinking himself strong in arms, St. Cyr accosted the killer and tried extortion. And maybe he was right—St. Cyr, I mean. Maybe he was now strong enough to confront the murderer, and that was why the man donned his mail and stabbed St. Cyr in the back."

"That was how St. Cyr had acquired a pound of silver to buy that forged betrothal. God in heaven, the murder had nothing to do with Loveday at all."

"Only indirectly," Bell said. "The extortion was so he could marry Loveday, but likely he would have tried that game even if Loveday had fallen willingly into his arms."

Magdalene shuddered. "So who is it?" she asked. "Who could have killed Lord Sutton's daughter?"

Slowly Bell shook his head. "We all knew her, even I did. Jules knew her best, perhaps, but unless he killed St. Cyr and Arras killed him . . ."

"No. I do not think Arras intended to kill the murderer—at least not now. He was dead set—" she hesitated and swallowed at the ugly appropriateness of the words she had chosen by chance "—on doing something about that lodging that would . . . he said 'spoil game.' I suppose he meant he would spoil the killer's game—maybe disgrace him. I think now that Arras wanted a harsher punishment for the killer than a swift death. Who else?"

"Ferrau knew her too. He served in Lord Sutton's Household. But he had left that service before Sutton's daughter was killed."

"And Ormerod was about to be betrothed to her." Magdalene made a face. "Oh, surely he would not kill her because he did not wish to marry her. That is ridiculous! All he had to do was refuse."

"Unless his father was strongly determined on the marriage. From what Ormerod has said to me about that stupid farm his father bought, I am sure he was in awe of his father and also loved him very much. It is not impossible that he thought the girl's life—" Bell's lips turned down with distaste "—she wasn't a very nice girl—was less important than his father's disappointment in him."

"I would not have believed it of him," Magdalene said, shaking her head. "He was always kind to my women, even to Ella, and you know how she can try the patience of a sensible man."

Magdalene's voice suddenly sounded very loud, and she looked toward the window, realizing the heavy rush of rain and occasional thunder had stopped. Bell realized it too, and opened the shutter wider so he could see better. Not only had the downpour diminished to a drizzle, but the clouds had rolled off to the south and at the northern edge of what he could see there was a ribbon of blue.

"Let us chance it," Magdalene said, taking her cloak from a peg on the wall.

Bell looked at her, opened his mouth, closed it and shrugged. If he refused her, likely she would go later on her own. He closed the shutter, belted on the sword he had removed when Magdalene had helped him remove his mail, and stepped out of the door. While Magdalene locked it, he asked about a cloak and was delighted when Florete said she had one to lend him. It had been left by a drunken client who, so far, had not returned to claim it. She looked at Bell's rather elegant attire and said, grinning, that it would suit him much better than Rand's or Ogden's, being less grease-stained and lousy.

As they stepped out of the Soft Nest, Magdalene asked Bell about Monseigneur, and he laughed and said he had left the destrier at the stable. He did not want his precious horse to drown, but more than that, he said, laughing again, he did not want to squelch when he sat in his saddle again. Magdalene laughed too. The oiled leather of the saddle would shed water for a while, but if left out in the rain too long would get soaked and transfer the wet to the rider's seat.

When they reached the Carfax, Magdalene turned left on Castle Street. Bell started to speak, but then fell silent. Magdalene knew Oxford. His mouth tightened. It was not impossible that she had trod this road to the castle when she was summoned to futter some nobleman. Perhaps she had walked this road to Lord William's bed. His teeth set hard together. She would do it again, too, if Lord William summoned her.

The road ended at the wall of the castle, although with the great gates open it led directly to the inner bailey. In the time of Robert D'Oigli, who had built the keep, there had been an outer bailey too, and St. Peter's Church had been erected in that bailey. However, as the vill of Oxford had grown into a city and the wall around the city was erected, the wooden wall that protected the outer bailey had either been pulled down or allowed to fall. Moreover, various noblemen had received permission to build houses along the road and around the church.

The houses nearest the Carfax and thus nearest the Corn-market were obviously the dwellings and shops of very wealthy or well-established merchants. Those nearest the market showed large windows on the street floor, closed now to keep out the rain, but capable of dropping open shutters, that fastened on the bottom, to form counters. Farther along were houses built back from the street and protected by courtyards with hitching posts for horses.

Magdalene put back the hood of her cloak and pointed ahead. "Just beyond that lane is St. Peter's. I wonder whether

Arras meant the houses directly across from the church, or
those on this side of the lane?"

"Do you know who is in the houses?" Bell shook his head.
"I feel like an idiot! I have ridden up and down this road four
times a day for the last two? three? days, and I never looked."

Magdalene smiled at him. "You had other things on your
mind. I can tell you some of those who used to own them five
years ago, but doubtless they've gone out of town with their
families during the Council, unless they had business with the
king. Anyway, I don't think any of those houses are big
enough. There might be room for fifteen or twenty men on
the shop floor, leaving the solar for the nobleman and his
captains. According to Diccon, that's what the armorer's
house—where William's men are staying—is like. Only, of
course, William is in the castle so there are only the captains
in the solar and a few of his most trusted men-at-arms in the
house. The rest are camped out of the city."

"Poor things. This is no weather to be camping out." Bell's
voice was sincerely sympathetic as he recalled his own expe-
riences.

They walked past the houses, which were very quiet. No
men lounged in the courtyards, nor were any horses tied to
the posts out front. Magdalene glanced at them as she passed.

"What I think," she said, "is that most likely three or four
gentlemen who have real and pressing business with the king
are quartered in each house. Each man probably has four or
five men-at-arms as escort—as Ormerod did on the road.
Across the lane, though—that would have been the other side
of the bailey wall, when there was a wall—the houses are all
owned by the king. Some are quite large. I think Waleran has
one of those."

"Oh, yes? Interesting. At least I am not such a fool as not
to have noted where Salisbury is lodged. He is in that group
of houses, too. You can see it from here: the very large stone
built house at the very end, before the wall of the inner bailey
begins. I heard that the earl who built it had quite an eye to
the main chance. He left servants in the place and if any respectable person wanted to stay in Oxford, he could stay in
the earl's house . . . for a price. Which was why it was called
an inn."

Magdalene laughed. "He did not come to my house when I
was here." Then she sobered and glanced up the street at Salisbury's lodging. "Hmm. One would think the lodging was
chosen to keep Salisbury as far as possible from his men. No,
that is unfair. I would lay odds that there is a footpath from
the churchyard to the back of that house. It is too bad that
Salisbury has so much business as justiciar that that big house
is full of clerks."

"It is not only the business of justiciar. He is a bishop, too,
and has clerks receiving petitions and recording decisions
about the diocese." Bell touched his hair, upon which a heavy
drop had landed, looked up, and added, "Damn and blast this
weather. It is starting to rain harder again. Is there anywhere
we can go for shelter?"

Magdalene nodded and drew up her hood. She hurried forward into the lane that ran by the east side of the church. A
good deal of noise was coming out of it, and Magdalene hesitated, then, as the rain grew heavier yet, drew Bell forward.
There was one grand house, which might well be the lodging
that Arras was talking about, and they might be allowed in,
but if not, there was a handsome stable toward the back where
they could wait.

"You brought me here apurpose," Bell said, lips tight. "You want the murderer to see you and attempt to silence you."

"No. If he sees me with you, he should know that it is useless to silence me. I would have told you already."

"Oh, good," Bell remarked, looking as if he had tasted an unripe apple, "you want him to try to kill me as well as you."

Magdalene giggled and yanked on the bell cord that hung by the door. It was opened promptly, not by a servant but by a grizzled veteran of unmistakable authority. He looked at them with an expression of shocked surprise.

"Who are you?" he asked.

"Only passersby caught in the rain," Magdalene said sweetly. "We ask no more than a few moments shelter, until the rain will allow us to go our way."

The man's mouth opened, closed. He looked down at Magdalene, who obligingly put her hood back so he could see her face. His mouth opened again, closed again. He looked up at Bell, whose face was blank, then over his shoulder at the two trestle tables at the far side of the room. About twenty men sat at the tables. There was room for at least six more tables. Beyond the tables was a door leading to a room or a shed at the back of the house. The door was open, and through it Magdalene could hear the clank of pots and ladles. Then the man looked out, as if to judge the amount of rainfall.

"Yes, of course, come in," he said, shutting the door behind them. "I am sorry I cannot ask you to sit down with us and join us. Our master is . . . very rigid in his ways and does not like us to invite strangers to our table. However, I cannot well put you out into the rain. If you would be satisfied to wait out this rain in the kitchen, the servants would dry you off and even offer you something to eat."

Bell's mouth opened, but before he could speak, Magdalene said, "Thank you. I am more concerned with my comfort than my dignity. I will be willing to wait in the kitchen for the weather to improve."

Whereupon the older man turned and walked toward the other end of the room, pausing and gesturing as he came abreast of the tables. Magdalene thought she heard a gasp, but she did not bother to look for who had uttered the sound; it was a frequent enough occurrence when men had not seen her before. The man at the end of the table rose to lead them into the kitchen. There, he told the servants to dry their clothing and to give them dinner if they wanted to eat.

"And," he said, "you are making too much noise. I will close the door. Leave it closed until you are ready to serve." He turned to Magdalene and Bell. "If you wish to leave before the meal is served, I hope you would not mind going out this way." He waved at a back door. "There is a good path around the house."

Magdalene had a grip on Bell's hand. He looked down at her, then nodded brusquely at their guide. Meanwhile, Magdalene swung her cloak off her shoulders and handed it to a manservant who was gawking at her. A moment later, Bell did the same.

The kitchen was far larger than needed to serve food to the number of men in the common room. Magdalene looked at the servants, then said to Bell, "Take two stools and let us get out of the way of these busy folk."

Bell nodded, picked up two stools, and crossed to the unoccupied end of the kitchen. As he put down the stools, his back to the servants, he said softly, "I recognized the badges. We are in the lodging of Alain of Brittany."

"Then Ferrau is the murderer?" Magdalene whispered as she sat down on the stool Bell had placed for her. "But you said he was no longer in Sir Sutton's household when the daughter died."

Bell put his own stool very close beside hers and leaned forward to murmur into her ear. "That was what he told me, and I had no reason before to doubt his word. But if Arras was right and the man who lodged here was the one St. Cyr recognized, it must be Ferrau. We know Ormerod is not acquainted with Count Alain. Remember, he wanted Ferrau to present him or to raise the question of the disputed farm. And even if he had been presented, he is not of sufficient importance to be invited as a frequent visitor. Nor, as you pointed out, are the Hardels likely to have come here often."

Magdalene noticed somewhat uneasily the small smile that tugged at Bell's lips. He could hold a grudge, could Bell, and hold it hard. No matter what he had said on the road, he had not forgotten or forgiven the beating Ferrau had given him. She knew Bell was fair enough not to try to load a crime on an innocent man, but if Ferrau was guilty, Bell was going to enjoy it.

"And Sir Jules is dead and could not have killed Arras," she said.

Bell nodded. "So it must be Ferrau," he said, satisfaction clear in his voice though he kept it very low. "Even if he told the truth about leaving Lord Sutton's service before the girl was killed," Bell continued, "there was nothing to stop Ferrau from coming back to Culham or from staying in the village. It is not quite a town, but there are two merchants with decent houses. I will ride over to Culham . . . oh, God," he glanced at the door to the common room. "I don't know when I'll be free to go."

Magdalene's glance had followed his to the closed door. "For now this is more important," she said. "Whatever happens here will happen soon. In there they are waiting for something right now, which is why that sergeant-at-arms is answering the door instead of a servant and why he wanted us out of that room."

"I think so too," Bell agreed. "And from his surprise at seeing us, he was expecting someone else—perhaps a group from Salisbury's men to ask for lodging?"

"That could be. Also, piecing together what Arras said to me, I see now that he was not wandering. The last thing he said was the word 'tried' and his eyes were full of tears. I thought it was pain or because he had not been able to tell me what I wanted to know, but it wasn't that. It was because he had *tried* to avenge St. Cyr and failed."

"You said he didn't intend to confront the murderer."

"True. He had intended to spoil the killer's game. And I think the killer's game is to embroil Salisbury's men with Alain of Brittany's."

"That would do it," Bell said, lips thinning grimly. "That would be an offense against the king's peace."

"And considering the weather, not so hard to create. I would say someone told Salisbury's men that this house is near empty—or they have seen it for themselves. Would it not be only common sense for them to ask for shelter because of the rain? I am surprised they did not do so sooner."

"I can guess the reason for that," Bell said. "To demand better lodging the first day it rained would have made them seem like proud whiners. As it was, in Court the king's toadies were saying that no bishop should need so large a meiny, and that there would have been room for them had there been fewer. But Salisbury had his defenders, and the sentiment from the uncommitted barons was that it was shameful not to find room for them. I think they were told to endure for a day or two in the hope that the dissatisfaction in Court would force the king to make some arrangement for them."

"I see. But since no relief was forthcoming, they might just have lost patience." She paused, bit her lip, and went on slowly, "I think Arras tried to warn them their discomfort was being deliberately inflicted to make them react. He said 'tell them not to go there,' but you know what he looked and sounded like. They wouldn't listen to him."

Bell stood up. "They will listen to me," he said.

CHAPTER 22

27 May morning, By St. Peter's Church;
27 May evening, The Soft Nest

Bell seized his cloak and went out the back door, feeling more hopeful because the rain had stopped again. He intended to cross over to the churchyard of St. Peter's and make clear to whoever was in charge that they had been left without shelter in the expectation they would commit some outrage. He had some authority as the papal legate's knight, and in this case was prepared to use it. And the fact that the downpour had stopped might make his order more palatable.

Magdalene went with him. Bell opened his mouth once to protest that it would do his authority no good to be in the company of a woman; however, he dared not leave her alone in Count Alain's house where Ferrau might be among the men, although they had not seen him. At the churchyard, he thought, he would tell her to wait outside the gate for him or go into the church, and he hurried out without speaking.

It was already too late. As he and Magdalene rounded the corner of Count Alain's lodging, a man burst out of the front door holding his head as if he had been hurt. His tunic was torn; one sleeve was gone and the right breast, where his house badge might have been, was flapping over so it could not be seen. Most of his face was hidden too, and he was bent to the side as if his ribs hurt. He staggered across the lane, suddenly beginning to scream for succor for Salisbury's men.

Bell rushed toward him, shouting for him to hold his tongue, but the man released his head to draw his sword, swung around lithely with no sign of pain, and launched a terrific blow. Bell ducked and slipped in the mud, going down on one knee. Magdalene shrieked and ran forward, pulling off her cloak in the hope of tangling the man's sword in it, but he did not press his attack on Bell. He had already turned back toward St. Peter's, calling for help against his pursuer and shouting that Count Alain's men were beating the deputation who had come to ask for shelter.

"Wait! Wait!" Bell shouted, on his feet again, sword drawn, also running toward the churchyard. "Do not go! It is a trap."

Too late again. Several idlers who had been standing by the churchyard gate watching to see the result of their comrades' appeal for shelter rushed out into the street. One snatched up a cudgel; another drew his belt knife; both ran toward Bell. The third shouted back to those in the churchyard that their friends had been greeted with blows and insults. The news was repeated, and in two heartbeats other men began to run through the gate into the street. Behind them a growing noise rose from many voices shouting protests and curses and retelling the news still again.

Bell managed to avoid the two coming at him because they were distracted by their deputation rushing out of Count Alain's door calling for help. Bell's voice was lost in the shouts of rage from the men now pouring out of the churchyard, and from Count Alain's men cursing those who fled for attacking them without cause. Both parties crashed together, a variety of weapons in hand.

The man who had started the upheaval had disappeared into the growing crowd. Bell continued trying to make the men nearest him hear sense, although he knew it was useless. He also scanned the faces of those closest to him, hoping he would recognize one of Salisbury's officers who could help him. Hopelessly, he began to flail around with the flat of his blade, yelling, "Remember the king's peace, you fools! Put up your weapons!"

It was hopeless, and he knew it, but it was not in him to do nothing, and then faintly, because the pitch was so high, he heard a woman scream above the shouting of the men.

"Magdalene!" he bellowed.

Around him, the two groups crashed together, trapping him in a wall of men in front and behind. More curses of rage and howls of pain were interspersed with thuds and thunks as weapons made contact. The riot had gone too far to be stopped. Bell continued to bellow for Magdalene, pushing and pulling men out of his path, striking some who tried to struggle against him, straining this way and that for a sight of her hooded cloak.

He had not heard another female cry, but he was panting with terror, only realizing now that the man who caused the riot by shouting for help from Salisbury's men had been Ferrau. He had been so caught up in rage and anxiety during his pursuit that the glimpse he had had of the man's face had not come home to him. And he had left Magdalene to face the murderer alone.

*   *   *

Magdalene had skittered out of the way of the oncoming men as soon as she saw that Bell was on his feet, sword in hand, and that his attacker had no advantage over him—in fact had abandoned him. She heard the man cry out again of the mistreatment visited on Salisbury's men and the response from the churchyard. She muttered a few curses under her breath, but she had no intention of trying to stop what was happening. All she wanted to do was find a safe place to wait out the riot she could see developing.

Her first thought had been to go into the church, but there was no way she could pass through the growing crowd of furious men rushing out of the churchyard gate and reach Castle Street. And then the number of men coming out began to dwindle and she realized she could get to the church through the churchyard, once it was empty. She ducked and dodged around the men on the fringe of the conflict, not that she feared the men would be interested in her or wish to hurt her—they were all too intent on relieving their misery and frustration by beating Alain of Brittany's people—but because she feared being knocked to the ground and trampled.

Magdalene had almost reached her goal, a place where the wall would shelter her, not too far from the gate, when a man's shout of triumph almost in her ear made her start violently to the side. Her upper arm was seized in a grip that wrung a cry of pain from her, and she saw the man's free hand rise, holding a blade poised to strike. She screamed loud and long, wordlessly at first, then forming the word "help."

Ferrau paused and grinned, enjoying her terror. "I did a public service by killing Carl Butcherson, but you couldn't leave well enough alone," he said, pulling her nearer, close enough for her to hear him over the noise of the crowd. "Had to go listen to the looby, didn't you?"

His knife hand rose higher. Magdalene struggled wildly but could not get free. She screamed for help again, but her voice was choked with fear.

"Hoy!" A man's rough voice overrode her muffled cry as the speaker staggered out of the churchyard gate. His eyes were bleary, his gait uncertain, his brow wrinkled in a puzzled frown. "What'cher doin'? Don't knife a woman no matter what she done."

With the words, he lifted the cudgel he carried, but Ferrau was quicker. He took a swift step toward the man, dragging Magdalene with him, but he tilted the raised knife away from her. Then he brought it down hard, with the clear intention of burying it in the man's neck. His drunkenness saved his life, for in the same moment he staggered sideways right into Ferrau so that the knife struck his shoulder instead of his throat and lodged under his collarbone. He screamed and waved his cudgel wildly, wrenching himself away from the pain and twisting Ferrau's knife from his hand.

The cudgel struck Ferrau a glancing blow. In the same moment, Magdalene tore free of his loosened grip and ran for the churchyard, hoping there were other stragglers there or that she would be able to get into the church and find the protection of the priest. But the church door was too far away and the churchyard seemed empty now.

Ferrau was virtually on her heels with the fallen man's cudgel in his hand. He struck at her. She dodged between and around sodden tents, barely leaping over some soaking wet bedrolls that threatened to trip her. She knew that if she fell or was caught again, she was dead.

The cudgel swished again. Magdalene leapt away, heard Ferrau laugh, saw that she was being herded away from the church door. Behind a low, drooping tent she stopped to catch her breath, swinging around to face him and keeping the tent between them. Her eyes flickered from side to side as she sought a path to escape. Ferrau flourished the cudgel and grinned at her.

"Better way to kill a woman than a knife anyway," he said. "Stand still and you'll never feel a thing. I'll hit you on the head, not break your bones first like I did to that little Culham bitch. She got with child apurpose to tell her father I'd done it."

"It's useless to kill me," she gasped. "Bell knows."

"Loose-mouthed bitch!"

As he spoke, he suddenly leaned forward over the tent and struck viciously toward Magdalene, but she had been watching him warily. She had breath now and jumped backward, screaming again at the top of her lungs.

"No use yelling for your fancy man," Ferrau snarled. "Salisbury's men'll kill him."

He lunged toward her, only to have the tent collapse under him so that he staggered forward off balance. Magdalene turned and ran, but in the open space in the center of the churchyard, where the men had had their cookfires, he was close enough to catch at her sleeve. She turned and threw the cloak she was still clutching into his face and won free again. But he was still between her and the church door.

She ran again toward the tents, knowing he could catch her more easily in the open space. But this time her luck had run out. Before she could dodge behind the canvas shelter, her foot caught in a bedroll. She staggered, catching at the tent for support, feeling it sway and begin to collapse under her hands, feeling the cudgel rise behind her.

"Enough!"

The bellow loosened Magdalene's knees and she sank right to the ground, pressed against the tent's wet side. The cudgel swished by her, deflected by the edge of the tent, barely striking her shoulder. Her face was pressed into the canvas in her attempt to make herself the smallest target, and she could see nothing.

"Draw," Bell snarled, his voice close now and slightly breathless, as if he had been running or fighting, "or I will copy your custom and kill you from behind."

"Not before I kill her," Ferrau shouted, and leapt right over Magdalene, the cudgel poised over her. "Drop your sword or I will break her to pieces."

Magdalene heard the soft squelch and thud as Bell's weapon hit the ground. "No!" she shrieked and squirmed back, right on to Ferrau's feet. She knew from bitter experience that the angle was wrong for the full force of a blow from a stick or a strap to fall on her. Then she twisted around, seizing Ferrau's ankles so he could not kick her away.

As she wriggled closer she felt something heavy pass over her. Ferrau cried out and toppled backward. Legs hit her back and Magdalene knew that Bell had launched himself at Ferrau, knocked him down, and fallen atop him. She heard the cudgel strike but felt nothing, so she knew it had struck Bell, and then she felt Ferrau convulse and heard him scream. She saw the cudgel flung away, but Ferrau shuddered again. Then his legs twitched feebly and were still.

A knee in much-muddied but once red hose came down almost on her hand. Magdalene released her grip on Ferrau's ankles. The other leg that had burdened her lifted, and she squirmed away.

"Are you hurt, Magdalene?" Bell asked anxiously, his voice only raised a little because the roar of the riot was muffled by the churchyard wall and the tents around them.

She turned over and sat up. "No, only bruised a little. Are *you* hurt? I heard the cudgel hit you."

"There was no force in the blow. I am hurt only in my pride." He sighed. He was sitting too, but out of the mud, atop Ferrau. "I have never felt such a jackass in all my life. I do not even know whether it is right or wrong that the king should curb Salisbury's power, and I let myself get so caught up in stopping the bishop's men from attacking Count Alain's that I forgot it was Ferrau who was inciting them and that he intended to kill you." He sighed again.

"He still has an eating knife," Magdalene warned Bell. "He will try to use it as soon as he comes to his senses."

Bell looked at her and smiled. "He will never come to his senses again. He is dead, Magdalene." He looked down at his right hand, which Magdalene now saw was stained red, but his lips did not loose their satisfied curve. "He should have met me sword to sword. Perhaps he would have survived that, but with a knife in my hand, I kill."

Magdalene stared at the bloody hand and then at the body on which Bell was sitting so casually. She shuddered, imagining how the scene would look to other eyes.

"Clean the knife and put it away," she said, struggling to her feet. She reached down, grasped Bell's unbloodied left hand, and pulled urgently at him. "Wipe your hand, too. A little mud will hide the blood."

"Why should I hide it? He was a murderer four times over—

five times if you count Sutton's daughter's maid. I—"

"Likely he was also the king's tool in this matter of Salisbury." Magdalene tugged at his hand again. "You do not want to be mixed into that, especially not you! Do you want to drag Winchester into your folly?"

"Oh, my God!" he gasped, twisting around to pull his knife from Ferrau's chest and wiping it on Ferrau's tunic. He got to his feet and went around her to pick up his sword. "But Winchester had nothing to do with this, nothing! The last news the bishop had was that all seemed well. Why should he order me to kill a man he did not even know?"

"Never mind giving reasons to me." Her voice was thin and breathless. "If we are gone from here, no one will know you had anything to do with this. Winchester need not be involved at all, even by distant implication. Ferrau will just have been one more man killed in this broil. Come, let us go into the church. With any luck we can claim to be innocent bystanders who were caught in the street, knocked to the ground and rolled in the mud by the fighting men."

Fortunately no one was there to question them. They assumed the priests were outside, trying to quell the riot or to assist the wounded and dying. From their haven, they heard the fighting as a distant growling heightened now and again by a particularly high and anguished shriek. Bell pulled up his tunic and used his shirt to clean his knife and sword, then pulled the tunic down again to hide the soiling. Later, but no long time later, they heard hoofbeats.

"Someone has sent a troop to quiet them," Bell said.

"Good," Magdalene murmured, lifting her head from Bell's shoulder. "When the fighting is nearly stopped, I think we can slip out and away without being noticed."

For a time the noise grew louder and then it began to diminish. Magdalene and Bell went to the front door of the church and looked out cautiously. It was raining again, but not very hard. Magdalene started to turn toward the back door where her cloak lay in the mud of the churchyard, but stopped. There was nothing on it that would identify her and she did not think it could be saved. It was better to leave it there than to take a chance on being seen trying to retrieve it. She brushed ineffectually at the mud caked on her gown and tried to secure the sleeve Ferrau had torn.

Bell shook his head over her efforts to repair the damage and took off his cloak. It had some mud on it, but not very much because it had been pushed far back out of his way when he was fighting. He put it around Magdalene. She did not thank him, only looked up, her eyes glazed with shock and fatigue. Still, he thought, she was not about to fail. She gathered the cloak around her, hiding her mud-soaked gown and its torn sleeve, and pulled up the hood. Bell's clothing, aside from the muddied chausses, was only spattered here and there.

Together but silent they walked from the church door through the porch and down to the street. There was a crowd at the intersection of Castle Street and the lane on which Alain's lodging stood, but the people were all staring in at the lane, from which there was a greatly diminished sound—only a few raised voices protesting innocence, some moans from the wounded, and a few louder cries for help. Magdalene and Bell walked around the onlookers, pausing to peer into the street where the riot had been, as if naturally curious, but no one took notice of them, and they hurried on.

At the Carfax, still wordless, they parted, Bell moving quickly north through the market toward the stable where

Monseigneur guarded his saddle bags. His need to appear in Court had only increased, and he needed clean clothing. He blessed the dean's sudden uneasiness and his, which had made him decide to carry all his possessions with him on the off chance that he would need to ride to Winchester in a hurry. No longer an off chance, he would have to ride for Winchester this very night, but he needed to see just what the king's response to the riot would be.

Magdalene turned south to go to the Soft Nest. If Florete was surprised to see her return wearing the cloak that had been lent to Bell, she kept it to herself. Magdalene found her pocket still tied safely around her waist, extracted her key, and let herself into her room.

She was not much aware of how the next few candlemarks passed. She must have washed and changed her clothing, and she remembered sitting at the table with her head hidden in her arms, shivering and weeping, for a long time. But whether that was before or after she washed and changed, she had no idea. She remembered, too, that Diccon had come in to ask whether she wanted dinner and that she had ordered a whole pasty, two roasted chickens, stew, greens, two loaves of bread, and a generous portion of sweet pudding. Diccon looked at her as if she were mad, but she could not explain what she was doing—and she did not eat any of the food when he returned with it, nor did she offer him any. She just put it away and went to lie down in her bed and weep some more.

She had no idea why she was crying—certainly not for Ferrau—and she fell asleep wondering about it. However, when she woke, hearing Bell call her name, the confusion was gone. She knew very well why she had ordered all that food and why she had been crying.

"What are you doing alone in the dark?" Bell asked from the doorway.

She fumbled her way to the table and took a candle from the holder there, slipped by Bell, and lit the candle from the one in the corridor.

"I was tired . . . and frightened," she said. "I fell asleep."

Bell followed her into the room carrying the large, heavy, leather-covered roll that she knew held his mail. He put it down on the table, watching her collect enough torchettes to fill every holder on the walls and go around lighting them. Then she lit both night candles, and came back to the table to light the branch of candles that sat on it. When she was done, the room was bright as day.

She caught at Bell's hand before he could ask what she was doing, and said, "What happened? What did the king say to Salisbury about the riot?"

Even in the golden light of the candles and torchettes, he looked gray. "God, you were right about not mixing Winchester into this business. Stephen got what he wanted. I had hoped he knew nothing about it, that it was Meulan and Count Alain that mixed this mess of poison, but the king knew. I should have known how treacherous he could be, after he appointed Theobald archbishop instead of his own brother—"

Magdalene reached up and put her fingers gently over his mouth. "Do not say it, love. It could be taken as a reflection of Winchester's thoughts. Everyone knows you are a favorite with him."

"But no doubt you will tell Lord William!"

She dropped her hand and moved back a step. "I tell William only what he needs to know for his own safety, and you and Winchester are presently no threat to him. Tell me what happened at Court. You need not fear I will recount that to William. I am sure he was there."

He turned away a little and began to unwrap the leather-covered roll, baring his gambeson, which was wrapped around his mail shirt. "I reached the castle soon after the king rose from dinner. He had already sent for Salisbury, who came in soon after me. The king accused the bishop of failing to keep the king's peace. Salisbury made light of the matter, saying it was a small fracas among a few hotheads. He said he was sorry about it, but that the men had been miserable from camping out in the constant rain, since no provision had been made to lodge them. They had become envious of Count Alain's retainers, who were few and lodged in a hall much too large for them." Bell paused, looked down at his armor, which he was absently stroking. "He made a mistake."

"Who?"

"Salisbury. He spoke to Stephen as he must have spoken when the king was a boy fostering in King Henry's Household, in a kind, understanding way, as if he did not need to make explanation and did so out of indulgence. I think he was frightened, sought to remind Stephen of their long association, and misjudged. Stephen then said, quite sharply, that if the bishop had not brought more men-at-arms than the king himself had, there would have been room enough."

"I imagine Salisbury changed his tune?"

"Oh, yes, but then it was too late—if it had not been too late before he even came to this accursed Council. Then he said he would make restitution to those who were injured and apologized more contritely, but the king replied that he now realized it was not meet nor fitting for a man of God, a bishop who should be overseeing the souls of those in his cure, to be burdened with the secular care of so many armed men. It was clear that he could not control his secular followers and thus it was not safe for him to hold so many strong castles, and he demanded the keys of Salisbury's strongholds, not only the royal castles that he held by the king's will, but those he had built himself."

"Will he give them up?" Magdalene breathed, seeing in her mind's eye William assaulting those strong keeps.

"I do not know. He demurred, begging for time, but one thing I do know—the king's peace is broken and Oxford will not be a safe place. Those in Salisbury's debt may try to rescue him. There will be bitterer quarrels among the men-at-arms and more riots. The sheriff, the Watch, they are not fit to control what will happen. I must ride to Winchester, of course, but I want you to come with me. I am sure the bishop will give me permission to take you home to London or provide some other escort for you if I must ride back here."

Magdalene's throat closed and for a moment all she could do was shake her head. This was why she had been crying. She had been too shocked by the attempt on her life, too exhausted, to formulate the thoughts clearly, but she had known it would come to this, that Bell would have to leave Oxford, that he would want to take her with him. There was even some truth in what he said: Oxford would be more dangerous now. But this crisis was why William had summoned her. It was now that William would have to talk to men who were Salisbury's supporters, men who would not want their friends to know that they were dealing with the king's man. Yet William must induce them to talk to him, to listen to him, if he were to keep the kingdom from breaking apart.

Finally she forced out words. "Do not be so silly, Bell. No

one will blame a whore for a conflict between the king and his chief minister."

"Not even one who entertains the king's prime enforcer? Whose men do you think went to make sure that Salisbury came to the king?"

"Mine." The well-known voice was loud and flat.

No one in the Soft Nest would dare speak a word to William of Ypres unless he asked a question. He had walked past Florete and her men and had opened the door silently. Now he stood in the doorway, examining the well-lit room.

"William!" Magdalene exclaimed. "I did not think you would have time to come here today."

"I don't. I happened to be riding to the South Gate, so I stopped to tell you that we will be six for the evening meal tonight . . . I hope." He turned to look at Bell. "Bruno of Jernaeve told me you were right in the middle of that fracas outside St. Peter's. What were you doing there? Is Winchester—"

"No! Good God, no! He knows nothing of this."

"No?"

"William, we were there by accident."

"You were there too?" Now Ypres's voice made the flames on the candles shiver.

Magdalene did not shrink back or wince; she smiled at him. "Yes, I was. Bell escorted me to see who had the lodging opposite St. Peter's churchyard. I was told that the murderer of St. Cyr lodged there."

"I thought I told you I wasn't interested in that any more," William said impatiently.

"So you did, but I was interested."

William snorted with irritation but shrugged indulgently.

"Do you want me to ask him—with a hot iron on the side, so he's quick to answer?"

"He's dead. He was the man who ran out of Alain of Brittany's lodging screaming for help from Salisbury's men. He is Alain of Brittany's man, and he instigated the riot."

William's face froze, but Magdalene thought she saw a flicker of pain in his eyes. After a moment, too softly, he said, "I see. Who killed him?"

"I did," Bell said.

"Clever man!" William muttered approvingly, his small eyes closing and then opening wide with relief. "At least any questions must end in his grave. Who was he?"

Bell's lips thinned at that cynical remark. Whether or not any questions could be answered, the trail of deceit led straight to the king. But all he said was, "His name was Sir Ferrau de Surtaine, and he was a murderer five times over."

William thought a moment, then shook his head. "Never heard of him. It does not matter, since Count Alain is on his knees, apologizing profusely for what happened. He takes the full blame for his men having responded with force but insists they were assaulted first."

Bell shrugged. "It is possible, I suppose, that Salisbury's men struck first—given the right prodding. They were already wet and cold and furious."

William did not seem to have heard him. He smiled and said, "Actually we are well met, Sir Bellamy. I know you are Winchester's man and that he trusts you."

"I hope he does. He has reason for it."

William's little blue eyes stared, blinked, stared. "I assume you will be riding to Winchester to report on what happened here?"

"You assume correctly." Bell's voice had gone hard, his lips stiff, his hand dropped to his sword hilt.

William raised a placating hand. "I am not trying to interfere with your duty," he said, his expression intent. "I only wish you to tell your master that the king offered no challenge to the Church nor to Salisbury's wielding the full power of his Church office. All King Stephen demanded was his own *secular* property, the castles Salisbury held as royal grants, and the *secular* castles that Salisbury had erected without royal grant."

"I will report faithfully what I saw with my eyes and heard with my ears," Bell said.

"Do not be a fool!" For once William's voice was low, but there was as much force in it as when he shouted. "There is nothing so terrible as a full civil war. A little rebellion here and there is one thing. Every man's hand against every other is another. Tell the bishop of Winchester to keep the Church quiet and—"

Bell laughed, harsh and humorless. "I am the bishop of Winchester's knight. He trusts me—yes, but only to wield my sword as he directs. He would not take my advice if I offered it, and I am not likely to offer advice so much against common sense and decency."

"You mean it would be more decent for the king to wait until Robert of Gloucester landed and Salisbury used those castles he has stuffed and garnished for war to overthrow the anointed king? Stephen was *anointed* king and his claim to the throne was validated by the pope only three months ago."

"No one has challenged his right to the throne!"

William's expression was bleak. "No one has challenged the right of the bishop of Salisbury to be a bishop. The king may change the officers of his realm at his own will. When a man leaves his office, he must return to the king what he held from the king during that office. That is all that has happened. All. Will you tell the bishop of Winchester so much in my name?"

Bell relaxed, nodded. "If I may use your name and say you bade me say those words, I will."

"Thank you." William nodded at him, then turned his head to look at Magdalene. "Remember, Chick, six for the evening meal. Tell the whoremistress to keep five girls for us. I do not know if anyone will be in a temper fit for using a woman, but if inquiries are made, the whoremistress will be able to say that those girls were with those men."

Having said that, he walked right past her, opened the door, at which two men were standing guard, and went out. Magdalene dropped her head and let out a long sigh. *William at his worst,* she thought, and then felt guilty because she knew his mind was occupied with half a dozen other things . . . and it was William who faced assaulting the bishops' keeps and taking them if Salisbury and his nephews did not yield.

"Five girls?" Bell's voice was choked. "Then he intends to sleep with you!"

"I doubt any of the men will be bothering with women tonight," Magdalene said tiredly, although she was reasonably sure that William probably would stay the night. She was glad she had cried herself out during the day. Her eyes were dry now, although she feared what was coming.

"He does not even care that this whorehouse might be marked by the concourse of great men suddenly coming to it? There is an alehouse full of men-at-arms right next door. They could easily be paid or driven to attack this place."

"He cares, but he is busy now trying to keep everyone quiet until their first fine fury subsides and they have time to think.

Once men begin to think, they are less likely to fly to arms. And as for the men-at-arms next door, they are more likely to come to the aid of the Soft Nest than to attack it. Please do not worry about me. I am too insignificant to be a target."

"You are known as William of Ypres's woman—and if you were not before, you will be now. There will be those who think you can tell them what he plans. There will be those who will think he can be constrained by holding you hostage." He put out a pleading hand. "Come with me. Do you fear he will turn on you if you do not obey him?"

"No."

That was not completely true. William might indeed punish her if she went with Bell, not for disobedience but for betrayal. But she was not staying out of fear of William. Partly she was staying because William needed her, trusted her so completely that he used neither bribes nor threats to keep her in Oxford even though he must have known that Bell would urge her to leave. And partly she was staying because if she went with Bell, she would be his and only his in her own mind and heart, and she did not believe she could survive the pain when he called her whore and turned away from her.

"Then why?" Bell cried.

She could not tell him her fears and listen to his easy assurances that he would never think of her as a whore and drive her away. Sooner or later, he would. So instead she said, "Because I love William, too. Because he needs me more than you do right now."

"You said you owed him. You said nothing of love . . ." He choked and began to wrap his gambeson and armor back into the leather.

She saw what he was doing and tears stung her eyes but she

did not let them fall. "When you owe a man as much as I owe William and do not hate him with every fiber of your being . . . why, then you love him. You should have known that without my telling you. I do not love him as . . . as I love you, Bell, but love him I do, and I will stand by him and give him whatever help he will take with my body or my wits or my very soul—whether he asks it of me or not—as long as he needs me."

Bell's face was white gray and looked as if it were carved of granite. "Fare thee well, Magdalene," he said. "May only good befall you and may the Merciful Mother keep you." And he picked up the untidy bundle of armor and went out of the room.

For a long time Magdalene stood looking at the closed door. She knew that whether the bishop of Winchester sent him back to Oxford or not, she would not see Bell again. She did not weep; she had done her weeping already. Finally she went out and asked Florete for another stool. William might not want to sit in the high chair if he intended to cajole Salisbury's friends so she would need an extra stool, unless she wanted to stand. Then she scrubbed the table and put out the cups she had bought and the flagon of wine.

When William's guests began to arrive, she smiled at each with apparent pleasure, extending a graceful hand in welcome, lowering her lids over her eyes in modest acceptance of the compliments about her beauty from those who did not know her. She served the wine, then the food. Once the serious talk began, she sighed and looked utterly bored, retreating to a corner and coming forward only to refill cups as needed. She started with well-simulated surprise when one of the men spoke to her and again when another asked her what she thought.

She laughed then, making clear that she was totally indifferent to what they said to each other.

Much later, when the guests were all gone either to their lodgings or to the women waiting for them and she was lying beside William, whose breathing had deepened into sleep rhythms, tears began to trickle down her face again and an occasional sob shook her. A heavy arm fell across her and gathered her close.

"Not to worry, Chick," William murmured sleepily. "He'll be back. Can't remember how many times I swore I'd be done with you, that I was a fool to trust a whore. Well, I was wrong about that, but I didn't know it then. Came back anyway. So will he."

AUTHOR'S NOTE

Political infighting in the reign of King Stephen might not have been *quite* as complicated as that in the early twenty-first century, but in many ways it was more interesting because it was less a matter of vague, faceless corporate and national interests and more driven by individual personalities. For those who are interested, or only confused by the personal relationships and conflicts, I hope this author's note will be of help.

A very brief summary of the history of England from the conquest to the beginning of Stephen's reign was given in the Author's Note to my previous book, *A Personal Devil*. Here I hope to explain the events that led up to Stephen's dismissal of the bishop of Salisbury and his kin from the highest offices of the country.

The Council at Oxford in June of 1139 was a turning point in the reign of King Stephen, who had not been the one and only possible heir to the throne of England when he succeeded King Henry I. King Henry's only legitimate son, William the Aethling, had drowned in a crossing of the English Channel on 25 November, 1120. His death left three contenders with varying claims.

First and foremost was Henry's daughter Matilda, to whom King Henry had forced the barons to swear fealty in 1126; however, Matilda was a woman, and of less importance but still significant, she had a strong and unpleasant personality. Second was his eldest illegitimate son, Robert of Gloucester, who was deeply respected and admired by many of the barons of England; but Robert was a bastard, and his strong sense of honor restrained him from pushing his claim. Finally there was Stephen of Blois, a nephew greatly favored by the king, who always treated him like a son; Stephen had been raised mostly in the English Court, had been richly endowed with lands by his uncle, and was known and liked by much of the nobility.

When Henry I died, Matilda made no move to seize her inheritance. Robert of Gloucester dutifully remained with Henry's body to see him decently interred. Stephen set out from Boulogne as soon as he heard of his uncle's death, and after being refused permission to land at Dover and repulsed at Canterbury—both of which owed homage to Robert of Gloucester—he sailed up the Thames to London. There he was enthusiastically received. He promised the Londoners that he would "gird himself with all his might to pacify the kingdom for the benefit of them all." (John T. Appleby, *The Troubled Reign of King Stephen 1135–1154*. New York, Barnes and Noble Books, 1995, page 22.)

Meanwhile Henry, bishop of Winchester, who was also Stephen's younger brother, was hard at work convincing William Pont de l'Arche, the keeper of Henry I's treasure, to welcome Stephen into Winchester Castle, which he did. Equally important, Henry convinced Roger, bishop of Salisbury, King

Henry's chief justiciar, to accept Stephen. Salisbury was King Henry's most trusted servant; he had been left as regent in England when Henry had cause to travel abroad. When Salisbury acknowledged Stephen's claim to the throne, many of the nobility followed his lead. Moreover Salisbury and the bishop of Winchester joined forces to convince William of Corbeil, the archbishop of Canterbury, to crown Stephen king. Once anointed, to the medieval mind whether his was the best claim or not, Stephen *was* king.

Thus, with the crown, King Stephen inherited the bishop of Salisbury, who was of course confirmed in all his honors and possessions. Salisbury had held great power for a long time and had, as was the custom of the time, elevated his relatives to positions of power. Thus his nephew Nigel was bishop of Ely and the king's Treasurer, and his son, Roger le Poer (because he wasn't yet a bishop), was the king's Chancellor. Among them they controlled the entire government of England. Salisbury had also, with King Henry's approval—and sometimes when the king was abroad without specific approval but with his trust and concurrence—appointed most of the sheriffs, who ran the governments of the individual shires. Thus, indirectly, Salisbury also influenced the local governments.

The advantage of this inheritance to Stephen was that there was no disruption at all in the government of England when he became king. The disadvantage was that Stephen—no administrative genius—had not the faintest idea of how the realm was governed. Over the first few years of Stephen's reign, the advantages of the inheritance far outweighed the disadvantages. There were minor rebellions of nobles who were dissatisfied with Stephen's failure to right what they considered their wrongs, and there was an invasion by the Scots, whose king had sworn to support Matilda as queen and used that oath as an excuse to attempt a seizure of English territory.

Dealing with these matters was of prime importance, and Stephen managed them for the most part satisfactorily so that his grip on the country became more secure. Perhaps, as more and more of the barons gave him oaths of fealty, he began to believe that the machinery of government, which he did not understand, was unimportant.

Nor, in truth, did the king have time, even had he been willing, to learn the intricacies of government. There were problems abroad, in Normandy, and those were not concluded so satisfactorily. One of Stephen's favorites, the leader of his Flemish mercenaries, William of Ypres, tried to rid Stephen of Robert of Gloucester (the second claimant to the throne), but the attempt at ambush failed, multiplied Stephen's problems, and cost William of Ypres much of the king's confidence.

William of Ypres was not Stephen's only favorite. The king had also reestablished relationships that had weakened over the years while he was away from England after his marriage to Matilda of Boulogne. The strongest of these relationships was with Waleran, count of Meulan, head of the great Norman family of Beaumont. Waleran was clever and a good soldier, but self-seeking and very ambitious. He too had a family whose power he wished to extend, but one prime favorite stood in his way. The man closest to the king was his brother, Henry, bishop of Winchester, who had done so much to win the throne for him.

In 1136, William of Corbeil, the archbishop of Canterbury who had anointed Stephen king, died. Henry, bishop of Winchester (and most of the other bishops of England) expected that the king would appoint him to that position at once, but he did not. It was possible that Stephen realized his brother was cleverer than he, and Henry certainly had a stronger personality. It was not impossible that Stephen feared if Henry became archbishop of Canterbury, ruler of the Church of England, that there would be two kings in the realm, and the archbishop would be the stronger. Still, Stephen could not appoint any other English bishop without a violent breach with his brother, not to mention that there was not another English bishop equally fitted for the office.

Thus the archbishopric was kept vacant for two years and then, in December of 1138, Theobald, abbot of Bec, was elected to the office when Henry had been conveniently involved in Church business at a distance. Theobald had only been abbot of Bec for two years and was virtually unknown— except by Waleran de Meulan, who was the lay patron of Bec. Was it too much to suspect that Waleran had proposed Theobald to Stephen, and that Theobald's primary qualification for the office was that he was *not Henry?*

There is no hard evidence one way or the other, but the appointment of Theobald accomplished one thing that Waleran must have desired. It opened a gulf between the brothers; Henry was angry and bitter, Stephen felt guilty. The ease and confidence that had existed between them was gone. Henry was no longer the first advisor to the king.

Other problems had also arisen. William of Ypres's action in Normandy had borne bitter fruit. Robert of Gloucester, who had actually sworn fealty to Stephen in 1136, withdrew that fealty in June 1138. And in 1139, Matilda at last began to move against Stephen. She appealed to the pope against Stephen, who she said had not only committed perjury in violating his oath to receive her as heir to King Henry, but had usurped the throne as well.

Meanwhile Waleran had not been idle. In 1138, he was made earl of Worcester. His twin brother Robert was already earl of Leicester; William de Warenne, his half brother, was earl of Surrey; his first cousin, Roger de Beaumont, who was married to Waleran's half-sister, was earl of Warwick; his younger brother, Hugh Pauper—because he was not yet as well endowed as his older brothers—was soon created earl of Bedford; his brother-in-law, Gilbert de Clare, was created earl of Pembroke.

By 1139 when Theobald left for Rome to receive his pallium from the pope accompanied by five other bishops, part of whose duties was to defend the king against Matilda's appeal, Waleran and his close kin held six of the earldoms of England. Earl was then the highest rank of English nobility, but although the earls of a county were supposed to oversee the work of the sheriffs and defend the counties, the government under Salisbury operated so efficiently that being earl was essentially a functionless honor. The path to real power for Waleran and his kin was blocked by Salisbury and his.

Stephen knew his uncle, King Henry, had trusted Salisbury and his coterie enough to leave Salisbury as regent of the kingdom when he was absent, and Salisbury had been among the first to welcome him. However, in the year since Robert of Gloucester had cried defiance and Matilda had appealed to the pope to restore her kingdom to her, Salisbury had strengthened the castles that he held for the king and those he had built himself—he said for the glory and safety of his diocese—and had stocked them with all kinds of supplies, as if for war or against siege.

It is not impossible that Stephen, who was a good war leader, noticed these uncomfortable facts for himself. It is equally possible that Waleran also made note of what was happening, drew it to the king's attention, and asked whether Salisbury might be preparing to use those keeps and supplies to support Robert of Gloucester when he invaded England, which was expected.

There had been enough rebellions by dissatisfied nobles and some who were truly distressed over their violated oaths to Matilda that Stephen had grown mistrustful. He was suspicious also of the bishop of Ely's (Salisbury's nephew) management of the finances of the realm. The constant wars Stephen had been fighting were an expensive business, and he was growing poorer while Salisbury grew richer. Better safe than sorry, the king must have thought, and decided to be rid of Salisbury. In fact, the suspicions were most likely justified. Although there was a tremendous uproar over the way the situation was handled, no one really attempted to deny that Salisbury and his supporters were plotting treason.

Being rid of them was easier said than done, however. Stephen feared the reaction of his barons if he simply dismissed Salisbury and his kin without a reasonably obvious cause. He certainly did not want to use his suspicion that Salisbury intended to abandon him and espouse the cause of Robert of Gloucester. It was all too likely that many nobles of the kingdom would follow his lead, as they had in acknowledging Stephen.

Nor did Stephen want any quarrel with the Church. In an attempt to mend fences with his brother, the king had appealed to the pope to name Henry the papal legate. Since this would give Henry authority even over the newly appointed archbishop, Stephen hoped Henry would be appeased. Unfortunately he was not. Henry understood all too well that the legatine authority lasted only during the lifetime of the pope who had issued it; an archbishop would be archbishop until he himself died.

Stephen needed to walk a sword's edge between allowing Salisbury to do whatever he wanted and bringing down on himself the wrath of the Church. What seems to have been arranged was that the bishop's armed retainers were provoked into a clash with the retainers of Alain, count of Brittany. In the fight one knight was killed, Alain's nephew was badly wounded, and Alain's men were put to flight.

This was a breach of the king's peace, which was prohibited behavior during any Council called by the king. The bishops were summoned to Stephen's presence, and he required them to give up possession of their castles as guarantees of their trustworthiness. Carefully, Stephen made no demands on the property of the Church nor did he require the bishops to abate their authority over their dioceses. He was asserting, as his predecessors back to the days of William the Bastard had done before, "that his ministers were answerable to him for their actions, that castles could be held only at the king's pleasure and must be surrendered on demand, and that ecclesiastics who held secular offices were accountable for their conduct of those offices." (Appleby, *op. cit.*, page 69.)

Unfortunately Salisbury and his kin had committed no real act that was questionable, nor had the bishops failed in their conduct of their offices. To many of the nobility and all of the clergy, Stephen's behavior was high-handed and based on a patently fabricated cause. Although there is a strong possibility that he was right in his suspicions, and it was certainly his right to dismiss and appoint officers in his government, the king's methods were violent and unacceptable. He, himself, had broken the king's peace.

The results of Stephen's action were disastrous in the long run—although it is entirely possible that the disasters would have occurred even if he had not acted. However, the events of *Bone of Contention* end with the summoning and demands on the bishop of Salisbury and his son and nephews. Further events will be addressed in later books.

Roberta Gellis
Lafayette, Indiana